the unexplained

Other anthologies edited by Ric Alexander

Cyber-killers

the unexplained

STORIES OF THE PARANORMAL

Edited by Ric Alexander

Introduced by Peter James

ORION

First published in Great Britain in 1998 by
Orion
An imprint of Orion Books Ltd
Orion House, 5 Upper St Martin's Lane, London WC2H 9EA

A CIP catalogue record for this book is available
from the British Library.

ISBN 0 75281 004 9 (hardcover)
0 75281 005 7 (trade paperback)

Typeset by Deltatype Ltd, Birkenhead, Merseyside
Printed in Great Britain by
Clays Ltd, St Ives plc

The Archives

ARCHIVE 4: TIME WARPS

··

ARCHIVE 5: URBAN LEGENDS

··

There is so much material on the paranormal. I think there is an infinite number of spiritual, physical and psychological questions to explore.

Chris Carter,
creator, *The X-Files.*

Foreword: Peter James

'I don't know what's going on and I guess I'm not smart enough to understand if someone were to explain it to me. All I can do is hang around, try to be calm and friendly, and have a nice time until it's over.' Kurt Vonnegut Jnr.

In 1920 a survey taken among those doughty rationalists in white lab coats, otherwise known as the scientific community, revealed, rather surprisingly, that forty-four percent of scientists believed in God. In 1997 the same survey was conducted again. It revealed that forty-four percent of scientists believe in God.

Er – hello?

Er, what planet are we on here? This is Earth, the third rock from the sun, the mechanistic reductionist centre of the universe. What's with these boffins? Are they a few nanoseconds short of a millennium? Where have these forty-four percent of our planet's total scientific manifest been hiding for the past eight decades? Up in some black hole that spat them out before they had even entered it?

Well, no, I don't think so, actually. I'm not at all surprised that the figure has remained constant. Much less has changed this century in our search for the Big Answers to the Big Questions than the advancements of science and technology would have us believe. Ever since Queen Victoria trashed the microscope for being 'A ludicrous object that enables us to see things so closely we cannot tell what they are,' we have been on a rollercoaster ride of shattering techological progress but blinkered thinking. We can travel faster than our planet's own clock, we can amass and process data at speeds that gobsmack us (even though this is done by machines far dumber and slower than the human brain) and we no longer get the night sweats worrying about our next trip to the dentist, because it doesn't hurt anything like as much as it used to.

And yet, what have we learned this century about the origins of man that we didn't know in the previous one? That we may or may not have come out of Africa, but little more. We still have no real idea how old Homo sapiens is. The link between us and the apes is still just as AWOL as it was for Charles Darwin.

Despite sending rodents, dogs, apes, humans and robots out into space, what have we learned about the origins of this planet that Edgar Allan Poe didn't tell us when in his own writings he pre–empted the Big Bang theory by a century and a quarter? We still don't know how old it is, nor do we have any real idea how big the Universe is. Nor what it is. Nor where it sits in the overall scheme of things. It is probably bigger than Professor Richard Dawkins' ego, but smaller than God's.

In 1876 the Professor of Physics at Harvard University advised his students there was no point in majoring in physics any more, because every important discovery had now been made. This great visionary had failed to anticipate the first motor car, which appeared twelve months later, the first X-ray, eleven years later, along with most of the other discoveries and inventions that since his time have entirely changed the horizons and expectations of mankind.

He wasn't the only man born on this planet with a foresight bypass. In 1876 an internal Western Union memo warned, 'This "telephone" has too many shortcomings to be seriously considered as a means of communication. The device is inherently of no value to us.' And in 1899, a mere twenty-three years after the Harvard professor's famous clanger, someone did it again: this time it was Charles H. Duell, Commissioner of the US Patent Office, who advised that the Patent Office should now be closed down, since 'there is nothing of significance left to mankind to invent.'

Moving right along into the twentieth century, in 1943, the first great technological guru of our time, Thomas Watson, founder and chairman of IBM, declared, 'I think there is a world market for maybe five computers.' Clearly not wanting to be left off the list of Limited Mental Bandwidth Award nominees, in 1981 that great visionary of visionaries, Bill Gates, announced that in his opinion, '640K ought to be enough for anybody.'

We laugh at the above, we are smart, we know such an absurdity could never happen again, now that we are certain we are on the brink of dotting the 'i's and crossing the 't's on the Absolute Completely and Utterly Final Unified Theory of Everything.

But we'd do well to remember that there is nothing new about scientists believing they were nearing the end of the superhighway of discovery. In 1885 the London Society of Psychical Research was founded by some of the greatest brains of their time. The original committee included eleven Oxbridge dons; Arthur Balfour, who became Prime Minister, and Sir Oliver Lodge, one of the inventors of radio. Plus one eminent author – Arthur Conan Doyle. This venerable team believed with utter certainty that by the end of the century they would have proved the existence of life after death, and in this way, have arrived at a complete unified theory of everything.

Imagine for a moment you are reading this not now, but in high–tech 1898. You would have felt as modern as you do now. There has been a telegraph line between England and France for forty-seven years. It is thirty-three years since antiseptics began to be used in surgery. It is twenty-two years since the invention of the telephone, and since the appearance of the first motor car. Three years ago Marconi sent the first ever wireless radio signal. We are just seven years away from man's first flight. But we are still almost a quarter-century away from the first direct flight across the Atlantic – right now this is beyond all dreams.

Imagine everything that was in front of people in 1898. Is there any reason to doubt that there is just as much in front of us now in 1998? I believe that one day our super-tekky postmodernist late 1990s world will look as out–of–date as the Victorians do to us. What is ahead of us in the next one hundred years? And in the next thousand years? What is out there in the universe that we cannot see? What lies all around us in dimensions we have not yet learned to access?

Who are the visionaries who can help us try to guess? Certainly not the bald men in white lab coats who saw such a short distance into the future, it didn't occur to them to program computers to make the changeover into the twenty-first century.

Nor will it be medics. Is the statement of Pierre Pachet, Professor of Physiology at Toulouse in 1872 that 'Louis Pasteur's theory of germs is ridiculous fiction', or our own Surgeon-Extraordinary to Queen Victoria, Sir John Eric Ericksen's statement that 'the abdomen, the chest, and the brain will forever be shut from the intrusion of the wise and humane surgeon' any less ludicrous than those made today by many eminent medics and scientists, which declare that the science of freezing people will never become a reality – despite the fact that thousands of human beings born into this decade began life as frozen embryos?

In 1970 a lecturer in computing science at Massachusetts Institute of Technology told me that by the year 2000 we would have replicated human consciousness in a computer and proved, by definition, that God did not exist. For the past quarter-century the quest for a sentient computer has been the holy grail of Artificial Intelligence. But we are now in 1998 and the world's smartest computer is, in sentient terms, only somewhere between a cockroach and a mouse, and not showing signs of getting much smarter.

There has been huge disillusionment in the field of artificial intelligence, with many of its exponents starting to consider where there might be a crucial element to human consciousness which exists outside time and space as we currently understand it, and into which we are all in some way tuned. A concept that in many ways mirrors Jung's Collective

Unconscious – something that was for him not a theory but an absolute certainty.

It seems as we tap away on our keyboards the closing handful of months of this millennium, that we are not much closer than a hundred years ago to the ultimate answers to two of the biggest questions for the human race: how was the universe created? And what will really happen when we die? Of course, science is as divided as ever. In one corner we have the reductionist Theories of Everything brigade. They say that life is an accident, a result of two bits of dust colliding out in space and causing the Big Bang. We are nothing but specks in an ever-expanding universe and we will become as extinct as the dinosaurs before us.

In a second corner are those who say that all human existence is progressing towards immortality. When we have achieved that, and we will do so – perhaps within the next twenty years, but without any doubt whatsoever within the next hundred – we will ourselves, each and every one of us, have become a 'god'.

And in the third corner are those who believe that there is a supernatural dimension to existence. They think we are incapable of knowing the real truth behind human existence until we can replicate consciousness, and because consciousness exists outside of time and space we can never reach it from the human form. We can reach it only through dying or maybe we can ultimately reach it through technology. Perhaps even through cyberspace.

The great visionary Danny Hillis, founder of Thinking Machines Corporation, the pioneer of the parallel processor supercomputer, once said, 'Neurophysiologists suspect that lurking somewhere in the brain – most likely in a formation at the base of the brain stem – lies a facility that makes us feel under the right conditions like we're in communication with gods or that we have voyaged out to meet some Higher Presence. Certain configurations of data delivered to the brain by electronic stimulation could flood this region of the brain with hallucinogenic chemicals that could trigger that oceanic all–embracing feeling known so well to mystics and psycho–tropical beachcombers.

'But let's not stop here with this portrait of cyberspace as some kind of electronic designer drug! It's hard not to wonder why the brain has this weird facility to make us feel like we're talking to God. Is something so irrelevant to survival and yet so distinctively human just a neurochemical accident, an evolutionary bi-product of the sheer complexity of the nervous system? Is it, as Immanuel Kant suggested two centuries ago, that the laws of the "in here" are the same as the laws of "out there": our minds are tuned to universal harmonies. Perhaps the brain is prepped to receive divine telegrams because there is, after all, an intelligence informing the cosmos toward which universal evolution gropes – a Cosmic Anthropic Principle. Perhaps virtual reality technology will be one of the ways of opening the hailing frequency.

'Surely we are no less likely to find transcendence in cyberspace than we are in any other space, whether a Gothic cathedral or a Himalayan monastery or the pages of the Talmud. Cyberspace could be our civilisation's burning bush.'

I think the answer to who are the true visionaries will be, as it always has been, writers. I don't think there can ever have been a time in history when writers have had such a wealth of material on which to draw. As J. B. S. Haldane famously said: 'the universe is not only stranger than we think . . . it is stranger than we *can* think.'

Where did the world first hear about so many seemingly fantastic things that have now become a reality? H. G. Wells let the time genie out of the bottle. Arthur C. Clarke invented the concept of satellite communications. Gene Roddenberry – the flip-up mobile phone. Almost every popular writer in history, from Sophocles to Shakespeare to Stephen King has fuelled our interest in the paranormal.

I see great writing as the means of examining the often irrational fears which beset the child in all of us. The fear of being alone in the dark, the fear of what else might be in the house that we cannot see, the fear of what will really happen when we die. I see it too as the means of pushing back those white picket fences of mediocrity inside which lesser minds seek constantly to fence us.

All of us who share a love for this quality of thought provoking, mind–expanding writing owe a great debt to Ric Alexander. In this anthology he has put together a truly unique and extraordinary collection of treasures spanning this century, and he has produced it in a brilliantly inventive way. I hope it will have a special place on the bookshelves of the present and the future, because it deserves it. And of course we share this debt with the writers, many fortunately still with us and at the height of their powers, whose work is included.

To single any for praise is not to lessen the others. But David J. Schow's *Red Light* has a startling spin; anything by Graham Masterton is always a treat, and *The Irish Question* is one of the finest stories I've read of his and a beautiful evocation of Ireland. Harry Bates really freaked me with his smart roaches, and J. G. Ballard's *Unidentified Flying Objects* is as convincing as it is exquisitely written.

I've always been a sucker for urban legends, perhaps because secretly I really, really want them to be true . . . and believe that there is no smoke without fire. All four of the writers have done this category proud. And of course, what anthology of the supernatural could be complete without a Ramsey Campbell entry?

All these writers are explorers of another world. Urban legends, time warps, alien encounters, psychic phenomena and supernatural mysteries go back to the earliest days of storytelling, and reach forward to wipe the condensation off the lens that peers into an ever-elusive future.

As the biologist J. B. S. Haldane so chillingly and elegantly said, 'This is my prediction for the future. Whatever hasn't happened will happen. And no one will be safe from it.'

Peter James
scary@pavilion.co.uk
November 1997

archive 1
supernatural mysteries

File classification: Zombie
Location: New Orleans, USA

Title: The Job
Writer: *Richard Laymon*

Briefing: *Zombie – a corpse reanimated by supernatural powers; originally from Africa and now associated in America with Voodoo.* New Orleans is known as 'Murder Capital, USA', the place where modern crime battles with the ancient power of voodoo for control of the city's mean streets. Two off-duty cops, Mark and Stacy, on their way home after a night out, see a giant black man carrying the apparently unconscious body of a white woman dressed only in a nightgown. It looks like something straight from an old B-movie about The Undead. But when the man ignores all the officer's warnings, what *can* the law do in the face of the inexplicable?

Author: Richard Laymon is the best-selling writer of horror fiction that all the other top authors in the genre admire. Dean Koontz has said that 'no one writes like Laymon', and Stephen King has added, 'If you've missed Laymon, you've missed a treat.' Born in Chicago, Laymon grew up in California and got an MA from Loyola University, Los Angeles, before working as a schoolteacher, librarian, mystery magazine editor, report writer for a law firm and, finally, full-time writer. Among his most successful novels have been *Flesh* (1988), which was named 'Best Horror Novel of the Year'; *Funland* (1989), shortlisted for the prestigious Bram Stoker award, and *Quake* (1995), the terrifying story of a pervert on the loose in a city lying shattered in the aftermath of an earthquake. 'The Job' is also about *something* at large in the city and was written especially for this book.

'Oh, man,' Mark said.

'What?'

'Check it out. Over there. The black guy.'

Stacy, behind the wheel, swung his gaze to the right. He spotted the man halfway up the block. Probably six feet six and two hundred eighty pounds, walking away with stiff, slow strides. His muscle-bound body gleamed under the streetlights as if he'd been rubbed with oil. He wore skimpy white underpants, and nothing else.

Someone in a wispy white nightgown was cradled in his arms.

'What's he got there?' Mark asked. 'A woman?'

Stacy couldn't see much of the limp body – just its legs, dangling by the man's side. They were bare, slender and white. 'Yeah, I think it's a woman.'

'Oh, man,' Mark said. It sounded much like a moan.

In silence, they stared at the couple. Stacy took his foot off the gas pedal, and his car lost speed. When they rolled by, Stacy kept his eyes on the road ahead, but Mark turned his head to continue watching.

'What do you think?' Stacy asked.

'It's a white female, and it doesn't look like she's conscious.'

'Any signs of injury?'

'Not that I can see. But Mr Universe looks like he's stoned.'

'I'm pulling over.'

'Yeah, okay.' Mark didn't sound very happy about it. He glanced over his shoulder. Then he turned to Stacy and said, 'You think we oughta get involved in this?'

'I don't wanta, that's for damn sure.'

It had been a long day at work. They'd topped it off by attending a double header at Dodger Stadium. During the ballgames, they'd each put away several hotdogs, bags of peanuts and tall, cold beers. Enough beer, as Mark had put it, 'to float a canoe.' Stacy wanted to get home and go to bed.

We should've just stayed on the freeway, he thought. We'd be stuck in traffic, yeah – but we wouldn't be running into some sort of damn *situation.*

'I mean,' Mark said, 'it's not exactly like we're on duty or anything.'

Eyes on the rearview mirror, Stacy watched the man's approach. Mark watched in the side mirror.

'Well,' Stacy said, 'I guess it couldn't hurt to talk with the guy. Maybe nothing's going on.'

Mark let out a snort. 'Yeah, like maybe it's his daughter.'

'If he has a white wife . . .'

'Hey, maybe *she's* his wife.' Mark chuckled.

'Certainly possible,' Stacy said.

Whoever she is, Stacy thought, she's either asleep or out cold. Or dead.

He saw how her head drooped and her blonde hair swayed. Both her legs swung with the motion of the man's stiff, jerky strides.

In the pale glow of streetlamps, with his view distorted by the mirror and rear window of his car, he couldn't see her face well enough to judge her age. He couldn't even tell if she was pretty. She had a good figure, though. The thin, clingy nightgown made that obvious. She was no child. Either a teen or an adult woman.

'She isn't wearing much,' he said.

'Maybe she got snatched out of bed,' Mark suggested. 'And what's *he* doing in his skivvies?'

'Walking home from a weigh-in?'

Mark laughed. 'Yeah, that's gotta be it.' Trying to sound like Brando, he said, 'Maybe da guy's a contender.'

'Could be.'

They stopped talking, and turned their heads to watch the man stride by. He gazed straight forward with eyes that bulged as if they might pop out of their sockets.

'Catch those eyes?' Stacy asked.

'Freaky.'

'He's stoned, all right.'

'I'd say so.'

''Less maybe he be hyp-mo-tized.'

'Looks like a fuckin' zombie, that's what he looks like. A buggy-eyed zombie.'

'Whatever he is,' Stacy said, 'we can't just let him walk *away* with this gal.'

'Man, I *hope* it's his daughter. If we have to stop him . . .'

'Piece of cake,' Stacy said.

'Yeah. Right. It'll be our assess.'

Stacy glanced over his shoulder to check for traffic. Nothing was near enough to worry about, so he swung out and sped up the road. Half a block ahead of the man and woman, he pulled to the curb. He stopped the car, shut off the engine and headlights, and took out the ignition key.

'Ready?' he asked.

'Let's get it over with.'

They both swung open their doors and climbed from the car. As Stacy eased his door shut, he scanned the area. There wasn't much traffic. As far as he could see up and down the street, nothing seemed to be open.

Certainly, all the nearby businesses were shut. Most had steel gates across their display windows and doors. Some, closed for the night, had dim lights glowing inside. Others, closed for good, were dark. Many of those had boarded windows.

The entryway of every shop was cluttered with litter.

In some of them, dark shapes lurked.

A real pip of a neighbourhood, Stacy thought.

But at least there weren't many citizens milling around.

Aside from the derelicts hunched inside dark entryways, he saw only a few isolated figures scattered about in the distance. Mostly drunks and druggies, he figured.

Not enough to form a mob, if things went bad.

As Stacy walked around the front of the car, he pulled out his police shield and flipped open its leather case. Holding it straight out in front of him, he stepped over the curb. He joined Mark on the sidewalk.

The approaching man didn't react. He just gazed straight forward as if oblivious of them and kept on coming.

'Police officers, sir,' Stacy called. 'We'd like to ask you a few questions.'

He kept on coming.

'Ma'am?' Mark called. 'Are you all right?'

She lay limp, cradled against the man's muscular chest. Her eyes were shut. Her face looked peaceful and sweet. Stacy pegged her age at about nineteen or twenty. He saw no blood or other signs of injury. Though he couldn't detect any motions of breathing, she appeared to be alive.

Asleep, or knocked out. Maybe drugged.

Her nightgown was very thin. Stacy could see that she wore nothing underneath it.

The man kept coming.

His bulging eyes seemed to be frozen in an empty stare.

Mark cast a nervous glance at Stacy.

'Maybe he's blind,' Stacy muttered.

'Deaf, too?'

They both faced him. He kept coming.

'Please stop right where you are, sir,' Stacy said in a more forceful voice than before. 'We're police officers. We want to talk to you and the woman.'

He kept coming.

'Sir! Stop!'

He was almost on them. Side by side, they started backing away from him.

'Come on, mister,' Mark said. He used a calm voice as if trying to reason with an obstinate buddy. 'Just cut it out, okay? You don't want to make trouble for yourself. We're police officers. We're not here to cause you any trouble. We just want to talk to you.'

He kept lumbering toward them. They kept backing away.

'Who's the woman?' Stacy demanded.

Nothing.

'What's the matter with her, mister?' Mark asked. 'Did you do something to her?'

'We're not going away,' Stacy told the man. 'Don't think we're just going to walk away from this and let you take her. Ain't gonna happen. This is the end of the road. So stop and talk to us.'

He didn't stop. He didn't talk.

'What're we gonna *do*, Stace? He ain't stopping.'

'I know, I know.'

'What're we gonna do?'

'We'll take care of him. Don't worry.'

'He's awfully big.'

'I know. I noticed.'

'Built like Schwarzenegger, for godsake.'

Shoulder to shoulder, they stepped backward off the curb at the end of the block. They glanced both ways, checking for traffic. The nearest car seemed to be a couple of blocks away.

The man stepped off the curb.

'We're so screwed I can't believe it,' Mark said.

'We're fine. Calm down.'

'We can't even *shoot* the asshole.'

'I know, I know.'

'I mean, he's in his fucking *underwear*. We'd be toast.'

White cops in this city had been crucified, Stacy knew, for plenty less than shooting an unarmed black man. And this guy couldn't be more *obviously* unarmed, lumbering down the street in nothing but his skivvies.

If they had to use their weapons, there would be a storm of public outrage. The D.A. would cave in and prosecute them for murder. Right off the bat, before even going to trial, they'd be marked as rogue cops, racists, murderers. They'd lose their jobs. Their incomes.

If the jury found them not guilty, the city would burn like it did after the Rodney King verdict. No juror would want that on his conscience, so the verdict would have to be guilty. Then it would be years in prison for Stacy and Mark.

'We'd be dead ducks,' Mark muttered.

'We can't just let him go,' Stacy said.

Coming to the other side of the street, they climbed backward onto the curb.

Mark glanced at Stacy and grimaced. 'Where're the damn cops when you need 'em, huh?'

'This guy's starting to piss me off.'

'Hey, look,' Mark said. 'How about you stick with him and I'll go and call for some backup?'

'No. Don't.'

'I just gotta get to a phone that works. Won't take . . .'

'This is a lose-lose situation, partner. The backup would go down with us. Let's just keep it to ourselves if we can.'

'Then we'd better take care of it fast.'

'Let's do it,' Stacy said.

Though the summer night was mild enough for short sleeves, both men wore lightweight jackets to conceal their sidearms. Still holding his shield out toward the suspect, Stacy used his other hand to unholster his 9 mm semi-auto. Mark drew his .38 revolver. They stopped backing away, stood firm and took aim.

'Halt where you are!' Stacy shouted.

'Stop and put the woman down!' Mark shouted.

The guy paid no attention.

'Stop!'

'You're under arrest! Put down the woman!'

'Put down the woman!'

'Set her down!'

'Halt!'

'Put her down, buddy! Put her down!'

'You're not walking away from this!'

'This is it!'

'Put her down, asshole!'

'Now! Now! Put her down!'

Somewhere nearby, car brakes screamed.

Stacy jerked his head toward the noise.

Across the street, the door of a stopped car flew open and a woman leaped out – an attractive young woman with flowing blonde hair. She was dressed in a white T-shirt and jeans and sneakers and she carried a video camcorder.

'Oh, shit,' Stacy muttered.

Mark glanced over at her. '*Shit!*'

Rushing toward them, she raised her video camera.

The suspect was almost on top of them.

Stacy slapped Mark's arm with his shield hand. 'Back off! Back off! We gotta back off!'

They backpedalled, lowering their weapons.

'Let 'em by?' Mark asked.

'Yeah, yeah, yeah.'

They leaped apart, Stacy toward the curb and Mark toward the gated display window of a pawn shop.

The enormous man, as if totally unaware of the two officers – and of everything else – strode between them and past them and kept on walking.

Walking away with the girl in his arms.

Stacy holstered his weapon and faced the camera lens. 'We've got a situation here, ma'am. Why don't you get back into your car and be on your way?'

Keeping the camcorder in front of her face, the woman reached up with her free hand and touched a button. A light came on, glaring in Stacy's eyes. He squinted and turned his head away.

'Lady!' he snapped.

'You're interfering with police business,' Mark yelled at her. 'Get that camera out of our faces!'

'Oh, don't pay any attention to me,' she said, sounding calm and amused. 'Please. Just go on about your business. Pretend I'm not even here. I believe you were about to shoot the man. Don't let me stop you.'

Stacy glared at her.

'They're getting away,' Mark mentioned.

'Yeah, yeah.' Stacy turned his head and saw the huge man walking away with slow, stiff strides. 'Shit!'

'Let's have a pow-pow, Stace.' Mark grabbed his arm and pulled him toward the store front. 'Lady, you keep away from us!'

They ducked into a recessed entryway. No derelict was using this one for a bedroom, but Stacy tripped over an old telephone book and almost fell. Mark caught him. 'Thanks, buddy.'

They leaned in close together. The woman stayed back, but she kept her camera on them.

'What're we gonna do?' Mark asked.

Stacy put his back to the woman. 'Cover your mouth,' he whispered, ' 'less you want the whole world reading your lips.'

'Shit. Oh, shit, man. This is one big clusterfuck. We never should've stopped. We're dead meat. What're we gonna do?'

'We're screwed no matter what.'

'Want me to whack the bitch?' Mark asked.

'Gimme a break.'

'I know, man. I know. But what're we gonna do?'

'I know what I'm *not* gonna do. I'm not gonna let that bastard walk away with that girl.'

'How you gonna stop him?'

'Any way I have to.'

'Shit, man.'

'Look. No use both of us going down the hole. You stay here. Or go back to the car. Whatever. Wait! Here's the plan. I'll deal with Goliath, you go ahead and find a phone and call in some backup.'

'I thought you said . . .'

'It'll be over before they get here. I'll make sure of it. This way, nobody goes down but me.'

'Shit, Stace.'

'Hey, it was bound to happen. It's the Job.'

'I can't let you . . .'

'You just keep your nose clean, okay? Stay out of the way, don't give 'em any excuses. Don't say shit to *this* babe. I know her type. Just look at her funny, she'll sign a complaint. So *ignore* her and go off and find a phone. You got it?'

'Yeah, but . . .'

'Go.' He slapped Mark on the shoulder, then broke away and ran up the sidewalk. The guy had a good head start on him. Stacy poured on the speed. 'Police!' he shouted. 'Stop and put down the woman! Stop and put her down!'

The man kept walking.

Stacy gained on him fast.

'You're under arrest! Stop and put down the woman!'

He didn't.

Stacy drew his pistol.

In the distance behind Stacy, a woman cried out, 'Don't! Get away from me! Let go!'

He glanced back and saw Mark rip the camcorder out of the woman's hands.

No!

But it was done.

Damn it, Mark! Damn it!

Why'd you have to do that?

Tears suddenly flooding his eyes, Stacy raced the final few strides and crashed the barrel of his pistol down on top of the man's bald, shiny head with all the power he could muster.

It sounded like hammering a coconut.

The pistol bounced off.

The man's head bobbed a bit under the impact, but he didn't flinch or cry out in pain, didn't stagger, didn't fall to his knees, didn't keel over unconscious.

Nor did he bleed.

He just kept walking.

Stacy lunged at him and slammed the pistol barrel against the side of his head, laying open his scalp an inch above his ear.

The split skin looked raw in the streetlights.

But didn't bleed.

Stacy noticed shouts behind him.

'You bastard! You bastard! Give that back to me! That's private property! You have no right!'

Stacy dodged the suspect, rushed in front of him and whirled around. The guy kept trudging forward, eyes buggy, a calm look on his face as if he were lost in a daydream.

Behind him, Mark was dashing up the sidewalk with the camcorder in his hands and its owner hot on his tail. 'You've got no right!' she yelled as she chased him. 'It's mine! Stop, you bastard!'

Holstering his pistol, Stacy threw himself forward and tried to wrestle the girl free. But the giant clutched her too tightly. His hot, slippery arms were thick with solid muscles.

Stacy couldn't budge them.

Nor could he stop the man, who just kept walking, his massive body shoving Stacy backward.

Stacy let go and scurried clear.

Mark, charging in from behind, raised the camcorder high overhead with both hands and crashed it down on top of the suspect's head.

'No!' the woman cried out. 'You fuckin' dirty pig!'

The camcorder bounced off the man's shiny black scalp, tumbled sideways and fell. It struck his shoulder then dropped to the sidewalk. He didn't seem to notice.

Mark jumped on his back and applied a choke hold.

The 'modified carotid'.

Deadly force.

In the eyes of the world, the same as shooting.

Feet in the air, Mark dangled and rode him.

The outraged owner of the camcorder rushed past Mark and the giant and bore down on Stacy. 'Did you see what he did? Did you see? He stole my camera. He *destroyed* it. I want you to arrest him.'

'Get outa here, lady.'

'I *demand* you arrest him.'

'Please get out of my way.'

They both backed up, staying ahead of the giant – who now lumbered along unfazed with the girl in his arms and Mark on his back.

The choke hold should have dropped him by now – cut off the circulation of blood to his brain in a matter of seconds, and rendered him unconscious.

But it seemed to be having no effect at all.

'Get off him!' Stacy shouted.

Mark hung on.

'It isn't working! Let go, Mark!'

Mark let go and fell from the man's back. He staggered for a few steps, but managed to stay on his feet.

Stacy barked, 'Go get the woman's camera!'

Asking no questions, Mark swung around and ran to retrieve it.

'What good's *that* gonna do?' the woman whined. 'It's *broken*! He *demolished* it! I don't *want* it back!'

'We'll buy you a new one, lady.'

They kept scurrying backward to keep a safe distance between themselves and the bug-eyed, powerful suspect.

'I want you to arrest that officer,' the woman said.

'Are you *blind*, lady? Have you taken a good look at this situation here? This asshole is *kidnapping* this woman.'

'That's none of my business.'

'It was your business enough to *tape* us trying to stop him, you worthless . . .'

'So go ahead and stop him. I'm not taping you *now*, am I?'

Mark came running toward them, the broken camcorder in one hand.

'The tape still in there?' Stacy asked.

'Yeah,' Mark gasped as he jogged past the black man.

'Take it out.'

Mark cut in front of the man, then slowed down and studied the camera.

'Watch out!'

He glanced over his shoulder, gasped, and picked up his pace.

'You're going to be in *so much* trouble!' the woman cried out. 'If you don't give me that tape . . . !'

'It's evidence,' Stacy said. 'Evidence of *you* obstructing justice.'

'Bullshit!'

Mark pulled out the tape cassette. 'Got it!' He tossed the camcorder aside and it crashed against the sidewalk.

'You fucking pig Nazi bastard!' the woman blurted.

'Take it easy, lady,' Stacy told her. 'Why don't you just go on . . .'

'Give me that tape!' she shouted.

'It's police . . .'

Suddenly, she rushed Mark.

A look of surprise on his face, he raised the cassette overhead.

As she leaped at him, reaching high, he dodged her.

She squealed and slammed into the cradled girl. Stacy saw the limp body jerk with the impact. But the collision had no effect at all on the black man. He just kept lumbering foward, carrying his captive.

The woman bounced off them as if she'd thrown herself against a granite wall.

She fell to the sidewalk.

The girl in the giant's arms turned her head and stared toward Stacy, blinking.

She's okay!

But a startled, frightened look came to her face as the black man tripped over the sprawled woman and plunged headlong. He hurtled forward out of control – a dazed, vacant look on his face as if he didn't care, as if he wasn't even aware of his trouble.

He'll crush her!

Stacy rushed forward and hurled himself against the girl. Even as he clutched her under the back and legs, he was being carried backward like a child hit by a wild surf.

Suddenly, the blast of a gunshot crashed through the night.

The huge, shiny head above Stacy jerked to the right. Blowback erupted from its left temple. At almost the same instant, the right side of the head seemed to explode. The exiting bullet smacked through a store window. As the window started to fall apart, it was splashed by a red gush mixed with pieces of brain and skull.

Falling backward, Stacy kept his hold on the girl.

At least I'll break her fall.

And the bastard's dead.

He kept his head up as he slammed the sidewalk. An instant later, the enormous man pounded the girl against his chest.

The terrible weight only pressed down on him for a few seconds.

At first, he thought Mark must be pulling the body away.

But then he realized that the black man was pushing himself up.

No way. His brains are blown out.

A moment later, he was kneeling over Stacy.

But Stacy still had the girl.

Though the guy had the same blank expression on his face, he was busy slipping a forefinger into the entry wound in his left temple as if curious about its depth.

'Stacyyyyy!'

Mark's voice sounded high and somewhat mad.

Stacy turned his head and saw Mark in the street, staggering backward, the revolver dangling by his side.

'Stacyyyy? What's he DOING?'

The man's forefinger was *way* in there, now – all the way to the knuckle.

'What's he doing with his finger, Stacyyyyy?'

Stacy heard a squeal of tires, then the deep *THUMP THUMP* of a radio's roaring, pounding base. Headlights swept across Mark. But Mark didn't seem to notice, just gaped at the rising dead man.

'MARK! Look out!'

The speeding car smashed through him and roared away, its music thudding like a savage drum.

Mark, tumbling high and limp, looked like a trampoline artist who'd been gunned down in midair.

He landed hard in the street.

'NO!' Stacy cried out.

The dead man, now standing, turned slowly toward the street as if curious about Mark's fate.

It was impossible. Stacy knew this guy couldn't possibly be alive – not after catching a .38 through the head that way – but he was on his feet anyway.

And looking the other way.

Fast as he could, Stacy rolled over, letting go of the girl. On her back, she blinked up at him through her tears. She was sobbing wildly.

'You'll be all right,' he whispered. 'We're gettin' outa here. Are you hurt?'

Glancing over his shoulder, he saw the dead man turning toward him.

Outa time!

Stacy scooped up the girl and ran. She bounced in his arms, her head jerking up and down. She was larger than she'd looked in the arms of the giant. And heavier than he'd expected. But Stacy was strong and he carried her well and fast.

Soon, he realized they weren't being chased.

He glanced over his shoulder. Then he slowed down and stopped and turned around.

The dead man hadn't chased them at all. He stood in the middle of the sidewalk a block away.

Facing Stacy.

Like Stacy, holding a blonde woman cradled in his arms.

His woman, however, didn't seem to be conscious. Instead of a white nightgown, she wore a white T-shirt, blue jeans and sneakers.

He stared across the distance at Stacy and his previous captive.

Then he slowly turned around.

Slowly, stiffly, he walked away.

Stacy looked over at Mark crumpled on the pavement.

He brought his gaze back to the sidewalk again just in time to see the huge man lurch into an alley with his prize.

When they were out of sight, he looked around and spotted a pay phone across the street. It might be too late for Mark – probably was – but you never know.

He ran for the phone, carrying the girl that he and Mark, together, had saved from . . .

God-only-knows-what.

Stacy didn't want to know.

But a certain young lady would probably be finding out.

'Too bad she can't videotape it,' Stacy muttered.

'Huh?' the girl asked.

'Nothing,' he said.

File classification: Elemental
Location: Isle of Man, UK

Title: The Trespassers
Writer: *Nigel Kneale*

Briefing: *Elemental – a disembodied spirit belonging to, produced by, or inhabiting an ancient site: sometimes categorized as a ghost or poltergeist.* As soon as the Pritchards move into their new bungalow on the island's legend-haunted coast, strange things begin to happen. A tap squirts water of its own accord. Huge cracks appear mysteriously in the walls and food decomposes, suddenly and revoltingly. But when a huge pile of soil explodes through the back door one morning, the Pritchards realize that a terrifying supernatural power is now threatening their very *lives*.

Author: Nigel Kneale is recognized as one of Britain's foremost scientific rationalizers – a writer who takes ancient legends and superstitions and attempts to explain them against the background of dramatic contemporary situations. Originally trained as an actor at RADA, Kneale turned his hand to writing and in 1953 created the famous pioneer television science fiction serial, *The Quatermass Experiment*. This made him a household name while simultaneously demonstrating the attraction of sf to television audiences. *Quatermass* generated a movie and three sequels, and has since inspired a number of other quasi-scientific television drama series. Since this success, Kneale has written almost exclusively for films and television, with his interest in the supernatural very evident in productions like *The Road* (1963), where ghosts of twentieth-century technology are seen two hundred years earlier, *The Chopper* (1971), about a phantom biker, and *Season of the Witch* (1983) – the third in the *Halloween* movie series – in which microchips made from an ancient monolith are used as weapons of destruction at Halloween. The force at work in 'The Trespassers' is also very evidently ancient and terrifyingly destructive . . .

The estate agent kept an uncomfortable silence until we reached his car. 'Frankly, I wish you hadn't got wind of that,' he said. 'Don't know how you did; I thought I had the whole thing carefully disposed of. Please get in.'

He pulled his door shut and frowned. 'It put me in a rather awkward spot. I suppose I'd better tell you all I know about that case, or you'd be suspecting me of heaven-knows-what kind of chicanery in your own deal.'

As we set off to see the property I was interested in, he shifted the cigarette to the side of his mouth. 'It's quite a distance, so I can tell you on the way there,' he said. 'We'll pass the very spot, as a matter of fact, and you can see it for yourself. Such as there is to see . . .'

It was way back before the war, the estate agent said. At the height of the building boom. You remember how it was: ribbon development in full blast everywhere; speculative builders sticking things up almost overnight. Though at least you could get a house when you wanted it in those days.

I've always been careful what I handle, I want you to understand that. Then one day I was handed a packet of coast-road bungalows, for letting. Put up by one of these gone-tomorrow firms, and bought by a local man. I can't say I exactly jumped for joy, but for once the things looked all right – and business is inclined to be business.

The desirable residence you heard about stood at the end of the row. Actually, it seemed to have the best site. On a sort of natural platform, as it were, raised above road level and looking straight out over the sea.

Like all the rest, it had a simple layout – two bedrooms, lounge, living-room, kitchen, bathroom. Red tiled roof, roughcast walls, Ornamental portico, garden strip all round. Sufficiently far from town, but with all conveniences.

It was taken by a man named Pritchard. He was a cinema projectionist, I think. Wife, a boy of ten or so, and a rather younger daughter. Oh – and a dog, one of those black, lop-eared animals. They christened the place 'Minuke,' M-I-N-U-K-E . . . My Nook. Yes, that's what I thought too. And not even the miserable excuse of its being phonetically correct.

Well, at the start everything seemed quite jolly. The Pritchards settled in and busied themselves with rearing a privet hedge and shoving flowers in. They'd paid the first quarter in advance, and as far as I was concerned were out of the picture for a bit.

Then about a fortnight after they'd moved in, I had a telephone call from Mrs P. to say there was something odd about the kitchen tap. Apparently the thing had happened twice. The first time was when her sister was visiting them, and tried to fill the kettle: no water would come through for a long time, then suddenly it squirted violently and almost soaked the woman. I gather the Pritchards hadn't really believed this – thought she was trying to find fault with their little nest. It had never happened before, and she couldn't make it happen again.

Then about a week later it did. With Mrs Pritchard this time. After her husband had examined the tap and could find nothing wrong with it, he decided the water supply must be faulty, so they got on to me.

I went round personally, as it was the first complaint from any of these bungalows. The tap seemed normal and I remember asking if the schoolboy son could have been experimenting with their main stopcock, when Mrs Pritchard, who had been fiddling with the tap, suddenly said, 'Quick, look at this! It's off now!' They were quite cocky about its happening when I was there.

It really was odd. I turned the tap to the limit, but – not a drop! Not even the sort of gasping gurgle you hear when the supply is turned off at the main. After a couple of minutes, though, it came on. Water shot out with, I should say, about ten times normal force, as if it had been held under pressure. Then gradually it died down and ran steadily.

Both children were in the room with us until we all dodged out of the door to escape a soaking, so they couldn't have been up to any tricks. I promised the Pritchards to have the pipes checked. Before returning to town, I called at the next two bungalows in the row: neither of the tenants had had any trouble at all with the water. I thought that localized it, at least.

When I reached my office there was a telephone message waiting from Pritchard. I rang him back and he was obviously annoyed. 'Look here,' he said, 'not ten minutes after you left, we've had something else happen! The wall of the large bedroom's cracked from top to bottom. Big pieces of plaster fell, and the bed's in a terrible mess.' And then he said, 'You wouldn't have got me in a jerry-built place like this if I'd known!'

I had plasterers on the job next morning, and the whole water supply to 'Minuke' under examination. For about three days there was peace. The tap behaved itself, and absolutely nothing was found to be wrong.

I was annoyed at what seemed to have been unnecessary expenditure. It looked as if the Pritchards were going to be difficult – and I've had my share of that type: fault-finding cranks occasionally carry eccentricity to the extent of a little private destruction, to prove their point. I was on the watch from now on.

Then it came again.

Pritchard rang me at my home, before nine in the morning. His voice sounded a bit shaky.

'For God's sake, can you come round here right away?' he said. 'Tell you about it when you get here.' And then he said, almost fiercely, but quietly and close to the mouthpiece, 'There's something damned queer about this place!' Dramatizing is a typical feature of all cranks, I thought, but particularly the little mousy kind, like Pritchard.

I went to 'Minuke' and found that Mrs Pritchard was in bed, in a state of collapse. The doctor had given her a sleeping dose.

Pritchard told me a tale that was chiefly remarkable for the expression on his face as he told it.

I don't know if you're familiar with the layout of that type of bungalow. The living-room is in the front of the house, with the kitchen behind it. To get from one to the other you have to use the little hallway, through two doors. But for convenience at meal-times there's a serving-hatch in the wall. A small wooden door slides up and down over the hatch-opening.

'The wife was just passing a big plate of bacon and eggs through from the kitchen,' Pritchard told me, 'when the hatch door came down on her wrists. I saw it and I heard her yell. I thought the cord must've snapped, so I said, "All right, all right!" and went to pull it up, because it's only a light wooden frame.' Pritchard was a funny colour, and as far as I could judge it was genuine.

'Do you know, it wouldn't come! I got my fingers under it and heaved, but it might have weighed two hundredweight. Once it gave an inch or so, and then pressed harder. That was it – it was pressing down! I heard the wife groan. I said, "Hold on!" and nipped round through the hall. When I got into the kitchen she was on the floor, fainted.

'And the hatch door was hitched up as right as ninepence. That gave me a turn!' He sat down, quite deflated: it didn't appear to be put on. Still, ordinary neurotics can be almost as troublesome as out-and-out cranks.

I tested the hatch gingerly. The cords were sound and it ran easily.

'Possibly a bit stiff at times, being new,' I said, 'They're apt to jam if you're rough with them.' And then, 'By the way, just what were you hinting on the phone?'

He looked at me. It was warm sunlight outside, with a bus passing. Normal enough to take the mickey out of Frankenstein's monster. 'Never mind,' he said, and gave a sheepish half-grin. 'Bit of – well, funny construction in this house, though, eh?'

I'm afraid I was rather outspoken with him. Apart from any nonsense about a month-old bungalow being haunted, I was determined to clamp down on this 'jerry-building' talk. Perhaps I was beginning to have doubts myself.

I wrote straight off to the building company when I'd managed to trace them – they were busy developing an arterial road three counties away. I dare say my letter was on the insinuating side: I think I asked if they had any record of difficulties in the construction of this bungalow.

At any rate, I got a sniffy reply by return, stating that the matter was out of their hands: in addition, their records were not available for discussion. Blind alley.

Meanwhile, things at 'Minuke' had worsened to a really frightening degree. I dreaded the phone ringing. One morning the two Pritchards senior awoke to find that nearly all the bedroom furniture had been moved around, including the bed they had been sleeping in. They had felt absolutely nothing. Food became suddenly and revoltingly decomposed. All the chimney pots had come down, not just into the garden, but on the far side of the high road, except one that appeared, pulverized, on the living-room floor.

I managed to find a local man who had been employed during the erection of the bungalows – he had worked only on the foundations of 'Minuke', but what he had to say was interesting.

They had found the going slow because of striking a layer of enormous flat stones, apparently trimmed slate, but as the site was otherwise excellent they pressed on, using the stone as foundation where it fitted in with the plan, and laying down rubble where it didn't.

The concrete skin over the rubble – my ears burned when I heard about that, I can tell you – this wretched so-called concrete had cracked, or shattered, several times. Which wasn't entirely surprising, if it had been laid as he described. The flat stones, he said, had not been seriously disturbed. A workmate had referred to them as 'a giant's grave', so it was possibly an old burial mound. Norse, perhaps – those are fairly common along this coast – or even very much older.

Apart from this – I'm no diehard sceptic, I may as well confess – I was beginning to admit modest theories about a poltergeist. There were two young children in the house, and the lore has it that kids are often unconsciously connected with phenomena of that sort, though usually adolescents. Still, in the real-estate profession you have to be careful, and if I could see the Pritchards safely off the premises without airing these possibilities, it might be kindest to the bungalow's future.

I went to 'Minuke' the same afternoon.

It was certainly turning out an odd nook. I found a departing policeman on the doorstep. That morning the back door had been burst in by a hundredweight or so of soil, and Mrs Pritchard was trying to convince herself that a practical joker had it in for them. The policeman had taken some notes, and was giving vague advice about 'civil action', which showed that he was out of his depth.

Pritchard looked very tired, almost ill. 'I've got leave from my job to look after the children,' he said, when we were alone. I thought he was wise. He had given his wife's illness as the reason, and I was glad of that.

'I don't believe in – unnatural happenings,' he said.

I agreed with him, non-committally.

'But I'm afraid of what ideas the kids might get. They're both at impressionable ages, y'know.'

I recognized the symptoms without disappointment. 'You mean, you'd rather move elsewhere,' I said.

He nodded. 'I like the district, mind you. But what I—'

There was a report like a gun in the very room.

I found myself with both arms up to cover my face. There were tiny splinters everywhere, and a dust of fibre in the air. The door had exploded. Literally.

To hark back to constructional details, it was one of those light, hollow frame-and-plywood jobs. As you'll know, it takes considerable force to splinter plywood: and this was in tiny fragments. The oddest thing was that we had felt no blast effect.

In the next room I heard their dog howling. Pritchard was as stiff as a poker.

'I felt it!' he said. 'I felt this lot coming. I've got to knowing when something's likely to happen. It's all around!'

Of course I began to imagine I'd sensed something too, but I doubt if I really had; my shock came with the crash. Mrs Pritchard was in the doorway by this time with the kids behind her. He motioned them out and grabbed my arm.

'The thing is,' he whispered, 'that I can still feel it, stronger than ever! Look, will you stay at home tonight, in case I need – well, in case things get worse? I can phone you.'

On my way back I called at the town library and managed to get hold of a volume on supernatural possession and what-not. Yes, I was committed now. But the library didn't specialize in that line, and when I opened the book at home, I found it was very little help. 'Vampires of South-Eastern Europe' kind of stuff.

I came across references to something called an 'elemental', which I took to be a good deal more vicious and destructive than any poltergeist. A thoroughly nasty form of manifestation, if it existed. Those Norse gravestones were fitting into the picture uncomfortably well; it was fashionable in those days to be buried with all the trimmings, human sacrifices and even more unmentionable attractions.

But I read on. After half a chapter on zombies and Rumanian werewolves, the whole thing seemed so fantastic that I settled down with a whisky, and began to work out methods of exploding somebody's door as a practical joke. Even a totally certifiable joker would be likelier than vampires.

When the phone rang I was hardly prepared for it.

It was a confused, distant voice, gabbling desperately, but I recognized it as Pritchard. 'For God's sake, don't lose a second! Get here – it's all hell on earth! Can't you hear it? My God, I'm going crazy!' And in the background I thought I was able to hear something. A sort of bubbling, shushing 'wah-wah' noise. Indescribable. But you hear some odd sounds on telephones at any time.

'Yes,' I said, 'I'll come immediately. Why don't you all leave–' But the line had gone dead.

Probably I've never moved faster. I scrambled out to the car with untied shoes flopping, though I remembered to grab a heavy stick in the hall – whatever use it might be. I drove like fury, heart belting, straight to 'Minuke', expecting to see heaven knows what.

But everything looked still and normal there. The moon was up and I could see the whole place clearly. Curtained lights in the windows. Not a sound.

I rang. After a moment Pritchard opened the door. He was quiet and seemed almost surprised to see me.

I pushed inside. 'Well?' I said. 'What's happened?'

'Not a thing, so far,' he said. 'That's why I didn't expect—'

I felt suddenly angry. 'Look here,' I said, 'what are you playing at? Seems to me that any hoaxing round here begins a lot nearer home than you'd have me believe!' Then the penny dropped. I saw by the fright in his face that he knew something had gone wrong. That was the most horrible, sickening moment of the whole affair for me.

'Didn't you ring?' I said.

And he shook his head.

I've been in some tight spots. But there was always some concrete, actual business in hand to screw the mind safely down to. I suppose panic is when the subconscious breaks loose and everything in your head dashes screaming out. It was only just in time that I found a touch of the concrete and actual. A child's paintbox on the floor, very watery.

'The children,' I said. 'Where are they?'

'Wife's just putting the little 'un to bed. She's been restless tonight: just wouldn't go, crying and difficult. Arthur's in the bathroom. Look here, what's happened?'

I told him, making it as short and matter-of-fact as I could. He looked ghastly. 'Better get them dressed and out of here right away,' I said. 'Make some excuse, not to alarm them.'

He'd gone before I finished speaking.

I smoked hard, trying to build up the idea of a hoax in my mind. After all, it could have been. But I knew it wasn't.

Everything looked cosy and normal. Clock ticking. Fire red and mellow. Half-empty cocoa mug on the table. The sound of the sea from beyond the road.

I went through to the kitchen. The dog was there, looking up from its sleeping-basket under the sink. 'Good dog,' I said, and it wagged its tail.

Pritchard came in from the hall. He jumped when he saw me.

'Getting nervy!' he said. 'They won't be long. I don't know where we can go if we – well, if we have to – to leave tonight—'

'My car's outside,' I told him. 'I'll fix you up. Look here, did you ever hear things? Odd noises?' I hadn't told him that part of the telephone call.

He looked at me so oddly I thought he was going to collapse.

'I don't know,' he said. 'Can you? At this moment?'

I listened. 'No,' I said. 'The clock on the shelf. The sea. Nothing else. No.'

'The sea,' he said, barely whispering. 'But you can't hear the sea in this kitchen!'

He was close to me in an instant. Absolutely terrified. 'Yes, I have heard this before! I think we all have. I said it was the sea, so as not to frighten them. But it isn't! And I recognized it when I came in here just now. That's what made me start. It's getting louder: it does that.'

He was right. Like slow breathing. It seemed to emanate from inside the walls, not at a particular spot, but everywhere. We went into the hall, then the front room: it was the same there. Mixed with it now was a sort of thin crying.

'That's Nellie,' Pritchard said. 'The dog. She always whimpers when it's on – too scared to howl. My God, I've never heard it as loud as this before!'

'Hurry them up, will you!' I almost shouted. He went.

The 'breathing' was ghastly. Slobbering. Stertorous, I think the word is. And faster. Oh, yes, I recognized it. The background music to the phone message. My skin was pure ice.

'Come along!' I yelled. I switched on the little radio to drown the noise. The old National Programme, as it was in those days, for late dance music. Believe it or not, what came through that loudspeaker was the same vile sighing noise, at double the volume. And when I tried to switch off, it stayed the same.

The whole bungalow was trembling. The Pritchards came running in, she carrying the little girl. 'Get them into the car,' I shouted. We heard glass smashing somewhere.

Above our heads there was an almighty thump. Plaster showered down.

Halfway out of the door the little girl screamed, 'Nellie! Where's Nellie? Nellie, Nellie!'

'The dog!' Pritchard moaned. 'Oh, curse it!' He dragged them outside.

I dived for the kitchen, where I'd seen the animal. Plaster was springing out of the walls in painful showers. In the kitchen I found water everywhere, one tap squirting like a fire-hose and the other missing, the water belching across the window from a torn end of pipe.

'Nellie!' I called.

Then I saw the dog. It was lying near the oven, quite stiff. Round its neck was twisted a piece of painted piping with the other tap on the end.

Sheer funk got me then.

The ground was moving under me. I bolted down the hall, nearly bumped into Pritchard. I yelled and shoved. I could actually feel the house at my back.

We got outside. The noise was like a dreadful snoring, with rumbles and crashes thrown in. One of the lights went out. 'Nellie's run away,' I said, and we all got into the car, the kids bawling. I started up. People were coming out of the other bungalows – they're pretty far apart and the din was just beginning to make itself felt.

Pritchard mumbled, 'We can stop now. Think it'd be safe to go back and grab some of the furniture?' Just as if he was at a fire – but I don't think he knew what he was doing.

'Daddy – look!' screeched the boy.

We saw it. The chimney of 'Minuke' was going up in a horrible way. In the moonlight it seemed to grow, quite slowly, to about sixty feet, like a giant crooked finger. And then it burst. I heard bricks thumping down. Somewhere somebody screamed.

There was a sudden glare like an ungodly great lightning flash.

Of course we were dazzled, but I thought I saw the whole of 'Minuke' fall suddenly and instantaneously flat, like a swatted fly. I probably did, because that's what happened, anyway.

There isn't much more to tell.

Nobody was really hurt, and we were able to put down the whole thing to a serious electrical fault. Main fuses had blown throughout the whole district, which helped this theory out.

There wasn't much recognizably left of 'Minuke'. But some of the bits were rather unusual. Knots in pipes, for instance – I buried what was left of the dog myself. Wood and brick cleanly sliced. Small quantities of completely powdered metal. The bath had been squashed flat, like tin foil. In fact, Pritchard was lucky to land the insurance money for his furniture.

My professional problem, of course, remained. The plot where the wretched place had stood. I managed to persuade the owner it wasn't ideal for building on. Incidentally, lifting those stones might reveal something to somebody some day – but not to me, thank you!

I think my eventual solution showed a touch of wit: I let it very cheaply as a scrap-metal dump.

I know I've never been able to make any sense out of it. I hate telling you all this stuff, because it must make me seem either a simpleton or a charlatan. In so far as there's any circumstantial evidence in looking at the place, you can see it in a moment or two. Here's the coast road . . .

The car pulled up at a bare spot beyond a sparse line of bungalows. The space was marked by a straggling, tufty square of privet bushes. Inside I could see a tangle of rusting iron: springs, a car chassis, oil drums.

'The hedge keeps it from being too unsightly,' said the estate agent, as we crossed to it. 'See – the remains of the gate.'

A few half-rotten slats dangled from an upright. One still bore part of a chrome-plated name. 'MI—' and, a little farther on 'K'.

'Nothing worth seeing now,' he said. I peered inside. 'Not that there ever was much – Look out!'

I felt a violent push. In the same instant something zipped past my head and crashed against the car behind. 'My God! Went right at you!' gasped the agent.

It had shattered a window of the car and gone through the open door opposite. We found it in the road beyond, sizzling on the tarmac.

A heavy steel nut, white-hot.

File Classification: Witch
Location: London, England

Title: The Gap
Writer: *Ramsey Campbell*

Briefing: *Witch – a person regarded as having supernatural or magical powers and knowledge; a practitioner of the black arts.* Despite all the research Lionel Tate has put into his witchcraft novel, he still says it is all a thing of the past. Not even Don Skelton, author of the occult best-seller *The Black Road*, can convince him that modern science, far from destroying the old powers, has actually given people more tools with which to work. 'Telephones, cameras – so many ways to announce power,' Skelton insists. It is only when Tate begins to sense that he is being dogged by a hallucinatory figure in denim that his certainty starts to crumble.

Author: British writer Ramsey Campbell is known as 'the modern master of suggestion' and has received more awards for his horror fiction than any other author. A former civil servant and librarian, Campbell arrived on the publishing scene as a teenager with a series based on H. P. Lovecraft's Cthulhu Mythos, but quickly found his own voice with a number of tales of evil and alienation set against the background of contemporary urban settings. After the success of his collection, *Demons By Daylight* (1973), he went on to confirm his status as perhaps the best writer working in the British weird fiction tradition with his novels, *The Doll Who Ate His Mother* (1976) and *The Face That Must Die* (1979). One of Campbell's most important influences has been Fritz Leiber, the American writer who focused a number of his best short stories and a novel, *Conjure Wife* (1943), on his conviction that witchcraft continues to flourish in modern society, albeit very different from the traditional concept. Campbell, too, has developed this idea further in tales such as 'Lilith's', 'The Seductress', 'The Trick', 'Baby', 'The Fit' and, perhaps most effectively of all, in 'The Gap', written in 1980.

Tate was fitting a bird into the sky when he heard the car. He hurried to the window. Sunlit cars blazed, a double-stranded necklace on the distant main road; clouds transformed above the hills, assembling the sky. Yes, it was the Dewhursts: he could see them, packed into the front seat of their Fiat as it ventured into the drive. On his table, scraps of cloud were scattered around the jigsaw. The Dewhursts weren't due for an hour. He glanced at the displaced fragments and then, resigned, went to the stairs.

By the time he'd strolled downstairs and opened the front door, they were just emerging from the car. David's coat buttons displayed various colours of thread. Next came his wife, Dottie: her real name was Carla, but they felt that Dave and Dottie looked a more attractive combination on book covers – a notion with which millions of readers seemed to agree. She looked like a cartoonist's American tourist: trousers bulging like sausages, carefully silvered hair. Sometimes Tate wished that his writer's eye could be less oppressively alert to telling details.

Dewhurst gestured at his car like a conjuror unveiling an astonishment. 'And here are our friends that we promised you.'

Had it been a promise? It had seemed more a side effect of inviting the Dewhursts. And when had their friend turned plural? Still, Tate was unable to feel much resentment; he was too full of having completed his witchcraft novel.

The young man's aggressive bony face was topped with hair short as turf; the girl's face was almost the colour and texture of chalk. 'This is Don Skelton,' Dewhurst said. 'Don, Lionel Tate. You two should have plenty to talk about, you're in the same field. And this is Don's friend, er—' Skelton stared at the large old villa as if he couldn't believe he was meant to be impressed.

He let the girl drag his case upstairs; she refused to yield it to Tate when he protested. 'This is your room,' he told Skelton, and felt like a disapproving landlady. 'I had no idea you wouldn't be alone.'

'Don't worry, there'll be room for her.'

If the girl had been more attractive, if her tangled hair had been less inert and her face less hungry, mightn't he have envied Skelton? 'There'll be cocktails before dinner, if that's your scene,' he said to the closed door.

The jigsaw helped him relax. Evening eased into the house, shadows deepened within the large windows. The table glowed darkly through the last gap, then he snapped the piece home. Was that an echo of the snap behind him? He turned, but nobody was watching him.

As he shaved in one of the bathrooms he heard someone go downstairs. Good Lord, he wasn't a very efficient host. He hurried down, achieving the bow of his tie just as he reached the lounge, but idling within were only Skelton and the girl. At least she now wore something like an evening dress; the top of her pale chest was spattered with freckles. 'We generally change before going out to dinner,' Tate said.

Skelton shrugged his crumpled shoulders. 'Go ahead.'

Alcohol made Skelton more talkative. 'I'll have somewhere like this,' he said, glancing at the Victorian carved mahogany suite. After a calculated pause he added, 'But better.'

Tate made a last effort to reach him. 'I'm afraid I haven't read anything of yours.'

'There won't be many people who'll be able to say that.' It sounded oddly threatening. He reached in his briefcase for a book. 'I'll give you something to keep.'

Tate glimpsed carved boxes, a camera, a small round gleam that twinged him with indefinable apprehension before the case snapped shut. Silver letters shone on the paperback, which was glossy as coal: *The Black Road*.

A virgin was being mutilated, gloated over by the elegant prose. Tate searched for a question that wouldn't sound insulting. At last he managed, 'What are your themes?'

'Autobiography.' Perhaps Skelton was one of those writers of the macabre who needed to joke defensively about their work, for the Dewhursts were laughing.

Dinner at the inn was nerve-racking. Candlelight made food hop restlessly on plates, waiters loomed beneath the low beams and flung their vague shadows over the tables. The Dewhursts grew merry, but couldn't draw the girl into the conversation. When a waiter gave Skelton's clothes a withering glance he demanded of Tate, 'Do you believe in witchcraft?'

'Well, I had to do a lot of research for my book. Some of the things I read made me think.'

'No,' Skelton said impatiently. 'Do you *believe* in it – as a way of life?'

'Good heavens, no. Certainly not.'

'Then why waste your time writing about it?' He was still watching the disapproving waiter. Was it the candlelight that twitched his lips? 'He's going to drop that,' he said.

The waiter's shadow seemed to lose its balance before he did. His trayful of food crashed onto a table. Candles broke, flaring; light swayed the oak beams. Flaming wax spilled over the waiter's jacket, hot food leapt into his face.

'You're a writer,' Skelton said, ignoring the commotion, 'yet you've no idea of the power of words. There aren't many of us left who have.' He smiled as waiters guided the injured man away. 'Mind you, words are only part of it. Science hasn't robbed us of power, it's given us more tools. Telephones, cameras – so many ways to announce power.'

Obviously he was drunk. The Dewhursts gazed at him as if he were a favourite, if somewhat irrepressible, child. Tate was glad to head home. Lights shone through his windows, charms against burglary; the girl hurried towards them, ahead of the rest of the party. Skelton dawdled, happy with the dark.

After his guests had gone to bed, Tate carried Skelton's book upstairs with him. Skelton's contempt had fastened on the doubts he always felt on having completed a new book. He'd see what sort of performance Skelton had to offer, since he thought so much of himself.

Less than halfway through he flung the book across the room. The narrator had sought perversions, taken all the drugs available, sampled most crimes in pursuit of his power; his favourite pastime was theft. Most of the scenes were pornographic. So this was autobiography, was it? Certainly drugs would explain the state of the speechless girl.

Tate's eyes were raw with nights of revision and typing. As he read *The Black Road*, the walls had seemed to waver and advance; the furniture had flexed its legs. He needed sleep, not Skelton's trash.

Dawn woke him. Oh God, he knew what he'd seen gleaming in Skelton's case – an eye. Surely that was a dream, born of a particularly disgusting image in the book. He tried to turn his back on the image, but he couldn't sleep. Unpleasant glimpses jerked him awake: his own novel with an oily black cover; friends snubbing him; his incredulous disgust on rereading his own book. Could his book be accused of Skelton's sins? Never before had he been so unsure about his work.

There was only one way to reassure himself, or otherwise. Tying himself into his dressing-gown, he tiptoed past the closed doors to his study. Could he reread his entire novel before breakfast? Long morning shadows drew imperceptibly into themselves. A woman's protruded from his open study.

Why was his housekeeper early? In a moment he saw that he had been as absurdly trusting as the Dewhursts. The silent girl stood just within the doorway. As a guard she was a failure, for Tate had time to glimpse Skelton at his desk, gathering pages from the typescript of his novel.

The girl began to shriek, an uneven wailing sound that seemed not to need to catch breath. Though it was distracting as a police car's siren, he kept his gaze on Skelton. 'Get out,' he said.

A suspicion seized him. 'No, on second thoughts – stay where you are.' Skelton stood, looking pained like the victim of an inefficient store detective, while Tate made sure that all the pages were still on his desk. Those which Skelton had selected were the best researched. In an intolerable way it was a tribute.

The Dewhursts appeared, blinking as they wrapped themselves in dressing-gowns. 'What on earth's the matter?' Carla demanded.

'Your friend is a thief.'

'Oh, dear me,' Dewhurst protested. 'Just because of what he said about his book? Don't believe everything he says.'

'I'd advise you to choose your friends more carefully.'

'I think we're perfectly good judges of people. What else do you think could have made our books so successful?'

Tate was too angry to restrain himself. 'Technical competence, fourth-form wit, naive faith in people, and a promise of life after death. You sell your readers what they want – anything but the truth.'

He watched them trudge out. The girl was still making a sound, somewhere between panting and wailing, as she bumped the case downstairs. He didn't help her. As they squeezed into the car, only Skelton glanced back at him. His smile seemed almost warm, certainly content. Tate found it insufferable, and looked away.

When they'd gone, petrol fumes and all, he read through his novel. It seemed intelligent and unsensational – up to his standard. He hoped his publishers thought so. How would it read in print? Nothing of his ever satisfied him – but he was his least important reader.

Should he have called the police? It seemed trivial now. Pity about the Dewhursts – but if they were so stupid, he was well rid of them. The police would catch up with Skelton if he did much of what his book boasted.

After lunch Tate strolled towards the hills. Slopes blazed green; countless flames of grass swayed gently. The horizon was dusty with clouds. He lay enjoying the peace of the sky. At twilight the large emptiness of the house was soothing. He strolled back from the inn after a meal, refusing to glance at the nodding shapes that creaked and rustled beside him.

He slept well. Why should that surprise him when he woke? The mail waited at the end of his bed, placed there quietly by his housekeeper. The envelope with the blue-and-red fringe was from his New York agent – a new American paperback sale, hurrah. What else? A bill peering through its cellophane window, yet another circular, and a rattling carton wrapped in brown paper.

His address was anonymously typed on the carton; there was no return address. The contents shifted dryly, waves of shards. At last he stripped off the wrapping. When he opened the blank carton, its contents spilled out at him and were what he'd thought they must be: a jigsaw.

Was it a peace offering from the Dewhursts? Perhaps they'd chosen one without a cover picture because they thought he might enjoy the difficulty. And so he would. He broke up the sky and woodland on the table, and scooped them into their box. Beyond the window, trees and clouds wavered.

He began to sort out the edge of the jigsaw. Ah, there was the fourth corner. A warm breeze fluttered in the curtains. Behind him the door inched open on the emptiness of the house.

Noon had withdrawn most shadows from the room by the time he had assembled the edge. Most of the jumbled fragments were glossily brown, like furniture; but there was a human figure – no, two. He assembled them partially – one dressed in a suit, one in denim – then went downstairs to the salad his housekeeper had left him.

The jigsaw had freed his mind to compose. A story of rivalry between authors – a murder story? Two collaborators, one of whom became resentful, jealous, determined to achieve fame by himself? But he couldn't imagine anyone collaborating with Skelton. He consigned the idea to the bin at the back of his mind.

He strolled upstairs. What was his housekeeper doing? Had she knocked the jigsaw off the table? No, of course not; she had gone home hours ago – it was only the shadow of a tree fumbling about the floor.

The incomplete figures waited. The eye of a fragment gazed up at him. He shouldn't do all the easy sections first. Surely there must be points at which he could build inwards from the edge. Yes, there was one: the leg of an item of furniture. At once he saw three more pieces. It was an Empire cabinet. The shadow of a cloud groped towards him.

Connections grew clear. He'd reached the stage where his subconscious directed his attention to the appropriate pieces. The room was fitting together: a walnut canterbury, a mahogany table, a whatnot. When the shape leaned towards him he started, scattering fragments, but it must have been a tree outside the window. It didn't take much to make him nervous now. He had recognized the room in the jigsaw.

Should he break it up unfinished? That would be admitting that it had disturbed him: absurd. He fitted the suited figure into place at the assembled table. Before he had put together the face, with its single eye in profile, he could see that the figure was himself.

He stood finishing a jigsaw, and was turning to glance behind him. When had the photograph been taken? When had the figure in denim crept behind him, unheard? Irritably resisting an urge to glance over his shoulder, he thumped the figure into place and snapped home the last pieces.

Perhaps it was Skelton: its denims were frayed and stained enough. But all the pieces which would have composed the face were missing. Reflected sunlight on the table within the gap gave the figure a flat pale gleam for a face.

'Damned nonsense!' He whirled, but there was only the unsteady door edging its shadow over the carpet. Skelton must have superimposed the figure; no doubt he had enjoyed making it look menacing – stepping eagerly forward, its hands outstretched. Had he meant there to be a hole where its face should be, to obscure its intentions?

Tate held the box like a waste-bin, and swept in the disintegrating jigsaw. The sound behind him was nothing but an echo of its fall; he refused to turn. He left the box on the table. Should he show it to the Dewhursts? No doubt they would shrug it off as a joke – and really, it was ridiculous to take it even so seriously.

He strode to the inn. He must have his housekeeper prepare dinner more often. He was early – because he was hungry, that was all; why should he want to be home before dark? On the path, part of an insect writhed.

The inn was serving a large party. He had to wait, at a table hardly bigger than a stool. Waiters and diners, their faces obscured, surrounded him. He found himself glancing compulsively each time candlelight leapt onto a face. When eventually he hurried home, his mind was muttering at the restless shapes on both sides of the path: go away, go away.

A distant car blinked and was gone. His house's were the only lights to be seen. They seemed less heartening than lost in the night. No, his housekeeper hadn't let herself in. He was damned if he'd search all the rooms to make sure. The presence he sensed was only the heat, squatting in the house. When he tired of trying to read, the heat went to bed with him.

Eventually it woke him. Dawn made the room into a charcoal drawing. He sat up in panic. Nothing was watching him over the foot of the bed, which was somehow the trouble: beyond the bed, an absence hovered in the air. When it rose, he saw that it was perched on shoulders. The dim figure groped rapidly around the bed. As it bore down on him its hands lifted, alert and eager as a dowser's.

He screamed, and the light was dashed from his eyes. He lay trembling in absolute darkness. Was he still asleep? Had he been seized by his worst nightmare, of blindness? Very gradually a sketch of the room gathered about him, as though developing from fog. Only then did he dare switch on the light. He waited for the dawn before he slept again.

When he heard footsteps downstairs, he rose. It was idiotic that he'd lain brooding for hours over a dream. Before he did anything else he would throw away the obnoxious jigsaw. He hurried to its room, and faltered. Flat sunlight occupied the table.

He called his housekeeper. 'Have you moved a box from here?'

'No, Mr Tate.' When he frowned, dissatisfied, she said haughtily, 'Certainly not.'

She seemed nervous – because of his distrust, or because she was lying? She must have thrown away the box by mistake and was afraid to own up. Questioning her further would only cause unpleasantness.

He avoided her throughout the morning, though her sounds in other rooms disturbed him, as did occasional glimpses of her shadow. Why was he tempted to ask her to stay? It was absurd. When she'd left, he was glad to be able to listen to the emptiness of the house.

Gradually his pleasure faded. The warmly sunlit house seemed too bright, expectantly so, like a stage awaiting a first act. He was still listening, but less to absorb the silence than to penetrate it: in search of what? He wandered desultorily. His compulsion to glance about infuriated him. He had never realised how many shadows each room contained.

After lunch he struggled to begin to organize his ideas for his next book, at least roughly. It was too soon after the last one. His mind felt empty as the house. In which of them was there a sense of intrusion, of patient distant lurking? No, of course his housekeeper hadn't returned. Sunlight drained from the house, leaving a congealed residue of heat. Shadows crept imperceptibly.

He needed an engrossing film – the Bergman at the Academy. He'd go now, and eat in London. Impulsively he stuffed *The Black Road* into his pocket, to get the thing out of the house. The slam of the front door echoed through the deserted rooms. From trees and walls and bushes, shadows spread; their outlines were restless with grass. A bird dodged about to pull struggling entrails out of the ground.

Was the railway station unattended? Eventually a shuffling, hollow with wood, responded to his knocks at the ticket window. As he paid, Tate realized that he'd let himself be driven from his house by nothing more than doubts. There were drawbacks to writing fantastic fiction, it seemed.

His realization made him feel vulnerable. He paced the short platform. Flowers in a bed spelt the station's name; lampposts thrust forward their dull heads. He was alone but for a man seated in the waiting-room on the opposite platform. The window was dusty, and bright reflected clouds were caught in the glass; he couldn't distinguish the man's face. Why should he want to?

The train came dawdling. It carried few passengers, like the last exhibits of a run-down waxworks. Stations passed, displaying empty platforms. Fields stretched away towards the sinking light.

At each station the train halted, hoping for passengers but always disappointed – until just before London, Tate saw a man striding in pursuit. On which platform? He could see only the man's reflection: bluish clothes, blurred face. The empty carriage creaked around him; metal scuttled beneath his feet. Though the train was gathering speed, the man kept pace with it. Still he was only striding; he seemed to feel no need to run. Good Lord, how long were his legs? A sudden explosion of foliage filled the window. When it fell away, the strider had gone.

Charing Cross Station was still busy. A giant's voice blundered among its rafters. As Tate hurried out, avoiding a miniature train of trolleys, silver gleamed at him from the bookstall. *The Black Road*, and there again, at another spot on the display: *The Black Road*. If someone stole them, that would be a fair irony. Of the people around him, several wore denim.

He ate curry in the Wampo Egg on the Charing Cross Road. He knew better restaurants nearby, but they were on side streets; he preferred to stay on the main road – never mind why. Denimed figures peered at the menu in the window. The menu obscured his view of their faces.

He bypassed Leicester Square Underground. He didn't care to go down into that dark, where trains burrowed, clanking. Besides, he had time to stroll; it was a pleasant evening. The colours of the bookshops cooled.

He glimpsed books of his in a couple of shops, which was heartening. But Skelton's title glared from Booksmith's window. Was that a gap beside it in the display? No, it was a reflected alley, for here came a figure striding down it. Tate turned and located the alley, but the figure must have stepped aside.

He made for Oxford Street. Skelton's book was there too, in Claude Gill's. Beyond it, on the ghost of the opposite pavement, a denimed figure watched. Tate whirled, but a bus idled past, blocking his view. Certainly there were a good many strollers wearing denim.

When he reached the Academy Cinema he had glimpsed a figure several times, both walking through window displays and, most frustratingly, pacing him on the opposite pavement, at the edge of his vision. He walked past the cinema, thinking how many faces he would be unable to see in its dark.

Instinctively drawn towards the brightest lights, he headed down Poland Street. Twilight had reached the narrow streets of Soho, awakening the neon. SEX SHOP, SEX AIDS, SCANDINAVIAN FILMS. The shops cramped one another, a shoulder-to-shoulder row of touts. In one window framed by livery neon, between *Spanking Letters* and *Rubber News*, he saw Skelton's book.

Pedestrians and cars crowded the streets. Whenever Tate glanced across, he glimpsed a figure in denim on the other pavement. Of course it needn't be the same one each time – it was impossible to tell, for he could never catch sight of the face. He had never realized how many faces you couldn't see in crowds. He'd made for these streets precisely in order to be among people.

Really, this was absurd. He'd allowed himself to be driven among the seedy bookshops in search of company, like a fugitive from Edgar Allan Poe – and by what? An idiotic conversation, an equally asinine jigsaw, a few stray glimpses? It proved that curses could work on the imagination – but, good heavens, that was no reason for him to feel apprehensive. Yet he did, for behind the walkers painted with neon a figure was moving like a hunter, close to the wall. Tate's fear tasted of curry.

Very well, his pursuer existed. That could be readily explained: it was Skelton, skulking. How snugly those two words fitted together! Skelton must have seen him gazing at *The Black Road* in the window. It would be just like Skelton to stroll about admiring his own work in displays. He must have decided to chase Tate, to unnerve him.

He must glimpse Skelton's face, then pounce. Abruptly he crossed the street, through a break in the sequence of cars. Neon, entangled with neon afterimages, danced on his eyelids. Where was the skulker? Had he dodged into a shop? In a moment Tate's vision struggled clear of afterimages, the face was obscured by the crowd.

Tate dashed across the street again, with the same result. So Skelton was going to play at manoeuvring, was he? Well, Tate could play too. He dodged into a shop. Amplified panting pounded rhythmically beyond an inner doorway. 'Hardcore film now showing, sir,' said the Indian behind the counter. Men, some wearing denim, stood at racks of magazines. All kept their faces averted from Tate.

He was behaving ridiculously – which frightened him: he'd let his defences be penetrated. How long did he mean to indulge in this absurd chase? How was he to put a stop to it?

He peered out of the shop. Passers-by glanced at him as though he was touting. Pavements twitched, restless with neon. The battle of lights jerked the shadows of the crowd. Faces shone green, burned red.

If he could just spot Skelton . . . What would he do? Next to Tate's doorway was an alley, empty save for darkness. At the far end, another street glared. He could dodge through the alley and lose his pursuer.

Perhaps he would find a policeman; that would teach Skelton – he'd had enough of this poor excuse for a joke.

There was Skelton, lurking in a dark doorway almost opposite. Tate made as if to chase him, and at once the figure sneaked away behind a group of strollers. Tate darted into the alley.

His footsteps clanged back from the walls. Beyond the scrawny exit, figures passed like a peepshow. A wall grazed his shoulder; a burden knocked repetitively against his thigh. It was *The Black Road*, still crumpled in his pocket. He flung it away. It caught at his feet in the dark until he trampled on it; he heard its spine break. Good riddance.

He was halfway down the alley, where its darkness was strongest. He looked back to confirm that nobody had followed him. Stumbling a little, he faced forward again, and the hands of the figure before him grabbed his shoulders.

He recoiled gasping. The wall struck his shoulder-blades. Darkness stood in front of him, but he felt the body clasp him close, so as to thrust its unseen face into his. His face felt seized by ice; he couldn't distinguish the shape of what touched it. Then the clasp had gone, and there was silence.

He stood shivering. His hands groped at his sides, as though afraid to move. He understood why he could see nothing – there was no light so deep in the alley – but why couldn't he hear? Even the taste of curry had vanished. His head felt anaesthetized, and somehow insubstantial. He found that he didn't dare turn to look at either lighted street. Slowly, reluctantly, his hands groped upwards towards his face.

File classification: Vampire
Location: San Francisco, USA

Title: Red Light
Writer: *David J. Schow*

Briefing: *Vampire – one who feeds on the blood of sentient victims; also psychic vampire, an energy-draining predator.* Tasha Vode – once ordinary Claudia Katz – is an internationally famous model, budding cinema star and headliner who every magazine editor wants on their front cover. That is until she goes missing and the rumours start to fly that she's either in a lunatic asylum or been murdered by a lover. There is, though, someone who knows what's really happened – her original photographer. But now, it seems, Tasha is terrified of being photographed again *ever* . . .

Author: English-born David J. Schow is one of the new wave of uncompromising horror-story writers categorized as the 'splatter punks', and also the creator of the controversial movie, *The Crow* (1984), which has generated a cult following. He combines the careers of media historian (having authored the official guide to the legendary black and white Sixties television series, *The Outer Limits*, now back on the small screen in colour), Hollywood scriptwriter (*Leatherface* – the third *Texas Chainsaw Massacre* blood-epic – and two of the *Critters* movies), plus rock musician, novelist and short-story writer. *The Light at the End*, which he co-authored with Craig Spector in 1986 about a punk vampire loose on the New York subway system, and his short story, 'A Week in the Unlife', featuring an undead predator known only as 'The Vigilante', are certainly among the best contributions to the vampire story genre in recent years. 'Red Light' – about a psychic vampire seeking its victim's energy rather than its blood – makes it a hat-trick.

Tabloid headlines always make me laugh. You know: *I Aborted Bigfoot's Quints*, or *See Elvis' Rotting Nude Corpse*, or *Exclusive on Jack the Ripper's Grandfather*! Earlier today, while passing one of those Market Street news vendors, I saw similar hyperbolic screamers, and I laughed. I did not want to laugh; it came out as a sick coughing sound.

TASHA VODE STILL MISSING
Terrorist Kidnapping
of International Cover Girl
Not Ruled Out

What the hell did they know about her? Not what I knew. They were like vampires; they sucked, ethically. Morally.

But what did that make *me*?

At the top of the dungheap was the good old *National Perspirer*, the hot, steaming poop on Tasha's disappearance, and how one of three juicy fates had befallen her. One: She had pulled a Marilyn Monroe. Two: She had had a Dorothy Stratten pulled *on* her by some gonzo fruitbag lover. Three: She was tucked away in the Frances Farmer suite at some remote, tastefully isolated lunatic asylum.

Or maybe she was forking over richly to manufacture all this furious controversy in order to boost her asking price up into the troposphere – in a word, hoax time.

It was pathetic. It made my gut throb with hurt and loss, and downtown San Francisco diffused behind a hot salt-wash of welling tears. I blamed the emissions of the Cal Trans buses lumbering up and down the street, knowing full well I couldn't cop such a rationalization, because the buses ran off electricity, like the mostly defunct streetcars. Once, I'd nearly been decapitated by one of the rooftop conductor poles when it broke loose from the overhead webwork of wires and came swinging past, boom-low, alongside the moving bus, sparking viciously and banging off a potted sidewalk tree a foot above my head, zizzing and snapping. Welcome to the Bay Area.

I had no real excuse for tears now, and wiped my eyes with the heel of my hand. My left hand; my *good* hand. I was still getting used to the weight of the new cast on my other one. One of our famous denizens of the streets had stopped to stare at me. I stared back, head to toe, from the cloud of gnats around his matted hair to the solid-carbon crustiness of his bare, black feet. He had caught me crying, with his mad-prophet eyes, and the grin that snaked his face lewdly open suggested that yes, I *should* howl with grief, I *should* pull out a Mauser and start plugging pedestrians. I put my legs in gear instead, leaving him behind with the news kiosk, the scungy, sensationaíist headlines, and all those horrifyingly flawless pictures of her. The bum and I ceased to exist for each other the moment we parted.

I know what happened to Tasha. Like a recurring dream, she showed up unannounced on my doorstep just four days ago. Like a ghost then, like a ghost now.

People read *People*. The truth, they never really want to know, and for good reason.

Her real name was Claudia Katz. In 1975, nobody important knew my name, or either of hers, and I'd already shot thousands of pictures of her. When I replaced my el cheapo scoop lamps with electronically synchronized umbrella shades so new that their glitter hurt your eyes even when they *weren't* flashing, I commemorated the event by photographing her. New Year's Eve, 1974 – five seconds before midnight, I let a whole roll rip past on autowind, catching her as she passed from one year into the next. Edited down, that sequence won me a plaque. Today, it's noteworthy only because Tasha is the subject.

'Claudia Katz is too spiky and dykey,' she explained later, as she pulled off her workout shirt and aired a chest that would never need the assistance of the Maidenform Corporation, breasts that would soon have the subscribership of *Playboy* eating their fingernails. '*Claudia Katz* is somebody who does chain mail and leather doggie-collar spreads for Bitch Records. *Claudia Katz* is not somebody you'll find on the staple page in *Sports Illustrated*'s Swimsuit Issue.'

I pushed back an f-stop and refocused. 'Part your lips. Stop. Give me the tip of your tongue, just inside your teeth.' Her mouth was invitingly moist; the star-filters would trap some nice little highlights. *Click-whirr click-whirr.* 'Tilt your head back. Not so much . . . stop.' I got a magnified closeup of the muscles beneath her skin, moving through the slow, programmed dance of positions. My big fan was on, making her amber hair float. 'Hands together, arms back over your head. Turn, turn, turn . . . whoa, right there, stop!' *Click-whirr* – another thousandth of a second, immobilized. '*Sports Illustrated*? Why bother aiming it at a bunch of beer-swilling beat-offs in baseball caps, anyway?'

'You don't understand the way the world works, do you?' She spoke to the camera lens, because she knew I was in there, watching, 'You've got to make people look at your picture and either want you, or want to *be* you. When they anticipate your next picture, that means they're fantasizing about you. Saying to themselves, "Geez, I wonder what she looks like in bed, without that damned bathing suit on?"'

It was my privilege to know the answer to that one already. Grinning, I baited her: 'The women say that, do they?'

'No, not the women, you dork.' The warm, come-hither expression on her face was entirely contrary to her tone. She was, after all, very good at her job. *Click-whirr*. 'The men. When all the men in the country, in the world, lust for you, then you can say no to the lot of them. If all the men want you, then all the women lust to *be* you. Voilà.'

'Excluding lesbians, Tibetan lamas and some Kalahari bushmen.' Her reply begged my sarcasm. She expected it. 'Not that, um, lust and envy aren't *admirable* goals . . .'

If I had not been shooting, her brow would have rearranged and a familiar crease would appear between her eyes, indicating her annoyance at my childish, defeatist, irrelevant, smartass remark. And then she'd say –

'You just don't understand.' Right on cue. 'But I'll be on top someday. You'll see.'

'I'd like to see you on top after you finish your shower.' It flew out of my mouth before I could stop it. File a lawsuit if you want. 'It's your turn.'

She decided not to blow up, and rolled her eyes to keep from giggling. *Click-whirr*. My heart fumbled a beat. I'd just netted a shot of an honest-to-U.S.-Grant human being, peeking out from behind a cover-girl façade of plastic. Nude from the waist up, sensual not from flaunted sexuality, but because her expression let you in on the secret that the whole sham was strictly for laughs and wages. A real woman, not a fantasy image. I wanted that photo. It reduced the rest of the roll to an exhausted, mundane repertoire of tit shots – pretty billboard face, pasted-on bedroom eyes of that inhuman chromium color, the 'ideal', a dime per double-dozen from one shining sea to the next, from the four-star hookers at the Beverly Hills Hotel to the smartly attired, totally paranoid corporate ladies who took their Manhattan business lunches in neat quartets.

'To hell with the shower,' she had said then, lunging at me with mischief in her eyes.

I still have that photo. Not framed, not displayed. I don't make the effort to look at it any more. I can't.

Claudia – Tasha – got precisely what she wanted. That part you know, unless you've spent the last decade eating wallaby-burgers in the Australian outback. The tiny differences in the way we perceived the world and its opportunities finally grew large enough to wedge between us. Her astronomical income had little to do with it. It was me. I made the classic mistake of trying to keep her by blurting out proclamations of love before my career, my life, was fully mobilized. When you're clawing through the riptide of your twenties, it's like a cosmic rule that you cannot be totally satisfied by your emotional life and your professional life simultaneously. We had been climbing partners, until I put everything on hold to fall in love with her. So she left, and became famous. Not many people know my name even today. They don't have to; I pull down a plush enough income. But it did come to pass that everybody wanted Tasha. Everybody still does.

I was halfway through my third mug of coffee at the Hostel Restaurant when I admitted to myself that I was consciously avoiding going home. Bad stuff waited for me out there. A Latino busboy had made off with my plate. Past the smoky front windows, Geary Street was acruise with the bunboys that gave the Tenderloin its rep. In New York, where things are less euphemistic, they're called fudge-packers. I wondered what gays made of all the media fuss over Tasha.

Nicole was giving me the eye. She's my favourite combat-hardened coffeeshop waitress in the charted universe, an elegant willowsprout of West Indies mocha black, with a heaving bosom and a lilting, exotic way of speaking the English language. When I watch her move about her chores at the Hostel, I think she'd probably jump my bones on the spot if she thought I could *click-whirr* her into the Tasha Vode saddle – worldwide model, budding cinema star, headliner. And still missing. When I try to formulate some logical nonsense for what happened to her, I fail just like I did with the street bum. Nothing comes out. Instead, I watch Nicole as she strolls over to recharge my cup. She watches me watching her.

'How'd you know I wanted more, Nicole?'

She narrows her panther eyes and blesses me with an evil smile. 'Because you white boys *always* want more, hon.'

My house-*cum*-studio hangs off the north end of the Fieldings' Point Pier, which is owned by a white-maned, sea-salt type named Dickie Barnhardt, whom no mortal dares address as 'Richard', He sold me my home and plays caretaker to his pier. I live in a fabulous, indifferently planned spill-together of rooms, like building blocks dumped haphazardly into a corner. Spiderwebbing it together are twelve crooked little stairways, inside and out. At first I called it my Dr Seuss House. On the very top is a lighthouse tower that still works. Dickie showed me how to operate it, and from time to time I play keeper of the maritime flame because the notion is so irresistibly romantic. In return for spiffing up the place, I got another plaque – this one from the U.S. Lighthouse Society in San Francisco. Lighthouses have long been outmoded by navigational technology, and the Society is devoted to a programme of historical preservation. There's no use for my little beacon. But there are nights when I cannot bear to keep it dark.

After ten years without a postcard, Tasha knew exactly where to find me. Maybe she followed the light. I answered my downstairs door with the alkaline smell of developer clinging to my hands; the doorknob was greened from all the times I'd done it. And there she was.

Was I surprised? I knew instantly it was her, knew it from the way the ocean tilted and tried to slide off the edge of the world, knew it because all the organs in my body tried to rush together and clog up my throat.

'You look like you just swallowed a starfish,' she said. She was burrowed into a minky-lush fur that hid everything but the tips of her boots. The chill sea breeze pushed wisps of her hair around. I don't have to describe what her face looked like. If you want to know, just haul your ass down to Slater's Periodicals and check out the covers of any half-dozen current glamour and pop-fashion magazines. *That's* what she looked like, brother.

Her eyes seemed backed up with tears, but maybe tears alone were insufficient to breach the Tasha forcefield, or maybe she used some brand of eyeliner so expensive that it was tear-resistant. I asked her why she was crying, invited her in, and then did not give her room to answer me. I was too busy babbling, trying to race past ten years in ten minutes and disguise my nervousness with light banter. She sensed my disorientation and rode it out, patiently, the way she used to. I fixed coffee and brandy. She sipped hers with picture-perfect lips, sitting at the breakfast overlook I'd glassed in last summer. I needed the drink. She needed contact, and hinted at it by letting her leg brush mine beneath the booth-style table. My need for chitchat and my awareness of the past hung around, dumbing things up like a stubborn chaperone. Beyond the booth's half-turret of window-panes, green breakers crashed onto the rocks and foamed violently away.

Her eyes cleared, marking time between me and the ocean outside. They grew darkly stormy, registering the thunderheads that were rolling in with the dusk to lash the beach with an evening sweep of rain.

At last I ran out of stupid questions.

She closed my hand up in both of hers. My heartbeat meddled with my breathing. She had already guessed which of my odd little Caligari staircases led to the bedroom loft.

The night sky was embossed by tines of lightning somewhere between us and Japan. Fat drops splatted against the seaward hurricane glass and skidded to the right as a strong offshore wind caught and blew them. I had opened the shutters on the shore side, and the wooden blades of the ceiling fan cast down cool air to prickle our flesh, sweat-speckled from fervent but honest lovemaking.

A lot of women had drifted through my viewfinder after Tasha had left me. Except for two or three mental time-bombs and outright snow queens, I coupled enthusiastically with all of them. I forgot how to say no. Sometimes I was artificially nice; most of the time I was making the entire sex pay because one of their number had dumped me. The right people found out my name, yes. My studio filled up with eager young lovelies. No brag, just a living. I settled into a pattern of rejecting them about the time they tried to form any sort of lasting attachment, or tried to storm my meticulously erected walls. Some of them were annoyingly persistent, but I got good at predicting when they would turn sloppy and pleading . . . and that made snuffing their flames oddly fulfilling. I was consistent, if not happy. I took a perverse pleasure in booting cover girls out of my bed on a regular basis, and hoped that Joe Normal was envious as hell.

Lust. Envy. Admirable goals, I thought, as she lay with her hair covering my face, both of her legs hugging one of mine. We had turned out to be pretty much alike after all.

When I mumbled, she stirred from her doze. 'What . . . ?'

'I said, I want a picture of you, just like you are, right this moment.'

Her eyes snapped open, gleaming in the faint light. 'No.' She spoke into the hollow of my neck, her voice distant, the sound of it barely impressing the air. 'No pictures. No more pictures. Ever.'

The businessman part of my brain perked up: *What neurosis could this be?* Was Tasha Vode abandoning her career? Would it be as successful as her abandonment of me? And what was the difference? For what she earned in a month, I could buy the beach frontage below for several miles in both directions. What difference? I'd gotten her back, against all the rules of reality, and here I was looking for the loophole. Her career had cleaved us apart, and now it was making us cleave back together. Funny how a word can have opposing definitions.

After five minutes of tossing and turning, she decided not to make me work for it. 'Got anything warm?' She cracked a helpless smile. 'Down in the kitchen, I mean.'

'Real cocoa. Loaded with crap that's bad for you. Not from an envelope. Topped with marshmallows, also real, packed with whatever carcinogens the cocoa doesn't have.'

'Sounds luscious. Bring a whole pot.'

'You can help.'

'No. I want to watch the storm.' Water pelted the glass. Now and then lightning would suggest how turbulent the ocean had gotten, and I thought of firing up my beacon. Perhaps there was a seafarer out there who was as romantic about boats as I was about lighthouses, and he'd gotten caught in the squall without the latest in high-tech directional doodads.

I did it. Then I dusted off an old TV tray for use as a serving platter, and brought the cocoa pot and accoutrements up the narrow stairs, clanking and rattling all the way.

My carbon-arc beam scanned the surface of the water in long, lazy turns. She was facing her diaphanous reflection in the glass, looking through her own image into the dark void beyond.

I had pulled on canvas pants to make the kitchen run, but Tasha was still perfectly naked and nakedly perfect, a siren contemplating shipwrecks. She drifted back from the window. I pitied my imaginary seafarer, stuck out in the cold, away from the warmth of her.

'You know those natives in Africa?' she asked as I served. 'The ones who wouldn't let missionaries take their pictures because they thought the camera would trap their souls?'

'It's a common belief. West Indians still hold to the voodoo value of snapshots. *Mucho* mojo. Even bad snapshots.' I couldn't help that last remark. What a pro I am.

'You remember April McClanahan?' She spoke toward the sea. To my reflection.

'You mean Crystal Climax, right?'

She nodded. 'Also of wide renown as Cherry Whipp.'

All three were a lady with whom Tasha had shared a garret during her flirtation with the hardcore film industry in the early 1970s. Don't swallow the negative hype for a second – every woman who is anyone in film or modelling has made similar contacts. Tasha never moved beyond a couple of relatively innocuous missionary-position features, respectable porn for slumming middle-class couples; a one-week run at the Pussycat Theatre, max. April, on the other hand, moved into the porn mainstream – *Hustler* covers, videocassette toplines, 'Fully Erect' notices in the film ratings. And no, she didn't get strangled or blow her brains all over a motel room with a Saturday Night Special. Last I heard, she was doing TV commercials for bleach and fabric softener as 'Valerie Winston', sort of a Marilyn Chambers in reverse.

'April once told me she'd figured out, with a calculator, that she was responsible for more orgasms in one year than anybody else,' Tasha said, holding the big porcelain mug with both hands to warm her palms. 'She averaged out how many movie houses were showing her films, how many times per day, multiplied by however many guys she figured were getting their jollies in the audience per show. Plus whoever was doing likewise to her pictures in God knows how many stroke magazines. Or gratifying themselves to the sex advice column she did for *Leather Life*. I remember her looking at me and saying, "Think of all the energy that must produce. All those orgasms were born because of me. *Me*." '

'I'm sure there are legions of guys getting their jollies to your photos, too,' I said. 'No doubt, somebody is out there yanking his crank to Christie Brinkley's smile, right now.'

'It's not the same thing. April was tough. She got something back.' She sat on the bed facing me, tucking her legs beneath her. She reminded me of Edvard Eridsen's famous sculpture of the little mermaid, rendered not in bronze but shaped from milk-white moonstone, heated by living yellow electricity called down from a black sky, and warmed by warm Arctic eyes – the warmest blue there is in our world.

'You mean April didn't mind getting that porn-star rap laid on her – literally?'

I could see the sadness in her being blotted away by acid bitterness. 'The people in porn have it easier. The thuds out there in Bozo-land know in their tiny little hearts that porn stars fuck for jobs. Whereas cover girls or legit models who are rarely seen in the buff, or full-frontal, are suspect.'

'You can't deny the public their imaginary intrigues.'

'What it always boils down to is, "Climb off it, bitch – who did you *really* blow to get that last *Vogue* cover?" They feed off you. They achieve gratification in a far dirtier way, by wanting you and resenting you at the same time. By hating your success enough to keep all the tabloids in business. It's a draining thing, all taking and no giving, like . . .'

'Psychic vampirism?' It was so easy for someone in her position to sense that her public loved her only in the way a tumour loves its host. But a blacker part of my mind tasted a subtle tang of revenge. She'd left me to go chase what she wanted . . . and when she'd finally sunk in her teeth, she'd gotten the flavour of bile and chalk and ashes. I suppose I should have been ashamed of myself for embracing that hateful satisfaction so readily. And from the hurt neutrality on her face, she might have been reading the thoughts in my head. She watched her cocoa instead of drinking it – always a bad sign.

Just as much as I never said no, I never apologized. Not for anything.

After a cool silence, she said, 'You're saying to yourself, "She's got it made, for christsake. What right does she have to be dissatisfied with anything?" Right?'

'Maybe a tiny bit, yeah.' She let me take her hand regardless. She needed the contact. The missing ten years settled between us to fog the issue. I was resentful, yes. Did I want a to help her? Same answer. When I guiltily tried to pull back my hand she kept hold of it. It made me feel forgiven; absolved, almost.

'In science class, in eighth grade, they taught us that when you smell something, your nose is actually drawing in tiny molecular bits of whatever it is you're smelling. Particles.'

'Which means you clamped both hands over your mouth and nose whenever you passed a dog turd on the sidewalk after school, am I right?' My prescription for sticky emotional situations is rigid: Always – *always* joke your way out.

Her smile came and went. 'The idea stuck in my head. If you smelled something long enough, it would run out of molecules and poof – it wouldn't exist any more.'

'Uh-huh, if you stood around sniffing for a couple of eons.' Fortunately, I'd forgotten most of the junk with which school had tried to clog my head. About hard science I knew squat, like math. But I did know that there were billions or trillions of molecules in any given object.

'My point is that each one of us only has so much to give.' She cleared her throat, almost as though it hurt her, and pressed valiantly onward. 'What if you were to run out of pieces all of a sudden?'

'Happens all the-time,' I said airily. 'That's what a nervous breakdown is. Entertainers who can't give their audiences an ounce more, collapse onstage. Corporate guys get physically ill and can't go near a meeting room. People exceed their operational limit . . . and you're in one of the most high-pressure professions there is.'

'No.' She was shaking her head prevent me from clouding her train of thought. 'I mean run out of pieces literally. Suppose every photo of me ever taken was an infinitesimal piece? Every magazine ad, every negative, very frame of motion picture film – another tiny molecule of me, stolen away to feed an audience that is *never* satiated. And when someone is fully consumed – vampirized – they move on, still hungry, to pick their next victim by making him or her a star. That's why they're called consumers.'

I looked up from the muddy lees in my cup just in time to see the passing lighthouse beam blank the ghost of her reflection from the windowpanes. Just like her smile, it came and went.

Her voice had downshifted into the husky and quavering register of confession. Now I was really uncomfortable. 'I know there are celebrities who've had their picture taken two million more times than I have. But maybe they can afford it.' She stretched across the bed to place her head on my thigh and hug my waist, connecting herself. 'Maybe some of us don't have so many pieces . . .'

I held her while the storm rallied for a renewed assault. My modest but brave beam of lamplight chopped through it. She did not grimace, or redden, or sob; her tears just began spilling out, coursing down in perfect wet lines to darken my pantleg.

Did I want to help her?

She feared that consumers wanted so much of her that pretty soon there would be nothing left to consume. And Claudia Katz no longer existed, except in my head. I'd fallen in love with her, become addicted to her . . . and now she was clinging to me because Tasha Vode was almost used up, and after that, if there was no Claudia, there was nothing. She had not brought her exhaustion home to my stoop to prove she could still jerk my leash after ten years. She had done it because the so-called friends who had gorged themselves on her personality were now nodding and clucking about celebrity lifestyles and answering their machines and juggling in new appointments to replace her as the undertow dragged her away to oblivion.

I stroked her hair until it was all out of her face. The tears dried while the seastorm churned. She snoozed, curled up, her face at peace, and I gently disengaged. Then, with a zealot's devotion toward proving her fears were all in her imagination, I went downstairs to load up one of my Nikons.

I asked her how she felt the next morning. When she said terrific, I spilled the beans.

'You *what*—?'

'I repeat for clarity: I took pictures of you while you were asleep. Over a hundred exposures of you wound up in my dark blue sheets, sleeping through a gale. And guess what – you're still among the living this morning.' I refilled her coffee cup and used my tongs to pluck croissants out of the warmer.

She cut loose a capacious sigh, but put her protests on hold. 'Don't do that again. Or you'll lose me.'

I wasn't sure whether she meant she'd fade to nothingness on the spot, or stomp out if I defied her superstitions a second time. 'You slept like a stone, love. Barely changed position all night.' My ego was begging to be told that our mattress gymnastics had put her under, but when I saw the care she took to lift her coffee cup with both hands, I knew better.

'Look at this shit,' she said with disgust. 'I can barely hold up my head, let alone my coffee. I'm slouching. Models aren't supposed to *slouch*, for christsake.' She forced her sitting posture straight and smiled weakly. Her voice was a bit hoarse this morning, almost clogged.

'Hey, lady – slouch away.' Worry stabbed at my insides while I tried to sound expansive and confident. 'Do what thou wilt. Sleep all day if that's your pleasure. Just wait till you discover what I've learned to cook in the last ten years. Real salads. Stuff you have to sauté. Food with *wine* in it. I can artistically dish up all the squares you require. Loaf on the beach; read my library. I have said it; it is good.' I watched a glint of happiness try to burn away the caution in her eyes. She did so want to believe me. 'And no more photographs. Promise. Anybody who tries has gotta shoot through yours truly.'

She brightened at that. I'd gotten the reaction I wanted from her. It was the challenge-and-reward game. And goddamned if that tiny acid-drop of doubt didn't settle into my brain, sizzling – *what if what if what if.*

What if I was playing it safe because she might be right?

'I don't want to see those pictures,' she said. 'Don't even develop them.'

'I'll toss 'em in the woodstove right now, if that's what you'd like.' I'd made my point.

She gave a theatrical shudder. 'Don't burn them. That's too much like a horror story I read once. I might shuffle off the coil along with my own pictures.'

The rolls of film were lined up on my miscellaneous shelf downstairs, in the darkroom, the room with the red lightbulbs. Expose the film to anything but that mellow, crimson glow and it blanked into silver nitrate nothingness. The rolls could stay down there, sealed into their little black plastic vials. For ever, if that's what she wanted.

She kept watch on the sea while we destroyed our Continental breakfast. 'I thought maybe we could brave the overcast later, and drive down past Point Pitt for dinner,' I said. 'Steaks, salads and a bottle or two of Cabernet. If anybody asks whether you're Tasha Vode, just blink and say, "Who?"'

The life had surged back in to her expression. 'Maybe. Or maybe seafood. But I want you to do something for me, first.'

'Your wish . . .'

'Don't you have any work to do today?'

Who were we kidding? I think we both knew I'd do almost anything she asked. 'Nothing that can't wait.'

'Then carry me back up to the bedroom.'

My narrow little stairway was a tight shot, but we negotiated it successfully after a mild bump or two. Our robes got in the way, so we left them crumpled on the stairs about halfway up.

Her need for contact was vital.

Outside the bedroom window, it got dark. I did not notice. All I could see was her.

Her eyes were capable of a breath-catching syllabary of expressions, and

I felt my own eyes become lenses, trying to record them. I stopped being friend or lover to be a camera, to try and trap what it was about her that made strangers hear those jungle drums. There were thousands, maybe millions of men out there who fantasized being inside her the way I was, who played my role and spoke my half of the dialogue whenever they passed a newsstand. Their wanting never ceased.

Her eyes told me she knew what I was up to. They did not approve.

Hers was one of the few callings that made you a veteran before puberty was left behind. If you lucked out, it could make you wealthy while still a child; if you weren't so lucky it could leave you a burned-out has-been before you graduated high school. The attrition rate was worse than that for professional athletes, who could at least fall back on commercials for razors and lite beer when middle age called them out. But she did not seem the sort of human being who could relish the living death of celebrity game shows. Staying beautiful had been an unending war; each touchup a skirmish that stole away another irreclaimable chunk of time. Doing it ten years, and staying the best, had been draining. Her outside was being used up. Her hipbones felt like flint arrowheads beneath soft tissue paper.

Her hand slid down and felt the cingulum cinched drawstring tight above my balls. Comprehension dawned in her eyes, followed by that strange tolerance of hers for my various idiocies. I can't relate the exact sequence (to come was, for me, a necessary agony by now), but I was almost certain that her rapidfire contractions began the instant she slipped the knot of the cingulum. Unbound, I offloaded lavishly. Her fingers whitened with pressure on my shoulders, then relaxed, reddening with blood. I watched the pupils of those warm Arctic eyes expand hotly in the dimness as she took what was mine. Until that moment, her own orgasms had seemed insubstantial somehow. Disconnected from her. Spasms of her equipment more than sparky showers in her brain. Her breath had barely raised condensation on my skin. Now she came into focus, filled, flushed, and radiating heat.

After holding me for a lapse of time impossible to measure, she said, 'Don't try to impress. You're not performing with a capital *P*.' Her eyes saw that I had been intimidated by the imagined skills of her past decade of lovers, and thus the girdle cord trick. Stupid. 'Don't you see? You're the only one who ever gave anything back.'

'Tasha, you don't really believe that—'

'Try Claudia.' It was not a command but a gentle urging. But it, too, was vital. 'You're the only one who can give me back some of myself: replace what the others have taken. Give me more.' Her reverent tone bordered on love – the word I could rarely force myself to speak, even frivolously.

Who better to give her back some of herself? I was a goddamn repository of her identity. With other women I had never bothered worrying, and so had never been befuddled as I was now. I'd made love to Claudia, not the exterior self that the rest of the world was busy eating. And now she was steering.

I gave her back to herself; her eyes said so, her voice said so, and I tried to hush the voice in my head that said I was not being compensated for this drain. I tried to ignore the numberless black cannisters of film that beckoned me from the room with the red light. And later, past midnight, when the storm thundered in, I carefully took twice what I had given her. No matter how much we have, as Nicole the waitress would say, we always want more.

'Skull full of sparrow shit,' she said the following day, as we bumped knees and elbows trying to dress for dinner. 'Gorgeous but ditzy. Vacuous. Vapid. Pampered. Transient values. A real spoiled-rotten—'

'I think I get the stereotype,' I said. 'You're just not stupid enough to be happy as a model anymore, right?'

'Ex-model.' She watched the sea bounce back the glare of late afternoon. 'You don't believe me, do you?'

'What I believe scares the crap out of me.' I tried to veneer what I said with good humour, to defang my fears. 'I believe, for example, that you might be a ghost. And ghosts never stay.'

She waggled her eyebrows. 'I could haunt your lighthouse. Or maybe I'm just your wish-fulfilment.'

'Don't laugh. I've often thought that I'm not really earning a living as a photographer.' Merely speaking that last word caused the slightest hestitation in the natural flow of her movements; she was *that* sensitized to it. 'I'm not really sleeping with Tas . . . uh, Claudia Katz.' She caught that slip, too, but forgave it. 'Actually, I'm really a dirtbag litter basket picker up in the Mission. And all of this is a hallucinatory fantasy I invented while loitering near a magazine rack with Tasha Vode's picture at hand, hm?'

'Ack,' she said with mock horror. 'You're one of *them*. The pod-folk.'

'Are we gone, or what?'

She stepped back from the mirror, inside a bulky, deep-blue ski sweater with maroon patterning, soft boots of grey suede, and black slacks so tight they made my groin ache. Her eyes filled up with me, and they were the aquamarine color of the sunlit ocean outside. 'We're gone,' she said, and led the way down the stairs.

I followed, thinking that when she left me again I'd at least have those hundreds of photographs of her in my bed. Ghosts never stay.

Outside there was a son of a bitch, and an asshole.

The son of a bitch was crouched in ambush right next to my front door. His partner, the asshole, was leaning on my XLS, getting cloudy fingerprints all over the front fender. I had backed out the front door, to lock it, and heard his voice talking, before anything else.

'Miss Vode, do you have any comment on your abrupt—'

Tash – *Claudia* – started to scream.

I turned as she recoiled and grabbed my hand. I saw the asshole. Any humanity he might have claimed was obliterated by the vision of a huge, green check for an exclusive article that lit up his eyes. A pod man. Someone had recognized us in the restaurant last night, and sent him to ambush us in the name of the public's right to know. He brandished a huge audio microphone at us as though it was a scepter of power. It had a red foam windscreen and looked like a phallic lollipop.

Her scream sliced his question neatly off. She scrambled backward, hair flying, trying to interpose me between herself and the enemy, clawing at her head, crushing her eyes shut and *screaming*. That sound filled my veins with liquid nitrogen.

The son of a bitch was behind us. From the instant we had stepped into the sunlight, he'd had us nailed in his viewfinder. The video rig into which he was harnessed ground silently away; the red bubble light over the lens hood was on.

And Tasha screamed.

Maybe she jerked her hand away, maybe I let it go, but her grip went foggy in mine as I launched myself at the cameraman, eating up the distance between us like a barracuda. Only once in my whole life had I ever hit a man in anger, and now I doubled my own personal best by delivering a roundhouse punch right into the black glass maw of his lens, filling his face up with his own camera, breaking his nose, two front teeth, and the three middle fingers of my fist. He faded to black and went down like a medieval knight trapped by the weight of his own armour. I swarmed over him and used my good hand to rip out his electronic heart, wresting away portacam, tape and all. Cables shredded like torn ligaments and shiny tape viscera trailed as I heaved it, spinning, over the pier rail and into a sea the same colour as Tasha's eyes. The red light expired.

Her scream . . . wasn't. There was a sound of pain as translucent as rice paper, thin as a flake of mica, drowned out by the roar of water meeting beach.

By the time I cranked my head around – two dozen slow-motion shots, easy – neither of her was there any more. I thought I saw her eyes, in Arctic-cold afterburn, winking out last.

'Did you *see*—?'

'You're trespassing!' bellowed Dickie Barnhardt, wobbling toward the asshole with his side-to-side Popeye gait, pressed flat and pissed off. The asshole's face was flash-frozen into a bloodless bas-relief of shock and disbelief. His mouth hung slack, showing off a lot of expensive fillings. His mike lay forgotten at his feet.

'Did you see . . . did . . . she just . . .'

Dickie bounced his ashwood walking stick off the asshole's forehead, and he joined his fallen mike in a boneless tumble on the planks of the pier. Dickie's face was alight with a bizarre expression that said it had been quite a while since he'd found a good excuse to raise physical mayhem, and he was proud of his forthright defence of tenant and territory. 'You okay?' he said, squinting at me and spying the fresh blood on my hand.

'Dickie, did you see Tasha?' My own voice was switching in and out. My throat constricted. My unbroken hand closed on empty space. Too late.

He grinned a seaworthy grin at me and nudged the unconscious idiot at his feet, who remained slack.

'Who's Tasha, son?'

I drink my coffee left-handed, and the cast mummifying my right hand gives me something to stare at contemplatively.

I think most often of that videotape, decomposing down there among the sand sharks and the jellyfish that sometimes bob to the surface near Dickie's pier. I think that the tiny bit of footage recorded by that poor, busted-up son-of-a-bitch cameraman would not have mattered one damn, if I hadn't shot so much film of Tasha to prove she had nothing to fear. So many pieces. I pushed her right to the edge, cannibalizing her in the name of love.

The black plastic cans of film are still on the shelf down in my darkroom, lined up like inquisitors already convinced of my guilt. The thought of dunking that film in developer makes me want to stick a gun in my ear and pull the trigger, twice if I had the time.

Then I consider another way out, and wonder how long it would take me to catch up with her; how many pieces I have.

I never cried much before. Now the tears unload at the least provocation. It's sloppy, and messy, and unprofessional, and I hate it. It makes Nicole stare at me the way the street bum did, like I've tipped over into psycholand.

When she makes her rounds to fill my cup, she watches me. The wariness in her eyes is new. She sees my notice dip from her eyes to her sumptuous chest and back, in a guilty but unalterable ritual. I force a smile for her, gamely, but it stays pasted across my face a beat too long, insisting too urgently that everything is okay. She doesn't ask. I wave my unbroken hand over my cup to indicate *no more*, and Nicole tilts her head with a queer, new expression – as though this white boy is trying to trick her. But she knows better. She always has.

archive 2
psychic phenomena

File classification: Magic
Location: Kerry Peninsula, Ireland

Title: The Irish Question
Writer: *Graham Masterton*

Briefing: *Magic – a secret or mysterious power over the imagination or will; often called sorcery or enchantment in earlier times.* Antique dealer Sarah Bryce has come to Ireland to bid for two valuable Daniel Marot chairs. At Kenmare, where the auction is being held, she begins to have visions of people she *knows* cannot be there – including her much-loved father who died several years earlier. Sarah also finds herself strangely attracted to the mysterious Seáth Rider who calls himself an 'Acquisitor' and can – in his own words – 'find people what they want'. But is his power just Irish charm or something far more sinister?

Author: English author Graham Masterton has been one the country's most consistently inventive horror-story writers for over twenty years. Following an earlier career as a journalist and magazine editor, Masterton published his first novel, *The Manitou*, in 1975, in which he graphically recounted the story of a professional clairvoyant who releases the vengeful spirit of a Red Indian sorcerer who has been dead for over four hundred years. The book announced the arrival of a new talent and was filmed with Tony Curtis and Susan Strasberg. *The Manitou* has been followed by a number of equally chilling works including *Djinn* (1977), *The Pariah* (1983), *Ikon* (1983) and many more. As a result of his days as a journalist, the background to Masterton's work is always thoroughly researched – a fact that is evident in 'The Irish Question' which he wrote especially for this collection from his Irish home.

It was raining hard by the time Raymond left the hotel and hurried over to his rental car. He was already half an hour late, and it would be touch and go if he could get to Cork in time to catch the last flight to London. He shook out his umbrella, tossed it on to the back seat, climbed in the car and started up the engine. He shouldn't have stayed so long talking to Dermot Brien; but Dermot knew of some eighteenth-century landscapes that Raymond was very keen to get his hands on, as well as some rare etchings by Conor O'Reilly.

He drove out of the hotel and on to the narrow road that led to Kenmare. The rain was coming down so heavily now that it was almost like being at sea. Raymond's windshield kept steaming up, and he had to keep wiping it with his handkerchief. Mostly, the road was unlit, except for reflective road-signs and the gleaming eyes of startled hares.

He glanced at the clock. He would probably make it to Cork with twenty minutes to spare, but he would have to return his car and check in his suitcase. He put his foot down harder, and the Volvo jolted over the roughly metalled road and blurted through puddles. He nearly miscalculated a tight left-hand bend, and by the time he had steered his way out of it his heart was beating at twice its normal rate.

He hadn't been driving for more than ten minutes when he saw something light flickering in front of him. He wiped his windshield again, and peered at it hard. At first it looked like a sheet, flapping in the wind; but then he saw that it was a woman, dressed in white, running along by the side of the road. A large dog was running along beside her.

Raymond slowed down. It looked as if the woman was wearing nothing more than a sodden nightdress. He didn't know whether to stop or not, and offer her a lift. But he was late, and she could turn out to be trouble, especially dressed in her night things on a dark, wet night in the depths of Kerry – and he didn't fancy the look of her dog, either. The woman looked as if she was wearing flowers in her hair, which didn't exactly reassure Raymond that she was altogether sane.

He drew out so that he could pass her. But as he did so, she turned around, and stepped right into the road, with both of her arms lifted. For a split second he could see her face, white with panic.

He stepped on the brake, but the Volvo hit her head-on. There was a dull thumping sound like somebody dropping a sack of flour. Then the Volvo was spinning around, with Raymond scrabbling frantically at the wheel. It slid backwards into the ditch, and he heard the crackle of breaking hedge.

He sat behind the wheel for one long moment, quaking with shock. Then he managed to open the door and climb out on to the boggy verge. The rain lashed him in the face as if it wanted to punish him. Turning up his coat-collar, he hurried across the road, praying that the woman wasn't badly hurt – praying that he hadn't killed her.

He found the dog lying on its side. Its front legs were crooked at a peculiar angle and its skull was crushed. One mournful eye stared at him accusingly, while blood was washed and diluted by the rain. There were fresh weals on the dog's smooth-haired flanks, but they looked as if they had come from a systematic beating, rather than any collision with Raymond's car.

He looked around for the woman, but there was no sign of her. He walked back along the road, looking into the hedgerows and shouting out, 'Hello! Are you there? Is anybody there?'

There was no answer. He trudged back to the dog and wondered what to do. He was frightened that the impact of the collision might have hurled the woman over the hedge and into the fields, and that she was lying in the rain, fatally hurt. There was nothing else he could do: he would have to call the Garda.

He went back to his car and found his mobile phone.

'There's been an accident,' he said. 'I think I might have killed somebody.'

It took more than two hours of searching before the Garda decided that there was no woman anywhere around. Raymond sat miserably in his car with the rain drumming on the roof, drinking a cup of tea that had been brought for him by the landlady of a nearby bed-and-breakfast.

At last a police sergeant came over and tapped on his window, and he wound it down. 'There's no trace whatsoever of a woman, sir.'

'I saw her. I'm sure that I hit her.'

'Well, sir, if there was a woman, she must have run off, and be well clear by now. Do you think it might have been the dog that caused the impact, rather than her?'

'I don't know. It could have been. It all happened so fast.'

'You say the woman was wearing a white nightdress of sorts.'

'That's right. And something in her hair, like a garland.'

'You mean flowers, sir?'

'Something like that, yes. White flowers, I think, with green leaves.'

The sergeant was silent for a long time. The rain dripped off the peak of his cap.

'Is anything wrong?' Raymond asked him.

'Not exactly wrong, sir. But there's more than one kind of individual out here, if you follow my meaning. Some that live with us, and some that live next to us, so to speak.'

'I don't know what you mean.'

'Well, sir, think of people living in *parallel*, as it were. They're here, but not on the same plane as we are. Except of course if they want to escape from *their* world into ours. Then we see them, now and again.'

Raymond was beginning to wonder if the sergeant was drunk.

'You say the woman was running, sir?'

Raymond nodded, and said, 'Yes. And she was running quite fast.'

'As if somebody were after her, would you say?'

'I suppose so. But I didn't *see* anybody after her.'

'No, well, you wouldn't.'

'I don't know what you're getting at,' Raymond protested. 'Are you trying to tell me she wasn't real?'

'Oh, she was real, sir, and I believe you saw her. But let's just say that she wasn't in the same reality as you and me.'

'But the dog's real.'

'The dog is something else altogether.'

The sergeant stood up. 'We'll search again in the morning, sir, but I doubt that we'll find anything. Meanwhile, why don't you stay here the night, and I'll talk to you again tomorrow.'

'All right,' Raymond agreed. He felt exhausted and shivery. 'Can you ask one of your men to move the car for me? I don't think I could manage it just yet.'

'Oh, sure, no problem.'

'There's one thing more.'

'Yes, sir?'

'You said that somebody could be after her. Do you have any idea *who*?'

The sergeant gave him a long, expressionless look, and then turned away without answering.

Sarah arrived at Cork Airport just as the clouds began to stain the sky like Indian ink blotted on a damp sheet of paper, and the wind began to get up. By the time she had crossed the concrete to the terminal building it was already starting to rain. Her friend Shelagh had told her that it always rained in Ireland, every quarter of an hour for fifteen minutes, and now she believed it. She went to the car-rental desk with her hair hanging down in long, dark-blonde rat's-tails.

'Ah, Mrs Bryce,' smiled the carroty-haired man behind the counter. 'It's you that were wanting the Corsa.'

'Yes, that's right,' she said, trying to be composed, with rainwater dripping off the tip of her nose. She looked bedraggled, but she didn't look as bad as she felt: a tall, slim woman in her early 30s, with brown, wide-set eyes and firm bone structure. She could have been a *Vogue* model for sensible country clothes, or the wife of a senior Army officer.

In fact, she was neither. She was an antiques dealer, the recently divorced wife of a lovable but chronically unfaithful artist called Ken who had shown too much appreciation for one of his models just once too often. She missed him; but she relished her freedom. His childish dependence on her had kept her tethered for six years like a sacrificial goat. Now she could travel wherever she liked, whenever she wanted – see who she liked, eat what she liked, and watch whatever television channel she liked, which was one of the greatest new freedoms of all. Like a curiously large number of artists, Ken had been an avid football fan.

The carroty-haired man gave her the car-keys. 'You'll find the little fellow in space 21. Enjoy your visit.'

She hurried through the puddles and found her rental – a tiny Opel in metallic emerald, very appropriate for Ireland. Gratefully she stowed her bag in the back and climbed inside. She pulled down the sun-vizor and combed her wet hair in the mirror and dabbed her face with her handkerchief. The rain pattered on the roof and ran down the windshield in herringbone patterns.

She was just about to start up the car when she became aware of a man watching her from the other side of the parking lot. He was very tall and very dark, almost Spanish-looking, although his face was pale. What was strange about him was that he was standing in the pouring rain without a coat and without an umbrella, his hands in his pockets, staring at her unflinchingly, as if he had seen her before and was trying to remember who she was. The runnels of rain distorted her image of him. For a moment he appeared to have a hunched back, and then a twisted torso, and then his face became long and devilish. Sarah started up the Corsa's engine and switched on the windshield wipers, and the man became a normal man again. All the same, she couldn't think why he was staring at her like that.

She drove out of the parking lot and the man turned around to watch her go. She kept checking her rear-view mirror to make sure that he wasn't getting into a car and following her, but he stayed where he was until she had driven round the curve in the airport roadway and he disappeared from view.

The rain continued to lash down as she negotiated Cork's south-western suburbs, past factories and roadworks and mean rows of bungalows and semi-detached houses. At last she found the main road westward to Macroom, and began to make her way out into the countryside; although the rain was so torrential now that the windshield wipers couldn't keep up with it, and she could barely see where she was going. She drove for over half an hour along an empty, winding road, before she found herself in a small town with a church and a long stone wall and a sign that announced that she had reached Bandon, miles out of her way south-westward.

She stopped the car by the side of the road, and breathed, 'Shit.'

She could turn back, and try to find the Macroom road again, but turning back was never in her nature. If she was careful, and followed the map, she could keep going westward, and then follow a convoluted road over the mountains that would take her to Bantry, and then north to Kenmare, which was where she was originally headed. Six or seven haughty London dealers had been on the same plane with her, and if she turned up late she would have to suffer the usual taunts about scatty women amateurs who couldn't empty piss out of a Georgian chamber-pot even if the instructions were written on the bottom.

A small boy in a tweed cap and a sodden sleeveless sweater came up to her car and knocked on the window. He was pale and freckled and very earnest-looking.

'Are you lost, miss?' he wanted to know.

'Well, a bit,' she admitted. 'I'm trying to find the road to Bantry.'

'Sure and that's easy,' he told her. 'You follow the main road till you nearly get to the church. Then you turn right and go up the hill. Then left again, till you reach the main road. The turning for Bantry is halfway up.'

'Thanks,' she said, and wound up her window before she realized that he had failed to tell her how far 'halfway up' might be. Oh, well, she thought, that's Ireland for you. At least the Irish are mad on purpose.

Although it was still raining, Sarah managed to find the narrow turnoff that would lead her over the hill. Through the frantically whipping windshield-wipers, she saw a wild, green landscape of mountains and boulders, and valleys veiled with drifting rain, like processions of ghostly brides.

She carried on driving for another half-hour, gradually making her way over the mountains toward Bantry. In all this time she saw only one other vehicle, a speeding farm van, with its windows all steamed up. It overtook her at nearly sixty miles an hour and then went careering off in a plume of spray.

Just before two o'clock she reached a small village, two pubs and a post-office, and she pulled up outside the least derelict-looking of the pubs, The Russet Bull, and climbed out of the car. Rain poured down the pub's steeply sloping slate roof and gurgled into its gutters. Inside, there was a long, smoky room with a flagstoned floor and battered old wooden settles. A noisy group of young people were drinking and laughing in one corner. At the far end, two determined-looking men with the tweedy jackets of farmers and the hard faces of terrorists were playing snooker. A tape was playing a Celtic lament, all violin-strings and haunted voices.

A plump fair girl behind the bar asked her what she was having.

'A sandwich, if it's not too late.'

'Too *late*?' asked the girl, in mild perplexity, as if she couldn't understand what sandwiches had to do with the time of day.

Sarah sat opposite the noisy young people with a huge wholemeal sandwich filled with slices of fresh ham and a half-pint of Guinness. The men with terrorists' faces gave her a good looking-over and then went back to their game, although one of them glanced over at her and said something to the other one, who laughed a sharp, knowing laugh.

On the creamy-plastered walls of the pub hung pieces of arcane agricultural equipment, with blackened iron prongs and chains and leather straps, like instruments of torture from the Inquisition, alongside framed sepia photographs of downtrodden-looking men in cloth caps and tightly buttoned-up jackets. The rain kept on sprinkling against the windows and the endless laments elegantly wailed of lost loves and times gone by, and Sarah began to feel as if she had been here for ever and would never leave.

She had almost finished her sandwich when she noticed the man sitting in the far corner, in the gloomiest shadows, half-hidden by the trailing cigarette smoke from the snooker table. He was dark, with slashed-back hair, and his cheekbones were knobby as a steer's skull found in the desert. From where Sarah was sitting, his eyes were drowned in shadow, but she could tell that he was watching her. One hand rested on the small table in front of him, a long-fingered hand with a heavy silver ring.

He looked so much like the man who had stood watching her at Cork Airport that she felt deeply unsettled. She knew that it couldn't possibly be him. He couldn't have reached this village ahead of her, even if he had taken the Macroom road; and how could he know that she was going to come this way, and stop here?

She finished her sandwich and barely tasted it. The plump fair girl behind the bar said, 'God speed, then,' and she was embarrassed because she hadn't thought of saying goodbye. 'May you find your heart's desire,' the girl added, as if it were a perfectly normal thing to say, like 'take care' or 'see you later'. Outside it was raining even more heavily, and she had to run across to her car.

As she drove away from The Russet Bull she glanced several times in the rear-view mirror to see if the man was following her. But the pub door remained closed and soon she was round the bend and well on her way toward Bantry.

It was getting late now, and she made her way through the mountains as fast as she dared. The rain was pelting almost horizontally across the road, and the wind buffeted the car as if it was determined to blow it off the edge of the ridge and send it rolling four hundred feet into the valley below. Water cascaded from the crags on either side, and gushed down cracks and crevices into the heather. Sarah's windshield wipers could barely cope.

But as she reached the coastal road, and started to drive northward to Kenmare, between caravansites and bed-and-breakfasts, the skies began to clear with almost unnatural swiftness; and by the time she drove into Kenmare itself, the sun was shining and the roads were dry, as if it had never been raining at all.

Kenmare was a small tourist town with two main streets, each of them lined with souvenir shops and pubs and restaurants, all painted in solid reds and greens and yellows, O'Leary's Pub and O'Sullivan's Diner and Shamrock Souvenirs. Sarah drove through it slowly, looking out for antique shops. Even in a town as over-commercialized as Kenmare, it was still possible to discover good-quality antiques at reasonable prices – especially chairs and sideboards that had been auctioned off from some of the local country houses. She saw a Regency chiffonier that she liked the look of, and made a note of the shop's telephone number. Then she drove out of Kenmare, heading westward on the narrow road that would take her out on to the Kerry peninsula.

She reached the grand gates of the Parknasilla Hotel and drove into the grounds. The afternoon was brilliant now, and the subtropical palms and bamboo bushes that lined the driveway gave her the feeling that she had driven out of Ireland and into some colonial other-reality, a memory of Mandalay. The hotel itself was a huge Gothic building, looking out over the glittering waters of the Kenmare estuary, with a view of the Caha mountains on the opposite side, still half-concealed by grey pillowy rainclouds.

The light was extraordinary. It was reflected from the ripples of the river in all directions, and gave the whole promontory a spangled, theatrical shine.

Sarah recognized several dealers from London and Brighton, and smiled in particular at Ian Caldecott, a dapper, florid-faced furniture expert from Surrey, who had taught her all about William and Mary chairs and card-tables. He raised his Panama and came over to greet her.

'My dear Sarah, I didn't know you were coming,' he said. 'We could have travelled together.'

'I didn't know I was coming, either, not until the last moment. Then Fergus told me that they were going to be selling two Daniel Marot chairs.'

'Really? They're not in the catalogue.'

'Late entries, apparently,' said Sarah. 'They come from the Kearney estate.'

'Well, well. I hope we shan't be bidding too frantically against each other.'

'We can always join forces.'

Ian tapped the side of his nose with his finger. 'Very naughty, Sarah. We don't want to be accused of auction-rigging, now do we?'

'If the chairs are good, I want them,' Sarah warned him.

A porter came out to take her bag, and she went into the hallway to register. Inside, the hotel was as Gothic and grand as it was outside, with a wide staircase and sunlit lounges with deep, heavily upholstered chairs. Sarah was taken to her room by a grinning boy with sticking-out ears.

'Hope you enjoy staying here twice as much as we enjoy having you,' he said. She tipped him a punt and he was gone before she understood what he had said; and even then she couldn't be sure that he had understood it himself.

She kicked off her shoes and started to run herself a bath. As she took off her jacket and unbuttoned her blouse she walked toward the window, which looked out over the gardens and the river, and the mountains in the distance. It was odd to think that less than two hours ago, she had been driving through those mountains in devastating rain, and yet here the weather was balmy and bright. She hung up her blouse and she had just reached behind her to unfasten her bra when she saw a man standing in the garden, partially hidden by the shadow of a yucca tree – a man who appeared to be staring up at her window.

He was tall, and dark-haired, and dressed in black. His face was as white as a sheet of notepaper. He didn't move, but there was no way in which Sarah could tell for sure that he was actually watching *her* window. It was just that he looked so much like the man she had seen at the airport, and the man she had seen at The Russet Bull.

She retreated into the room so that he wouldn't be able to see her. She sat on the end of the bed and she suddenly found that her mouth was dry, and that her heart rate had quickened. *Come on, Sarah, she thought: dozens of men dress in black; and dozens of men look at you; you're still quite attractive, after all.* It was probably a coincidence; three different men who just happened to look similar. Apart from the sheer logical impossibility of the man in The Russet Bull reaching Parknasilla before her, why on earth would anybody want to follow her? She didn't have very much money. She was attractive but she wasn't a movie star. And as far as she knew – even in the devious world of buying and selling antiques – she hadn't cheated anybody, or trodden on anybody's toes. She had once sold a bureau to a well-known horse trainer on the understanding that it was a Hodson; and when it had turned out to be a fake he had threatened to burn her shop down if she didn't give him his money back, but that was the most alarming thing that had ever happened to her. And she *had* given him his money back.

She bathed and washed her hair and changed into a light grey collarless suit. The first event of the day was a champagne reception for the dealers, to be followed by a viewing of some of the most important lots on sale. She went downstairs into the bar where she found most of the dealers already well into their third glass of Lanson, telling each other jokes and laughing too loudly.

'– and I said, if you want to believe that's a jardinière, my dear, then who am I to say it isn't? But make sure you tell people to take out the potted palm before they piss in it!'

'– squeezed his nose to stop himself from sneezing and found that he'd put in the top bid for two elephant howdahs, parasols, ladders and all!'

Sarah took a glass of champagne from the waiter and circled the room. Although she knew so many of the dealers, very few of them acknowledged her with anything more than a nod, and only one came over to welcome her, Raymond French, an art dealer who specialized in paintings of dogs. Raymond was tall and thin and very intense, with a wonderfully hooked nose and an accent that could have cut diamonds.

'Sarah, you're looking as soignée as ever,' he said. 'I didn't think this was your kind of thing.'

'I'm looking for some chairs,' said Sarah.

'Oh, chairs! Well, you were always *very* up on chairs, weren't you? I don't know. There's something about chairs that leaves me cold.'

'These are *supposed* to be Daniel Marots,' said Sarah, under her breath.

'Sorry, you've lost me. But ask me to find you a Stebbings. He did beautiful cocker spaniels, you have no idea.'

'Raymond, you don't understand. These chairs could be really significant. Daniel Marot was a French furniture designer, but he was forced into exile in Holland because he was a Protestant. He designed furniture for William of Orange, and when William of Orange acceded to the English throne, Marot came to England and had a *huge* influence on English furniture. He was totally Baroque. I mean, up until Marot, English chairs had been terribly plain; but Marot gave them high backs, covered in carving, and tasseled seats, and curved legs. His designs had so much *life*.'

'Oh, well, I don't know. As far as I'm concerned, Sarah, a chair is a chair. It may have four legs but there isn't much point in throwing a stick for it, is there?'

'You're impossible,' laughed Sarah.

It was just at this moment that Sarah became conscious that somebody else was standing very close to her. She could sense his tallness next to her shoulder. She half turned to the left, and found herself face to face with the dark, thin man who had been staring up at her window.

Close up, he appeared much more handsome, in a black-eyebrowed, saturnine way. His skin was very white and pitted, but he had a sharply cut profile and amber eyes. A white scar ran from the right side of his mouth all the way down his chin. His suit and his shirt were dead black, funeral black, and his necktie was black, too. He smelled of something faintly attractive but very old-fashioned, bay rum and lavender, and the tightly closed rooms of expensive hotels.

'Excuse me for interrupting,' he said. His voice was deep and soft, Irish-accented, like rubbing up the fur of a big black cat in the wrong direction. 'I couldn't help overhearing the name of Daniel Marot.'

'You're in furniture?' asked Sarah; and again she could feel her heartbeat quickening.

The man slowly smiled. 'I'm in . . . finding people what they want.'

'And that includes Marots?'

'That includes everything, Mrs Bryce.'

Sarah felt herself blushing. 'I'm surprised that you know my name.'

'You're the only woman dealer . . . it wasn't difficult to guess who you were. But let me introduce myself. Seáth Rider.'

'You're a dealer, too?'

'Well, in a sense, yes. But it's a strange business, isn't it, this matter of taking paintings and furniture from people's houses and selling it on, as if you were taking all of their lives to pieces, dismantling their existence, so to speak.'

'I suppose it is, if you put it like that.' Sarah couldn't help but feel conscious of Seáth Rider's aura. He was charged up, almost electrical. She felt that if she touched him, sparks would crackle out of her fingertips. She had never felt like this about a man before, and she didn't know what to make of it. It was partly sexual; but it was partly to do with fear, too. He didn't seem like a man who could be easily disagreed with, or crossed.

'There are two Marot chairs and I've seen them,' he said.

'Do you know about furniture? What kind of condition are they in?'

He made a circle with his finger and thumb, and gave her a smile that barely curled his lips. 'They're perfect, Mrs Bryce. Seventeen-oh-five or thereabouts, I'd say, soon after Marot published his collection of designs. They were made in London by Shearley, so far as I know, on a special order, and brought out here when Ballyclavan House was first built.'

'Are you bidding?' asked Sarah bluntly.

Seáth Rider shook his head: 'I've no interest in them myself, Mrs Bryce; although I know that you have.'

'And how do you know that?' She watched him as he lifted his champagne glass and took a small sip. There was a heavy silver ring on his finger, embossed with the design of a beast's face. She couldn't have sworn that it was identical to the ring worn by the man in The Russet Bull but, all the same, it was almost too much of a coincidence to be true.

'I'm always here and there, back and forth,' Seáth Rider told her. She liked the delicate Irish way he said 'fort' instead of 'forth'. 'I know when people have their heart set upon something, and the lengths to which they'll go to get it.'

'Do you have a shop?' Sarah asked him.

'Not a shop as such. But a sort of imaginary market, where you can buy whatever you want. Here—' he said, and handed her a business card. *Seáth E. Rider, Acquisitor, Dublin & London*. There was no address, only a mobile telephone number. 'For instance, if you had urgent need of an eighteenth-century teapoy, I could find you one and bring it to you within the blink of an eye. Or if you had urgent need of anything else, for that matter.'

'Well, that's very interesting, Mr Rider. Perhaps I can keep you in mind.'

Seáth Rider gave her the faintest hint of a smile. 'I was hoping that you'd do that, Mrs Bryce.'

With that, he gave her a nod, and disappeared into the crowds of dealers, almost sliding rather than walking, like a character in a children's cut-out theatre.

'Well, what do you make of *him*?' asked Raymond. 'Rather *louche*, wasn't he? And what's an "Acquisitor" when it's at home? I don't think there's any such word.'

'I don't know,' said Sarah, still trying to see where Seáth Rider had gone. 'I thought he was quite attractive, in a shifty kind of way.'

'That's the trouble with women,' Raymond retorted. 'Give them a good, trustworthy man and they won't look twice at him. But give them a rat, and they fall on their backs with their legs in the air.'

Sarah looked at him narrowly. 'Do you know something, Raymond, I do believe that *you* thought he was attractive, too.'

*

That evening, after dinner, when the sun was sinking over the Kenmare estuary, Sarah went for a walk in the hotel gardens. There was a light breeze blowing from the south-west, but the air was warm and smelled of the sea, and gulls were still circling overhead. She walked through a succession of small, secret gardens, each surrounded by a high hedge. In each there were cast-iron Victorian chairs and tables, all empty now, some tipped over. She felt that she was walking through a garden from *Alice Through The Looking Glass*, or one of Edward Gorey's drawings of Gashlycrumb Hall.

She thought how much her father would have loved this place. He had always adored a bit of grandeur, and she had never forgotten the first time he had taken her for dinner at the Savoy. He hadn't been wealthy: in fact, he had run a toyshop in a suburb of South London. But he had always been kind, and smartly dressed, and gentlemanly, and Sarah had been devastated when he died last year, only 61 years old, of a massive heart attack.

As she walked between the dark, enclosed gardens, Sarah was sure that she could hear people talking; but every garden was empty, and growing darker, too, as the sun began to sink even lower. She could hear a girl's voice, persistently arguing, and a man trying to reason with her. Yet she couldn't work out where they were. Perhaps they were somewhere behind the hedges, and their voices were being carried on the breeze.

She came out onto the shoreline, where the tidal waters splashed clear and shallow against the rocks. There were two small islands offshore, which had been connected to the hotel grounds by a causeway built of planks. Each island was overgrown with trees, and was silhouetted now against the sky. There were probably less than twenty minutes of daylight left. The clouds above the mountains were already black, and a huge pillar of cumulus had risen in the west, threatening thundery rain. It looked like a demon, with horns and billowing wings, risen from out of the furnace of the setting sun.

Sarah had thought that she was alone. But as she walked along the causeway, she saw that somebody else was ahead of her, walking in the same direction. It was a tall, white-haired man in a navy-blue blazer and grey pants. He was walking quite quickly, but with an interrupted step, because of the gaps between the planks.

Sarah stopped and shaded her eyes. She was sure she recognized him. There was something so familiar about his slightly stooped shoulders, and the way he flapped up his hand to beat away the midges. There was something so familiar about his hair. She always remembered her father saying that you can disguise your face but you can never disguise the way you look from the back.

'*Dad?*' she whispered, too frightened to say it out loud. Then, when he kept on walking, 'Dad!'

He had reached the end of the first stretch of causeway, and was crossing a small rocky point where the hotel had built bathing-huts and benches for guests to sit on while their children swam. Now he was turning toward the woods.

Shocked, thrilled, frightened, Sarah shouted, 'Dad! It's me, Sarah! Dad!'

She snatched off her shoes and started to run along the causeway barefoot. The man had almost reached the shadow of the woods, but she shouted at him again. 'Dad! Just wait a minute! Wait for me!'

Even as she ran, she knew that it couldn't be him. He was dead, how could it be him? But it *was* him. It looked so much like him. She couldn't believe that there could be two people on God's earth with the same hair and the same stooping walk and the same irritable way of flapping his hand at insects.

She reached the bathing-huts and balanced herself against one of the benches while she pulled her shoes back on. She could still see the man, walking away from her along the tree-shadowed path that led to the islands. About a hundred feet away, he paused for a moment, and looked around, and although she couldn't see his face clearly she was even more convinced that it was her father.

'Dad! Stop!' she cried out, and ran toward him. Her feet pelted through last autumn's leaves. But whether he heard her or whether he didn't, he turned into the woods and vanished behind the trees.

Sarah came to the turning in the path and stopped. From here, she could see all the way down a narrow, root-entangled path that led to an inlet between the islands. The water gleamed between the trees, but there was no sign of the white-haired man. She listened, but all she could hear was the shushing of the waves on the rocky beach, and the chirping of insects in the woods. Quite close to her, a single leaf quivered excitedly on a branch, making a soft whirring sound, but that was all.

She stayed where she was for almost two minutes, still listening, but it was obvious that there was nobody here. It had all seemed so real, but she must have imagined it. Maybe she was tired, after travelling across the mountains, and spending the whole afternoon talking antiques. She had drunk half a bottle of Chablis with her dinner, and that might have induced a hallucination, or a mirage, or a memory, or whatever it was.

She put her hand up to her face and found that tears were sliding down her cheeks. She had wanted so much to see her father one more time. She had wanted so much for him not to be dead. It had taken her more than six months to come to terms with the fact that he had gone, and even now she found herself unexpectedly crying when she heard one of his favourite songs, or smelled pipe tobacco, or heard a man tunelessly whistling in the street.

She turned around, and literally jumped. Standing less than ten feet away from her was Seáth Rider, his hands in his pockets, watching her.

'God, you scared me.'

'I'm sorry. I didn't mean to. I saw you marching off to the islands and wondered if you wanted some company.'

'I don't think so, thank you. Besides, I'm going back now. It's getting too late.'

'Well, that's a shame. It's a charming walk and it won't take us more than fifteen minutes.'

'I'm cold,' she said, and tried to push past him; but he took hold of her arm, not roughly, but very insistently.

'You've been piping your eye.'

'It's nothing. Hay fever, that's all.'

'And you want me to believe that?'

'Quite frankly, I don't care what you believe.'

'Oh, come on, now,' he said, in that soothing, cat's-fur voice. 'There's no need to be offish about it, is there? I'm only trying to be sociable. I know what it's like when you've lost somebody dear to you. Everybody thinks that you can get over it, but you never can.'

She stared at him, face to face. 'How did you know?' she demanded.

'I'm sorry. How did I know what?'

'How did you know why I was crying?'

He gave her a look like no man had ever looked at her before. It was a mixture of desire and teasing and something that was close to greed. She had the disturbing feeling that he had an erection. 'I'm always here and there,' he said. 'You know. Back and forth.'

'But you knew why I was crying.'

'Well . . . don't think anything of it. It's only intuition. You know what the Irish are like. Tribal, touchy, maudlin, over-sentimental, quick as a flash to take offence and preternaturally slow to forget it. Magical, too; though not in the way that tourists think. None of your little people and your leprechauns' crossings, your Blarney stone and all that tosh. Different magic, that's what.'

Sarah waited for a while to see if he was going to explain himself further, but he didn't; and so she drew her arm away. 'I'm tired,' she said. 'I think I'm going back.'

'You're missing something, believe me.'

'I expect I am. But then we can't always have what we want, can we?'

His eyes glittered in the twilight. He was tall and dark and crowned with midges. 'Oh, you're wrong there,' he told her. 'We can *always* have what we want.'

Sarah hesitated for a moment longer, she didn't know why; but then she made her way back toward the bathing-huts.

The estuary was lilac when she got there, lilac and grey, and the waters still persistently lapping. She glanced back once, but she couldn't see Seáth Rider at all, because the shadows were so deep, or perhaps he had carried on walking. She didn't understand what had happened. She didn't understand how she could have imagined seeing her father, and how he had vanished so completely. She didn't understand how Seáth Rider could have such an acute sense of what she was feeling. *Here and there, back and forth*, what the hell did that mean?

She walked back through the gardens. This time she heard no voices, only the sound of laughter from the hotel lobby and car doors slamming. She went back inside, where it was noisy and lively, and went to the bar to see if she could have a nightcap with anyone she knew.

On the whole, the auction was disappointing. Some of the best lots had been withdrawn, including paintings by Jack Butler Yeats and Sir John Lavery, and a set of pen-and-ink sketches by William Orpen. A large breakfront bookcase had been taken out, too, much to Ian Caldecott's fury, because he had been specially commissioned to bid for it by a wealthy rock musician who wanted it for his library.

Oddly, Sarah found that she was pleased that so many paintings and so many articles of furniture were staying in Ireland. She kept thinking of what Seáth Rider had said about 'taking people's lives to pieces, so to speak'. But she still wanted her Daniel Marot chairs. She had inspected them this morning, in daylight, and they were perfect. High-backed, exquisitely carved, with curved legs and curved stretchers; and their original upholstery, in faded rose-pink, with fringes. They had been cared for so well that they could have been nearly new. She had run her hands over the carvings, and they had felt almost as if they were flesh, rather than wood, because they were so warm and smooth.

She was sitting at the back of the conference room where the auction was being held. There must have been two or three hundred dealers there, illuminated by the sunshine that came through the windows like parishioners in church, a bald head over here shining through its last traces of carefully combed hair; and over there a large pair of ears glowing red. There, some smeary thumbprinted spectacles; and here, too close for comfort, a black jacket liberally sprinkled with dandruff.

The auctioneer was bald and pink and smooth as a billiard ball, with wiry half-glasses and a formal suit. His accent was Kerry-trying-to-be-Posh, and since Kerry is incomprehensible anyway, even to Irishmen from other counties, and Posh meant saying 'fornitchewer' and 'harty facts', it was difficult for most of the dealers to follow what was going on, and Ian Caldecott became even more enraged when he missed an important Regency writing-table.

At the very end, the Daniel Marot chairs were brought in, and set up on the rostrum. Ian Caldecott glanced back at Sarah and she knew then that she was in trouble. He wanted these badly, almost as badly as she did, and since he still had plenty of money to spend, the chances were that he was going to push her as high as he could.

'Well then lot 167a two upright chairs to the design of Daniel Marot and attributed to Josiah Shearley of London *circa* 1705. Can we start at three thousand punts the pair.'

Sarah waved her prospectus and at the same time Ian Caldecott lifted a single finger. This time he didn't look back at her.

'Three thousand five hundred do I hear you now.'

Again, Sarah waved her prospectus and Ian Caldecott lifted his finger.

'Four thousand is it now.'

Sarah had guessed that the two chairs could probably be retailed at £3,750 each, but even that was stretching it. To make any kind of profit, she would have to stop bidding at £6,000. If she went above that, she wouldn't even be able to cover her air fare and her hotel bill and the hire of her emerald-green car. But she did badly want those chairs. They were historic, and they were simply beautiful. They represented the moment when English furniture first came truly alive.

'Four thousand five hundred is that what I'm hearing.'

Sarah waved her prospectus. Ian Caldecott lifted his finger.

'Is it five thousand now.'

A low murmuring went through the auction-room. It was obvious that the price of the chairs had almost reached their premium trade value, and that the bidding was becoming a personal contest between Sarah and Ian Caldecott, the experienced connoisseur and his assertive young pupil.

'Five thousand five,' said the auctioneer. There was a pause, and he raised his gavel. 'Any takers at five thousand five.'

Ian Caldecott hesitated for a moment, then bid. Sarah bid too.

'Six is it then. Six thousand punts.'

Ian Caldecott bid, but this time Sarah hesitated. This was the very limit of what she could spend. Then again, she thought, she could always raise the extra money from a few quick sales. She had a Welsh dresser that she had just bought in Lymington which would probably fetch £650, even though it was unrestored, and she had two Thompson Hobbs paintings that she had been intending to have cleaned but which would raise another £400–£500.

'Going for six thousand,' said the auctioneer; but Sarah waved her prospectus again.

For the first time, Ian Caldecott turned around to look at her. She tried to smile at him, but the expression on his face was so furious that her smile died at birth.

'Six thousand five. Seven. Seven thousand five.'

Now Sarah knew that she was way beyond her budget. If she bid more than £7,500 she would never get her money back, and she wouldn't be able to buy anything else here at Parknasilla in the hope of cutting her losses. All the same, she waved her prospectus one more time.

'Seven thousand five. Is it any more than seven thousand five. Going to Mrs Bryce then for seven thousand five.' *They're mine*, thought Sarah, with a surge of triumph. *I've done it!*

Ian Caldecott lifted his finger.

'Eight,' said the auctioneer. Everybody turned in their seats to look at Sarah, and right at that moment she could have burst into tears. She had already taken far too much of a risk, and even though she was absolutely desperate to show Ian Caldecott that she could beat him at his own game, she knew that she couldn't commit financial suicide for the sake of two chairs.

'Going for eight thousand to Mr Caldecott; gone.'

Sarah got up from her seat and left the auction-room without looking back. She went outside, where the sun was shining on the water and the yuccas were rustling. For the first time in seven years she felt like a cigarette. For the first time in three years she wished that Ken were here, so that she could talk to him. For all of his faults, for all of his tantrums, he had always cheered her up when she was disappointed, and made her laugh.

She leaned against the rail overlooking the estuary, her hair blowing in her face. She heard quiet footsteps, and saw a shadow on the flagstones, and then Seáth Rider came up and leaned on the rail beside her, black-suited as always.

'Another fine day,' he remarked. 'There's a story that you could see the lost city of Atlantis from here, under certain weather conditions, reflected in the sky.'

Sarah said nothing but brushed back her hair with her hand.

'You're looking glum,' said Seáth Rider. 'You lost the chairs, I'll bet.'

'Yes, Mr Rider, I lost the bloody chairs. They went for eight thousand and I just couldn't match it.'

'That's a terrible pity. They're fine chairs, the both of them.'

'God knows how Ian's going to get his money back. They're scarcely worth six.'

'Maybe he wasn't looking to get his money back. Maybe he just didn't want you to have them. You know what some of these dealers are like – dogs in the manger. Especially when it comes to women. They're very sensitive about women, and a whole lot of old queens, most of them.'

'I'd pack and go home except I haven't bought anything yet.'

He smiled at her and shook his head. 'You musn't start thinking like that. No good ever came of giving in.'

She didn't reply. She didn't really know what to say. After a while she left him standing by the rail and went back into the hotel. In the lobby she met Ian Caldecott, looking bright-eyed and pleased with himself.

'You gave me quite a run for my money, there, Sarah,' he effused. 'You must let me buy you a glass of champagne to commiserate.'

'You really are a stupid old bastard, aren't you?' Sarah retorted. 'You could have agreed not to bid against me and we could have shared the profit. You knew how much I wanted those chairs. Now neither of us have ended up with anything.'

'Just remember who taught you everything you know,' said Ian.

'I haven't, and I never will. Because one thing I know now is that a pupil should never trust her teacher. Especially when her teacher grows jealous.'

She went upstairs to her room, and threw her prospectus on to the table. Outside her window, the gardens were dappled with sunlight, and even the mountains were clear, for a while. Seáth Rider was still leaning against the rail, but he wasn't watching the water. He was watching her, although he was too far away to see if he was serious or smiling. She stood close to the curtains, so that he wouldn't be able to see her, and she wondered who he really was, and why he took such an interest in her. Perhaps he behaved in the same way with every woman he met. But she had never seen him talking to any other woman the way he talked to her; and she had never seen him staring at any other woman's window.

She began to feel that he was intimately connected with her, in an inexplicable way – that their futures were somehow intertwined. A nemesis, a shadow, a promise of unknown days to come. The kind of man you meet in dreams.

She came back to the window almost an hour later and he was still watching.

The next day was fresher and cooler and so she dressed in jeans and a white cable-knit sweater. After breakfast, she drove first to the little village of Sneem where she sat in O'Sullivan's Pub with a half of Guinness and wrote postcards to all of her friends. Then she went on to the west, through the fields and the mountains, with bright sandy glimpses of the Kenmare estuary off to her left, and then the Atlantic Ocean, pale and green, listlessly heaping its seaweed on to the beaches.

She drove as far as the little town of Cahirciveen and then she parked by the side of the main street and went looking for antique shops. She found a good prie-dieu with a Berlin tapestry seat; and a china display cabinet, a vitrine, which she bought for less than £400; a Sutherland fall-leaf table; and a beautiful pâpier-maché chair, an original Jennens & Bettridge, inlaid with mother-of-pearl and gilded with flowers.

She was leaving the last antique shop when she thought she saw her ex-husband Ken turning into a pub along the street. He couldn't have been Ken; but he was wearing the same blue linen jacket that Ken always wore when he painted, and he had the same shock of brown hair, and even the same shoes, those awful tan-coloured Hush Puppies that he wore every day of the week.

Sarah turned back to the woman in the antique shop, and said, 'Have you ever seen anybody dead?'

'Well, there's a question,' said the woman, all pink-cheeked and flustered. 'I saw my ma and my da in their caskets, of course; and my Uncle Joe.'

'But you've never seen anybody dead walking around the streets? Or anybody who couldn't conceivably be there, dead or alive?'

The woman was wiping her hands on a tea-towel. She gave Sarah a peculiar, bulgy-eyed look. 'I can't say that I have. And I think if I did I'd run a mile.'

'I'm sorry,' said Sarah. 'I'll arrange for the shipping and let you know.'

She walked cautiously along the street. The afternoon was windy now, and the moving clouds were reflected in every window, like televisions in a television store, with all the same programme playing. The pub was painted liver-red outside, with decorative shamrocks. O'Hagans Pub & Restaurant, Guinness, Murphys and Caffreys, and those were just to quench your thirst before you started on the Bush.

She stepped inside. A single doleful man with gray hedgehog hair and cavernous cheeks was wiping up glasses. He looked like Samuel Beckett's untalented brother.

'Are you open?' she asked. He turned and blinked at her as if he had never expected to have a customer, never, not of any early afternoon.

'Of course we're open. How would you have got in?'

Sarah turned back toward the door. 'I would have – yes, I see. I see what you mean.'

'We're quiet of course. There's not much trade on a Tuesday. Would you care for a drink?'

'Yes, yes please. A Guinness will do.'

She turned and there he was, sitting just in front of a strong triangle of sunshine, his hand on the table with its silver ring, a glass of whiskey in front of him catching the light. She left her Guinness on the bar to settle and walked across to him and dragged out a chair.

'Something's going on,' she told him, before he could speak. 'Something I don't understand. I thought I saw my ex-husband coming in here, but now it's turned out to be you.'

'You didn't have to follow me,' he said.

'No, I didn't. But I did. I don't know how you managed to look like Ken. I can't begin to imagine how you know what Ken looks like. But it was you, wasn't it? And last night, out on the island, my father was you. You have a knack for it, don't you? Knowing what I want, knowing what I need. What is it, hypnotism, something like that? Or do I make myself so bloody obvious that you don't even need to hypnotize me? Is it a trick? What is it? And what do you want?'

Seáth Rider looked at her ruefully. 'Why are you giving me such a hard time, Mrs Bryce, when all I want to do is to please you?'

'What? By following me? By making me think that—'

'Please, Mrs Bryce. I'm not making you think anything. Whatever you think, whatever you want, that's up to you.'

She said, 'Anyway, I'm leaving tomorrow morning, first thing. I didn't get the Daniel Marot chairs; but I think I've made enough to cover my expenses.'

Seáth Rider lifted his glass. 'I'll drink to that, Mrs Bryce.'

And for all that she didn't understand him, and found him so strange and threatening, Sarah lifted her glass, too.

When she returned to her room at the Parknasilla, the chairs were there, waiting for her. She walked in and there they were, side by side, slightly angled, as if two people had been sitting in them, talking, only minutes before. She approached them in disbelief, and touched them, and they were real. Solid, carved, but brilliantly imagined, with tall backs and stretchers that curved as if they were alive. She was always amazed how few people realized that furniture – just as much as paintings, or sculptures, or music – didn't begin to exist until somebody had imagined it, and turned that imagination into something that other people could see and touch. Yes, and even sit on.

She sat on her bed and stared at them. Surely Ian Caldecott couldn't have been so remorseful that he had let her have the chairs? Even if he had, he wouldn't have taken them up to her room, surely? Once they were sold, they were due to be crated and shipped directly back to London.

She had a strange feeling that Seáth Rider was involved in this. She had no proof, of course, but it seemed like his style. She just hoped that he hadn't bullied Ian Caldecott into letting her have them; or something worse. She picked up the phone and asked reception to put her through to Mr Caldecott's room.

'I'm sorry, Mrs Bryce, would you repeat the name?'

'Caldecott, Ian Caldecott. I don't know his room number, but he's one of the antique dealers.'

'Caldecott, did you say? Well, there's no one of that name registered here.'

'There must be. I saw him this morning.'

'Are you sure he was resident with us, Mrs Bryce, and didn't just come for the auction?'

'Of course I'm sure. He even told me how much he liked his room. Listen – why don't you put me through to the auctioneers? They may know where he is.'

She waited for nearly five minutes, listening to 'Greensleeves' over and over again. Finally a cultured voice said, 'O'Shaughnessy and Drum, Mr Drum speaking.'

'Oh, hallo, Mr Drum. This is Mrs Bryce.'

'Well, now, Mrs Bryce. What can I do for you? Congratulations on the chairs, by the way. You got yourself a bargain there, wouldn't you say?'

'But I didn't get the chairs. Ian Caldecott outbid me.'

'I'm sorry?'

'I was outbid by Mr Caldecott. But now the chairs have turned up here in my room.'

'Where you said you wanted them, Mrs Bryce, so that you could have a chance to admire them for a while before we packed them up for shipping.'

Sarah was so confused that she could hardly speak. 'Mr Drum – there must be some mistake. I didn't – I didn't even—'

'I'm sorry, Mrs Bryce, did we misunderstand your instructions somehow? If you wish us to pack up the chairs directly, we will be only too happy to oblige.'

'But they're not my chairs, Mr Drum! Mr Caldecott bought them!'

There was an embarrassed silence. Then Mr Drum said, 'The records show otherwise, Mrs Bryce. There were two principal bidders, yes; and one of them was you. But the other was Mr James McGuinness, and he stopped bidding at £5,500, which is when the chairs were knocked down to you.'

'I'm going mad,' said Sarah. 'Either that, or you're going mad. What about Mr Caldecott?'

Another silence, even longer than the first. Then, 'I'm sorry, Mrs Bryce. I hate to contradict a favoured client, such as yourself. But to my knowledge there was no Mr Caldecott present at the auction; and I have never heard of any antique dealer by that name. The only Caldecott I know of is the children's book illustrator, Randolph Caldecott. And of course he died more than a hundred years ago.'

'You've never heard of Ian Caldecott?'

'No, Mrs Bryce. Never.'

Sarah lowered the receiver. She could hear Mr Drum's tiny voice saying '*Hello? Hello?*' like an insect in a matchbox. She had seen Mr Drum talking to Ian Caldecott; she had seen him shake his hand. How could be possibly say that he had never heard of him?

'*Hello? Hello?*' Mr Drum persisted; so Sarah hung up.

She went back to the chairs and stood between them, with a hand on each one. They were beautiful; they were almost magical; and in some extraordinary way they seemed to be hers. But how? And what had happened to Ian Caldecott? At a stretch, she could imagine that Ian had felt guilty after outbidding her, and had let her have the chairs as a gesture of goodwill. But that sort of spontaneous generosity wasn't really in his nature. She had seen him talk to another woman dealer for almost half an hour, dissuading her from buying a cane-seat Regency chair because it was 'obviously fake', and then buying it himself for less than half what it was really worth.

She was still looking at the chairs when there was a quick, sharp knock at her door. She went to open it, expecting the maid. Instead, it was Seáth Rider, looking pale but excited. He stalked into the room before she could stop him, and walked straight up to the chairs, although he didn't touch them.

'There! They're very fine, aren't they? And are you pleased with them, now?'

'I think they're beautiful. But they still don't belong to me.'

Seáth Rider twisted around and stared at her, as if he couldn't believe what he was hearing. 'What do you mean, they don't belong to you? You bid for them fair and square, didn't you? You paid for them?'

'Ian Caldecott outbid me.'

'Ian Caldecott? Now who would he be?'

'You know exactly who he is. God, you're beginning to sound like all the rest of them now.'

Seáth Rider approached her and his face was very serious, almost tragic. 'There is no Ian Caldecott, Mrs Bryce. There never was. You bought those chairs. Look at your cheque-book if you want the proof.'

Sarah went to her purse, opened it up, and took out the Gucci cheque-book wallet that Ken had given her for her birthday, after selling two paintings to the Oswald Gallery in Bond Street. That was probably the only time that he had ever had any money of his own. She opened her cheque-book, and there it was, the cheque stub, in her own handwriting, in her own distinctive violet ink. *O'Shaughnessy & Drum, 4,500, DM Chairs.*

'I didn't write this,' she said, her voice wavering. She stepped up to Seáth Rider and shook the cheque-book under his nose. '*I didn't write this!*'

Seáth Rider shrugged, and said, 'Take it to a handwriting expert if you wish. You bid for the chairs, you topped the bidding and you took out your cheque-book. Confident as any woman I've ever seen – a queen amongst dealers, I'd say.'

'Something's happened, hasn't it?' said Sarah.

'Happened? What would you mean by that?'

'Something's happened to Ian Caldecott . . . You've bribed him, or you've threatened him, or something. He wouldn't have given me those chairs for anything!'

Seáth Rider said, 'There is no Ian Caldecott. There never was.'

'I don't understand you. I don't understand any of this.'

'But it's very simple, especially if you know your Irish legends. There was always magic here, of a kind, which people fancified and turned into stories of little people and all that guff. But there's another world here, Mrs Bryce, there always has been; and there was a whole people, Lir's people, the people of the Tuatha, back in ancient times, who disappeared from human view. Vanished!'

'I still don't understand.'

'You will if you realize that the portals of the invisible kingdoms were never completely closed, and there were those who could travel with ease from one to the other, having friends and even lovers in both existences.

'The Fianna could do that: they were warriors, trained in every skill; and among them was Iollan, who kept a fairy mistress called Fair Breast. She was his heart's desire, the most beautiful creature that you ever saw, and all Iollan had to do was breathe her name, wherever she was, and she would appear, and she would do anything for him, whatever he wanted. For all of the pleasure she gave him, she asked only one thing in return, and that was his fidelity.'

'What the – what the *hell* are you talking about?' Sarah demanded. 'I want to know what's happened to Ian Caldecott – not some ridiculous fairy-story!'

'But that's what I'm trying to tell you,' said Seáth Rider. 'Iollan fell in love with a human woman, and married her, and made her pregnant with twin boys. So when Fair Breast found out what had happened, she turned Iollan's wife into a dog, and dragged her off to live with a man who hated dogs, so that she would be starved and whipped. And to Iollan she said: I will turn her back into a woman, if you come and live with me for ever, in the invisible kingdom. So what could he do, poor fellow, but agree?

'The only snag was that his sons, who had both been born as dogs, would have to remain as dogs for the rest of their lives.'

'All right,' said Sarah. 'Tell me what it means. Tell me what you're talking about. And where's Ian Caldecott?'

Seáth Rider went over to the window and looked out over the gardens and the estuary. The mountains were plumed with clouds. 'You can always have whatever you desire, Mrs Bryce; just as Iollan of the Fianna had what he desired. But somebody always has to pay the price. It's the magical version of Newton's Law, if you like. No action without a reaction. Maybe the reaction doesn't affect you, but it always affects somebody.'

Sarah said nothing, but stood waiting for him to say what she knew he was going to say: her fists clenched, her heart beating fast.

Seáth Rider turned away from the window and said, 'If there was ever a man called Ian Caldecott, he would have outbid you for these chairs, and taken them away. But now, there never was. Ian Caldecott was never born, and he never grew up, and he never went to university or started a dealership. You will never find a photograph of him in the South of France; you will never find a school report or a dental record or a social security card. You will never find a tot that knew him, when he was tiny. You will never find a woman who kissed him at his first party. He has evaporated, Mrs Bryce, as if he never existed.'

'You've murdered him,' said Sarah. She was shaking with shock.

'Of course I haven't. How can you murder somebody who never existed?'

'Then you've – Christ, I don't know what you've done! What have you *done*?'

'I've expunged him, I'd say that's the word. He's not gone completely, if you get my meaning. Matter can neither be created nor destroyed. But he's certainly not *here*, that's the message, and never was here, ever.'

'For two chairs? For two stupid chairs?'

Seáth Rider frowned at her. He looked hurt. 'You said those chairs were your heart's desire. What does it matter to you whether Ian Caldecott ever existed or not? *He* doesn't mind: he never existed. His family doesn't mind: they never ever knew him. People get killed every day. Shot, or drowned, or knocked down on pedestrian crossings because they were thinking about what they could eat for their tea, instead of looking. That never worries you does it, so why are you so worried about Ian Caldecott? You have your chairs, and everything's hunky-dory.'

Sarah had to sit down. 'I can't take this in. You erased his entire life, *everything*, just because you wanted me to have these chairs?'

'Oh no, Mrs Bryce. You wanted the chairs, not me. I'm an acquisitor, not a collector. But that was the price, yes. That was the only way to do it.'

'But *how*? How do you rub out somebody's whole existence?'

Seáth Rider pointed to the mountains, covered in grey, thunderous clouds; and to the Kenmare estuary, sparkling with sunshine. 'If you want me to put it simply, Mrs Bryce, there are visible kingdoms and invisible kingdoms; and here in Ireland the doors are still open for those who know how to tread between. And, yes, it was me who watched you at the airport; and it was me sitting at The Russet Bull; and here, too, when you arrived.'

'I'm going to have to give the chairs back,' said Sarah.

'To whom?' Seáth Rider demanded. 'Not to Ian Caldecott, because there is no Ian Caldecott. Not to his family, because they won't know who he was. They're yours, Mrs Bryce. You bid for them, you paid for them, they're yours.'

'And what do *you* get out of this?' asked Sarah.

Seáth Rider smiled, a genuine smile this time. 'I get my commission, Mrs Bryce. Don't you worry about that.'

Unexpectedly, he kissed her on the cheek. It was a kiss like no other kiss she had experienced before: soft, yet positive; unusually salacious; a kiss that told her that he wanted more. For some reason she found it incredibly erotic, and when he left the room and closed the door behind him, she stood stiff and wide-eyed, her right hand straight down by her side, her left hand clutching her right elbow, rigid, like a woman who has just witnessed a serious traffic accident.

In the night she dreamed of her father. She was sitting on his lap and he was reading to her. She could smell tobacco and cologne and old tweed coat. Outside the library windows the sky was a bright shade of aniline purple, and the clouds moved as if they were cut out of cardboard. Sarah knew that she was safe for the moment, but she felt a small, nagging anxiety that when her father reached the end of the story that he was telling her, something terrible would happen; and so she kept begging him to read on and on and on.

The story was like no story that she had ever heard before. 'The razormen came when the night was darkest and sneaked through the house calling and singing. Everybody knew they were there but nobody dared to open a door. They had razors in their fingers and razors in their backs. They had razors in the palms of their hands. If they once took hold of you, why then you were blood all over before you knew it. They had razors between their teeth and they wanted to kiss you.'

She clutched at her father's prickly tweed lapel in fear; and for security, too. Inside his waistcoat his voice was a warm, reassuring rumble. She couldn't think why he was trying to frighten her so much. The razormen! She could see them crawling along the corridor, their backs embedded with two-edged blades, enduring the agony because nobody would dare to touch them when they emptied out your drawers full of jewellery or raped your daughters in a blood-drenched bed. She heard somebody screaming, and she felt somebody jump on the bed.

She woke up, abruptly, and caught herself kicking the mattress with her heels and making a peculiar gargling noise. She lay back, gasping and sweating, and took ten deep breaths.

A dream, she told herself. *That's all it was. A ridiculous, terrifying dream.* The moon was high and it shone between the curtains and illuminated the two chairs. She propped herself up on one elbow and stared at them. It was well past 3.00 in the morning and she felt exhausted and disoriented. She hadn't bought the chairs, she knew that. Somebody else had bought them. Somebody called –

Somebody called –

At first she couldn't think of his name. She could remember his face, but she simply couldn't think of his name. Ian Somebody. Ian Coldwell. Ian Cottesmore. Something like that. Her memory of him was fading like a photograph left in the sun. But she looked at the chairs and she could remember what Seáth Rider had done for her; giving her just what she wanted.

She climbed out of bed and went into the bathroom to splash her face with cold water. She stared at herself in the mirror and thought that she looked distinctly different. Not older, but different. When you live with somebody, you use your partner's face as a mirror, instead of a real mirror. You see your smiles reflected; you see your anger rising before you even know that you're angry. You see sarcasm, you see affection. But when you live on your own, you have to rely on glass mirrors, with silver backs, and there was never a glass mirror with a silver back that ever told the truth.

Sarah's father had once said, 'Mirrors are only good for one thing: to hold over a dead man's lips, to make sure that he isn't breathing any longer.' And that had scared her, too.

She suddenly thought of seeing her father out on the island; and the more she thought about it, the more convinced she became that she hadn't imagined it, and that Seáth Rider had been involved in conjuring him up. Maybe he had done it to tempt her; to excite her. But then again, maybe he had done it to show her what he was capable of doing. Maybe the chairs were nothing more than a teaser, a way of warming her up.

After all, if he had managed to manipulate history to expunge the man who had originally bought these chairs, this Ian somebody, couldn't he manipulate history to bring her something she wanted even more? Couldn't he alter time and events so that her father hadn't really died?

She realized that the thought was blasphemous. But she had seen her father, alive. Not an illusion, not a trick of the light. And if Seáth Rider could bring him back to her, the way he had brought her these chairs . . .

She went back to bed. It was only 4.00 but she wished it were morning. She was too tired to read but she was too excited to sleep. In the end, however, she *did* sleep, from 5.15 until way past eight. She talked constantly, strange unintelligible sentences, and once or twice she cried, and tears dripped down her cheeks.

She met Seáth Rider outside. The morning was misty, so misty that it was almost raining; but the only concession that Seáth Rider had made to the weather was to turn up his collar.

'Did you sleep well?' he asked her.

'No. I kept worrying about those bloody chairs.'

'Ah, you'll get used to them. They're housetrained.'

'As a matter of fact, I kept worrying about you, what else you could do.'

He turned and stared at her in exaggerated surprise. 'What *else* I could do? Now what do you mean by that?'

'I was just wondering if you could do other things . . . apart from making that man disappear, so that I could have my chairs.'

'Don't they always say that women are never satisfied?'

'It's not that . . . it's just that I saw my father, out on the island. I was wondering whether that was anything to do with you.'

'Your father's dead.'

'The man who bought those chairs was once alive.'

Seáth Rider wiped his face with his hand. 'You're not trying to suggest that I've got any power over life or death? Because I haven't. All I can do is get you what you want.'

She stood beside him, watching him. She was afraid of him and the consequences of knowing him but her need was greater than her fear. 'Supposing I want my father.'

He looked at her without speaking.

'Supposing *that's* my heart's desire?'

'Well, then,' he said, 'that would be something of an acquisition now, wouldn't it? But of course it would cost you.'

'Is it possible? Is it really possible?'

'I didn't say that it was and I didn't say that it wasn't. All I said was, it would cost you.'

'How much?' she demanded.

'Seáth Rider shook his head. 'More than you could afford, I should say.'

'How much? I'll give you anything you want.'

'No,' he said. 'You'd only welsh.'

'Mr Rider, if you could bring my father back to me, I swear on my life that I would never go back on my word, no matter what you asked me for.'

'I ask only what Fair Breast asked of Iollan. Your fidelity.'

'Are you asking me to sleep with you, is that it?'

'Nothing of the kind; unless you wish it. I just want your faithfulness, that's all.'

'I don't really understand.'

'Your father never taught you what fidelity was? Cleaving to a person through thick and thin; through rain and shine; staying true?'

Sarah was confused. She couldn't think what Seáth Rider wanted her to do. But all the same she said, 'Yes, you can have my fidelity, if that's the price of bringing my father back.'

'For ever and ever?'

'Yes, for what that's worth.'

Seáth Rider shrugged. 'Very well, then, if that's what you want.'

Sarah waited. 'Is that it? Is that all there is to it?'

The rain dripped from the tip of Seáth Rider's nose, and trickled down his cheeks as if he were crying. 'What more did you want? A flash of lightning and a rumble of thunder?' It still made her shiver when he said 'tunder'.

'But he's going to come back?'

'You'll just have to wait and see, won't you? You can give me a kiss if you care to.'

She stood facing him for a long time and the rain grew steadily heavier. At last she stepped forward, and laid her hands on his shoulders, and kissed him, on the lips.

'You're rare,' he said. 'You're very rare.'

She was about to turn away, but she found that she couldn't resist kissing him again, rain-wet lips touching rain-wet lips, scarcely more than a graze, but enough for the nerve-endings in her lips to tingle, and her eyes to close.

She stared directly into his eyes, but it occurred to her that she didn't even know what she was looking for. 'Thank you,' she whispered, and then she walked back toward the hotel.

During the afternoon the clouds unravelled and the rain cleared away. Sarah went for a walk around the hotel grounds, and out to the islands. She saw two or three other guests, and exchanged 'good days', but she saw no sign of her father. She began to suspect that Seáth Rider had been deceiving her with all his talk of giving people whatever they wanted, and his 'fidelity'. Irish blarney, that's all it was.

Just after three o'clock she drove into Kenmare to take a look at the shops. She bought two fine linen tablecloths and a set of silver spoons, and was tempted by a small walnut cabinet, but decided that she had probably spent enough on her Daniel Marot chairs. At five she was beginning to feel hungry so she went into O'Leary's Restaurant for a half of Guinness and a prawn sandwich. O'Leary's had a bar on one side and a large, airy restaurant on the other, with gilded mirrors on the walls and old-fashioned fans rotating on the ceiling. Sarah was about to go into the bar, which seemed cosier and jollier, when she noticed a man sitting at one of the tables in the restaurant with his back to her. An elderly man, in a green tweed jacket. Beside him on the tabletop lay a pipe and a tobacco-pouch.

She felt a crawling sensation all the way down her back. It couldn't be him, surely. Not here, in this crowded restaurant, in Kenmare.

She thought: no, it can't be him. She had hoped and prayed that Seáth Rider could give her what she wanted, but at the bottom of her heart she hadn't really believed that it was possible. The dead can't come back – not after five years, anyway.

All the same, she found herself walking across the restaurant, circling around tables until she was standing close behind him. She closed her eyes for a moment. She didn't know what would upset her the most: if it *were* him, or if it *weren't*. But then she reached out and touched his shoulder, and he turned around.

And it was.

Neither of them spoke. Her father pushed back his chair, and stood up, and took her in his arms. For a long, long time the two of them stood in the middle of the restaurant, holding each other, with tears streaming down their faces. A few people looked and a few people smiled, but in Ireland that sort of dearness is never anything to be ashamed of, and that's why they cry when they play their laments.

'My dearest Sarah,' said her father, at last. 'How I've missed you, you've no idea.'

'Oh, Daddy, I've missed you too.'

They sat down, and held hands across the red-checkered tablecloth. Sarah couldn't believe how young her father looked, and how fit. *He's dead*, she thought, *and I think he looks fit!* It was like one of those awful Jewish jokes about the husband who died after a holiday in Florida, with all the relatives at the funeral home saying how well he looked. She found herself laughing at her own stupidity, but also with pleasure, just to have him back again.

'How have you been keeping?' her father asked her. 'You look different. Your hair's different. How's that idle husband of yours?'

'Ken? We're divorced.'

'Oh, I'm sorry to hear that. I always rather liked poor old Ken.'

'Daddy,' she said. 'I'm so glad to have you back. Mummy won't know what to say, will she, when I bring you back home?'

Her father lowered his eyes. 'How is Mummy? Did she take it really badly?'

Sarah nodded, with a lump in her throat. 'You'll make her so happy, coming back. We can be a family again, with Sunday lunches and walks and everything.'

Her father didn't look up. 'I can't do it, Sarah. I can't come back.'

'But you're *alive*. You were dead, but now you're alive. Of course you can come back!'

The woman at the next table gave her the oddest of looks, and then went back to her conversation about making jam.

'Perhaps it's physically possible, my darling. But I've got another life now quite different from the life I had before. I passed from one life into the next; and now I have friends who need me and people who rely on me. I *could* come back, but to tell you the truth—'

He squeezed her hands tight, and his eyes filled with tears. 'I love you, Sarah, with all my heart. But the life I spent with you and Mummy is over now, and no amount of wishing can bring it back. I *could* come back, but I've been living in a very different place – a place of great affection and complete fulfilment – and I simply don't want to.'

The waitress brought Sarah's sandwich. She pushed it to one side. She couldn't eat anything now if she tried.

'What are you going to do?' she asked her father. 'How long are you going to stay here?'

'Just long enough to tell you that I love you; and goodbye. I didn't have the chance to say goodbye before, did I?'

'You can't go,' Sarah begged him. 'I've brought you back, Daddy. I need you so much; and Mummy needs you more.'

He gave her the saddest of smiles. 'I'm sorry, darling. I really am. But I have to move on. There's so much waiting for me.'

He stood up, and the sun came through the restaurant window behind him and dazzled her, so that she couldn't see his face. He said, 'I love you, Sarah, and I wish you well,' and then he turned and walked out of the restaurant, leaving her sitting alone. She saw him pass by the window, more like a reflection than a real person, but then he was gone. She could have run out after him, and begged him to come back; but she knew that it wasn't any use. *I could come back, but I simply don't want* to . . . and what could be more specific than that?

The waitress came over, all concerned. 'Is there something wrong with your sandwich?' she asked.

Sarah shook her head and tried to sound bright. 'No. Not at all. There's something wrong with me.'

'Well, don't worry, dear, I won't charge you for it if you didn't like it.'

Sarah couldn't speak. Tears flooded out of her eyes, and all she could do was cover her face with her hands and let out a series of deep, muted sobs.

The waitress sat down next to her and put her arm around her. 'What's the matter, then? Is it something I can help you with?'

'No,' said Sarah. 'Nobody can.'

The waitress held her and shushed her while she sat on her bentwood chair and let out the longest burst of uncontrollable grief since her father had died.

When she returned from Kenmare it was evening and she found Seáth Rider waiting for her in the bar, with a glass of neat vodka in front of him. He looked darker than ever; edgy and dissatisfied.

'Well?' he said. 'What's the matter with you?'

She sat down opposite, on a large loudly upholstered sofa. Sonny Loony, the barman, came across and asked her what she wanted to drink. 'Dry white wine, very cold.'

Sonny gave Seáth Rider a sideways look as if to say, don't you so much as breathe on one hair of this young lady's head, or you'll have me to answer to. Seáth Rider, in return, gave him a black look back.

'You saw your father, is that it?'

'That's it. I went to Kenmare and there he was.'

'So where is he now? As if I didn't know.'

Sarah clamped her hand over her mouth to prevent herself from sobbing. She looked around the room and willed her eyes not to fill up with tears.

'You knew, didn't you?' she managed to ask him.

'I didn't know for sure. But it's par for the course. You ask a 20-year-old if he wants to be 16 again, and he won't be having it. You ask a 40-year-old if he wants to be 27 again, and he'll say no, even if he's full of envy. Or you ask a 60-year-old if he wants to be 45, and he'll scoff at you. We *progress*. We change. And after we die, there it is, waiting for us, the invisible kingdom, the same the Fianna could visit, full of light and hope and heavenly charms. I warned you, Mrs Bryce, but you didn't listen to what I saying. The dead will never come back to us. They've gone on, the dead, and they've left us behind.'

'I didn't know,' said Sarah, with as much dignity as she could summon up.

'Well now you do. You got what you wanted; but what you wanted didn't want you. It happens all the time, believe me.'

Sonny brought Sarah's wine, and she sipped it gratefully. She hadn't realized how thirsty she was; and hungry, too.

'You'll have dinner with me,' asked Seáth Rider.

'No, thanks. I'm going to have a bath, and wash my hair. I'm going to make an early start tomorrow.'

'I beg your pardon.'

'I said, "I'm going to make an early start." I'm going to fly back to London tomorrow.'

Seáth Rider sat up in his seat, bony and dark, his face as pale as a lantern. 'Now look here, you made an agreement with me, now didn't you? You promised me fidelity. On your life, you promised me fidelity. So what's all this talk of going back to London?'

Sarah almost laughed. 'Fidelity doesn't mean staying in Ireland for the rest of my life!'

'Perhaps not. But it means staying close to me; and since I'm Irish, and choose to live in Ireland, for all of its many faults, this is where you'll be.'

'Don't be absurd. I have to be back in London by lunchtime. I'm having a meeting with Sotheby's.'

Seáth Rider finished his vodka and lifted his glass for another. 'Did you not meet your father?'

'Yes, I did.'

'So did I not do what I said I was going to do? You had your heart's desire – your chairs, your father.'

'Mr Rider,' Sarah protested, 'I'm very grateful for the chairs; but my father's gone back to wherever dead people go back to, and I'm left with nothing at all.'

'You promised me fidelity. I fulfilled my part of the bargain, did I not? If your father chose not to stay, well, that was none of my doing, now was it?'

'Mr Rider, this is absurd.'

He snatched hold of her hand and held her tight. 'Was it absurd when you were standing in the rain begging me to bring your father back? Was it absurd then?'

Sarah stared at him coldly, and after a while he let go of her hand, and sat back. All the same, her heart was beating like the rain on the rooftops.

'I think I'd better go to my room and pack,' she said.

He made a dismissive face, as if she could do whatever she liked, and it would make no difference to him. She left the bar and walked quickly through the lobby. She felt deeply disturbed; not only by what had happened today in the restaurant in Kenmare, but by Seáth Rider's insistence that she keep her promise. She had seen what influence he had, and she was terrified that he was going to *make* her keep it, no matter what.

As she rushed up the staircase, she almost collided with a man coming down, carrying a travelling-bag. She looked up at him, and said, 'Sorry!' before she saw who it was. Ken, her ex-husband, his hair longer than it was before, in a crumpled blue-linen suit. His broad, Celtic face looked well and tanned, and even his eyebrows had gone blond.

'*Ken*! What on earth are *you* doing here?'

He flushed. 'I'm sorry, Sarah. I was trying to leave without you seeing me.'

'But what are you *doing* here? I thought you were still in France.'

'I was, until last week. Then I decided to do something which I've been wanting to do for a very long time. I came looking for you.'

'You followed me all the way here?'

He looked around. 'Listen – is there somewhere we can talk?'

They went upstairs to the hotel library, dedicated to George Bernard Shaw. It was huge and gloomy and completely empty. Sarah sat on one of the sofas and Ken pulled up a chair and sat close to her.

'I saw you in Cahirciveen, going into a pub,' said Sarah. 'I thought it was – well, I thought it was somebody else. But it *was* you.'

'I was following you. I wanted to see you, that's all. But then I saw that boyfriend of yours sitting there waiting for you, so I went out the back way.'

'You were following me? Why?'

'It was stupid, I suppose. But I wanted to find out if there was any chance of us getting back together again. I've changed, Sarah. I've been thinking about where we went wrong, and how much of it was my fault. I've been working and painting and I've really turned myself around.'

'Oh, Ken,' she said, and took hold of his hand.

'That's why I followed you here . . . to see if we could give it another try. But then I saw you talking to that boyfriend of yours, and I realized that I'd obviously left it too late. I saw you out on the terrace, too, having a bit of a tête-à-tête, and that's when I decided to pack my bag and leave you to it. I still love you, Sarah; I always will. But I'm not going to stand in your way.'

'Ken, why didn't you *try* to talk to me, at least? Seáth Rider isn't my boyfriend! He isn't even my friend! He's just a man I met at the auction.

He helped me to buy two Daniel Marot chairs, and we got chatting, but that was all.'

'I saw you kissing him.'

'Well . . . he promised to do me a favour, that's all; and I was grateful for it.'

'Oh, yes? What kind of favour?'

'Listen, you can't start acting jealous. You're my *ex*-husband, remember?'

'I'm sorry.'

Sarah glanced at her watch. 'Listen, are you leaving right now?'

'I've got to pay first – but, yes.'

'Then give me five minutes to stuff my things in my bag, and I'll come with you.'

He blinked at her. 'You mean it? Back to London?'

'That's right. And on the way you can tell me all about what you've been doing, and how much you've changed.'

Ken hesitated for a moment, then nodded, and said, 'Right, then! I'll see you downstairs in five minutes!'

He leaned over and kissed her cheek. Neither of them saw the pale face looking in through the library door, or the lean, dark shadow that flitted across the ceiling.

Ken was still waiting in the lobby more than quarter of an hour later. If he waited much longer, they were in danger of missing the last flight to Heathrow. He paced up and down, looking at the pictures on the walls, but in the end he went to the reception desk and asked if he could use the telephone.

'I want Mrs Bryce's number.'

The receptionist ran her finger down the guest-list. 'Mrs Bryce, did you say? We don't have anybody of that name staying here – oh, wait, here's a Bryce, but this is Mr.'

'That's me. I've only just checked out. Perhaps she registered under another name.'

'Well, why don't you ask the porter, sir? Just describe her to him: he's got a wonderful memory for faces.'

Ken went across to the porter's desk, where the porter was arranging copies of the evening's papers. 'I'm looking for a woman who registered here two days ago. Blonde, 34 years old. Very smart dresser. She came for the antiques auction.'

The porter frowned, and then slowly shook his head. 'We've had nobody of that description, sir. Not for a week or two, and certainly not to the auction.'

'I'm sorry, but you have. She's my ex-wife. I was talking to her in the library only twenty minutes ago.'

Again the porter shook his head. 'You'll have to forgive me, sir. Usually I can remember every single face, but that description has me beat.'

Ken went back to the lobby. He waited another half-hour, and then he picked up his bag. The receptionist gave him a sad, sympathetic smile. He should have known that Sarah wouldn't want him back. She had probably gone back up to her room, and started to remember all of the arguments, all of the throwing of pots and pans, all the times that he had left her at parties to chat to younger girls. Well, he couldn't blame her. It was just that she had seemed so keen to come with him.

He left the hotel and walked toward the car park. The evening was dark and drizzly. He was halfway there before he became aware of a tall, dark man standing by the fence. It was the same man that Sarah had been talking to – and kissing. The man who had promised to do her a favour.

'Leaving us, are you?' the man said, as Ken approached. His voice was a soft as cat's-fur.

'Yes,' said Ken. 'I have to be back in London tonight.' He paused. 'Listen, if you see Mrs Bryce, can you tell her that I don't bear her any ill-will. Tell her that I understand.'

'Oh, you think you understand, do you?'

Ken frowned at him. 'I beg your pardon. What do you mean by that?'

'I mean that you no more understand than a stone understands calculus.'

'I still don't know what you mean.'

'I mean that Mrs Bryce has promised to be faithful; and faithful she wasn't; but faithful she'll have to be. She's staying here, in Ireland, but not in Ireland, and they can look for her till their eyes drop out, but they'll never find her.'

'What the hell are you talking about? Are you drunk? Where is she?'

'She's here still, like I told you.'

Ken put down his bag. 'In that case, I want to see her, and I want to see her now.'

'Oh, you shall,' said Seáth Rider. 'You shall see her now and always. You shall see her to your heart's desire.'

Ken was about to say something else when he felt as if somebody had hit him, very hard, right at the base of his skull. He dropped forward on to his knees, his head bursting with pain. He thought he could hear Seáth Rider talking to him, but his voice seemed to echo, like a man talking down a drain. He put out his hands to stop himself from pitching forward, and crouched on the tarmac on all fours, trying to understand what had happened to him. He felt as if his brain were shrinking, as if his face were being sucked in. He felt his ribcage being pulled in, and his legs tightening. He tried to speak, but his jaws felt as if they been clamped together.

His whole body contracted. It was more painful than anything he had ever experienced in his life, and he screamed as loud as he could, but even his larynx seemed to have contracted into a small, inflexible knot, and all he could manage was a strangled howl.

He found himself naked and shivering in the rain, his faculties dimmed, his feet scratching on the pavement. He had lost all of his perception of who he was and what he was doing here. He looked up at Seáth Rider and all he could feel was fear.

'There now,' said Seáth Rider. 'There's a good fellow. Let's go and see what Sarah's doing, shall we?'

Sarah came downstairs with her bag packed, but there was no sign of Ken. She went to reception and asked if they had seen him, or if he had left a message, but the receptionist shook her head.

'No, Mrs Bryce; there's been nobody.'

'Perhaps he's gone back to his room. Can you tell me what number it is?'

The receptionist looked through the register. 'There's Mrs Bryce, but that's you. No record of anybody called *Mr* Bryce.'

'Are you sure? He told me he was staying here all weekend.'

'You can look for yourself, if you want to.'

She was still searching through the register when Seáth Rider came in through the door, with a brindled dog, straining at its leash.

'Ah, then, you're ready,' he said.

'Where's Ken?' she asked him, in rising alarm.

'Ken?' he said, trying to sound innocent.

'My ex-husband. He was here. I saw him, I spoke to him. I want to know what you've done with him.'

'Now surely why should I do anything with him? And why should you care? You pledged your fidelity to me, remember.'

The brindled dog tried to jump up but Seáth Rider briskly smacked it across its muzzle with the back of his hand. 'You can't be too strict with these mongrel mutts, now can you.' The dog miserably subsided, and circled around the back of Seáth Rider's legs.

'We're off then,' said Seáth Rider. 'I've taken care of your bill.'

'I'm not going off anywhere,' said Sarah. 'I'm driving to Cork, and then I'm flying back to—' She paused. She knew she was flying somewhere, but where?

'I have to get back to my mother,' she said, in desperation. 'I have to get back to my business – back to my shop.'

Seáth Rider pulled the dog-leash tighter, so that the dog began to breathe in thin, asphyxiated gasps. 'You're not going anywhere, Mrs Bryce, except with me. Your mother won't remember you. You never existed, as far as she's concerned. You never went to school, you never grew up. Sarah Thompson? they'll say, I never heard of anybody called Sarah Thompson. Nor Sarah Bryce, neither, when she was married. They won't find a speck of a mention of you anywhere, not in christening notes nor school magazine nor local newspaper. You've gone, vanished, you're invisible, except for here.'

Sarah looked around. 'I don't understand. This is still the same hotel.'

Seáth Rider passed his hand across his face like a camera-shutter. 'There isn't any such thing as "the same hotel", Mrs Bryce. There are thousands of Parknasillas, one for each guest who came here; just as there are millions of Irelands, layer upon layer, depth upon depth. The gates are still open in Ireland, Mrs Bryce, and people still walk through.'

'You're trying to tell me that I'm here, but I'm somewhere else?'

Seáth Rider nodded. 'You'll be happy here, Mrs Bryce. Happy as Larry. You'll see things that you never imagined possible; and you'll talk to people who'll set your ears ablaze. You'll grow to love me, too, I shouldn't wonder, and you and I will be the best of companions.'

He took her hand and led her out into the night. It was still drizzling, but the bright hotel lights made it look as if they were being showered with fairy dust. The dog yapped, and Seáth Rider slapped it again, sharp and short, right across the muzzle. 'You behave yourself now, you cur.'

Raymond French went to her room to say goodbye to her. He found the door open and the chambermaid already stripping the bed. To his surprise, however, the two Daniel Marot chairs were still there. He couldn't imagine that she would have left without seeing them packed up for shipping.

'Have you seen the woman whose room this was?' he asked the chambermaid.

The chambermaid shook her head.

Raymond walked into the room and looked around. The closets were empty; the bathroom had been cleared of cosmetics. The only evidence that anyone had been here was a business card, left in the ashtray, folded in half.

Downstairs, in the lobby, there was no sign of Sarah anywhere. But Raymond was just about to go to the reception desk and ask about her when he ran into Dermot Brien.

'Oh, Dermot – just the man I want to see! You were going to give me the name of that fellow in Dublin who bought those landscapes.'

By the time he had finished talking to Dermot, he was running late. It had started to rain much harder, and if he didn't hurry he was going to miss the last flight to London.

Something else had happened, too.

He had completely forgotten about Sarah, as if she had never existed.

By the next morning, the rain had cleared, and the sky was as blue as a baby's eyes. On the Atlantic shore at Ballinskelligs Bay, a man and a woman walked across the beach. He was tall and dark and dressed in black. She wore white, a fine linen gown trimmed with Kerry lace, and there was a garland of wild flowers in her hair. Her gown trailed on the wet reflecting sand but she seemed not to notice; or perhaps she didn't care.

'I love it down here in the morning,' the man said, stopping and looking out to sea, his hand shading his eyes. 'It's always so fresh. Like the world born anew.'

The woman said nothing but kept on walking. Eventually he caught up with her and took hold of her arm. 'You mustn't pine for what was,' he told her. 'That life is gone now, don't you see? That's what your father was trying to tell you, that it's no good trying to go back. That running away last night, what folly that was; and look what happened to my poor dog. Besides, didn't I keep my part of the bargain? I'm only expecting you to keep yours.'

She turned and looked at him. Her face was filled with resentment and bitterness. 'You gave me nothing.' she said. 'You gave me nothing and I owe you nothing.'

He gave her a quick frown, as if her words had badly hurt him. But then he said, 'This is just the beginning, you know. You'll see what I can give you, given time. It's a strange life, but a fair one. You'll meet all kinds of people just like yourself; rich and beautiful, some of them; and some of them ragged and odder than tinkers. And I'll show you what magic is, too. Real magic. Walking through hillsides and having no concern for time or space. I'll show you how to feed on blood and spiders and baby's breath; and how to win all of the men you could possibly want, and steal them away; the same way that I stole you.'

Just then, a man appeared around the rocks, walking his dog. The dog was darting and barking at the sea, but when it caught sight of them it came trotting up and stood a little way away from them, its head cocked to one side, making a high-pitched whining sound.

'Here boy, come on boy,' the man called him. 'What's got into you?'

The man came nearer and nearer. The woman slowly raised her hand, but the man walked right past her, missing her by only a few inches. He didn't even look at her.

The woman turned around as if to call him; but then she looked at her dark companion in absolute horror. 'He couldn't see me,' she said, her voice trembling. '*He couldn't see me!*'

Her companion started to laugh. He walked away, still laughing, and shaking his head.

The woman stayed where she was, mortified, while the sea ebbed slowly away on all sides.

Raymond caught the midday flight to London. The Garda had carried out another intensive search of the ditches and hedges alongside the Kenmare road, but they had found no trace of a woman's body. They called into the bed-and-breakfast and told Raymond that he was free to go.

It was while he was drinking his first vodka-and-tonic on the plane that he began to wonder what he had been looking for, just before he left Parknasilla. He remembered searching through somebody's room, but for the life of him he couldn't remember whose it was, or what he had been looking for. There was something about chairs but he couldn't remember that either.

Later, when he was looking for a pen, he discovered the folded business card out of his jacket pocket. 'Seáth E. Rider, Acquisitor, Dublin & London.'

He regularly tried to solve *The Daily Telegraph* crossword, but it didn't occur to him that 'Seáth E. Rider' was an anagram of 'Heart's Desire'.

Title: Girl of my Dreams
Writer: *Richard Matheson*

Briefing: *Second Sight – ancient gift of prophetic vision possessed by certain people; sometimes referred to as clairvoyance or prevision.* Carrie can 'see' future tragedies. At night she dreams about the dangers which lie in wait for people that she has never met – and then her greedy, unfeeling partner, Greg, exploits this knowledge to extort money from the unsuspecting victims. But dreams, of course, can also turn into nightmares – and not *just* for the dreamer.

Author: American novelist and scriptwriter Richard Matheson is one of the foremost contemporary writers of fantasy and horror fiction. He is especially highly regarded for the vampire story, *I Am Legend* (1954) and *Duel*, the edge-of-the-seat account of a car being relentlessly pursued by a monster lorry and its unseen driver which Stephen Spielberg turned into a movie classic in 1970. Born in New Jersey, Matheson was first published in the *Brooklyn Eagle* at the tender age of nine, but did not start seriously writing fiction until after he had left college. His interest in psychic phenomena and clairvoyance surfaced in his early short stories and also his powerful novel. *A Stir of Echoes* (1959). Matheson's work brought him to the attention of Hollywood and he scripted a number of the Sixties cult movies made by Roger Corman as well as several films based on his own fiction. Apart from scripts for the cinema and television, Matheson has continued to write outstanding short stories and the occasional novel, including the highly praised tale of the afterlife, *What Dreams May Come* (1978). In 'Girl of My Dreams', he combines the very contemporary human emotions of love, hatred and greed with another of the oldest psychic talents.

He woke up, grinning, in the darkness. Carrie was having a nightmare. He lay on his side and listened to her breathless moaning. Must be a good one, he thought. He reached out and touched her back. The nightgown was wet with her perspiration. *Great*, he thought. He pulled his hand away as she squirmed against it, starting to make faint noises in her throat; it sounded as if she were trying to say 'No'.

No, hell, Greg thought. Dream, you ugly bitch; what else are you good for? He yawned and pulled his left arm from beneath the covers. Three-sixteen. He wound the watch stem sluggishly. Going to get me one of those electric watches one of these days, he thought. Maybe this dream would do it. Too bad Carrie had no control over them. If she did, he could really make it big.

He rolled onto his back. The nightmare was ending now; or coming to its peak, he was never sure which. What difference did it make anyway? He wasn't interested in the machinery, just the product. He grinned again, reaching over to the bedside table for his cigarettes. Lighting one, he blew up smoke. Now he'd have to comfort her, he thought with a frown. That was the part he could live without. Dumb little creep. Why couldn't she be blonde and beautiful? He expelled a burst of smoke. Well, you couldn't ask for everything. If she were good-looking, she probably wouldn't have these dreams. There were plenty of other women to provide the rest of it.

Carrie jerked violently and sat up with a cry, pulling the covers from his legs. Greg looked at her outline in the darkness. She was shivering. 'Oh, no,' she whispered. He watched her head begin to shake. 'No. No.' She started to cry, her body hitching with sobs. Oh, Christ, he thought, this'll take hours. Irritably, he pressed his cigarette into the ashtray and sat up.

'Baby?' he said.

She twisted around with a gasp and stared at him. 'Come 'ere,' he told her. He opened his arms and she flung herself against him. He could feel her narrow fingers gouging at his back, the soggy weight of her breasts against his chest. Oh, boy, he thought. He kissed her neck, grimacing at the smell of her sweat-damp skin. Oh, boy, what I go through. He caressed her back. 'Take it easy, baby,' he said, 'I'm here.' He let her cling to him, sobbing weakly. 'Bad dream?' he asked. He tried to sound concerned.

'Oh, Greg.' She could barely speak. 'It was horrible; oh, God, how horrible.'

He grinned. It *was* a good one.

'Which way?' he asked.

Carrie perched stiffly on the edge of the seat, looking through the windshield with troubled eyes. Any second now, she'd pretend she didn't know; she always did. Greg's fingers tightened slimly on the wheel. One of these days, by God, he'd smack her right across her ugly face and walk out, free. Damn freak. He felt the skin begin to tighten across his cheeks. 'Well?' he asked.

'I don't—'

'*Which way, Carrie?*' God, he'd like to twist back one of her scrawny arms and break the damn thing; squeeze that skinny neck until her breath stopped.

Carrie swallowed dryly. 'Left,' she murmured.

Bingo! Greg almost laughed aloud, slapping down the turn indicator. *Left* – right into the Eastridge area, the money area. You dreamed it right this time, you dog, he thought; this is It. All he had to do now was play it smart and he'd be free of her for good. He'd sweated it out and now it was payday!

The tyres made a crisp sound on the pavement as he turned the car onto the quiet, tree-lined street. 'How far?' he asked. She didn't answer and he looked at her threateningly. Her eyes were shut.

'How far? I said.'

Carrie clutched her hands together. 'Greg, please—' she started. Tears were squeezing out beneath her lids.

'Damn it!'

Carrie whimpered and said something.

'What?' he snapped.

She drew in wavering breath. 'The middle of the next block,' she said.

'Which side?'

'The right.'

Greg smiled. He leaned back against the seat and relaxed. That was more like it. Dumb bitch tried the same old I-forgot routine every time. When would she learn that he had her down cold? He almost chuckled. She never would, he thought; because, after this one, he'd be gone and she could dream for nothing.

'Tell me when we reach it,' he said.

'Yes,' she answered. She had turned her face to the window and was leaning her forehead against the cold glass. Don't cool it too much, he thought, amused; keep it hot for Daddy. He pressed away the rising smile as she turned to look at him. Was she picking up on him? Or was it just the usual? It was always the same. Just before they reached wherever they were going, she'd look at him intently as if to convince herself that it was worth the pain. He felt like laughing in her face. Obviously, it was worth it. How else could a beast like her land someone with his class? Except for him, her bed would be the emptiest, her nights the longest.

'Almost there?' he asked.

Carrie looked to the front again. 'The white one,' she said.

'With the half-circle drive?'

She nodded tightly. 'Yes.'

Greg clenched his teeth, a spasm of avidity sweeping through him. Fifty thousand if it was worth a nickel, he thought. Oh, you bitch, you crazy bitch, you really nailed it for me this time! He turned the wheel and pulled in at the curb. Cutting the engine, he glanced across the street. The convertible would come from that direction, he thought. He wondered who'd be driving it. Not that it mattered.

'Greg?'

He turned and eyed her coldly. 'What?'

She bit her lip, then started to speak.

'*No*,' he said, cutting her off. He pulled out the ignition key and shoved open the door. 'Let's go,' he said. He slid out, shut the door and walked around the car. Carrie was still inside. 'Let's *go*, baby,' he said, the hint of venom in his voice.

'Greg, please—'

He shuddered at the cost of repressing an intense desire to scream curses at her, jerk open the door and drag her out by her hair. His rigid fingers clamped on the door handle and he opened the door, waited. Christ, but she was ugly – the features, the skin, the body. She'd never looked so repugnant to him. '*I said let's go*,' he told her. He couldn't disguise the tremble of fury in his voice.

Carrie got out and he shut the door. It was getting colder. Greg drew up the collar of his topcoat, shivering as they started up the drive toward the front door of the house. He could use a heavier coat, he thought; with a nice, thick lining. A real sharp one, maybe black. He'd get one one of these days – and maybe real soon too. He glanced at Carrie, wondering if she had any notion of his plans. He doubted it even though she looked more worried than ever. What the hell was with her? She'd never been this bad before. Was it because it was a kid? He shrugged. What difference did it make? She'd perform.

'Cheer up,' he said, 'it's a school day. You won't have to see him.' She didn't answer.

They went up two steps, onto the brick porch and stopped before the door. Greg pushed the button and, deep inside the house, melodic chimes sounded. While they waited, he reached inside his topcoat pocket and touched the small, leather notebook, Funny how he always felt like some kind of weird salesman when they were operating. A salesman with a damned closed market, he thought, amused. No one else could offer what he had to sell, that was for sure.

He glanced at Carrie. 'Cheer *up*,' he told her. 'We're helping them, aren't we?'

Carie shivered. 'It won't be too much, will it, Greg?'

'I'll decide on—'

He broke off as the door was opened. For a moment, he felt angry, disappointed that the bell had not been answered by a maid. Then he thought: Oh, what the hell, the money's still here and he smiled at the woman who stood before them. 'Good afternoon,' he said.

The woman looked at him with that half-polite, half-suspicious smile most women gave him at first. 'Yes?' she asked.

'It's about Paul,' he said.

The smile disappeared, the woman's face grew blank. 'What?' she asked.

'That's your son's name, isn't it?'

The woman glanced at Carrie. Already, she was disconcerted, Greg could see.

'He's in danger of his life,' he told her. 'Are you interested in hearing more about it?'

'*What's happened to him?*'

Greg smiled affably, 'Nothing yet,' he answered. The woman caught her breath as if, abruptly, she were being strangled.

'You've taken him,' she murmured.

Greg's smile broadened. 'Nothing like that,' he said.

'Where is he then?' the woman asked.

Greg looked at his wristwatch, feigning surprise. 'Isn't he at school?' he asked.

Uneasily confused, the woman stared at him for several moments before she twisted away, pushing at the door. Greg caught hold of it before it shut. 'Inside,' he ordered.

'Can't we wait out—?'

Carrie broke off with a gasp as he clamped his fingers on her arm and pulled her into the hall. While he shut the door, Greg listened to the rapid whir and click of a telephone being dialled in the kitchen. He smiled and took hold of Carrie's arm again, guiding her into the living room. 'Sit,' he told her.

Carrie settled gingerly on the edge of a chair while he appraised the room. Money was in evidence wherever he looked: in the carpeting and drapes, the period furniture, the accessories. Greg pulled in a tight, exultant breath and tried to keep from grinning like an eager kid; this was It all right. Dropping onto the sofa, he stretched luxuriously, leaned back and crossed his legs, glancing at the name on a magazine lying on the end table beside him. In the kitchen, he could hear the woman saying.

'He's in Room Fourteen, Mrs Jenning's class.'

A sudden clicking sound made Carrie gasp. Greg turned his head and saw, through the black drapes, a collie scratching at the sliding glass door; beyond, he noted, with renewed pleasure, the glint of swimming-pool water. Greg watched the dog. It must be the one that would—

'*Thank you,*' said the woman gratefully. Greg turned back and looked in that direction. The woman hung up the telephone receiver and her footsteps tapped across the kitchen floor, becoming soundless as she stepped onto the hallway carpeting. She started cautiously toward the front door.

'We're in here, Mrs Wheeler,' said Greg.

The woman caught her breath and whirled in shock. 'What *is* this?' she demanded.

'Is he all right?' Greg asked.

'*What do you want?*'

Greg drew the notebook from his pocket and held it out. 'Would you like to look at this?' he asked.

The woman didn't answer but peered at Greg through narrowing eyes. 'That's right,' he said, 'We're selling something.'

The woman's face grew hard.

'*Your son's life,*' Greg completed.

The woman gaped at him, momentary resentment invaded by fear again. Jesus, you look stupid, Greg felt like telling her. He forced a smile. 'Are you interested?' he asked.

'Get out of here before I call the police.' The woman's voice was husky, tremulous.

'You're not interested in your son's life, then.'

The woman shivered with fear-ridden anger. 'Did you hear me?' she said.

Greg exhaled through clenching teeth. 'Mrs Wheeler,' he said, 'Unless you listen to us – *carefully* – your son will soon be dead.' From the corners of his eyes, he noticed Carrie wincing and felt like smashing in her face.

That's right, he thought with savage fury. Show her how scared you are, you stupid bitch!

Mrs Wheeler's lips stirred falteringly as she stared at Greg. 'What are you talking about?' she finally asked.

'Your son's life, Mrs Wheeler.'

'Why should you want to hurt my boy?' the woman asked, a sudden quaver in her voice. Greg felt himself relax. She was almost in the bag.

'Did I say that we were going to hurt him?' he asked, smiling at her quizzically. 'I don't remember saying that, Mrs Wheeler.'

'Then—?'

'Sometime before the middle of the month,' Greg interrupted, 'Paul will be run over by a car and killed.'

'What?'

Greg did not repeat.

'What car?' asked the woman. She looked at Greg in panic. 'What car?' she demanded.

'We don't know exactly.'

'Where?' the woman asked. 'When?'

'That information,' Greg replied, 'is what we're selling.'

The woman turned to Carrie, looking at her frightenedly. Carrie lowered her gaze, teeth digging at her lower lip. The woman looked back at Greg as he continued.

'Let me explain,' he said. 'My wife is what's known as a "sensitive". You may not be familiar with the term. It means she has visions and dreams. Very often, they have to do with real people. Like the dream she had last night – about your son.'

The woman shrank from his words and, as Greg expected, an element of shrewdness modified her expression; there was now, in addition to fear, suspicion.

'I know what you're thinking,' he informed her. 'Don't waste your time. Look at this notebook and you'll see—'

'Get out of here,' the woman said.

Greg's smile grew strained. 'That again?' he asked. 'You mean you really don't care about your son's life?'

The woman managed a smile of contempt. 'Shall I call the police now?' she asked. 'The *bunco* squad?'

'If you really want to,' answered Greg, 'but I suggest you listen to me first.' He opened the notebook and began to read. '*January twenty-second: Man named Jim to fall from roof while adjusting television aerial. Ramson Street. Two-storey house, green with white trim.* Here's the news item.'

Greg glanced at Carrie and nodded once, ignoring her pleading look as he stood and walked across the room. The woman cringed back apprehensively but didn't move. Greg held up the notebook page. 'As you can see,' he said, 'the man didn't believe what we told him and did fall off his roof on January twenty-second; it's harder to convince them when you can't give any details so as not to give it all away.' He clucked as if disturbed. 'He should have paid us, though,' he said. 'It would have been a lot less expensive than a broken back.'

'Who do you think you're—?'

'Here's another,' Greg said, turning a page. 'This should interest you. *February twelfth, afternoon: Boy, 13, name unknown, to fall into abandoned well shaft, fracture pelvis. Lives on Darien Circle*, etcetera, etcetera, etcetera. You can see the details here,' he finished, pointing at the page. 'Here's the newspaper clipping. As you can see, his parents were just in time. They'd refused to pay at first, threatened to call the police like you did.' He smiled at the woman. 'Threw us out of the house, as a matter of fact,' he said. 'On the afternoon of the twelfth, though, when I made a last-minute phone check, they were out of their minds with worry. Their son had disappeared and they had no idea where he was – I hadn't mentioned the well shaft, of course.'

He paused for a moment of dramatic emphasis, enjoying the moment fully. 'I went over to their house,' he said, 'they made their payment and I told them where their son was.' He pointed at the clipping. 'He was found, as you can see – down in an abandoned well shaft. With a broken pelvis.'

'Do you really—?'

'—expect you to believe all this?' Greg completed her thought. 'Not completely; no one ever does at first. Let me tell you what you're thinking right now. You're thinking that we cut out these newspaper items and made up this story to fit them. You're entitled to believe that if you want to—' his face hardened '—but, if you do, you'll have a dead son by the middle of the month, you can count on that.'

The smile began to fade. 'And it *is* going to happen, Mrs Wheeler, whether you believe it or not.'

The woman, still too dazed by fright to be completely sure of her suspicion, watched Greg as he turned to Carrie. 'Well?' he said.

'I don't—'

'*Let's have it,*' he demanded.

Carrie bit her lower lip and tried to restrain the sob.

'What are you going to do?' the woman asked.

Greg turned to her with a smile. 'Make our point,' he said. He looked at Carrie again. '*Well?*'

She answered, eyes closed, voice pained and feeble. 'There's a throw rug by the nursery door,' she said. 'You'll slip on it while you're carrying the baby.'

Greg glanced at her in pleased surprise; he hadn't known there was a baby. Quickly, he looked at the woman as Carrie continued in a troubled voice, 'There's a black widow spider underneath the playpen on the patio, it will bite the baby, there's a—'

'Care to check these items. Mrs Wheeler?' Greg broke in. Suddenly, he hated her for her slowness, for her failure to accept. 'Or shall we just walk out of here,' he said, sharply, '*and let that blue convertible drag Paul's head along the street until his brains spill out?*'

The woman looked at him in horror. Greg felt a momentary dread that he had told her too much, then relaxed as he realized that he hadn't. 'I suggest you check,' he told her, pleasantly. The woman backed away from him a little bit, then turned and hurried toward the patio door. 'Oh, incidentally,' Greg said, remembering. She turned. 'That dog out there will try to save your son but it won't succeed; the car will kill it too.'

The woman stared at him, as if uncomprehending, then turned away and, sliding open the patio door, went outside. Greg saw the collie frisking around her as she moved across the patio. Leisurely, he returned to the sofa and sat down.

'Greg—?'

He frowned grimacingly, jerking up his hand to silence her. Out on the patio, there was a scraping noise, as the woman overturned the playpen. He listened intently. There was a sudden gasp, then the stamping of the woman's shoe on concrete, an excited barking by the dog. Greg smiled and leaned back with a sigh. Bingo.

When the woman came back in, he smiled at her, noticing how heavily she breathed.

'That could happen any place,' she said, defensively.

'Could it?' Greg's smile remained intact. 'And the throw rug?'

'Maybe you looked around while I was in the kitchen.'

'We didn't.'

'*Maybe you guessed.*'

'And maybe we didn't,' he told her, chilling his smile. 'Maybe everything we've said is true. You want to gamble on it?'

The woman had no reply. Greg looked at Carrie. 'Anything else?' he asked. Carrie shivered fitfully. 'An electric outlet by the baby's crib,' she said. 'She has a bobby pin beside her, she's been trying to put it in the plug and—'

'Mrs Wheeler?' Greg looked inquisitively at the woman. He snickered as she turned and hurried from the room. When she was gone, he smiled and winked at Carrie. 'You're really on today, baby,' he said. She returned his look with glistening eyes. 'Greg, please don't make it too much,' she murmured.

Greg turned away from her, the smile withdrawn. Relax, he told himself; relax. After today, you'll be free of her. Casually, he slipped the notebook back into his topcoat pocket.

The woman returned in several minutes, her expression now devoid of anything but dread. Between two fingers of her right hand she was carrying a bobby pin. *'How did you know?'* She asked. Her voice was hollow with dismay.

'I believe I explained that, Mrs Wheeler,' Greg replied. 'My wife has a gift. She knows exactly where and when that accident will occur. Do you care to buy that information?'

The woman's hands twitched at her sides. 'What do you want?' she asked.

'Ten thousand dollars in cash,' Greg answered. His fingers flexed reactively as Carrie gasped but he didn't look at her. He fixed his gaze on the woman's stricken face. 'Ten thousand . . .' she repeated dumbly.

'That's correct. Is it a deal?'

'But we don't—'

'Take it or leave it, Mrs Wheeler. You're not in a bargaining position. Don't think for a second that there's anything you can do to prevent the accident. Unless you know the exact time and place, it's going to happen.' He stood abruptly, causing her to start. 'Well?' he snapped, 'what's it going to be? Ten thousand dollars or your son's life?'

The woman couldn't answer. Greg's eyes flicked to where Carrie sat in mute despair. 'Let's go,' he said. He started for the hall.

'Wait.'

Greg turned and looked at the woman. 'Yes?'

'How – do I know—?' she faltered.

'You don't,' he broke in, 'you don't know a thing. *We* do.'

He waited another few moments for her decision, then walked into the kitchen and, removing his memo pad from an inside pocket, slipped the pencil free and jotted down the telephone number. He heard the woman murmuring pleadingly to Carrie and, shoving the pad and pencil into his topcoat pocket, left the kitchen. 'Let's go,' he said to Carrie who was standing now. He glanced disinterestedly at the woman. 'I'll phone this afternoon,' he said. 'You can tell me then what you and your husband have decided to do.' His mouth went hard. *'It'll be the only call you'll get,'* he said.

He turned and walked to the front door, opened it. 'Come on, come on,' he ordered irritably. Carrie slipped by him, brushing at the tears on her cheeks. Greg followed and began to close the door, then stopped as if remembering something.

'Incidentally,' he said. He smiled at the woman. 'I wouldn't call the police if I were you. There's nothing they could charge us with even if they found us. And, of course, we couldn't tell you then – and your son would have to die.' He closed the door and started for the car, a picture of the woman printed in his mind: standing, dazed and trembling, in her living room, looking at him with haunted eyes. Greg grunted in amusement.

She was hooked.

Greg drained his glass and fell back heavily on the sofa arm, making a face. It was the last cheap whisky he'd ever drink; from now on, it was exclusively the best. He turned his head to look at Carrie. She was standing by the window of their hotel living room, staring at the city. What the hell was she brooding about now? Likely, she was wondering where that blue convertible was. Momentarily, Greg wondered himself. Was it parked? – moving? He grinned drunkenly. It gave him a feeling of power to know something about the car that even its owner didn't know: namely, that, in eight days, at two-sixteen on a Thursday afternoon, it would run down a little boy and kill him.

He focused his eyes and glared at Carrie. 'All right, say it,' he demanded. 'Get it out.'

She turned and looked at him imploringly. 'Does it have to be so much?' she asked.

He turned his face away from her and closed his eyes.

'Greg, does it—?'

'*Yes*!' He drew in shaking breath. God, would he be glad to get away from her.

'What if they can't pay?'

'*Tough*.'

The sound of her repressed sob set his teeth on edge. 'Go in and lie down,' he told her.

'Greg, he hasn't got a chance!'

He twisted around, face whitening. 'Did he have a better chance before we came?' he snarled. 'Use your head for once, God damn it! If it wasn't for us, he'd be as good as dead already!'

'Yes, but—'

'I said go and lie down!'

'You haven't seen the way it's going to happen, Greg!'

He shuddered violently, fighting back the urge to grab the whisky bottle, leap at her and smash her head in. '*Get out of here*,' he muttered.

She stumbled across the room, pressing the back of a hand against her lips. The bedroom door thumped shut and he heard her fall across the bed, sobbing. Damn, wet-eye bitch! He gritted his teeth until his jaws hurt, then poured himself another inch of whisky, grimacing as it burned its way into his stomach. They'll come through, he told himself. Obviously, they had the money and, obviously, the woman had believed him. He nodded to himself. They'll come through, all right. Ten thousand; his passport to another life. Expensive clothes. A class hotel. Good-looking women; maybe one of them for keeps. He kept nodding. One of these days, he thought.

He was reaching for his glass when he heard the muffled sound of Carrie talking in the bedroom. For several moments, his outstretched hand hovered between the sofa and the table. Then, in an instant, he was on his feet, lunging for the bedroom door. He flung it open. Carrie jerked around, the phone receiver in her hand, her face a mask of dread. 'Thursday, the fourteenth!' she blurted into the mouthpiece. 'Two-sixteen in the afternoon!' She screamed as Greg wrenched the receiver from her hand and slammed his palm on the cradle, breaking the connection.

He stood quivering before her, staring at her face with widened, maniac eyes. Slowly, Carrie raised her hand to avert the blow. 'Greg, please don't—' she began.

Fury deafened him. He couldn't hear the heavy, thudding sound the earpiece made against her cheek as he slammed it across her face with all his might. She fell back with a strangled cry. 'You bitch,' he gasped. 'You bitch, you bitch, you bitch!' He emphasized each repetition of the word with another savage blow across her face. He couldn't see her clearly either; she kept wavering behind a film of blinding rage. Everything was finished! She'd blown the deal! The Big One was gone! *God damn it, I'll kill you!* He wasn't certain if the words exploded in his mind or if he were shouting them into her face.

Abruptly, he became aware of the telephone receiver clutched in his aching hand; of Carrie lying, open-mouthed and staring on the bed, her features mashed and bloody. He lost his grip and heard, as if it were a hundred miles below, the receiver thumping on the floor. He stared at Carrie, sick with horror. Was she dead? He pressed his ear against her chest and listened. At first, he could hear only the pulse of his own heart throbbing in his ears. Then, as he concentrated, his expression tautly rabid, he became aware of Carrie's heartbeat, faint and staggering. She wasn't dead! He jerked his head up.

She was looking at him, mouth slack, eyes dumbly stark.

'Carrie?'

No reply. Her lips moved soundlessly. She kept on staring at him. 'What?' he asked. He recognized the look and shuddered. '*What?*'

'Street,' she whispered.

Greg bent over, staring at her mangled features. 'Street,' she whispered, ' . . . night.' She sucked in wheezing, blood-choked breath. 'Greg.' She tried to sit up but couldn't. Her expression was becoming one of terrified concern. She whispered, 'Man . . . razor . . . you – oh, *no!*'

Greg felt himself enveloped in ice. He clutched at her arm. 'Where?' he mumbled. She didn't answer and his fingers dug convulsively into her flesh. 'Where?' he demanded. 'When?' He began to shiver uncontrollably. 'Carrie, *when?!*'

It was the arm of a dead woman that he clutched. With a gagging sound, he jerked his hand away. He gaped at her, unable to speak or think. Then, as he backed away, his eyes were drawn to the calendar on the wall and a phrase crept leadenly across his mind: *one of these days*. Quite suddenly, he began to laugh and cry. And before he fled, he stood at the window for an hour and twenty minutes, staring out, wondering who the man was, where he was right now and just what he was doing.

File classification: *Psychokinesis*
Location: *Wirral Peninsula, UK*

Title: A Modern Magician
Writer: *Olaf Stapledon*

Briefing: *Psychokinesis – an individual's supernormal ability to bring about death by will-power; a psychic killer.* Jim boasts he has 'powers'. To win the affections of pretty Helen, he demonstrates by killing flies, beetles, even a dog. He also shows her how he can stop a car's engine without being near the vehicle. But Jim's thoughts of love turn to revenge when he unexpectedly sees his lover in the company of another man . . .

Author: The English-born writer and philosopher Olaf Stapledon investigated psychic faculties in a number of his major works. He was particularly intrigued by the idea of supernormal intelligence as is revealed in his mammoth novels, *Last and First Men* (1930) and *Odd John* (1935). Stapledon began his career as a teacher, saw action in the First World War, and then studied philosophy and psychology. The idea of a university career was, however, abandoned after the success of *Last and First Men* and in company with the later triumph of *Star Maker* (1937), about the ultimate development of the super-mind, his books have been acclaimed as the best sf novels ever written. Some critics consider his influence to be second only to H. G. Wells, and Arthur C. Clarke has named him as one of his most important influences. Among Stapledon's other novels featuring psychic minds are *Sirius* (1944), about a dog with enhanced intelligence, and *The Flames* (1947), in which an alien race makes contact with the supernormals. 'A Modern Magician' was written shortly before Stapledon's death in 1950 and its theme of an individual's abuse of psychic powers can be seen as the predecessor to a whole range of similar stories, perhaps most notably Stephen King's best-selling trio *Carrie* (1974), *The Dead Zone* (1979) and *Firestarter* (1980).

They confronted each other across a tea table in a cottage garden. Helen was leaning back, coldly studying Jim's face. It was an oddly childish, almost foetal face, with its big brow, snub nose and pouting lips. Childish, yes; but in the round dark eyes there was a gleam of madness. She had to admit that she was in a way drawn to this odd young man, partly perhaps by his very childishness and his awkward innocent attempts at love-making; but partly by that sinister gleam.

Jim was leaning forward, talking hard. He had been talking for a long time, but she was no longer listening. She was deciding that though she was drawn to him she also disliked him. Why had she come out with him again? He was weedy, and self-centred. Yet she had come.

Something he was saying recaptured her attention. He seemed to be annoyed that she had not been listening. He was all worked up about something. She heard him say, 'I know you despise me, but you're making a big mistake. I tell you I have *powers*. I didn't intend to let you into my secret, yet; but, damn it, I will. I'm finding out a lot about the power of mind over matter. I can control matter at a distance, just by willing it. I'm going to be a sort of modern magician. I've even killed things by just willing it.'

Helen, who was a medical student, prided herself on her shrewd materialism. She laughed contemptuously.

His face flushed with anger, and he said, 'Oh very well! I'll have to show you.'

On a bush a robin was singing. The young man's gaze left the girl's face, and settled intently on the robin. 'Watch that bird,' he said. His voice was almost a whisper. Presently the bird stopped singing, and after looking miserable for a while, with its head hunched into its body, it dropped from the tree without opening its wings. It lay on the grass with its legs in the air, dead.

Jim let out a constricted squawk of triumph, staring at his victim. Then he turned his eyes on Helen. Mopping his pasty face with his handkerchief, he said, 'That was a good turn. I've never tried it on a bird before, only on flies and beetles.'

The girl stared at him silently, anxious not to seem startled. He set about telling her his secret. She was not bored any more.

He told her that a couple of years earlier he had begun to be interested in 'all this paranormal stuff'. He had been to seances, and read about psychical research. He wouldn't have bothered if he hadn't suspected he had strange powers himself. He was never really interested in spooks and thought transference, and so on. What fascinated him was the possibility that a mind might be able to affect matter directly. 'Psychokinesis', they called this power; and they knew very little about it. But he didn't care a damn about the theoretical puzzles. All he wanted was power. He told Helen about the queer experiments that had been done in America with dice. You threw the dice time after time, and you willed them to settle with the two sixes uppermost. Generally they didn't; but when you had done a great many experiments you totted up the results, and found that there had been more sixes than would have turned up by sheer chance. It certainly looked as though the mind really had some slight influence. This opened up terrific possibilities.

He began to do little experiments on his own, guided by the findings of the researchers, but also by some of his own ideas. The power was fantastically slight, so you had to test it out in situations where the tiniest influence would have detectable results, just tipping the scales.

He didn't have much success with the dice, because (as he explained) he never knew precisely what he had to do. The dice tumbled out too quickly for him. And so he only had the slight effect that the Americans had reported. So he had to think up new tricks, that would give him a better opening. He had had a scientific training, so he decided to try to influence chemical reactions and simple physical processes. He did many experiments, and learned a lot. He prevented a minute spot of water from rusting a knife. He stopped a crystal of salt from dissolving in water. He formed a minute crystal of ice in a drop of water, and finally froze the whole drop by simply 'willing away' all the heat, in fact by stopping all the molecular movement.

He told Helen of his first success at killing, a literally microscopic success. He brewed some very stagnant water, and put a drop on a slide. Then through the microscope he watched the swarm of micro-organisms milling about. Mostly they were like stumpy sausages, swimming with wavy tails. They were of many sizes. He thought of them as elephants, cows, sheep, rabbits. His idea was that he might be able to stop the chemical action in one of these little creatures, and so kill it. He had read up a lot about their inner workings, and he knew what key process he could best tackle. Well, the damned things kept shifting about so fast he couldn't concentrate on any one of them for long enough. He kept losing his victim in the crowd. However, at last one of the 'rabbits' swam into a less populous part of the slide, and he fixed his attention on it long enough to do the trick. He willed the crucial chemical process to stop, and it did stop. The creature stopped moving, and stayed still indefinitely. It was almost certainly dead. His success, he said, made him 'feel like God'.

Later he learned to kill flies and beetles by freezing their brains. Then he tried a frog, but had no success. He didn't know enough physiology to find a minute key-process to check. However, he read up a lot of stuff, and at last he succeeded. He simply stopped the nerve current in certain fibres in the spinal cord, that controlled the heartbeat. It was this method also that he had used on the robin.

'That's just the beginning,' he said. 'Soon I shall have the world at my feet. And if you join up with me, it will be at your feet too.'

Throughout this monologue the girl had listened intently, torn between revulsion and fascination. There was a kind of bad smell about it all, but one couldn't afford to be too squeamish in these days. Besides, there was probably nothing in morality, anyhow. All the same, Jim was playing with fire. Strange, though, how he seemed to have grown up while he was talking. Somehow he didn't look gawky and babyish any more. His excitement, and her knowledge that his power was real, had made him look thrillingly sinister. But she decided to be cautious and aloof.

When at last Jim was silent, she staged a concealed yawn, and said, 'You're clever, aren't you! That was a good trick you did, though a horrid one. If you go much farther, you'll end on the gallows.'

He snorted, and said, 'It's not like you to be a coward.'

The taunt stung her. Indignantly she answered, 'Don't be ridiculous! Why should I join with you, as you call it, merely because you can kill a bird by some low trick or other?'

In Jim's life there had been certain events which he had not mentioned. They seemed to him irrelevant to the matter in hand, but they were not really so at all. He had always been a weakling. His father, a professional footballer, despised him, and blamed the frail mother. The couple had lived a cat-and-dog life almost since their honeymoon. At school Jim had been thoroughly bullied; and in consequence he had conceived a deep hatred of the strong, and at the same time an obsessive yearning to be strong himself. He was a bright lad, and had secured a scholarship at a provincial university. As an undergraduate, he kept himself to himself, worked hard for a scientific degree, and aimed at a career of research in atomic physics. Already his dominant passion was physical power, so he chose its most spectacular field. But somehow his plans went awry. In spite of his reasonably good academic qualifications, he found himself stuck in a low-grade job in an industrial lab, a job which he had taken on as a stopgap till he could capture a post in one of the great institutions devoted to atomic physics. In this backwater, his naturally sour disposition became embittered. He felt he was not getting a fair chance. Inferior men were outstripping him. Fate was against him. In fact, he developed something like a persecution mania. But the truth was that he was a bad co-operator. He never developed the team spirit, which is so necessary in the immensely complex work of fundamental physical research. Also, he had no genuine interest in physical theory, and was impatient of the necessity of advanced theoretical study. What he wanted was power, power for himself as an individual. He recognized that modern research was a co-operative affair, and that in it, though one might gain dazzling prestige, one would not gain any physical power as an individual. Psychokinesis, on the other hand, might perhaps give him his heart's desire. His interest rapidly shifted to the more promising field. Henceforth his work in the lab was a mere means of earning a livelihood.

After the conversation in the cottage garden he concentrated more eagerly than ever on his venture. He must gain even more spectacular powers to impress Helen. He had decided that for him, at any rate, the promising line was to develop his skill at interfering with and checking small physical and chemical processes, in lifeless matter and in living things. He learned how to prevent a struck match from lighting. He tried to by-pass the whole of atomic research by applying his power of psychokinesis to the release of energy pent up in the atom. But in this exciting venture he had no success at all, perhaps because in spite of his training, he had not sufficient theoretical knowledge of physics, nor access to the right kind of apparatus for setting the experiment. On the biological side he succeeded in killing a small dog by the same process as he had applied to the robin. He was confident that with practice he would soon be able to kill a man.

He had one alarming experience. He decided to try to stop the sparking of his motor-cycle engine. He started up the bike on its stand, and set about 'willing' the spark to fail. He concentrated his attention on the points of the sparking plug and the leaping spark, and 'willed' the space between the points to become impenetrable, an insulator. This experiment, of course, involved a far greater interference with physical processes than freezing a nerve fibre or even preventing a match from lighting. Sweat poured from him as he struggled with his task. At last the engine began to misfire. But something queer happened to himself. He had a moment of horrible vertigo and nausea, and then he lost consciousness. When he recovered, the engine was once more running normally.

This mishap was a challenge. He had never been seriously interested in the mere theoretical side of his experiments for its own sake, but now he had perforce to ask himself what exactly was happening when by an 'act of will' he interfered with a physical process. The obvious explanation was that in some way the physical energy that should have crossed the gap between the points had been directed into his own body; in fact that he had suffered the electric shock that he would have had if he had touched the points. It may be doubted whether the true explanation was as simple as this, for his symptoms were not those of electric shock. It might be nearer the truth to say that the inhibition of so much physical energy caused some sort of profound physical disturbance in him; or else, to put the matter very crudely, that the physical energy was in some sense converted into physical energy in him. This theory is born out by the fact that, when he recovered consciousness, he was in a state of great excitement and mental vigour; as though he had taken some stimulating drug like benzedrine.

Whatever the truth of the matter, he adopted the simpler theory, and set about side-tracking the intruding energy, so as to protect himself. After much anxious experimentation, he found that he could do so by concentrating his attention both on the sparking plug and on some other living organism, which then 'drew off the electricity', and suffered accordingly. A sparrow sufficed. It died of the shock, while he himself remained conscious long enough to stop the engine. On another occasion he used his neighbour's dog as a 'lightning conductor'. The animal collapsed, but soon recovered consciousness, and careered about the garden barking hilariously.

His next experiment was more exciting, and much much more reprehensible. He went into the country and took up his position on a knoll, whence he could see a fairly long stretch of road. Presently a car came into sight. He concentrated his attention on the sparking plugs, and 'willed' the electrical energy to escape into the driver. The car slowed down, vacillated between the two sides of the road, and came to a standstill across the fairway. He could see the driver slumped over the steering wheel. There was no one else in the car. Greatly excited, Jim wanted to see what would happen. Presently another car came in the opposite direction, hooted violently and drew up with screeching brakes. The driver emerged, went to the derelict car, opened a door, and was confronted by the unconscious occupant. While the horrified newcomer was wondering what to do, the other recovered consciousness. There was an anxious conversation, and finally both cars went their several ways.

Jim now felt ready to impress his girl friend. Since the killing of the robin, they had occasionally met, and in his awkward and adolescent way he had tried to make love to her. She had always discouraged him; but she was obviously more interested in him since the robin incident. Though she sometimes affected to despise him, he felt that she was secretly drawn to him.

But one day he had an unpleasant surprise. He had boarded a bus to take him home from his work. He climbed the stairs and settled into a seat. Suddenly he noticed Helen sitting a few seats ahead with a curly-headed young man in a sports coat. The couple were deep in conversation, with their heads bent together. The girl's hair brushed his cheek. Presently she laughed, with a ring of happiness such as he had never before heard from her. She turned her face toward her companion. It was aglow with vitality, and love. Or so it seemed to the jealous lover three seats behind.

Irrational fury swept over him. He was so ignorant of the ways of girls, and so indignant that '*his* girl' (for so he regarded her) should take notice of another man, that jealousy wholly possessed him, to the exclusion of all other considerations. He could think of nothing but destroying his rival. His gaze seized upon the nape of the hated neck before him. He passionately conjured up images of the hidden vertebrae and the enclosed bundle of nerve fibres. The nerve-current must cease; must, must cease. Presently the curly head sank on Helen's shoulder, and then the whole body fell forward.

The murderer hurriedly rose from his seat and turned his back on the incipient commotion. He left the bus, as though ignorant of the disaster.

Continuing his journey on foot, he was still so excited that he had no thought but exultation over his triumph. But gradually his frenzy subsided, and he faced the fact that he was a murderer. Urgently he reminded himself that after all there was no point in feeling guilty, since morality was a mere superstition. But alas, he did feel guilty, horribly guilty; the more so since he had no fear of being caught.

As the days passed, Jim alternated between what he regarded as 'irrational' guilt and intoxicating triumph. The world was indeed at his feet. But he must play his cards carefully. Unfortunately his guilt gave him no peace. He could not sleep properly; and when he did sleep, he had terrifying dreams. By day his experiments were hampered by the fantasy that he had sold his soul to the Devil. This notion infuriated him with its very silliness. Yet he could not rid himself of it. He began drinking rather heavily. But he soon found that alcohol reduced his psychokinetic power, so he firmly broke himself of the habit.

Another possible form of relief from his obsessive guilt was sex. But somehow he could not bring himself to face Helen. He was irrationally afraid of her. Yet she must be quite ignorant that he had killed her lover.

At last he met her accidentally in the street. There was no possibility of avoiding her. She was rather wan, he thought, but she smiled at him, and actually suggested a talk over a cup of coffee. He was torn between fear and desire, but presently they were seated in a café. After some trivial remarks, she said, 'Please comfort me! I have had a terrible shock quite recently. I was on the top of a bus with my brother who has been in Africa for three years. While we were talking, he collapsed and died almost instantly. He seemed perfectly fit. They say it was some new virus in the spinal cord.' She noticed that Jim's face had turned deadly pale. 'What's the matter?' she cried. 'Are *you* going to die on me too?' He pulled himself together, and assured her that sheer sympathy for her had made him feel faint. He loved her so much. How could he help being upset by her misfortune? To his relief Helen was completely taken in by this explanation. She gave him, for the first time, the glowing smile he had seen her turn upon her brother.

Encouraged, he pressed home his advantage. He said he did so want to comfort her. They must meet again soon. And if she was at all interested in his experiments, he would show her something really exciting some time. They arranged a trip in the country for the following Sunday. He privately decided to repeat for her benefit his trick with a passing car.

Sunday was a bright summer day. Sitting together in an empty railway carriage, they talked a good deal about her brother. He was rather bored, but he expressed ardent sympathy. She said she never imagined he had such a warm heart. He took her arm. Their faces drew close together, and they looked into each other's eyes. She felt an overwhelming tenderness for his strange, rather grotesque though boyish face, wherein, she told herself, the innocence of childhood was overlaid by an adult consciousness of power. She felt the underlying grimness, and she welcomed it. Jim for his part was realizing that she was very desirable. The warm glow of health had returned to her face. (Or was it a glow of love?) The full, sweet lips, the kindly observant grey eyes, filled him not only with physical desire but a swooning gentleness that was new to him. The recollection of his guilt and present deception tormented him. An expression of misery came over his face. He let go her arm and bowed forward with his head in his hands. Perplexed and compassionate, she put an arm round his shoulders, and kissed his hair. Suddenly he burst into tears, and buried his head on her breast. She hugged him and crooned over him as though he were her child. She begged him to tell her what was the matter, but he could only blubber, 'Oh I'm horrible! I'm not good enough for you.'

Later in the day, however, he had quite recovered his spirits, and they walked arm in arm through the woods. He told her of his recent successes, culminating with the car incident. She was impressed and amused, but also morally shocked by the irresponsibility of risking a fatal accident merely to test his powers. At the same time she was obviously fascinated by the fanaticism that drove him to such lengths. He was flattered by her interest, and intoxicated by her tenderness and her physical proximity. For they were now resting on the little knoll where he intended to do his trick with the car, and he was lying with his head in her lap, gazing up at her face, where all the love that his life had missed seemed to be gathered. He realized that he was playing the part of an infant rather than a lover. But she seemed to need him to do so, and he was happy in his role. But soon sexual desire began to reassert itself, and with it masculine self-respect. He conceived an uncontrollable lust to demonstrate his godlike nature by some formidable display of his powers. He became the primitive savage who must kill an enemy in the presence of the beloved.

Looking up through Helen's fluttering hair, he saw a small object moving. For a moment he took it for a gnat then realized that it was a distant aeroplane approaching.

'Watch that plane,' he said; and she was startled by the abruptness of his voice. She looked up, and down again at him. His face was contorted with effort. His eyes glared, his nostrils dilated. She had an impulse to fling him from her, so brutal he looked. But fascination triumphed. 'Keep your eyes on the plane,' he commanded. She looked up, then down, then up again. She knew she ought to break the devilish spell. (There was something called morality, but a delusion, probably.) Fascination had triumphed.

Presently the advancing plane's four engines ceased one by one to fire. The plane glided for a while, but soon gave evidence of being out of control. It vacillated, staggered, and then was in a nose dive, spiralling. Helen screamed, but did nothing. The plane disappeared behind a distant wood. After a few seconds a black plume of smoke began to rise from behind the wood.

Jim raised himself from Helen's lap, and turning, pressed her backwards to the ground. 'That's how I love you,' he whispered fiercely. Then he furiously kissed her lips, her neck.

She made a violent effort to pull herself together and resist the impulses of self-abandonment to this lunatic. She struggled to free herself from his grip; and presently the two stood facing each other, panting. 'You're mad,' she cried. 'Think what you have done! You have killed people just to show how clever you are. And then you make love to me.' She covered her face with her hands and sobbed.

He was still in a state of crazy exaltation, and he laughed. Then he taunted her. 'Call yourself a realist! You're squeamish. Well, now you know what I am really like; and what I can do. And see! You're mine. I can kill you at any moment, wherever you are. I shall do whatever I like with you. And if you try to stop me, you'll go the way of the robin, and – the man on the bus.' Her hands dropped from her tearstained face. She stared at him in mingled horror and – tenderness. She said quietly, 'You're quite mad, you poor boy. And you seemed so gentle. Oh, my dear, what can I do about you?'

There was a long silence. Then suddenly Jim collapsed on the ground, blubbering like a child. She stood over him in perplexity.

While she was wondering what to do, and blaming herself for not breaking the spell before it was too late, he was in an agony of self-loathing. Then he started to use his techniques upon himself, so that no more harm should be done. It was more difficult than he expected; for as soon as he began to lose consciousness he also lost his grip on the operation. But he made a desperate effort of will. When Helen, noticing his stillness, knelt down by him, he was dead.

Title: Death of a Sensitive
Writer: *Harry Bates*

Briefing: *Parapsychology – psychical research; the study of phenomena such as telepathy where the mind gains knowledge by means other than normal perception.* Fred Warren is a journalist with more than a passing knowledge of parapsychology. When he is assigned to investigate the bizarre, reclusive behaviour of John Inglis – an identical twin who possesses acute psychic powers – Warren discovers the man living in a room full of cockroaches who are *communicating* with him. The journalist realizes he is in the presence of a unique telepathic mind – but one that is on the verge of insanity.

Author: American writer-editor Harry Bates created *The Day The Earth Stood Still*, the classic 1951 movie about the arrival of an alien and his robot companion on Earth. The film starred Michael Rennie as Klaatu, the extraterrestrial with the power to stop all the Earth's electrical equipment with his *mind*. Bates's original story on which the picture was based, 'Farewell To The Master', had actually been published a decade earlier in 1940 in *Astounding Stories* – a magazine whose success he had largely ensured during his tenure as editor. For a time, he also edited a stable-companion, *Strange Tales*, until the collapse of the publishers, The Clayton Group. Though he continued to publish the occasional piece of fiction during the next twenty years, Harry Bates vanished from the New York literary scene and was rarely heard of again until his death in 1981. It was then discovered he had been living for years in virtual poverty in a rundown apartment – events described with almost uncanny foresight in this story 'Death of a Sensitive', which he had written some thirty years earlier . . .

I bring you a most urgent message.

The man who charged me to deliver it is dead. He died to transmit it to you. I have just come from him. I was with him when he passed away.

I want you to ignore the confusion in the streets. Pay no attention to the Invaders! Read this to the end. There I shall give the message.

I cannot give you the message until I have described all that happened. For you would not feel *compelled*.

There is confusion here in the city room as I start. It churns all about me, it rises from the street, it comes in over the phones and the wire.

I think there is one of the Creatures on the roof.

Not far from here the body of John Inglis sits upright in a big armchair. At last the great sensitive is at peace. His wonderful head lies bent on his breast. His face is dead white, and there is a small hole in his wrist.

It is John Inglis who transmits the message.

I feel that he is guiding me now (this you will come to understand). I feel I can remember every word that was spoken.

(Interruption. A copy boy has just snatched from my hand the first page of the copy, the first 'take', and has run with it straight to the composing room. I had hoped for that. Since this story is bypassing the copy desk – and is not therefore to be edited – I shall not write it in the usual newspaper style, but shall tell it as a consecutive narrative.)

I must be fast!

Several hours ago this was a normal world.

I had just turned in a story, and the city editor handed me a phone memo. The superintendent of the building where John Inglis lived had phoned in, saying we might be interested to hear that the sensitive had gone 'off his trolley', as he put it. He had an apartment full of cockroaches. He was acting like a *friend* of the cockroaches. There were strange doings. He himself was very curious. Above the memo in the handwriting of the city editor were the words: 'Warren, I think you know this man. Feature?'

Everybody of course knows the name Inglis, and will remember how, ten years ago, the identical twin brothers, John and Robert, astounded the world with their feats in parapsychology. But the name Inglis meant something special to me. I was at Columbia at the same time they were piling up their records there, and I even shared some of their classes. They were the start of my own layman's interest in parapsychology.

It looked like a good assignment. I went to the newspaper's morgue to bring myself up to date. The clerk handed me a number of envelopes stuffed with clippings. At least once each year, in the ten years which have elapsed since their college performances, the Inglis brothers have been the subject of feature stories in the newspaper. One of these features, which appeared last year, was my own, so I already knew the background. All the stories, including mine, were rehashes of their great performances at Columbia as volunteer subjects of the famous parapsychologist Dr S. T. Whitman. They lived apart. They had always lived lives of seclusion and bleak poverty. The recurrent question of the features was: Why didn't they ever amount to something? Why, with such powers, did they remain so inconspicuous and poor? Specifically and vulgarly. Why didn't they 'clean up' on the races, or the stock market, and take a prominent place in the world?

I spent little time with the clippings, but went and picked up a photographer. I was assigned Willie. That is *not* his name. Willie is something of a louse. I don't approve of his methods. Naturally, he doesn't like me. But he is considered one of the best pic-men in the business.

Willie is a desiccated little gum-chewer, and a wise guy. As we drove off in my car I tried to warn him to behave.

'This man Inglis is a great sensitive and a mighty nice guy,' I informed him. 'I had a feature on him last year. This time I've a peculiar tip – something about cockroaches. It sounds like a good story and some swell pictures. Now, Willie, I want you to show him some manners. Lay off him till I'm through. Try to be decent for once. Don't try to catch him in an awkward moment; don't take any candid shots at all. Get his approval on everything. And don't try to force him into any vulgar poses. Got it?'

He was chewing gum, of course. Now he kept on chewing, and said nothing.

I said strongly, 'You hear?'

'You get your story and don't try to tell me my business,' he said, calloused and totally impervious.

'Well, I've told you your business,' I came back, a little ugly. 'Do you know what a sensitive is?'

'Do you?' he answered. Of course he is not very bright.

'A sensitive is a man who has powers not explainable by known physical laws,' I told him – for I doubted very much if he knew, and he'd never admit he didn't know something. 'He can perform feats of clairvoyance – that is, see things that exist or are happening at a distance. Or can foretell events which will occur in the future. Or can be the means of psychokinesis. In psychokinesis objects actually are moved without the use of known forces.'

He kept chewing away. I thought I knew what he would be thinking. I went on:

'They don't hold your hand in a dim room and tell your fortune, and they don't accept money. They do these things under controlled conditions, in front of scientists – yes, and sometimes in front of magicians, brought there to guard against possible trickery.'

'They're all a bunch of phonies,' he announced with contemptuous finality, hardly missing a chew.

'The scientists who work with them don't think so,' I answered.

'I never heard of one cleaning up on the races,' he said, enormously complacent. I could have smacked him.

'That's right, they don't clean up on the races,' I answered. 'For one reason, they don't try to.'

He grinned, and stuck a cigarette in his face and lit it. Thereafter he both chewed *and* smoked.

'For another reason,' I went on, 'they usually miss. Even the best of them hit only a fraction of the time, so that their success has to be evaluated statistically. It's that way with John Inglis. He, however, is in a class by himself. He and his brother Robert.'

He chewed and puffed. There was simply no way to get to him. I shut up.

I pulled up at the address on the memo – the same place of a year ago. It is an old-fashioned tenement house which has survived alone, lost among the two irregular rows of warehouses near the end of a half-deserted street over by the East River. Many of its windows were broken or boarded up. The entrance was a cracked and dirty marble doorway in the centre of the ground floor. Galvanized garbage barrels stood in stinking rows on either side of it.

We entered. The hallway was long, and very dark. At the far end was a decrepit door, its windows painted black. Through a break in the corner of one pane came a trace of dim light from a court in the back. To Inglis's door was tacked a small piece of cardboard containing his name, neatly printed by hand.

'Remember your manners,' I warned Willie, and then knocked.

There was no answer.

I knocked louder, and there was still no answer. I was still waiting, thinking someone would come, then Willie turned and began kicking at the door with his heel. He kicked much too hard. At the noise a man stuck his head out of the apartment door just behind us across the hall.

'I'm the super.' he whispered, holding one finger to his lips. He beckoned us into his glaringly oilclothed kitchen. 'You're the reporters?' he asked. 'It was me sent for you.'

'Isn't he home?' I asked.

'Yeah, he's home; he never goes out,' the man answered.

'What's this about cockroaches?' I asked.

'Well, that's the thing,' he answered. 'I don't rightly know what it is, but something's going on. There's a little girl lives in the house who does errands for him and yesterday she left the door open and I saw inside. Inglis is always neat as a pin, but I saw there's lots of cockroaches on his kitchen floor, most of them dead, but some of them alive. But that ain't what I mean. He's laid *boards* over the floor, a little bit off, so he can walk on the boards and not step on the cockroaches. He just walks on the boards. I think he's gone off his trolley.'

'How long has he had those boards?'

'I don't know. They weren't there a week ago.'

'Does he talk crazy?'

'No. Just the same as always. He don't never say much. Just goes around being quiet, his head a little on one side like he's thinking. He's always thinkin'.'

'Why doesn't he come to the door? He certainly heard us. Is there any way we can tell if he's in?'

'He's in all right. Come, I'll show you.'

Again touching his fingers to his lips, he led us down the hall to the door at the end and pulled it open. The blank brick wall of a building in the back seemed almost to hit me in the face, it was so close. It was so dark there that it would have been hard to read a newspaper.

The shades at the back of Inglis's apartment were pulled all the way to the ground.

There was a narrow concrete walk or alley, walled on the far side by another brick building, which led back along the side of the house parallel with the central hallway within. The super tiptoed around to the first window opening on this alley and put his face to the pane.

The shade there, too, was drawn all the way down, but it was torn, so that there was a small hole through which he could see the interior. He peeped through this hole, then turned to me and nodded a yes, and then I too peeped in. John Inglis, the man I remembered, was there. The room was lighted, and I could see his shoulder and the right side of his head. He was sitting quietly in a large armchair. At first I thought he was asleep, but when I was about to turn away I saw his head move a little.

I gave way to Willie and he put his eye at the hole. It seemed almost at once there was a click, and Willie had his first picture. I gave him a look but said nothing, for that shot certainly didn't have any value.

'He's in there and he's awake,' I said to the super. 'Why doesn't he answer our knock?'

The man shrugged. 'Sometimes he don't like to be bothered,' he said.

We went back to the hall entrance and knocked again, very loudly. Even then Inglis did not come to the door, nor did we hear any sound. I began to wonder.

Willie turned the knob. The door was locked. He took something out of his pocket and applied it to the crack of the door near the lock. I couldn't see it, but I knew from the office gossip that it was a very thin flat piece of flexible steel. Then he pushed. The door opened slowly inward and he stepped inside. It was an improper thing to do, but, hardly thinking, I followed him inside, the super following close at my heels.

It was completely dark. Willie produced a small pencil flash and swept the room with its narrow beam. We were in a rather large kitchen, the reverse in layout of the one across the hall. The beam cut to the floor and darted around.

The super was right. Two board walkways ran the length of the kitchen near the opposite walls, and connecting them at intervals lay several cross-walks. The walks were old planks, lifted four or five inches from the floor. The planks rested on wooden blocks set in tin plates filled with water. Here and there on the floor the thin beam of the flash picked out a cockroach or two, sometimes moving, usually dead.

Willie found a pull chain and jerked on the light. The floor leading into the rest of the apartment was closed, and I tiptoed toward it along one of the walks. As I went I heard a click. Willie had taken a second picture. I turned toward him in anger, and it was at that moment, behind and unseen by me, that John Inglis opened the closed door and entered the room.

The great sensitive stopped inside the door and stood motionless, looking right at me. I felt terribly embarassed at being caught that way in his place, and he saw it. With the faintest of smiles he said to me:

'That's all right.'

I blurted out something about having knocked several times and wondering what was wrong.

'That's all right; I wanted you to come,' he said kindly, and in his quiet voice.

My friends – all you who read this – John Inglis was a hell of a good guy.

He remained standing there, looking at one, then another.

I suppose all the world has seen his picture, but I had better describe him. He was 31 years old, a man of medium height, a little wide and a little thick. The thickness was not muscle, it was fat. Evenly, all over, he carried a thin layer of fat. The man never got any exercise.

Anyone seeing him for the first time would likely notice only his head. It was a striking head – large and broad, with hair a mass of coarse black ringlets. His complexion was milky white. He did not have the thin-skinned aesthetic face usually associated with sensitiveness. Quite the contrary: his face was full, the underlying bones large and strong, his skin looked rather thick, and no lines shown in it except around the eyes. But for his head and his eyes, and the relaxed way he stood there, he might have been taken for a truck driver. He was indeed wearing a truck driver's zippered jacket, now unfastened.

His wonderful eyes showed him as one apart. They were blue; even in the glaring, yellow light they showed their blueness; but whether they were light blue or dark I cannot tell you, for they seemed to change colour as he moved them, and they seemed to change with his words as he spoke. I think he might almost have conducted a conversation with those eyes. The whites, this time, were quite bloodshot, but even that did not seem to spoil their effect.

No doubt his gaze embarrassed the super too, for the man said stupidly:

'The door was unlocked so we just pushed in.'

'The door was not unlocked; but that is all right,' came the quiet voice. 'I hope you stayed on the planks,' he added, looking at Willie, who had one foot on a plank, the other on the floor. Slowly and contemptuously, I thought, Willie brought the other foot up. Inglis turned back to me.

'Some time early this morning I remember thinking it would be a good thing to ask you to come, Mr Warren,' he said. (He remembered my name!) 'I suppose I practically invited you – through our friend the superintendent.' At this the super's eyebrows went up. Inglis smiled slightly. 'But I only want to see Mr Warren,' he went on, looking at Willie, 'and it may take some time; so I suggest you go back and save your time. I'm sorry,' he said, dismissing the other two.

He turned and led the way past the inner door. I followed him through the next room, which was his bedroom, into the rearmost room, the one in which we had seen him through the window. Arrived there we found that Willie had come too. We looked at him.

'This must be private,' Inglis said evenly.

Willie's eyes narrowed.

'Look, I'm the photographer,' he said. 'You can't say anything to him you can't say to me.'

'Out,' I ordered. 'And no more pix.'

He sneered at me. I approached him and suddenly grabbed his camera.

He made a jump toward me, stopped, cursed, and then, after thinking things over a minute, turned and left. Inglis followed him to the kitchen door, closed it after him, and put a chair under the knob. Then he came back and asked me to be seated, he himself taking the large armchair he had sat in before. He sighed.

'That man disturbs me dreadfully,' he said in his quiet voice. He closed his eyes, and for a second the wrinkles deepened about them. I got down to business at once.

'I know how you feel about these interviews,' I said, 'but I think I can make this one brief and relatively painless. We have all the ancient history at the office. If you will just bring me up to date – tell me what you've been doing this last year – and then – well – tell me why you've got those planks on the floor.'

He said nothing.

'Why do you have them?' I asked directly. 'Are you afraid of stepping on the cockroaches?'

'That's right,' he said after a moment. 'I don't want to kill them.'

'Why?' I asked.

'I don't know,' he answered, his eyes still closed.

'Most people are only too glad to kill them,' I went on, feeling my way. 'I don't remember seeing any the last time I was here.'

He opened his eyes, and I thought I saw signs of distress in them.

'It is quite recent,' he said. 'They started coming a week ago. The people upstairs are doing something which drives them down. A nerve poison. At any rate they come down here to me, and then they die.'

'Well?' I asked after a moment. Again I saw the distress in his eyes. I said, 'But you don't remove them.'

'I know. But some of them are still alive. They run, and they'd be crippled,' he said.

'Is it so awful to kill a cockroach?'

All my questions seemed to cause feelings of distress in him. He moved his head slowly and said:

'I really don't know how to answer you. The planks seemed like a good idea.'

'Better than to kill them and sweep them up?'

'It – just – seemed – appropriate.'

There was no doubt at all that I was somehow torturing him. To lighten the moment I said, smiling, 'It does look odd.'

'I am aware of that,' he said, smiling faintly himself.

'You have no planks here, or in the bedroom.'

'They rarely come in here. When they do, I carefully shoo them back into the kitchen.'

He offered nothing further, but sat studying me. I saw that he had something heavy on his mind and was trying to decide about opening up. As I waited and wondered, I had an intuition. I asked:

'Mr Inglis, does this compulsion about the killing – about the planks – does it seem associated with your paranormal powers?'

'Yes,' he answered, looking me straight in the eyes.

'Is it a message?' I asked him.

'I think it is.'

'For you?'

'I don't know.'

For a moment I did not know what to say. Then I asked:

'It doesn't come clear?'

'That's just it,' he cried, showing a trace of excitement. 'It doesn't come clear.'

'How long has this been going on?'

'A week,' he answered, 'But early last evening there was something new.' He rose. 'Come with me to the kitchen,' he said, beckoning. and led the way back. I followed him, carefully keeping on the planks.

The light was still on, showing unpleasantly several scores of cockroaches along the edges of the floor and lower walls, most of them dead, but some moving. He pointed to a patch of white on the floor at a place just in front of the old-fashioned kitchen cabinet.

'That's flour,' he said. 'I spilled it preparing dinner last night. Later, when I went to clean it up, I found something.'

He stepped to the patch and carefully got down on his knees in front of it, moving carefully to avoid a live cockroach. Extremely curious and equally carefully I let myself down by his side.

Near one edge of the whited area lay a large cockroach, dead. Backward from it lay the trail it had made in its passage from the other side. The trail twisted and doubled; it looked like writing. Suddenly I saw that it *was* writing. Four words lay spelled out there in a wandering schoolboy hand, certain as can be! They read, 'do not kill us.' The last 's' was not quite finished, and the writer lay on its back, legs folded symmetrically inward, stopped by death at the point where the twisting trail ended.

Chills ran down my back. I stared at the words.

'The poor little devil,' Inglis murmured. 'It came in poisoned like the others. It died in pain like the others. But in dying it had a task.'

'A message,' I breathed.

'A message,' he said. '"Do not kill us."'

'It's psychokinesis!'

He nodded. He said, 'This happened yesterday – but I already had stopped killing them for a week.'

'Because you felt it "appropriate" not to kill them.'

'Because I felt it appropriate.'

I was frightened. The air around me seemed charged with unknown potential. Somewhere in space-time – somehow – an intelligence could conceive this – will this – possessed the undetectable force to effect this. For no one has ever credibly explained psychokinesis. It happens. It has even been produced in the laboratory. From some place unknown, from some thing or condition unknown, comes a force which can move a material object. The nature of the force cannot be detected. Its presence cannot be detected, except insofar as the object moves. It is not gravity, not electricity, not magnetism. It may move either inanimate objects or living matter. If in seances there is genuine contact with the dead – which is far from proved – it is likely that it is by psychokinesis that the vocal chords of mediums are manipulated in the production of the authentic-seeming voices of the dead ones who 'speak'.

'This is the rarest of paranormal phenomena!' I exclaimed, awed by what I was looking at.

'Who knows?' Inglis said thoughtfully. 'It may be the commonest of the normal.'

The implications of his words hit me suddenly, and like a ton of bricks. Again the chills ran down my back.

'Did you effect this?'

'Not that I know of,' was his answer.

'It was some entity, or force, or something working independently of you? Or were you in some sense the medium by which it happened?'

'I don't know. But I feel that I am involved in it somehow.'

'This cockroach has come – been sent – been made to actually write out the message to which you have already been responding for a week,' I said.

He sighed and the tortured look came again to his eyes.

'I can't catch it – I just can't catch it,' he said. 'I feel no particular urge not to kill cockroaches. It just began to seem appropriate not to kill them. There was no emotion involved. That is the common experience in receiving paranormal intelligence – though there are exceptions, sometimes striking exceptions.

'I just saw a cockroach or two and felt it appropriate not to kill them, and then I took steps not to kill them. I don't think I felt any particular emotion about the cockroaches as such . . . Now this. This is direct and specific. Yet even this message does not cause in me any emotion specific to cockroaches . . . There are theories and good men and even whole religions devoted to the ideal of not taking life, not even the life of the simplest creatures . . . and I have sometimes toyed with the thought . . . but I have always sheered away from such mysticism. As things are set up

in Nature, life lives on life, animal and plant, right down to the single cell
. . . As a sane person, and one of good will, I have merely killed as little as
is consistent with the maintainance of my own status as a live animal.
Germs I kill; insects, except pests, no. I eat meat. Of course I am
inconsistent,' he added, darkly contemplative; 'but I don't worry much
about that. It is a problem that can't be solved.'

He sighed, then wearily got to his feet and led the way back to his living
room, where he again slumped tiredly in his chair. I followed, greatly
disturbed. I wanted to help him.

'Someone, or something, is sending you a message,' I began. 'Or more
accurately, you keep receiving a message but you don't understand what it
means.'

'It is probably only part of a message,' he said, wearily. '"Don't kill
cockroaches" doesn't make sense.'

He closed his eyes and let his head rest on the back of the chair.

'I'm all in,' he said. 'I am oppressed by the feeling that I am failing in a
matter of great urgency. To be fruitful one must be relaxed; but I can't
relax. How can one relax after a week without sleep? I *try* to sense – what is
wrong – and sometimes I feel I am close; but it won't come; it just won't
come. I am at the end, Warren. I can't go on this way any longer.'

I felt terribly sorry for him. I ventured:

'Are there other conditions for optimum reception, and are you
complying with them?'

Best conditions usually are to merely to be quiet, to be alone, and to be
relaxed; but not always. I've been under great strain lately, but I've had
evidence of great sensitivity, more perhaps than ever in the past. But it's
not been enough.'

He opened his eyes; then, looking vaguely in my direction, he said:

'I am going to bring it to an end. I am going to commit suicide.'

I was astounded. He was quite serious. His words were spoken with quiet
firmness. For the first time, it struck me that he might be mentally
disturbed – I mean irrational – but this thought quickly passed from my
mind.

I could not at once find anything adequate to say, but only stared at
him, in distress myself. This man was no neurotic show-off, but a highly
mature, decent, intelligent but terribly bedevilled person. I had no doubt
that he was at the end of his endurance.

'You're talking very foolishly,' I said finally. 'You're tortured; you need
help. I'm going to call your brother. He can help you. Where's your
phone?'

'I haven't any phone,' Inglis sat without moving a muscle, except that I
think he smiled faintly. At last he explained.

'My brother is dead.'

I was shocked, then incredulous.

'But he's not dead!' I cried. 'He can't be dead. That would be a big story, and no word on such a thing has reached our office!'

'He died last night,' Inglis said quietly, still without moving.

'How do you know?' I asked. 'You were there?'

'I saw him,' he said, and to me he seemed to be seeing him again in his mind's eye. 'He came to me. At a little after three this morning. I was sitting in this chair, and at the moment of his death he came to me.'

For a moment I was speechless. That was one more paranormal phenomenon – not uncommon – known through the centuries. What unthinkable psychic forces were permeating this hapless man!

Suddenly a frightening suspicion flashed through my mind.

'Did he take his own life?'

'I feel he did.'

'You don't know for sure?'

'No, but I feel he did . . . He, like me, has been suffering. He was bearing the same burden.'

'Did he give you a message? How did he look? Tell me, for heaven's sake, man!'

'He was dressed as usual. He wore a jacket much like mine . . . I had been meditating. I looked up and there he was, just inside the door. He was solid and real. He took several steps toward me, then stopped and raised his right forearm. There was a gash in his wrist, and his wrist and hand were splotched with blood. In his left hand was a sheet of paper. He held out the paper – his lips moved – but I heard no words. My God, I could hear no words! . . . There was an expression of great suffering on his face. For a second or two he held out the paper; then his face softened and became most beautiful . . . and then he dissolved and was gone . . . '

How I felt as I sat and heard these things! I wanted to help Inglis, but I was way out of my depth! Inglis was such a good guy! Somehow I had to rescue him! But how? I sat there paralyzed. Who has ever been in a situation like that?

But my mind did keep working, it seems, for I produced another thought, eagerly I broached it.

'This Dr Whitman for whom you and your brother were subjects in school – he's a good friend of yours, isn't he?'

'He was.'

'Aren't you still friends?'

'Yes, in a way. I haven't seen him for several years, but that was my doing, not his. I have come to be something of a recluse; I seldom go out.'

'All right,' I began eagerly – but he interrupted me.

'I know. You want me to go fetch him. Perhaps he will be able to help me.'

'Yes!' I exclaimed. 'There's no one in the world knows you better. He has worked with you, he knows your powers – of course he can help you!'

'I had thought of him,' Inglis said. 'We used to get some wonderful results together.'

'You'll get some more!' I cried, quite excited. 'Inglis, it's ridiculous – it's all wrong for you to sit there and talk about taking your life! You need help; he can give it to you – positively; I'm going to get him.'

'Fred Warren,' he said, looking straight into my eyes, 'I have the feeling that several hours from now I'll be sitting in this chair dead, like my brother, and I will be with my brother. Wherever and whatever he now is. That I feel. I don't particularly want it, in a sense. I just feel it. I – I feel it is appropriate.'

'You have very often been wrong,' I retorted. I was standing. 'Inglis,' I said, 'I'm going to fetch him. You've got to give him a chance to try to help you. Will you promise not to do anything until I return with him? I will take your word.'

For a moment he did not answer, but looked thoughtfully through me, as it seemed; then he turned his head. He said:

'I had thought of asking him to come, but I felt, and still feel, that it would be useless.' He smiled slightly. 'You notice how I keep saying "I feel"? I usually *feel* nothing at all in the paranormal process, but when I do my feeling usually indicates a hit.' He took thought, and I waited. 'If he could only help me to dissolve the feeling of "appropriateness" . . .' he murmured, thinking out loud. 'It wouldn't hurt any . . . and he'll be an extra witness . . .' He turned back to me with an enigmatic expression. 'You know, Mr Warren, I wanted you here to witness my death. You have the three things needful: knowledge of parapsychology, competence as a reporter, and resonance with me as a man. It may be my death will give you something to write about. I don't want to put it into words, but perhaps you will sense what I mean. But it might be better with both of you . . . Yes, get Dr Whitman. I'm very fond of him. I give you my promise. And while you are gone I shall prepare my body.'

I choked down my objections to his last words. I asked:

'May I go to your brother's place? What if he's alive? And aren't you curious about the paper he was holding out to you?'

'He is dead,' he replied. 'I feel it will do no good. But you may go if you want to.'

I asked him the address and he told me. He took a small bunch of keys from his pocket and held them out. 'This is my set of keys,' he said.

I took them and rushed out with the feeling I held his life in my hands.

*

I had forgotten all about Willie; I saw him in the hall and hurried past without a word. As I entered the car I found him right behind me, and he took a place in the front seat at my side. He kept his mouth shut. He was much too sore and egotistical to ask any questions, but he was not going to miss anything if he could help it.

A few minutes later I was at Robert's house. It was a somewhat better building. His box told that he lived on the second floor, also in the back. The keys let us in without delay. I saw more cockroaches. Robert was there . . . he was dead . . . I can hardly bear to write this! He sat in a comfortable armchair much like his brother's, his head low over his breast, his face drained white. On a low table by his right side lay a white enamelled basin. His right forearm lay tied to the chair so that the hand lay out over its top. There was a gash in his wrist, and the basin was half full . . .

I kept thinking I was looking at John . . .

In Robert's left hand was a sheet of paper, just as his brother had described. I took it. On it were some marks. It looked like a drawing or a small piece of chaotic writing – very roughly like chromosomes during the process of cell division. It was meaningless to me. I stuck it in my pocket.

I can't remember exactly the shameful thing that happened then, but I know Willie made a grab for his camera, and I avoided his hand and hit him, and he stood there with his teeth bared, hate in his eyes. And I hated him too, fiercely. But when I left he was close behind me, and he rode up Columbia right by my side, neither of us speaking a word, only hating and hating . . .

I knew the campus like a book and without hesitation drove over the forbidden drives straight to the Parapsychology Building. By the time I was in the vestibule Willie again was fastened to me. The students must have thought us mad. I am sure I looked wild; I know I was soaked with perspiration. I took the stairs three at a time and in a moment was at the door of a certain lecture room well remembered from the old days. Without hesitation I pushed through, Willie still at my heels – and there, on the lecture platform, thank God, sat old Dr Whitman. Twenty or thirty pairs of eyes turned to look at us as I hurried up to the little table behind which the parapsychologist was sitting.

In the lowest voice I could muster I blurted out that I had come on a matter literally of life and death – the life of John Inglis – and the angry look that had come to his face dissolved instantly. He would have pulled me into his office, but when I whispered that I would explain in the car he dismissed the class and came hurrying along with me just as he was. I had never seen Dr Whitman on the campus with his head uncovered, but he didn't take time to pick up his hat.

I got Willie into the back seat of the car, and as I made the curved passage to the gates I began pouring out my story in bits and pieces. The good doctor was appalled. Again and again as we drove back through the streets he stopped my rush of words and made me repeat and amplify and make clearer. I told him about everything: the cockroaches, the walkways, the four written words, Robert's death appearance, the firm bent toward suicide, and finally the morbid scene that met my eyes in Robert's apartment. I showed him the paper. To him, too, the marks were meaningless.

'The man is tortured!' I kept telling him. 'He can't sleep! He has that message, and we can't tell what it means, or even if it's complete. It's worse than labour. You must believe him! He thinks only death will give him relief! He hopes that at the moment of death his message will come clear!'

Toward the end of the drive back Dr Whitman was exerting himself to calm *me*.

When we arrived the street was very quiet; the few trucks lay motionless at the curbs or stood at right angles, backed up to their loading platforms. There were hardly any people about; most of the trucking activity there occurred at night. We entered the house. I knocked on the door and at once escorted Dr Whitman inside. I pointed without speaking to the walkways and the cockroaches, then I led the way back to the living room.

Inglis met us at the door. He had changed his shirt, and I think he had shaved. The two friends shook hands with affection. Inglis invited us to be seated, and himself sat down in his big chair.

Dr Whitman sat on the edge of his chair and leaned tensely forward.

'What's all this Mr Warren has been telling me?' he asked. 'You talk about suicide? You shall do nothing of the kind. I am your friend. I probably am your best friend. I have worked intimately with you, and I know a good deal about you. Together we shall work this thing out. You are tortured? There is a devil in your skull? We shall exorcise it.'

Perhaps the good doctor's words and manner would have reassured many people, but here he was meeting a different order of experience. Inglis sighed deeply and looked away. He said:

'There's something I've got to know but can't catch. It's of greatest urgency. It's heavy. It permeates my body, it fills all the air around me, it weights me and it devils me. I smother!'

'We shall deliver you,' Dr Whitman said resolutely. 'First, let's try some word associations. Attend! I shall speak some single words. I want you to tell me the thoughts and feelings you associate with them. You know the process. Answer quickly. All right, are you ready?'

But Inglis was looking at Willie. He was standing at the door; I had forgotten all about him. Inglis said: 'I shall have to ask that man to go outside.'

Willie stood there and glared at him.

'Please go,' Inglis said. 'You disturb me very much.'

Willie didn't move, but he spoke. *'You're* off your nut,' he said hatefully.

It was shameful. 'Get out!' I told him. 'I'll call you if I want you.'

He turned with his hate toward me for a moment, cursed, I think, under his breath, then left the room. We heard the hall door bang.

'That man is not clean,' Inglis said.

'He's gone. Forget him,' said Dr Whitman. 'All right, John, the first word. Insect.'

Inglis did not respond. For a moment he sat looking vaguely up toward the ceiling; then he got to his feet, picked up a book lying on a coffee table nearby, and turned to the side window and placed it upright against the shade over the tear. I had just time to see through it a small motion.

Inglis then returned to his chair and sat leaning forward, his face clasped in his hands.

I said, 'I apologize for bringing that man here. But he's considered a good news photographer. He always gets his pictures, and the public eats them up. He's very good at posing a stricken mother weeping over a dead child in a gutter. He never fails to get the blood in, and baby, if there is one. He is ignorant, stupid, competitive and heartless, and a complete egotist; he knows only one thing: get the picture. Remember, you excluded him, and I took away his camera. I think you can understand his feelings.'

'I understand,' said Inglis. 'Each one has his flaw. God be merciful to us, animals that we are . . .'

He was very low for a while, and it took time to arouse him, but Dr William's considerate attentions at last brought him to the point where the exploration could begin again.

'There will be no more distractions,' he said. 'John, your associations. The first word. Cream.'

'Milk,' was the response.

'Book.'

'Words.'

'Brown.'

Inglis smiled a little. 'The eyes of the little girl who lives upstairs. She does my errands. Sometimes she comes in just to visit me. She sings coming down the stairs. Always she sings! She doesn't sing well, but she's not aware of that. She's still so little aware; she sings! She's a darling . . . and she twists my heart!'

He was deeply affected. We waited for him to recover. Dr Whitman gave the next word. We waited for him to recover. Dr Whitman gave the next word.

'Insect.'

'Cockroach.'

'Legs.'

'Cockroach.'

'Animal.'

Inglis writhed as if tortured. After a moment he said, 'Cockroach.'

'Creature.'

'No, no, you mustn't do this to me!' he cried. 'I can't stand it!' His head moved from side to side, and he breathed heavily. As we watched him I knew that Dr Whitman was probing his own mind, trying to understand.

I myself was tortured. I felt something frightening in that little room. It was in the air; it tingled me. For some time no one spoke. We recovered somewhat, and then I heard Dr Whitman speaking again.

'Mr Warren told me about the four words, John. Will you show them to me?'

Inglis led us out into the kitchen. 'Be careful where you step,' he said. He took a flashlight from somewhere and we stooped about the patch of spilled flour, while he held the light beam on it.

There lay the dead cockroach at the end of its torturous, torturous path. There lay the words, 'Do not kill us,' the little messenger had said, and so saying, died. I heard Dr Whitman gasp. The weird sensations of just before began to return to me, and my heart beat violently.

The psychologist turned his head and asked gently:

'What do you associate this with, John?'

'I can't give an answer. It's confused. It's terribly confused. It's torture.'

'Do you feel that this is somehow associated with you?'

'Oh, yes!'

We continued to kneel about the patch, looking, each thinking his own thoughts, feeling his own emotions. Dr Whitman murmured, 'This could have happened by chance only once out of – a page full of digits.'

As we were looking at the words, a large male cockroach appeared at one edge of the flour patch. It was sick. It had been poisoned. It rocked. Sometimes slowly, sometimes rapidly it moved, leaving behind a perfect record of its tortured trail. It passed just underneath the letters of the four words, and at the end it stopped and turned.

I watched it, breathless. It stood there listing a little to one side, obviously in distress. It kept stretching upward to maximum height, then lowering almost to the floor – up, down, up, down. Its antennae waved.

But then it began to move forward again. It went crazily as before, sometimes running, sometimes at a crawl; but sometimes now it stopped altogether and only made its tortured up and down movement. It was listing much more. It reached the side it had originally entered. It had retraced its path under the words, keeping just underneath the first trail!

'My God!' Dr Whitman murmured.

'It's underlined the words!' I exclaimed.

But it wasn't finished. It turned again. It started back for a third passage. It was extremely deranged now, and moved rapidly with wide convulsive jerks. It proceeded just beneath the second trail. When it was a little more than halfway across it came to a stop. Its up and down movements now were terrible and it was listing extremely. Suddenly it fell over on its back. Its legs waved wildly for a moment, then fell motionless, then folded back neatly and symmetrically over its abdomen. It did not move again.

Even now my heart beats so I can hardly write this. I was scared! I am sure we all were. There was something frightening in the air. It was all around us. I could not know if it was malevolent, but there was something present! Something that was active!

Inglis sobbed, got to his feet and went back to the living room. Without a word each of us again took his seat.

'Do not kill us,' murmured Dr Whitman. 'That is the message. It must be the entire message. It was underlined, not added to. Three times it was underlined.'

'I can't stand this any longer!' cried Inglis.

'Well, you're not going to take your life,' said Dr Whitman sharply. 'There's been progress. We know we have the message. We've only to find out what it means.'

'I can't stand any more,' repeated Inglis. 'Go away. Please go away! Let me handle this myself!'

'And take your life?'

'I have to!' said Inglis.

'So do crazy men and cowards feel they have to.'

'It's more than you know.' said Inglis. 'I now fore*see* my sitting here dead. I will be dead by my own hand within two hours. I have no wish for it to be otherwise. I have the strongest feeling that it is appropriate.'

This stopped Dr Whitman. I ventured to enlighten him.

'I think I know the meaning he attaches to the word "appropriate". Correct me if I'm wrong, Mr Inglis. It's a feeling that there has been a successful intuition. He feels it "appropriate" not to kill the cockroaches. He felt it "appropriate" to lay down the planks. To him this word expresses his awareness of a strong but indefinite compulsion or wish reaching him from the psychic ocean. He thinks that obedience to the compulsions is vital to the message?'

Dr Whitman reacted strongly against this idea.

'It's never "appropriate" for a healthy man of sound mind to destroy himself,' he said dogmatically. 'He's exhausted. He's plagued by a morbid fancy, nothing more. When he gets some sleep it will be gone.'

Inglis watched the doctor as he spoke, and smiled sadly. I watched him too, but I did not smile. I was sure he himself did not believe what he had said. I saw him bite his lip.

'I didn't speak honestly,' he admitted. 'I do think it is more than a fancy.'

Inglis looked fondly at his old master.

'Warren put it very well,' he said. 'Do you remember how, in our work together, I usually had no idea whether my tries were successful or not? There was no feeling of success when I hit. Only the figures later would show by how much I had exceeded the expectations of chance. You may recall that I told you it was that way even in the terrific series of 93 right calls of the dice.' He turned to me. 'There were six sides on the dice. Dr Whitman rolled it in a hotel room in Philadelphia – though I didn't know where he was. I was in the lab at Columbia. I called the number he rolled 93 consecutive times, then quit without a miss.' He turned back to the psychologist. 'But I hadn't the slightest feeling of correctness about a single one of those hits. This of course is the usual thing.

'But' – his voice rose – 'there were times in our work when I was sure. Sometimes I had a feeling about my call. When you and the others asked what the feeling was like, I would only say that it was a feeling of rightness all through my body. The right call satisfied something in me; it seemed to be "appropriate" I doubt if I ever used the word in those days, but it describes the feeling I have had this week. To stop killing cockroaches seemed "appropriate." Note that the feeling was finally confirmed by the written message; yes, and by the underlinings you yourself witnessed.'

Inglis roused and seemed to gather his forces. He continued strongly:

'Now this, Doctor. As fond as I am of you, and as much as I respect you professionally, and in spite of all you may say or do, I tell you I feel it is appropriate to let the blood from my veins; and shall act on the feeling. I shall do it and I know you won't stop me, for I also know that within two hours I shall be sitting in this chair dead.'

Inglis turned his head and looked across the room. His eyes fixed on a large plastic basin of the type used frequently for bathing babies. It was the same type of basin I had seen beneath the wrist that other Inglis, even then sitting dead and alone in his room.

'No!' cried Dr Whitman, and he rose to his feet.

'Yes,' said the afflicted man firmly, returning his eyes to the other's face.

As the two looked at each other the tension was broken by a sound at the hall door. We heard the door open, followed by the light patter of running feet coming in our direction. A little girl of perhaps five years came dashing in and almost threw herself at Inglis where he sat in the chair. She had hardly touched him before she twisted her limber body and stood erect between his knees taking us in. Wide-eyed, and with opened mouth, quite unselfconscious, she stood and wondered at us.

'This is my little friend,' said Inglis softly, touching her straying hair and shifting position a little so as to look better into her clear brown eyes. But she paid no attention to him and just kept on wondering at us. 'We are learning arithmetic,' he said.

At these words she became selfconscious; an impish smile spread over her face and she started to squirm. I think she must have been made of rubber, she bent so. At the end she was hanging backward in a sharp bow over Inglis's left knee, her hair dangling almost to the floor.

'How much are two and two?' Inglis asked her.

She squirmed even in that position; then suddenly she straightened up, ran to the door, and turned.

'Nine!' she cried triumphantly – and scampered back through the bedroom and away. We listened to her footsteps as long as they could be heard.

'How she sings!' Inglis murmured. 'What is her great secret?'

'Her secret is that she's a happy child, and your secret is that you need a few kids of your own,' said the psychologist. 'Well, you'll have them yet,' he promised grimly. 'Now look here, John – look – wake up!'

Slowly Inglis turned his eyes to him.

'Tell me, have you tried automatic writing?'

The effect of this was surprising.

'No, and I'm not going to!' he answered with much emotion.

'We're going to try it right now,' the doctor said firmly.

'No! Please! I can't stand that! It tears me apart!'

'Good,' the doctor retorted. 'It may let out your devil.'

Dr Whitman went to Inglis, pulled him to his feet and urged him toward a small table in front of some bookshelves. Earnestly protesting, the sensitive let himself be seated at it. The psychologist set before him a pad of paper which he found lying on the bookshelves and stuck his own pencil into his hand. Inglis kept protesting, but the other was inexorable.

'This may solve all your troubles,' he said firmly, 'but you've got to be cooperative. Please stop this childishness.'

Inglis quieted. He sat with the pad before him, the pencil just off its surface.

'Don't look at your hands,' said the psychologist.

Inglis turned his head so that he was looking at us over his right shoulder. His hand remained motionless. We waited, but nothing happened. Dr Whitman took out his handkerchief and threw it over the hand and pencil.

At once the hand began to move. It moved rapidly in large motions. When it came to the edge of the paper it moved back to the left and started another line. But Inglis never took his eyes from our faces. We were standing at his side, all but touching him. There was a look of anguish on his face; his eyes seemed to drain me with a deep unworded appeal. He began to breathe heavily, and sometimes made small gasps.

The hand moved faster. The handkerchief fell off to the side, but the hand kept up its rapid motion.

When the hand had written half a dozen lines and the paper was three-quarters full, there occurred a thing more extraordinary than even this. While the right hand continued to write, and with hardly a pause in its motion, Inglis's other hand darted to the pad, tore away the bottom half, reached into a pocket of his jacket and itself began to write on its own half of the pad. Both hands were working, the right rapidly, the left slowly – while the eyes of the man connected to the hands were turned from their work and remained fastened on Dr Whitman's only a foot away. Inglis was panting now, his face was contorted in anguish, he gasped loudly and almost rhythmically. But the end was at hand. When the right hand reached the bottom of the paper Inglis wrenched out a groan, threw both pencils at the wall, pushed away from the table and backed to the door of the bedroom. He stopped there, trembling, an indescribable expression on his face.

'I'm split!' he cried.

Dr Whitman snatched up the papers and looked at them. Over his shoulder I looked too.

The words written by the right hand were indicipherable. What was on the other paper caused my hair to rise. It was a drawing, or ideograph, or group of marks like those on the paper I had found in the hand of the dead Robert! Dr Whitman took from his pocket Robert's paper and compared the two. Yes, they were very much alike. Both looked something like a drawing of chromosomes in a cell. It was meaningless.

Inglis watched from the doorway with haunted eyes.

Dr Whitman stepped across the room to a small wall mirror and held the page written by the right hand so that its edge lay along the surface. I saw at once this was mirror writing. Words appeared, run together, still almost illegible; but gradually we were able to understand most of it. Inglis approached us to look upon the unconscious use of his hand, but the parapsychologist ordered him away.

These were the written words. Where something could not be deciphered I placed a question mark.

brown eyes in great distress (?) shameful in the (?) (cumulative?) effects of nosiness noisiness nosiness god save the mark the animals the poor things as if to be different is to be inferior I tell you it police is coming with another camera (?)

When I had read the last words I at once ran back through the apartment to the hall door. Willie wasn't there. He wasn't outside, either, and my car was gone. I returned with the news to the living room.

'The photographer is gone, and so is my car!' I told Dr Whitman. 'He may very well be going to get another camera.'

'And here's this word "police",' the psychologist added thoughtfully. 'Well, it's of no importance,' he concluded.

He studied the phrases, taking his time, now and then making a little nervous click with his tongue. Then he re-examined the left hand's paper, again comparing it with the paper I had found in the lifeless hand of Robert. John Inglis said:

'That's the paper my brother held in his hand when he came to me.'

He was pointing to it. He had not yet been permitted to see it. He asked, 'Are they alike?'

'Yes,' answered Dr Whitman. 'What's written on them?' he asked. He watched Inglis keenly.

'I don't know,' came the hesitant answer.

'Your reactions?'

'I don't know . . . It's confused. It's emotion. It's distressing.' After a moment he added, 'It's very important.'

We all looked at each other, baffled. We sat down as we were before. As for myself, I needed to sit down. The constant tension was exhausting me.

Dr Whitman studied the page of writing and prepared to proceed.

'I want your associations with these phrases, John,' he said. 'I'll read them one by one. All right, *"brown eyes in great distress,"* ' he read.

'I think of the little girl,' Inglis replied. 'She has brown eyes, but I associate nothing about her with distress.'

Dr Whitman turned this over in his mind, then went on:

' *"shameful in the"* '

'Nothing special.'

' *"cumulative"* (I think that's what it is); *"cumulative effects of nosiness noisiness nosiness."* '

'Nothing special. Of course I detest noise, and, as you know, I've had to endure a good deal of nosiness.'

'You know how these things are, John,' the doctor interjected. 'If we can find one significant thing in this small sample, just one; we'll be extremely lucky . . . *"god save the mark."* '

'Nothing. That's an old-time exclamation, I believe. I'm sure I myself have never used it. I've never even thought it, that I can remember.'

' *"the animals."* '

'That upsets me,' Inglis said. 'It's all emotion. It's a kind of anxiety.'

I could tell that from his face, without hearing his words. Dr Whitman went on:

' *"the poor things."* '

'Nothing much. Doesn't sound as if I could have written that. I don't talk or think that way.'

' *"as if to be different is to be inferior."* '

'Yes!' the sensitive exclaimed.

Dr Whitman leaned forward eagerly.

'What is there about that?' he asked.

Inglis seemed to feel the words. 'I don't know,' he said. 'I can't describe it. The words disturb me very much. It is not exactly unpleasant.'

'How would you explain your writing these words?'

'I – I – I was about to say they seem appropriate, but I don't want to say that exactly . . . As a concept, that has been in my mind ever since I can remember. It seems to tie in with my behaviour toward the cockroaches. Who is this "superior" man, that he should feel justified in taking the life of anything! Even the life of a cockroach! If to be an animal is to be inferior, than to be a man is to be superior; but this also works in reverse. If to be small and brown and have six legs and lurk in cracks is to be superior; then man is inferior to the cockroach. Is man really superior to the cockroach? That depends on the "if", and the "if" depends on whether it's the man or the cockroach who sets the standard. There are no "ifs" in natural laws.'

We turned this over in our minds; then, since Inglis volunteered nothing more, Dr Whitman continued. He said, 'I'll read all the rest in one piece, for it seems to have one group of thoughts except for an interruption. ' *"I tell you it police is coming back with another camera."* '

'Obviously that is simple clairvoyance or telepathy, if it's true,' Inglis said promptly. 'Mr Warren took away the photographer's camera and now he is coming back with another. It may or may not be so. And he could be bringing the police. He's very angry, and he thinks I'm crazy.'

I thought I detected in Dr Whitman a feeling of disappointment. He sat in thought a moment, then suddenly handed Inglis the two papers with similar marks – the one made by his brother and the one made by his own left hand.

Inglis reacted strongly. A surge passed through his body; he held his breath, then released it and breathed more rapidly. His eyes made quick wide movements, and his lips parted.

'This is the key!' he exclaimed.

'What are your associations?'

'I can't tell you! It's obscure, though very strong. All mixed up. It's all emotion . . .'

He stopped and seemed to be listening. The psychologist asked:

'Look at the marks. If you had to describe them to someone, how would you do it?'

'I'd say they look like drawings of chromosomes in cells. Fat, curly worms. Each a little different. Two sets, the left and right halves of each set symmetrically disposed.'

'What are your associations with the word "chromosome".?'

'Life. Persistence. Heredity. Mystery.'

'Your feelings?'

'Mild. Pleasant.'

'Are they feelings of appropriateness?'

'No.'

'Look at the marks again. Both you and Robert made those sets of "fat, curly worms" as you describe them. Do you have any feelings that your drawing them was what you call "appropriate"?'

'Yes!' Inglis pushed violently to his feet. 'Please don't do this to me!' he cried. 'You keep torturing me! You split me!'

Gently, Dr Whitman coaxed him back to his chair.

'Let's sum up,' he said. 'We know some important things. We know the message: it is the one written and underscored by the cockroaches. "Do not kill us." Your reaction to the words "animal" and "creature" was symptomatic – especially the word "creature". The word "cockroach", however much you have been concerned with cockroaches lately, does not affect you at all. You were powerfully affected by the words "as if to be different is to be inferior". You even gave us a little lecture. And now these two drawings, or whatever they are – no reaction to the word or concept "chromosome", but a marked reaction to the drawings of the fat, curly worms themselves, and a strong feeling that they are significant. There can be no doubt: The key lies in the nexus: drawings – animals – creatures – inferiority.'

He thought a moment. 'Have you ever seen an animal, or creature, that looks like the drawings?'

'No!' Inglis shouted.

'Why do you say "No" with so much emotion?'

'Because I feel it! – and you know that very well! You mustn't do this to me, Dr Whitman! I tell you, you split me!'

Dr Whitman sighed and sank back in his chair.

'Are you stuck?' Inglis asked.

'Yes,' was the admission. 'For the time . . . Well, there's only one thing to do. You've suffered far too much, John. You've got to sleep. I am going to take you home with me and give you an injection. Tomorrow, or the next day, when you're refreshed, we'll tackle this again.'

The afflicted man shook his head.

'I've told you,' he said; 'I've told you again and again; I feel it is appropriate that I die. That too is symptomatic.'

'But symptomatic perhaps only of exhaustion.'

Inglis regarded his old master firmly.

'I allowed Mr Warren to fetch you chiefly for one reason. That was the thought that it was only reasonable to afford you a chance to remove the feeling of "appropriateness" I have toward my death – if you could. I expected you to fail. You have failed. But since you came my feeling of necessity has been confirmed. I know now – I *know* – that shortly I will be sitting dead in this chair. I have seen myself so. I feel that it will be so. I feel that it is appropriate that it be so. Furthermore, I feel that there is a limitation of time. You cannot counter these intuitions, Dr Whitman. You cannot controvert my powers. I am being controlled, and you cannot controvert the controls.'

'You think that at the moment of death there may be a clear revelation?'

'I will not put into words what I think.'

'Isn't that being superstitious?'

'I don't know,' he said, at bay.

'It is important to you personally that you destroy yourself?'

'I don't know. It might be important for others.'

'Of course it *might*. And you would be dead.'

'I feel it appropriate.'

'Don't speak that word to me! I'm sure it is a trap!'

'Everything could be a trap.'

The parapsychologist shook his head with compassion.

'You are exhausted, John. You should see your eyes! Can you think I trust your feelings?'

'My powers this last week have been tremendous.'

Dr Whitman rose. 'Inglis,' he said determinedly, 'you are coming with me.'

'I am not,' said the other.

The doctor turned to me.

'Will you help me?'

I said, 'Do you think it likely that the two of us could handle him? Even if we could, would it do any good? A man really bent on suicide can't be prevented.'

This balked him. Once more he turned to Inglis and besought him with utmost earnestness to come and be given the means to sleep. Gently but inexorably Inglis shook his head.

The psychologist studied the sensitive for a moment. 'Sit down, John,' he begged. Slowly the afflicted man complied. Dr Whitman turned something over in his mind for a moment, then he began talking to him, quietly, soothingly.

'You are tired, John; you are very tired. I know. A week and no sleep? You show it. Have you seen your eyes? Have you ever seen such bloodshot eyes before? Well, I'm going to make one more attempt to help you. I think I can help you to loose some of your tension. I know I can. It should not be difficult; you are so tired. You may not realize it, but you are extremely sleepy. If you should want to close your eyes for a moment, go right ahead. I see it would not be hard for you to fall asleep.'

'I *am* so tired,' murmured Inglis. 'To sleep – just think! – to sleep then wake up with all my troubles gone!'

I saw the psychologist with opened mouth seeking a chance to interrupt, but Inglis ignored this and continued himself to speak. 'I should think you must be tired too, my old friend.' The doctor raised an arm, but Inglis would not let him break in. 'You *should* be tired,' he went on, never pausing. 'You're not as young as you were. You've experienced great excitements here. Let us all try and relax for a little. While we do, I'll tell you something. I assure you you'll be interested. But sit quietly; you too, Mr Warren. I never could talk to people who sit tense – especially those who are itching to interrupt. We've all been terribly overstrained, haven't we? Do you know the technique of relaxing? There *is* a technique; not many people know it. The routine is simple. I am going to tell you.'

His voice had picked up; his manner was actually compelling. I think I was surprised. I watched him with much interest; he was charming; he was actually magnetic. I'd never dreamed he could be so magnetic. He went on:

'First you relax the muscles of your right hand. Like this. Do it with me. So. Limp, utterly limp. So you can't feel anything. Not a thing. Let your thumb fall outward if it wants to. That's it. Now the left hand. Relax it. Do it, Dr Whitman. More. More. No feeling. There is no feeling at all. Now your arms. Both arms. Attend first to the right, then to the left. Alternate. Relax. Droop. Right, left, right, left. Do it, Dr Whitman. That's it. Now the same with your legs. Start at the toes. No tension. Relax. Let them sleep. Now your calves. One, then the other. Let them feel heavy. They do feel heavy, don't they?'

More and more command was coming into his voice. He never ceased speaking, and kept looking straight into his old master's eyes, with side glances into mine. I couldn't keep my eyes from his eyes. He kept using his hands, pointing with them, relaxing them, drooping them, demonstrating; I saw every motion they made – but my focus was on his compelling eyes. I *did* feel relaxed . . . more and more relaxed.

'Heavy legs,' he was saying. 'Heavy arms. Heavy eyelids, too. If you want to close your eyelids, just do so. Close them . . . soothingly . . . close them.' I closed my eyes. I couldn't keep them open. 'Soothingly close your eyes. That's right. Pretend I am your father. Yes, I am your father. You must obey your father. You are so sleepy. Sleep. Sleep. You are both so sleepy. Your father tells you to sleep. Sleep. Sleep more deeply. So.'

A new sharp tone came to his voice. 'You *are* asleep! You are sound asleep! You obey your father. You love your father and want to please him. If I should ask you to lift your left arm and your left leg you would do it, wouldn't you? Of course you would. I am going to ask you.' Sharply he commanded, 'Both of you. Lift your left arm and your left leg!' I obeyed. 'Good. Open your eyes.' I opened my eyes. I saw that Dr Whitman like me had raised his left arm and left leg. 'Lower your arms and legs.' We lowered them. 'You are both sound asleep,' he went on, 'even though your eyes are open. You will remain sound asleep. I am going to perform an experiment, a simple readjustment of space-time and matter. I too am going to sleep. I shall sleep very deeply. When you see me sound asleep you will wake up. *You* will stay asleep until you see *me* sound asleep, then you will wake up. And then you will remember everything that happened while you were asleep. You will do this, won't you? Answer me!'

'Yes,' we said.

He got to his feet, went and picked up the basin and placed it on the coffee table, then placed the table along the left arm of his chair. From his pocket he took a length of cord and a penknife, he opened a blade of his knife and set it on his knees. He bound his left forearm to the arm of the chair so that his wrist hung out over the edge. He bent back his hand. He placed the point of the knife blade near the turn of the wrist. He hesitated.

I saw his body firm. He jabbed.

The blood arced out in a solid stream. After a few seconds, the flow lessened and became a steady thick red cord. He watched it for a moment, then turned his head to the right and looked at us with an expression I cannot describe but will never forget.

'This is such a poor way to take leave of you!' he cried; 'but I had no choice! You were trying to hypnotize me, Dr Whitman! I had to beat you to it!'

His eyes turned back to the steady red cord, then returned to us.

'When I am sound asleep and quite motionless you will wake up,' he said firmly. 'Both of you will wake up. You will remember every word I speak. Later you will describe every little thing that I say and do. Do you understand? Answer.'

'Yes,' we said.

A faint smile came to his face.

'I really have something interesting to tell you. It's a confession, Dr Whitman. There was a period when you used to hypnotize me. Do you remember?'

'Yes,' was the answer.

'You were testing my powers under hypnosis, for one thing. Well, I played a trick on you one time. I hypnotized you! You had started to hypnotize me, but *I* hypnotized you. It was a prank and I shouldn't have done it, and I was fearful afterward lest you knew I did it; or found out that I did it; but you never did. I hypnotized you, and you never knew it! Of course I gave you the appropriate post-hypnotic suggestion . . . How unthinkably intermixed are the threads of our fates! Because once, long ago, I pulled a prank, I remembered it in my extremity and was confident I could do it again. Toward you, Mr Warren, I felt the same confidence for another reason. You are clean, and I've liked you. I've seen you sensitive and sympathetic. I knew you would respond to me.'

He turned his head and watched for a moment the cord of blood arcing slightly from his wrist. It was thinner now. He smiled, ever so faintly. 'I think I feel a little weak,' he said.

Time passed. He brooded. Suddenly he cried, 'Oh, how I wish I could talk normally with you! I know it could be done, but I don't dare try, I have been lucky enough . . . Answer me, Dr Whitman. Search your mind and answer truly. Did you ever suspect that I hypnotized you?'

'No,' was the reply; 'but there was one session at which I couldn't account for my time.'

The man who was dying smiled a little. After a moment he turned to me.

'Did you find my brother like – this?' he asked.

'Yes,' I said.

'Which arm did he use?'

'The other one. The right.'

'We were mirror-image twins,' Inglis said. 'We are,' he corrected. For a moment he was silent; then he announced quietly, 'Now I am really weaker . . . Well, I shall soon be with him, wherever or whoever or whatever he now is . . . I have had a tremendous piece of luck in my life; I was one of identical twins. You who are of single birth are half missing.

For the identical other is not a separate person; he is the other half of yourself. Day by day and side by side you grow, living extrapolations of all the million matrices of that first single potent pregnant cell; but your sum is always one. Everything the other does, you do; every experience you have, he shares. He is always there to play with, to associate with; what he thinks, you think, and what you feel he responds to in phase. Your pleasures, problems, friends, worlds, are alike. And to one person, at least, you are always important. You live together *en rapport*.

'But how much extra so was this with Robert and me, with our paranormal powers! Even when apart, consonance was continuous!

'We continued to deviate from the normal throughout life. By the nature of angles, as children we were not deviated far; but as we grew older our psychic peculiarity made us increasingly two freaks and misfits; but ours was the same deviation; we were alike; John plus Robert equalled one. That fine thing we had.

'Our paranormal powers were a tremendous burden. We were sensitive, but much too sensitive. The normal person lives within a shell which gives a measure of protection from the disharmonic waves of the psychic Mother Ocean; we seemed to lack that shell. We could be bruised by a look, wounded by a thought; we could be lifted and tossed and battered and half-drowned in the great swells and riptides of animal emotion from the great submerged herd. With increasing divergence we more and more sought quiet and seclusion. For years it was gladly we lived; but now, I assure you, I am not sorry to die ... When I say "I", I mean "We".'

Inglis brooded. Now his hand hung limp, and the inexorable red cord depended from the lithe fingers. He watched it. From time to time it broke, to instantly re-form with a little sound – *pip*. He said:

'Wonderfully, the body is mobilizing to defend its integrity. It will fail. Two quarts of my life are gone ... I am much weaker ... I feel at peace now, my dear old master. Can't you be glad for me? Peace for the first time – the first time in such a long time. Is peace an effect of weakness? Oh, definitions! I'm sure that half the troubles of the race of man are semantic ones!

'I wish we could really talk ...

'It is so peaceful and lovely. Just think, there are people who can feel this way once a week. For a week I was in torture, and now, with the letting of a little blood, I am at peace. What was my torture of the past week? I almost forget. There was a message. I thought I was intercepting, or being sent, a message. Confident, I brought you here, to witness the great Change. But I sink slowly into peace, while you remain behind in a new distress. Forgive me! I had thought there might be a message; it seemed so important; but I only subside ...

'I shall be with Robert soon. Wherever and whoever and whatever he now is. The Change is coming, and I shall know . . . The great Change . . . I have killed many insects; I have seen a hundred cockroaches die; they came to know, and soon I shall know. Life: they had it; I still for a moment have it. What is the difference between a cockroach and a man? I know there is one or so, but I can no longer see such little things. We both live, and then we die. Are there separate hereafters for cockroach and man? How can it be thought so? Where in the series does a man start being something special, to rate a special hereafter? Has the cockroach a soul? No. An ape? No. A man-ape? No. An ape-man? Maybe. But a man, yes! Oh, human vanity, what a quibbling! Experts in the unknowable are agreed that at some arcanic point between cockroach and man there appeared a new, tremendously valuable ticket – something entitling the accredited bearer to a reserved seat in human heaven; apes and cockroaches not admitted. I don't want to go to such a place . . .'

Inglis's head had for some time been lowering. Now it was low indeed; but from his words he did not appear to be aware how weak he had become. He was pausing not only between sentences, now, but sometimes between phrases. More often the red cord was breaking and re-forming with the little *pip*. I could not see how much of Inglis's life was in the basin, but he seemed far from unconsciousness. His head was lowered, but his eyes were open and still held forward.

'I am faint,' he said suddenly. '. . . There was to have been a message. I did think so . . . Or was it only a hope?'

There was a silence. He seem to rouse a little. His voice was now quite low, and the pauses longer.

'It is inconceivable. A man dies unexpectedly in London, and at the moment of his death he appears to his wife in New York. *Rapport* in life, communication in death . . . My brother, only a few blocks away . . . What force is this? How could I state where those artifacts were, buried twelve thousand years, entombed in a wilderness under twenty feet of earth? But they dug, and they found them, and they were as I had said. I did not vision them, I did not feel anything about them, I just said it; it seemed appropriate . . . that man in Melbourne, amnesia . . . a fugue . . . he didn't know himself who he was, but I spoke his name and around the world they found him. How is this? . . . have lived in an ocean of consciousness. Or is it an ocean of awareness? No more definitions. It is an ocean of awareness – shimmering, pulsing with intelligence, ineluctably interwoven, eons thick. Look upon the unthinkable distances between the universes. What lies beyond? The astronomers say there are a billion Earths, each teeming with its various life. Here we have cockroaches and human beings and apes and bacteria; but what are the creatures of the other Earths? They live. Our experts seem unaware of this and haven't got around to denying them a hereafter; but they are there – different, bizarre, alive. So very very many of them will be life forms superior to ours . . .

'Life forms – what does that mean? Life . . . It may be that living creatures never will know what life is; but motion is part of it. Is the virus alive. Will it go to virus heaven when it is no longer a whole? There are not so very many atoms in a virus molecule. They are the same atoms that cooperate to erect an elephant. Their electrons whirl, and all thy piety and all thy wit will not avail to stop them half a second. Eternally the electrons go about their atomic business; I am sure they are alive, momentously alive, until they meet their opposite charge and themselves experience the great Change. I am not thinking absurdly, my dear friends; it's just that I have nothing to speak with but words. Words. We are all choked with words . . .

'But I can come close to the truth. There is an infinite and everlasting ocean of Something. In one manifestation matter appears, and universes rush away. So radiantly! Out of the radiant energy more matter appears and takes its place, and the ultimate universes themselves dissolve back into energy, or are remanifested as energy, while the cosmic ocean heaves and shimmers. Yesterday and tomorrow, today and the light fading from my eyes and the blood out of my veins are one, variously manifesting, clotting and unclotting, seeming to speed and seeming to stand still. It is a One with aspects that our eyes see as changes; differences and changes; and somewhere in it, the ultimate miracle, there lies the possibility of love and kindness. Yes, the atom contains the capacity to be kind. Better, the atom in one aspect is kind . . .'

He stopped speaking, but his voice, edged with hoarseness from his speaking, still seemed to echo through the room. Now only drops were falling. Only their *pip* could be heard.

For a long time the silence held, but Inglis was still alive. His eyes remained open except for brief intervals, and his head kept lowering, and he kept bringing it back a little. I felt that he had spoken his last words.

But suddenly he spoke again. Head down, eyes closed, he said:

'Forgive me.'

The silence returned, and went on. Occasionally, very infrequently now, there was the *pip* of a falling drop. Ever so faintly I heard the noises of the great city around us: an attenuated clatter, the vibration from a passing truck, the faint whine of a jet plane far in the sky. We sat unmoving; sat, I think, unable to move. And the time passed. And the dripping ceased.

At some point I noticed that Inglis had raised his head. Just the least bit. And his eyes were open. Slowly his head continued to rise a little more, and as it did his eyes fixed on a point low on the opposite wall. As his head raised the eye focus shortened, until he seemed to be looking at something at a place in the air only a few feet in front of him, a little off the floor. My flesh creeped.

Inglis's bloodshot eyes watched that place as if it were the only thing in the universe. Back and forth between his eyes and that vacant place my own eyes travelled, while unknown forces crackled and prickled through my every cell. Inglis roused greatly. He turned to us and cried in triumph, 'You see?'

I saw nothing.

Again his eyes were back on that vacant place. Again he turned to us and cried, 'Do you hear?'

But I heard nothing.

'It's the message! – clear at last!' he cried. 'They've come! They're in the streets! They're not unfriendly! They're different, but not inferior! Be kind! do not kill them! Do not kill them!'

These were his last words. He panted; for a moment his eyes held on the vacant place near the floor; then slowly his head dropped to his breast, lower and lower, while his eyes moved upward, still holding on that vacant place, and holding there until the end.

His eyes did not close. He sat there, chin on his chest. For a long time I watched him and then I got to my feet and bent low over him, close, so close to that wonderful tortured head. Dr Whitman was there by my side.

I closed his eyes.

Dr Whitman said, 'With blood I could pull him back. Given five minutes I could still save his body, but his mind would be gone . . .'

I stood there resonating on a higher plane of awareness. And then I heard a click behind me. I turned. Willie was there. He was holding a camera. He had entered and taken a picture.

I hit him. I hit him hard. I took the camera and smashed it against the wall. I ran out to the street. My car was there, and near it a police car, but both were enclosed in an excited shoving crowd of truckmen. I jumped into my car, started the engine and inched forward. Reluctantly the excited men made way. I streaked through the dust for the office.

The Creatures had come! I'd seen one! It had fat, curly barbels! I saw it through the legs of the men! The men were poking the Creature with sticks!

I poured my story into the city editor's ears. He sat in the midst of chaos. He could hardly have understood my words, but he understood my emotion and waved me to my desk.

Now I have written it. *Here is the message! Hear it, everybody – hear it! The*

Creatures have come! They're not unfriendly! They are different, but not inferior! Restrain yourselves! Be kind! Do not kill them! Do not kill them! Do not kill them!

File classification: Extra-Sensory Perception (ESP)
Location: Sudbury, USA

Title: Cassandra
Writer: *C. J. Cherryh*

Briefing: *Extra-Sensory Perception – psychic talent outside the ordinary senses; generally accepted to include precognition and empathy.* Everyone knows Crazy Alis in the little town of Sudbury. She has spent a lifetime in and out of hospital, being treated with a whole range of drugs to try to cure the visions that haunt her troubled mind. But no matter *what* she sees lying in wait for the other townsfolk, is there any way she can avert disaster?

Author: American novelist Carolyn Janice Cherryh began writing when she was just ten years old, but it was not until she had become a teacher of Latin and Ancient History that she started submitting work for publication. Her short story debut was the remarkable tale of psychic phenomena, 'The Mind Reader', which appeared in *Astounding Science Fiction* in 1968. In 1976, after the publication of her heroic fantasy novel, *Gate of Ivrel*, Cherryh won the John W. Campbell Award for most promising new writer. Since then she has become an increasingly significant figure in sf, especially with her ongoing Future History novels known as the 'Union-Alliance' series that includes *Hestia* (1979), *Port Eternity* (1982) and *Voyager in the Night* (1984). Cherryh has also amassed many admirers for her 'Merovingen Nights' series and the 'Heroes in Hell' Shared-World novels co-created with Janet E. Morris. 'Cassandra', her aptly titled story of ESP, first appeared in the *Magazine of Fantasy and Science Fiction* in October 1978, and won that year's Hugo award for best short story.

Fires.

They grew unbearable here.

Alis felt for the door of the flat and knew that it would be solid. She could feel the cool metal of the knob amid the flames . . . saw the shadow-stairs through the roiling smoke outside, clearly enough to feel her way down them, convincing her senses that they would bear her weight.

Crazy Alis. She made no haste. The fires burned steadily. She passed through them, descended the insubstantial steps to the solid ground – she could not abide the elevator, that closed space with the shadow-floor, that plummeted down and down; she made the ground floor, averted her eyes from the red, heatless flames.

A ghost said good morning to her . . . old man Willis, thin and transparent against the leaping flames. She blinked, bade it good morning in return – did not miss old Willis's shake of the head as she opened the door and left. Noon traffic passed, heedless of the flames, the hulks that blazed in the street, the tumbling brick.

The apartment caved in – black bricks falling into the inferno, Hell amid the green, ghostly trees. Old Willis fled, burning, fell – turned to jerking, blackened flesh – died, daily. Alis no longer cried, hardly flinched. She ignored the horror spilling about her, forced her way through crumbling brick that held no substance, past busy ghosts that could not be troubled in their haste.

Kingsley's Cafe stood, whole, more so than the rest. It was refuge for the afternoon, a feeling of safety. She pushed open the door, heard the tinkle of a lost bell. Shadowy patrons looked, whispered.

Crazy Alis.

The whispers troubled her. She avoided their eyes and their presence, settled in a booth in the corner that bore only traces of the fire.

WAR, the headline in the vender said in heavy type. She shivered, looked up into Sam Kingsley's wraithlike face.

'Coffee,' she said. 'Ham sandwich.' It was constantly the same. She varied not even the order. Mad Alis. Her affliction supported her. A cheque came each month, since the hospital had turned her out. Weekly she returned to the clinic, to doctors who now faded like the others. The building burned about them. Smoke rolled down the blue, antiseptic halls. Last week a patient ran – burning –

A rattle of china. Sam set the coffee on the table, came back shortly and brought the sandwich. She bent her head and ate, transparent food on half-broken china, a cracked, fire-smudged cup with a transparent handle. She ate, hungry enough to overcome the horror that had become ordinary. A hundred times seen, the most terrible sights lost their power over her: she no longer cried at shadows. She talked to ghosts and touched them, ate the food that somehow stilled the ache in her belly, wore the same too-large black sweater and worn blue shirt and grey slacks because they were all she had that seemed solid. Nightly she washed them and dried them and put them on the next day, letting others hang in the closet. They were the only solid ones.

She did not tell the doctors these things. A lifetime in and out of hospitals had made her wary of confidences. She knew what to say. Her half-vision let her smile at ghost-faces, cannily manipulate their charts and cards, sitting in the ruins that had begun to smoulder by late afternoon. A blackened corpse lay in the hall. She did not flinch when she smiled good-naturedly at the doctor.

They gave her medicines. The medicines stopped the dreams, the siren screams, the running steps in the night past her apartment. They let her sleep in the ghostly bed, high above ruin, with the flames crackling and the voices screaming. She did not speak of these things. Years in hospitals had taught her. She complained only of nightmares, and restlessness, and they let her have more of the red pills.

WAR, the headline blazoned.

The cup rattled and trembled against the saucer as she picked it up. She swallowed the last bit of bread and washed it down with coffee, tried not to look beyond the broken front window, where twisted metal hulks smoked on the street. She stayed, as she did each day, and Sam grudgingly refilled her cup, that she would nurse as far as she could and then order another one. She lifted it, savouring the feel of it, stopping the trembling of her hands.

The bell jingled faintly. A man closed the door, settled at the counter.

Whole, clear in her eyes. She stared at him, startled, heart pounding. He ordered coffee, moved to buy a paper from the vender, settled again and let the coffee grow cold while he read the news. She had view only of his back while he read, scuffed brown leather coat, brown hair a little over his collar. At last he drank the cooled coffee all at one draught, shoved money onto the counter and left the paper lying, headlines turned face down.

A young face, flesh and bone among the ghosts. He ignored them all and went for the door.

Alis thrust herself from her booth.

'Hey!' Sam called at her.

She rummaged in her purse as the bell jingled, flung a bill onto the counter, heedless that it was a five. Fear was coppery in her mouth; he was gone. She fled the café, edged round debris without thinking of it, saw his back disappearing among the ghosts.

She ran, shouldering them, braving the flames – cried out as debris showered painlessly on her, and kept running.

Ghosts turned and stared, shocked – *he* did likewise, and she ran to him, stunned to see the same shock on his face, regarding her.

'What is it?' he asked.

She blinked, dazed to realize he saw her no differently than the others. She could not answer. In irritation he started walking again, and she followed. Tears slid down her face, her breath hard in her throat. People stared. He noticed her presence and walked the faster, through debris, through fires. A wall began to fall and she cried out despite herself.

He jerked about. The dust and the soot rose up as a cloud behind him. His face was distraught and angry. He stared at her as the others did. Mothers drew children away from the scene. A band of youths stared, cold-eyed and laughing.

'Wait,' she said. He opened his mouth as if he would curse her; she flinched, and the tears were cold in the heatless wind of the fires. His face twisted in an embarrassed pity. He thrust a hand into his pocket and began to pull out money, hastily, tried to give it to her. She shook her head furiously, trying to stop the tears – stared upward, flinching, as another building fell into flames.

'What's wrong?' he asked her. 'What's wrong with you?'

'Please,' she said. He looked about at the staring ghosts, then began to walk slowly. She walked with him, nerving herself not to cry out at the ruin, the pale moving figures that wandered through burned shells of buildings, the twisted corpses in the street, where traffic moved.

'What's your name?' he asked. She told him. He gazed at her from time to time as they walked; a frown creasing his brow. He had a face well-worn for youth, a tiny scar beside the mouth. He looked older than she. She felt uncomfortable in the way his eyes travelled over her: she decided to accept it – to bear with anything that gave her this one solid presence. Against every inclination she reached her hand into the bend of his arm, tightened her fingers on the worn leather. He accepted it.

And after a time he slid his arm behind her and about her waist, and they walked like lovers.

WAR, the headline at the newsstand cried.

He started to turn into a street by Tenn's Hardware. She balked at what she saw there. He paused when he felt it, faced her with his back to the fires of that burning.

'Don't go,' she said.

'Where do you want to go?'

She shrugged helplessly, indicated the main street, the other direction.

He talked to her then, as he might talk to a child, humouring her fear. It was pity. Some treated her that way. She recognized it, and took even that.

His name was Jim. He had come into the city yesterday, hitched rides. He was looking for work. He knew no one in the city. She listened to his rambling awkwardness, reading through it. When he was done, she stared at him still, and saw his face contract in dismay at her.

'I'm not crazy,' she told him, which was a lie, that everyone in Sudbury would have known, only *he* would not, knowing no one. His face was true and solid, and the tiny scar by the mouth made it hard when he was thinking; at another time she would have been terrified of him. Now she was terrified of losing him amid the ghosts.

'It's the war,' he said.

She nodded, trying to look at him and not at the fires. His fingers touched her arm, gently. 'It's the war,' he said again. 'It's all crazy. Everyone's crazy.'

And then he put his hand on her shoulder and turned her back the other way, toward the park where green leaves waved over black, skeletal limbs. They walked along the lake, and for the first time in a long time she drew breath and felt a whole, sane presence beside her.

They bought corn, and sat on the grass by the lake, and flung it to the spectral swans. Wraiths of passersby were few, only enough to keep a feeling of occupancy about the place – old people, mostly, tottering about the deliberate tranquillity of their routine despite the headlines.

'Do you see them,' she ventured to ask him finally, 'all thin and grey?'

He did not understand, did not take her literally, only shrugged. Warily, she abandoned that questioning at once. She rose to her feet and stared at the horizon, where the smoke bannered on the wind.

'Buy you supper?' he asked.

She turned, prepared for this, and managed a shy, desperate smile. 'Yes,' she said, knowing what else he reckoned to buy with that – willing, and hating herself, and desperately afraid that he would walk away, tonight, tomorrow. She did not know men. She had no idea what she could say or do to prevent his leaving, only that he would when some day he realized her madness.

Even her parents had not been able to bear with that – visited her only at first in the hospitals, and then only on holidays, and then not at all. She did not know where they were.

There was a neighbour boy who drowned. She had said he would. She had cried for it. All the town said it was she who pushed him.

Crazy Alis.

Fantasizes, the doctors said. Not dangerous.

They let her out. There were special schools, state schools.

And from time to time – hospitals.

Tranquillizers.

She had left the red pills at home. The realization brought sweat to her palms. They gave sleep. They stopped the dreams. She clamped her lips against the panic and made up her mind that she would not need them – not while she was not alone. She slipped her hand into his arm and walked with him, secure and strange, up the steps from the park to the streets.

And stopped.

The fires were out.

Ghost-buildings rose above their jagged and windowless shells. Wraiths moved through masses of debris, almost obscured at times. He tugged her on, but her step faltered, made him look at her strangely and put his arm about her.

'You're shivering,' he said. 'Cold?'

She shook her head, tried to smile. The fires were out. She tried to take it for a good omen. The nightmare was over. She looked up into his solid, concerned face, and her smile almost became a wild laugh.

'I'm hungry,' she said.

They lingered long over a dinner in Graben's – he in his battered jacket, she in her sweater that hung at the tails and elbows: the spectral patrons were in far better clothes, and stared at them, and they were set in a corner nearest the door, where they would be less visible. There was cracked crystal and broken china on insubstantial tables, and the stars winked coldly in gaping ruin above the wan glittering of the broken chandeliers.

Ruins, cold, peaceful ruin.

Alis looked about her calmly. One could live in ruins, only so the fires were gone.

And there was Jim, who smiled at her without any touch of pity, only a wild, fey desperation that she understood – who spent more than he could afford in Graben's, the inside of which she had never hoped to see – and told her – predictably – that she was beautiful. Others had said it. Vaguely she resented such triteness from him, from him whom she had decided to trust. She smiled sadly, when he said it, and gave it up for a frown and, fearful of offending him with her melancholies, made it a smile again.

Crazy Alis. He would learn and leave tonight if she were not careful. She tried to put on gaiety, tried to laugh.

And then the music stopped in the restaurant, and the noise of the other diners went dead, and the speaker was giving an inane announcement.

Shelters . . . shelters . . . shelters.

Screams broke out. Chairs overturned.

Alis went limp in her chair, felt Jim's cold, solid hand tugging at hers, saw his frightened face mouthing her name as he took her up into his arms, pulled her with him, started running.

The cold air outside hit her, shocked her into sight of the ruins again, wraith figures pelting toward that chaos where the fires had been worst.

And she knew.

'No!' she cried, pulling at his arm. 'No!' she insisted, and bodies half-seen buffeted them in a rush to destruction. He yielded to her sudden certainty, gripped her hand and fled with her against the crowds as the sirens wailed madness through the night – fled with her as she ran her sighted way through the ruin.

And into Kingsley's, where cafe tables stood abandoned with food still on them, doors ajar, chairs overturned. Back they went into the kitchens and down and down into the cellar, the dark, the cold safety from the flames.

No others found them there. At last the earth shook, too deep for sound. The sirens ceased and did not come on again.

They lay in the dark and clutched each other and shivered, and above them for hours raged the sound of fire, smoke sometimes drifting in to sting their eyes and noses. There was the distant crash of brick, rumblings that shook the ground, that came near, but never touched their refuge.

And in the morning, with the scent of fire still in the air, they crept up into the murky daylight.

The ruins were still and hushed. The ghost-buildings were solid now, mere shells. The wraiths were gone. It was the fires themselves that were strange, some true, some not, playing above dark, cold brick, and most were fading.

Jim swore softly, over and over again, and wept.

When she looked at him she was dry-eyed, for she had done her crying already.

And she listened as he began to talk about food, about leaving the city, the two of them. 'All right,' she said.

Then clamped her lips, shut her eyes against what she saw in his face.

When she opened them it was still true, the sudden transparency, the wash of blood. She trembled, and he shook at her, his ghost-face distraught.

'What's wrong?' he asked. 'What's wrong?'

She could not tell him, would not. She remembered the boy who had drowned, remembered the other ghosts. Of a sudden she tore from his hands and ran, dodging the maze of debris that, this morning, was solid.

'Alis!' he cried and came after her.

'No!' she cried suddenly, turning, seeing the unstable wall, the cascading brick. She started back and stopped, unable to force herself. She held out her hands to warn him back, saw them solid.

The brick rumbled, fell. Dust came up, thick for a moment, obscuring everything.

She stood still, hands at her sides, then wiped her sooty face and turned and started walking, keeping to the centre of the dead streets.

Overhead, clouds gathered, heavy with rain.

She wandered at peace now, seeing the rain spot the pavement, not yet feeling it.

In time the rain did fall, and the ruins became chill and cold. She visited the dead lake and the burned trees, the ruin of Graben's, out of which she gathered a string of crystal to wear.

She smiled when, a day later, a looter drove her from her food supply. He had a wraith's look, and she laughed from a place he did not dare to climb and told him so.

And recovered her cache later when it came true, and settled among the ruined shells that held no further threat, no other nightmares, with her crystal necklace and tomorrows that were the same as today.

One could live in ruins, only so the fires were gone.

And the ghosts were all in the past, invisible.

archive 3

alien encounters

File classification: *Unidentified Flying Objects (UFOs)*
Location: Santa Vera, USA

Title: The Encounter
Writer: *J. G. Ballard*

Briefing: *Unidentified Flying Objects – sightings of unexplained phenomena in the skies, allegedly space craft; popularly referred to as 'flying saucers'.* At Mount Vernon Observatory, Charles Kandinski is notorious as the man who claims to have seen a UFO and written a book about the experience, *The Landings from Outer Space.* He is a star speaker at local women's groups and much admired by the young – but among the scientific community he is regarded as a madman. However, when newcomer Dr Andrew Ward meets Kandinski, he finds him anything but a crank: especially when the author provides him with evidence of the alien landing.

Author: The English writer J. G. Ballard is currently regarded as one of the most controversial figures in the sf genre, although his work is rarely about traditional themes: more particularly near future disasters, ruined land-scapes and the wreckage of technology. After a traumatic childhood in a Japanese POW Camp in Shanghai (which later formed the basis of his best-selling novel, *Empire of the Sun* (1984) and was filmed by Steven Spielberg), Ballard returned to England and with the short stories later collected as *The Terminal Beach* (1964) announced himself as a unique figure in contemporary fiction. Another of his novels, *Crash* (1973), about the psychological and sexual gratification to be experienced from mutila-tion and death on the roads, was also filmed in 1996 by David Cronenberg and generated such controversy in the media that for a time it seemed unlikely to be publicly screened. Another form of psychology – that of people towards the UFO experience – is what inspired Ballard to write 'The Encounter' in 1963, less than a decade after the American, George Adamski of Mount Palomar, California, published *Flying Saucers Have Landed*, and initiated a controversy that shows no sign of diminishing . . .

When Dr Andrew Ward joined the Hubble Memorial Institute at Mount Vernon Observatory he never imagined that the closest of his new acquaintances would be an amateur star-gazer and spare-time prophet called Charles Kandinski, tolerantly regarded by the Observatory professionals as a madman. In fact, had either he or Professor Cameron, the Institute's Deputy Director, known just how far he was to be prepared to carry this friendship before his two-year tour at the Institute was over, Ward would certainly have left Mount Vernon the day he arrived and would never have become involved in the bizarre and curiously ironic tragedy which was to leave an ineradicable stigma upon his career.

Professor Cameron first introduced him to Kandinski. About a week after Ward came to the Hubble he and Cameron were lunching together in the Institute cafeteria.

'We'll go down to Vernon Gardens for coffee,' Cameron said when they finished dessert. 'I want to get a shampoo for Edna's roses and then we'll sit in the sun for an hour and watch the girls go by.' They strolled out through the terrace tables towards the parking lot. A mile away, beyond the conifers thinning out on the slopes above them, the three great Vernon domes gleamed like white marble against the sky. 'Incidentally, you can meet the opposition.'

'Is there another observatory at Vernon?' Ward asked as they set off along the drive in Cameron's Buick. 'What is it – an Air Force weather station?'

'Have you ever heard of Charles Kandinski?' Cameron said. 'He wrote a book called *The Landings from Outer Space*. It was published about three years ago.'

Ward shook his head doubtfully. They slowed down past the checkpoint at the gates and Cameron waved to the guard. 'Is that the man who claims to have seen extra-terrestrial beings? Martians or—'

'Venusians. That's Kandinski. Not only seen them,' Professor Cameron added. 'He's talked to them. Charles works at a cafe in Vernon Gardens. We know him fairly well.'

'He runs the other observatory?'

'Well, an old 4-inch MacDonald Refractor mounted in a bucket of cement. You probably wouldn't think much of it, but I wish we could see with our two-fifty just a tenth of what he sees.'

Ward nodded vaguely. The two observatories at which he had worked previously, Cape Town and the Milan Astrographie, had both attracted any number of cranks and charlatans eager to reveal their own final truths about the cosmos, and the prospect of meeting Kandinski interested him only slightly. 'What is he?' he asked. 'A practical joker, or just a lunatic?'

Professor Cameron propped his glasses on to his forehead and negotiated a tight hairpin. 'Neither,' he said.

Ward smiled at Cameron, idly studying his plump cherubic face with its puckish mouth and keen eyes. He knew that Cameron enjoyed a modest reputation as a wit. 'Has he ever claimed in front of you that he's seen a . . . Venusian?'

'Often,' Professor Cameron said. 'Charles lectures two or three times a week about the landings to the women's societies around here and put himself completely at our disposal. I'm afraid we had to tell him he was a little too advanced for us. But wait until you meet him.'

Ward shrugged and looked out at the long curving peach terraces lying below them, gold and heavy in the August heat. They dropped a thousand feet and the road widened and joined the highway which ran from the Vernon Gardens across the desert to Santa Vera and the coast.

Vernon Gardens was the nearest town to the Observatory and most of it had been built within the last few years, evidently with an eye on the tourist trade. They passed a string of blue and pink-washed houses, a school constructed of glass bricks and an abstract Baptist chapel. Along the main thoroughfare the shops and stores were painted in bright jazzy colours, the vivid awnings and neon signs like street scenery in an experimental musical.

Professor Cameron turned off into a wide tree-lined square and parked by a cluster of fountains in the centre. He and Ward walked towards the cafes – Al's Fresco Diner, Ylla's, the Dome – which stretched down to the sidewalk. Around the square were a dozen gift-shops filled with cheap souvenirs: silverplate telescopes and models of the great Vernon dome masquerading as ink-stands and cigar-boxes, plus a juvenile omnium gatherum of miniature planetaria, space helmets and plastic 3-D star atlases.

The cafe to which they went was decorated in the same futuristic motifs. The chairs and tables were painted a drab aluminium grey, their limbs and panels cut in random geometric shapes. A silver rocket ship, ten feet long, its paint peeling off in rusty strips, reared up from a pedestal among the tables. Across it was painted the cafe's name.

'The Site Tycho.'

A large mobile had been planted in the ground by the sidewalk and dangled down over them, its vanes and struts flashing in the sun. Gingerly Professor Cameron pushed it away. 'I'll swear that damn thing is growing,' he confided to Ward. 'I must tell Charles to prune it.' He lowered himself into a chair by one of the open-air tables, put on a fresh pair of sunglasses and focussed them at the long brown legs of a girl sauntering past.

Left alone for the moment, Ward looked around him and picked at a cellophane transfer of a ringed planet glued to the table-top. The Site Tycho was also used as a small science fiction exchange library. A couple of metal bookstands stood outside the cafe door, where a soberly dressed middle-aged man, obviously hiding behind his upturned collar, worked his way quickly through the rows of paperbacks. At another table a young man with an intent, serious face was reading a magazine. His high cerebrotonic forehead was marked across the temple by a ridge of pink tissue, which Ward wryly decided was a lobotomy scar.

'Perhaps we ought to show our landing permits,' he said to Cameron when after three or four minutes no one had appeared to serve them. 'Or at least get our pH's checked.'

Professor Cameron grinned. 'Don't worry, no customs, no surgery.' He took his eyes off the sidewalk for a moment. 'This looks like him now.'

A tall, bearded man in a short-sleeved tartan shirt and pale green slacks came out of the cafe towards them with two cups of coffee on a tray.

'Hello, Charles,' Cameron greeted him. 'There you are. We were beginning to think we'd lost ourselves in a time-trap.'

The tall man grunted something and put the cups down. Ward guessed that he was about 55 years old. He was well over six feet tall, with a massive sunburnt head and lean but powerfully muscled arms.

'Andrew, this is Charles Kandinski.' Cameron introduced the two men. 'Andrew's come to work for me, Charles. He photographed all those Cepheids for the Milan Conference last year.'

Kandinski nodded. His eyes examined Ward critically but showed no signs of interest.

'I've been telling him all about you, Charles,' Cameron went on, 'and how we all follow your work. No further news yet, I trust?'

Kandinski's lips parted in a slight smile. He listened politely to Cameron's banter and looked out over the square, his great seamed head raised to the sky.

'Andrew's read your book, Charles,' Cameron was saying. 'Very interested. He'd like to see the originals of those photographs. Wouldn't you, Andrew?'

'Yes, I certainly would,' Ward said.

Kandinski gazed down at him again. His expression was not so much penetrating as detached and impersonal, as if he were assessing Ward with an utter lack of bias, so complete, in fact, that it left no room for even the smallest illusion. Previously Ward had only seen this expression in the eyes of the very old. 'Good,' Kandinski said. 'At present they are in a safe deposit box at my bank, but if you are serious I will get them out.'

Just then two young women wearing wide-brimmed Rapallo hats made their way through the tables. They sat down and smiled at Kandinski. He nodded to Ward and Cameron and went over to the young women, who began to chatter to him animatedly.

'Well, he seems popular with them,' Ward commented. 'He's certainly not what I anticipated. I hope I didn't offend him over the plates. He was taking you seriously.'

'He's a little sensitive about them,' Cameron explained. 'The famous dustbin-lid flying saucers. You mustn't think I bait him, though. To tell the truth I hold Charles in great respect. When all's said and done, we're in the same racket.'

'Are we?' Ward said doubtfully. 'I haven't read his book. Does he say in so many words that he saw and spoke to a visitor from Venus?'

'Precisely. Don't you believe him?'

Ward laughed and looked through the coins in his pocket, leaving one on the table. 'I haven't tried to yet. You say the whole thing isn't a hoax?'

'Of course not.'

'How do you explain it then? Compensation-fantasy or—'

Professor Cameron smiled. 'Wait until you know Charles a little better.'

'I already know the man's messianic,' Ward said dryly. 'Let me guess the rest. He lives on yoghurt, weaves his own clothes, and stands on his head all night, reciting the Bhagavadgita backwards.'

'He doesn't,' Cameron said, still smiling at Ward. 'He happens to be a big man who suffers from barber's rash. I thought he'd have you puzzled.'

Ward pulled the transfer off the table. Some science fantast had skilfully pencilled in an imaginary topography on the planet's surface. There were canals, craters and lake systems named Verne, Wells and Bradbury. 'Where did he see this Venusian?' Ward asked, trying to keep the curiosity out of his voice.

'About twenty miles from here, out in the desert off the Santa Vera highway. He was picnicking with some friends, went off for a stroll in the sandhills and ran straight into the space-ship. His friends swear he was perfectly normal both immediately before and after the landing, and all of them saw the inscribed metallic tablet which the Venusian pilot left behind. Some sort of ultimatum, if I remember, warning mankind to abandon all its space programmes. Apparently someone up there does not like us.'

'Has he still got the tablet?' Ward asked.

'No. Unluckily it combusted spontaneously in the heat. But Charles managed to take a photograph of it.'

Ward laughed. 'I bet he did. It sounds like a beautifully organized hoax. I suppose he made a fortune out of his book?'

'About 150 dollars. He had to pay for the printing himself. Why do you think he works here? The reviews were too unfavourable. People who read science fiction apparently dislike flying saucers, and everyone else dismissed him as a lunatic.' He stood up. 'We might as well get back.'

As they left the cafe Cameron waved to Kandinski, who was still talking to the young women. They were leaning forward and listening with rapt attention to whatever he was saying.

'What do the people in Vernon Gardens think of him?' Ward asked as they moved away under the trees.

'Well, it's a curious thing, almost without exception those who actually know Kandinski are convinced he's sincere and that he saw an alien spacecraft, while at the same time realizing the absolute impossibility of the whole story.'

'"I know God exists, but I cannot *believe* in him"?'

'Exactly. Naturally, most people in Vernon think he's crazy. About three months after he met the Venusian, Charles saw another UFO chasing its tail over the town. He got the Fire Police out, alerted the Radar Command chain and even had the National Guard driving around town ringing a bell. Sure enough, there were two white blobs diving about in the clouds. Unfortunately for Charles, they were caused by the headlights of one of the asparagus farmers in the valley doing some night spraying. Charles was the first to admit it, but at 3 o'clock in the morning no one was very pleased.'

'Who is Kandinski, anyway?' Ward asked. 'Where does he come from?'

'He doesn't make a profession of seeing Venusians, if that's what you mean. He was born in Alaska, for some years taught psychology at Mexico City University. He's been just about everywhere, had a thousand different jobs. A veteran of the private evacuations. Get his book.'

Ward murmured non-committally. They entered a small arcade and stood for a moment by the first shop, an aquarium called 'The Nouvelle Vague,' watching the Angel fish and Royal Brahmins swim dreamily up and down their tanks.

'It's worth reading,' Professor Cameron went on. 'Without exaggerating, it's really one of the most interesting documents I've ever come across.'

'I'm afraid I have a closed mind when it comes to interplanetary bogey-men,' Ward said.

'A pity,' Cameron rejoined. 'I find them fascinating. Straight out of the unconscious. The fish too,' he added, pointing at the tanks. He grinned whimsically at Ward and ducked away into a horticulture store halfway down the arcade.

While Professor Cameron was looking through the sprays on the hormone counter, Ward went over to a news-stand and glanced at the magazines. The proximity of the observatory had prompted a large selection of popular astronomical guides and digests, most of them with illustrations of the Mount Vernon domes on their wrappers. Among them Ward noticed a dusty, dog-eared paperback, *The Landings from Outer Space*, by Charles Kandinski. On the front cover a gigantic space vehicle, at least the size of New York, tens of thousands of portholes ablaze with light, was soaring majestically across a brilliant backdrop of stars and spiral nebulae.

Ward picked up the book and turned to the end cover. Here there was a photograph of Kandinski, dressed in a dark lounge suit several sizes too small, peering stiffly into the eye-piece of his MacDonald.

Ward hesitated before finally taking out his wallet. He bought the book and slipped it into his pocket as Professor Cameron emerged from the horticulture store.

'Get your shampoo?' Ward asked.

Cameron brandished a brass insecticide gun, then slung it, buccaneer-like, under his belt. 'My disintegrator,' he said, patting the butt of the gun. 'There's a positive plague of white ants in the garden, like something out of a science fiction nightmare. I've tried to convince Edna that their real source is psychological. Remember the story "Leiningen vs the Ants"? A classic example of the forces of the Id rebelling against the Super-Ego.' He watched a girl in a black bikini and lemon-coloured sunglasses move gracefully through the arcade and added meditatively. 'You know, Andrew, like everyone else my real vocation was to be a psychiatrist. I spend so long analysing my motives I've no time left to act.'

'Kandinski's Super-Ego must be in difficulties,' Ward remarked. 'You haven't told me your explanation yet.'

'What explanation?'

'Well, what's really at the bottom of this Venusian he claims to have seen?'

'Nothing is at the bottom of it. Why?'

Ward smiled helplessly. 'You will tell me next that you really believe him.'

Professor Cameron chuckled. They reached his car and climbed in. 'Of course I do,' he said.

*

When, three days later, Ward borrowed Professor Cameron's car and drove down to the rail depot in Vernon Gardens to collect a case of slides which had followed him across the Atlantic, he had no intention of seeing Charles Kandinski again. He had read one or two chapters of Kandinski's book before going to sleep the previous night and dropped it in boredom. Kandinski's description of his encounter with the Venusian was not only puerile and crudely written but, most disappointing of all, completely devoid of imagination. Ward's work at the Institute was now taking up most of his time. The Annual Congress of the International Geophysical Association was being held at Mount Vernon in little under a month, and most of the burden for organizing the three-week programme of lectures, semesters and dinners had fallen on Professor Cameron and himself.

But as he drove away from the depot past the cafes in the square he caught sight of Kandinski on the terrace of the Site Tycho. It was 3 o'clock, a time when most people in Vernon Gardens were lying asleep indoors, and Kandinski seemed to be the only person out in the sun. He was scrubbing away energetically at the abstract tables with his long hairy arms, head down so that his beard was almost touching the metal tops, like an aboriginal halfman prowling in dim bewilderment over the ruins of a futuristic city lost in an inversion of time.

On an impulse, Ward parked the car in the square and walked across to the Site Tycho, but as soon as Kandinski came over to his table he wished he had gone to another of the cafes. Kandinski had been reticent enough the previous day, but now that Cameron was absent he might well turn out to be a garrulous bore.

After serving him Kandinski sat down on a bench by the bookshelves and stared moodily at his feet. Ward watched him quietly for five minutes, as the mobiles revolved delicately in the warm air, deciding whether to approach Kandinski. Then he stood up and went over to the rows of magazines. He picked in a desultory way through half a dozen and turned to Kandinski. 'Can you recommend any of these?'

Kandinski looked up. 'Do you read science fiction?' he asked matter-of-factly.

'Not as a rule,' Ward admitted. When Kandinski said nothing he went on: 'Perhaps I'm too sceptical, but I can't take it seriously.'

Kandinski pulled a blister on his palm. 'No one suggests you should. What you mean is that you take it too seriously.'

Accepting the rebuke with a smile at himself, Ward pulled out one of the magazines and sat down at a table next to Kandinski. On the cover was a placid suburban setting of snugly eaved houses, yew trees and children's bicycles. Spreading slowly across the roof-tops was an enormous pulpy nightmare, blocking out the sun behind it and throwing a weird phosphorescent glow over the roofs and lawns. 'You're probably right,' Ward said, showing the cover to Kandinski. 'I'd hate to want to take that seriously.'

Kandinski waved it aside. 'I have seen 11th-century illuminations of the pentateuch more sensational than any of these covers.' He pointed to the cinema theatre on the far side of the square, where the four-hour Biblical epic *Cain and Abel* was showing. Above the trees an elaborate technicolored hoarding showed Cain, wearing what appeared to be a suit of Roman armour, wrestling with an immense hydraheaded boa constrictor.

Kandinski shrugged tolerantly. 'If Michelangelo were working for MGM today would he produce anything better?'

Ward laughed. 'You may well be right. Perhaps the House of the Medicis should be re-christened "16th Century-Fox"'

Kandinski stood up and straightened the shelves. 'I saw you here with Godfrey Cameron,' he said over his shoulder. 'You're working at the Observatory?'

'At the Hubble.'

Kandinski came and sat down beside Ward. 'Cameron is a good man. A very pleasant fellow.'

'He thinks a great deal of you,' Ward volunteered, realizing that Kandinski was probably short of friends.

'You mustn't believe everything that Cameron says about me,' Kandinski said suddenly. He hesitated, apparently uncertain whether to confide further in Ward, and then took the magazine from him. 'There are better ones here. You have to exercise some discrimination.'

'It's not so much the sensationalism that puts me off,' Ward explained, 'as the psychological implications. Most of the themes in these stories come straight out of the more unpleasant reaches of the unconscious.'

Kandinski glanced sharply at Ward, a trace of amusement in his eyes. 'That sounds rather dubious and, if I may say so, second-hand. Take the best of these stories for what they are: imaginative exercises on the theme of tomorrow.'

'You read a good deal of science fiction?' Ward asked.

Kandinski shook his head. 'Never. Not since I was a child.'

'I'm surprised,' Ward said. 'Professor Cameron told me you had written a science fiction novel.'

'Not a novel,' Kandinski corrected.

'I'd like to read it,' Ward went on. 'From what Cameron said it sounded fascinating, almost Swiftian in concept. This spacecraft which arrives from Venus and the strange conversations the pilot holds with a philosopher he meets. A modern morality. Is that the subject?'

Kandinski watched Ward thoughtfully before replying. 'Loosely, yes.

But, as I said, the book is not a novel. It is a factual and literal report of a Venus landing which actually took place, a diary of the most significant encounter in history since Paul saw his vision of Christ on the road to Damascus.' He lifted his huge bearded head and gazed at Ward without embarrassment. 'As a matter of interest, as Professor Cameron probably explained to you, I was the man who witnessed the landing.'

Still maintaining his pose, Ward frowned intently. 'Well, in fact Cameron did say something of the sort, but I . . .'

'But you found it difficult to believe?' Kandinski suggested ironically.

'Just a little,' Ward admitted. 'Are you seriously claiming that you did see a Venusian spacecraft?'

Kandinski nodded. 'Exactly.' Then, as if aware that their conversation had reached a familiar turning he suddenly seemed to lose interest in Ward. 'Excuse me.' He nodded politely to Ward, picked up a length of hose-pipe connected to a faucet and began to spray one of the big mobiles.

Puzzled but still sceptical, Ward sat back and watched him critically, then fished in his pockets for some change. 'I must say I admire you for taking it all so calmly,' he told Kandinski as he paid him.

'What makes you think I do?'

'Well, if I'd seen, let alone spoken to a visitor from Venus I think I'd be running around in a flat spin, notifying every government and observatory in the world.'

'I did,' Kandinski said. 'As far as I could. No one was very interested.'

Ward shook his head and laughed. 'It is incredible, to put it mildly.'

'I agree with you.'

'What I mean,' Ward said, 'is that it's straight out of one of these science fiction stories of yours.'

Kandinski rubbed his lips with a scarred knuckle, obviously searching for some means of ending the conversation. 'The resemblance is misleading. They are not my stories,' he added parenthetically. 'This cafe is the only one which would give me work, for a perhaps obvious reason. As for the incredibility, let me say that I was and still am completely amazed. You may think I take it all calmly, but ever since the landing I have lived in a state of acute anxiety and foreboding. But short of committing some spectacular crime to draw attention to myself I don't see now how I can convince anyone.'

Ward gestured with his glasses. 'Perhaps. But I'm surprised you don't realize the very simple reasons why people refuse to take you seriously. For example, why should you be the only person to witness an event of such staggering implications? Why have *you* alone seen a Venusian?'

'A sheer accident.'

'But why should a spacecraft from Venus land here?'

'What better place than near Mount Vernon Observatory?'

'I can think of any number. The UN Assembly, for one.'

Kandinski smiled lightly. 'Columbus didn't make his first contacts with the North American Indians at the Iroquois-Sioux Tribal Conference.'

'That may be,' Ward admitted, beginning to feel impatient. 'What did this Venusian look like?'

Kandinski smiled wearily at the empty tables and picked up his hose again. 'I don't know whether you've read my book,' he said, 'but if you haven't you'll find it all there.'

'Professor Cameron mentioned that you took some photographs of the Venusian spacecraft. Could I examine them?'

'Certainly,' Kandinski replied promptly. 'I'll bring them here tomorrow. You're welcome to test them in any way you wish.'

That evening Ward had dinner with the Camerons. Professor Renthall, Director of the Hubble, and his wife completed the party. The table-talk consisted almost entirely of good-humoured gossip about their colleagues retailed by Cameron and Renthall, and Ward was able to mention his conversation with Kandinski.

'At first I thought he was mad, but now I'm not so certain. There's something rather too subtle about him. The way he creates an impression of absolute integrity, but at the same time never gives you a chance to tackle him directly on any point of detail. And when you do manage to ask him outright about this Venusian his answers are far too pat. I'm convinced the whole thing is an elaborate hoax.'

Professor Renthall shook his head. 'No, it's no hoax. Don't you agree, Godfrey?'

Cameron nodded. 'Not in Andrew's sense, anyway.'

'But what other explanation is there?' Ward asked. 'We know he hasn't seen a Venusian, so he must be a fraud. Unless you think he's a lunatic. And he certainly doesn't behave like one.'

'What is a lunatic?' Professor Renthall asked rhetorically, peering into the faceted stem of his raised hock glass. 'Merely a man with more understanding than he can contain. I think Charles belongs in that category.'

'The definition doesn't explain him, sir,' Ward insisted. 'He's going to lend me his photographs and when I prove those are fakes I think I'll be able to get under his guard.'

'Poor Charles,' Edna Cameron said. 'Why shouldn't he have seen a spaceship? I think I see them every day.'

'That's just what I feel, dear,' Cameron said, patting his wife's matronly, brocaded shoulder. 'Let Charles have his Venusian if he wants to. Damn it, all it's trying to do is ban Project Apollo. An excellent idea, I have always maintained; only the professional astronomer has any business in space. After the Rainbow tests there isn't an astronomer anywhere in the world who wouldn't follow Charles Kandinski to the stake.' He turned to Renthall. 'By the way, I wonder what Charles is planning for the Congress? A Neptunian? Or perhaps a whole delegation from Proxima Centauri. We ought to fit him out with a space suit and a pavilion – "Charles Kandinski – New Worlds for Old".'

'Santa Claus in a space-suit,' Professor Renthall mused. 'That's a new one. Send him a ticket.'

The next weekend Ward returned the twelve plates to the Site Tycho.

'Well?' Kandinski asked.

'It's difficult to say,' Ward answered. 'They're all too heavily absorbed. They could be clever montages of light brackets and turbine blades. One of them looks like a close-up of a clutch plate. There's a significant lack of any real corroborative details which you'd expect somewhere in so wide a selection.' He paused. 'On the other hand, they could be genuine.'

Kandinski said nothing, took the paper package, and went off into the cafe.

The interior of the Site Tycho had been designed to represent the control room of a spaceship on the surface of the moon. Hidden fluorescent lighting glimmered through plastic wall fascia and filled the room with an eerie blue glow. Behind the bar a large mural threw the curving outline of the Moon on to an illuminated star-scape. The doors leading to the rest-rooms were circular and bulged outwards like air-locks, distinguished from each other by the symbols male and female. The total effect was ingenious but somehow reminiscent to Ward of a twenty-fifth century cave.

He sat down at the bar and waited while Kandinski packed the plates away carefully in an old leather briefcase.

'I've read your book,' Ward said. 'I had looked at it the last time I saw you, but I read it again thoroughly.' He waited for some comment upon this admission, but Kandinski went over to an old portable typewriter standing at the far end of the bar and began to type laboriously with one finger. 'Have you seen any more Venusians since the book was published?' Ward asked.

'None,' Kandinski said.

'Do you think you will?'

'Perhaps.' Kandinski shrugged and went on with his typing.

'What are you working on now?' Ward asked.

'A lecture I am giving on Friday evening,' Kandinski said. Two keys locked together and he flicked them back. 'Would you care to come? Eight-thirty, at the high school near the Baptist chapel.'

'If I can,' Ward said. He saw that Kandinski wanted to get rid of him. 'Thanks for letting me see the plates.' He made his way out into the sun. People were walking about through the fresh morning air, and he caught the clean scent of peach blossom carried down the slopes into the town.

Suddenly Ward felt how enclosed and insane it had been inside the Tycho, and how apposite had been his description of it as a cave, with its residential magician incanting over his photographs like a down-at-heel Merlin manipulating his set of runes. He felt annoyed with himself for becoming involved with Kandinski and allowing the potent charisma of his personality to confuse him. Obviously Kandinski played upon the instinctive sympathy for the outcast, his whole pose of integrity and conviction a device for drawing the gullible towards him.

Letting the light spray from the fountains fall across his face, Ward crossed the square towards his car.

Away in the distance 2,000 feet above, rising beyond a screen of fir trees, the three Mount Vernon domes shone together in the sun like a futuristic Taj Mahal.

Fifteen miles from Vernon Gardens the Santa Vera highway circled down from the foot of Mount Vernon into the first low scrub-covered hills which marked the southern edge of the desert. Ward looked out at the long banks of coarse sand stretching away through the haze, their outlines blurring in the afternoon heat. He glanced at the book lying on the seat beside him, open at the map printed between its end covers, and carefully checked his position, involuntarily slowing the speed of the Chevrolet as he moved nearer to the site of the Venus landings.

In the week since he had returned the photographs to the Site Tycho, he had seen Kandinski only once, at the lecture delivered the previous night. Ward had deliberately stayed away from the Site Tycho, but he had seen a poster advertising the lecture and driven down to the school despite himself.

The lecture was delivered in the gymnasium before an audience of forty or fifty people, most of them women, who formed one of the innumerable local astronomical societies. Listening to the talk round him, Ward gathered that their activities principally consisted of trying to identify more than half a dozen of the constellations. Kandinski had lectured to them on several occasions and the subject of this latest instalment was his researches into the significance of the Venusian tablet he had been analysing for the last three years.

When Kandinski stepped onto the dais there was a brief round of applause. He was wearing a lounge suit of a curiously archaic cut and had washed his beard, which bushed out above his string tie so that he resembled a Mormon patriarch or the homespun saint of some fervent evangelical community.

For the benefit of any new members, he prefaced his lecture with a brief account of his meeting with the Venusian, and then turned to his analysis of the tablet. This was the familiar ultimatum warning mankind to abandon its preparations for the exploration of space, for the ostensible reason that, just as the sea was a universal image of the unconscious, so space was nothing less than an image of psychosis and death, and that if he tried to penetrate the interplanetary voids man would only plunge to earth liké a demented Icarus, unable to scale the vastness of the cosmic zero. Kandinski's real motives for introducing this were all too apparent – the expected success of Project Apollo and subsequent landings on Mars and Venus would, if nothing else, conclusively expose his fantasies.

However, by the end of the lecture Ward found that his opinion of Kandinski had experienced a complete about face.

As a lecturer Kandinski was poor, losing words, speaking in a slow ponderous style and trapping himself in long subordinate clauses, but his quiet, matter-of-fact tone and absolute conviction in the importance of what he was saying, coupled with the nature of his material, held the talk together. His analysis of the Venusian cryptograms, a succession of intricate philological theorems, was well above the heads of his audience, but what began to impress Ward, as much as the painstaking preparation which must have preceded the lecture, was Kandinski's acute nervousness in delivering it. Ward noticed that he suffered from an irritating speech impediment that made it difficult for him to pronounce 'Venusian', and he saw that Kandinski, far from basking in the limelight, was delivering the lecture only out of a deep sense of obligation to his audience and was greatly relieved when the ordeal was over.

At the end Kandinski had invited questions. These, with the exception of the chairman's, all concerned the landing of the alien space vehicle and ignored the real subject of the lecture. Kandinski answered them all carefully, taking in good part the inevitable facetious questions. Ward noted with interest the audience's curious ambivalence, simultaneously fascinated by and resentful of Kandinski's exposure of their own private fantasies, an expression of the same ambivalence which had propelled so many of the mana-personalities of history towards their inevitable Calvarys.

Just as the chairman was about to close the meeting, Ward stood up.

'Mr Kandinski. You say that this Venusian indicated that there was also life on one of the moons of Uranus. Can you tell us how he did this if there was no verbal communication between you?'

Kandinski showed no surprise at seeing Ward. 'Certainly; as I told you, he drew eight concentric circles in the sand, one for each of the planets. Around Uranus he drew five lesser orbits and marked one of these. Then he pointed to himself and to me and to a patch of lichen. From this I deduced, reasonably I maintain, that—'

'Excuse me, Mr Kandinski,' Ward interrupted. 'You say he drew five orbits around Uranus? One for each of the moons?'

Kandinski nodded. 'Yes. Five.'

'That was in 1960,' Ward went on. 'Three weeks ago Professor Pineau at Brussels discovered a sixth moon of Uranus.'

The audience looked around at Ward and began to murmur.

'Why should this Venusian have omitted one of the moons?' Ward asked, his voice ringing across the gymnasium.

Kandinski frowned and peered at Ward suspiciously. 'I didn't know there was a sixth moon . . . ' he began.

'Exactly!' someone called out. The audience began to titter.

'I can understand the Venusian not wishing to introduce any difficulties,' Ward said, 'but this seems a curious way of doing it.'

Kandinski appeared at a loss. Then he introduced Ward to the audience. 'Dr Ward is a professional while I am only an amateur,' he admitted. 'I am afraid I cannot explain the anomaly. Perhaps my memory is at fault. But I am sure the Venusian drew only five orbits.' He stepped down from the dais and strode out hurriedly, scowling into his beard, pursued by a few derisory hoots from the audience.

It took Ward fifteen minutes to free himself from the knot of admiring white-gloved spinsters who cornered him between two vaulting horses. When he broke away he ran out to his car and drove into Vernon Gardens, hoping to see Kandinski and apologize to him.

Five miles into the desert Ward approached a nexus of rock-cuttings and causeways which were part of an abandoned irrigation scheme. The colours of the hills were more vivid now, bright siliconic reds and yellows, crossed with sharp stabs of light from the exposed quartz veins. Following the map on the seat, he turned off the highway onto a rough track which ran along the bank of a dried-up canal. He passed a few rusting sections of picket fencing, a derelict grader half-submerged under the sand, and a collection of dilapidated metal shacks. The car bumped over the potholes at little more than ten miles an hour, throwing up clouds of hot ashy dust that swirled high into the air behind him.

Two miles along the canal the track came to an end. Ward stopped the car and waited for the dust to subside. Carrying Kandinski's book in front of him like a divining instrument, he set off on foot across the remaining three hundred yards. The contours around him were marked on the map, but the hills had shifted several hundred yards westwards since the book's publication and he found himself wandering about from one crest to another, peering into shallow depressions only as old as the last sand-storm. The entire landscape seemed haunted by strange currents and moods; the sand swirls surging down the aisles of dunes and the proximity of the horizon enclosed the whole place of stones with invisible walls.

Finally he found the ring of hills indicated and climbed a narrow saddle leading to its centre. When he scaled the thirty-foot slope he stopped abruptly.

Down on his knees in the middle of the basin with his back to Ward, the studs of his boots flashing in the sunlight, was Kandinski. There was a clutter of tiny objects on the sand around him, and at first Ward thought he was at prayer, making his oblations to the tutelary deities of Venus. Then he saw that Kandinski was slowly scraping the surface of the ground with a small trowel. A circle about 20 yards in diameter had been marked off with pegs and string into a series of wedge-shaped allotments. Every few seconds Kandinski carefully decanted a small heap of grit into one of the test-tubes mounted in a wooden rack in front of him.

Ward put away the book and walked down the slope. Kandinski looked around and then climbed to his feet. The coating of red ash on his beard gave him a fiery, prophetic look. He recognized Ward and raised the trowel in greeting.

Ward stopped at the edge of the string perimeter. 'What on earth are you doing?'

'I am collecting soil specimens.' Kandinski bent down and corked one of the tubes. He looked tired but worked away steadily.

Ward watched him finish a row. 'It's going to take you a long time to cover the whole area. I thought there weren't any gaps left in the Periodic Table.'

'The spacecraft rotated at speed before it rose into the air. This surface is abrasive enough to have scratched off a few minute filings. With luck I may find one of them.' Kandinski smiled thinly. '262. Venusium, I hope.'

Ward started to say: 'But the transuranic elements decay spontaneously . . . ' and then walked over to the centre of the circle, where there was a round indentation, three feet deep and five across. The inner surface was glazed and smooth. It was shaped like an inverted cone and looked as if it had been caused by the boss of an enormous spinning top. 'This is where the spacecraft landed?'

Kandinski nodded. He filled the last tube and then stowed the rack away in a canvas satchel. He came over to Ward and stared down at the hole. 'What does it look like to you? A meteor impact? Or an oil drill, perhaps?' A smile showed behind his dusty beard. 'The F-109s at the Air Force Weapons School begin their target runs across here. It might have been caused by a rogue cannon shell.'

Ward stooped down and felt the surface of the pit, running his fingers thoughtfully over the warm fused silica. 'More like a 500-pound bomb. But the cone is geometrically perfect. It's certainly unusual.'

'Unusual?' Kandinski chuckled to himself and picked up the satchel.

'Has anyone else been out here?' Ward asked as they trudged up the slope.

'Two so-called experts.' Kandinski slapped the sand off his knees. 'A geologist from Gulf-Vacuum and an Air Force ballistics officer. You'll be glad to hear that they both thought I had dug the pit myself and then fused the surface with an acetylene torch.' He peered critically at Ward. 'Why did you come out here today?'

'Idle curiosity,' Ward said. 'I had an afternoon off and I felt like a drive.'

They reached the crest of the hill and he stopped and looked down into the basin. The lines of string split the circle into a strange horological device, a huge zodiacal mandala, the dark patches in the arcs Kandinski had been working telling its stations.

'You were going to tell me why you came out here,' Kandinski said as they walked back to the car.

Ward shrugged. 'I suppose I wanted to prove something to myself. There's a problem of reconciliation.' He hesitated, and then began: 'You see, there are some things which are self-evidently false. The laws of common sense and everyday experience refute them. I know a lot of the evidence for many things we believe in is pretty thin, but I don't have to embark on a theory of knowledge to decide that the moon isn't made of green cheese.'

'Well?' Kandinski shifted the satchel to his other shoulder.

'This Venusian you've seen,' Ward said. 'The landing, the runic tablet. I can't believe them. Every piece of evidence I've seen, all the circumstantial details, the facts given in this book . . . they're all patently false.' He turned to one of the middle chapters. 'Take this at random – "A phosphorescent green fluid pulsed through the dorsal lung-chamber of the Prime's helmet, inflating two opaque fan-like gills . . . "' Ward closed the book and shrugged helplessly. Kandinski stood a few feet away from him, the sunlight breaking across the deep lines of his face.

'Now I know what you say to my objections,' Ward went on. 'If you told a 19th-century chemist that lead could be transmuted into gold he would have dismissed you as a mediaevalist. But the point is that he'd have been right to do so—'

'I understand,' Kandinski interrupted. 'But you still haven't explained why you came out here today.'

Ward stared out over the desert. High above, a stratojet was doing cuban eights into the sun, the spiral vapour trails drifting across the sky like gigantic fragments of an apocalyptic message. Looking around, he realized that Kandinski must have walked from the bus-stop on the highway. 'I'll give you a lift back,' he said.

As they drove along the canal he turned to Kandinski. 'I enjoyed your lecture last night. I apologize for trying to make you look a fool.'

Kandinski was loosening his boot-straps. He laughed unreproachfully. 'You put me in an awkward position. I could hardly have challenged you. I can't afford to subscribe to every astronomical journal. Though a sixth moon would have been big news.' As they neared Vernon Gardens he asked: 'Would you like to come in and look at the tablet analysis?'

Ward made no reply to the invitation. He drove around the square and parked under the trees, then looked up at the fountains, tapping his fingers on the wind-shield. Kandinski sat beside him, cogitating into his beard.

Ward watched him carefully. 'Do you think this Venusian will return?'

Kandinski nodded. 'Yes. I am sure he will.'

Later they sat together at a broad roll-top desk in the room above the Tycho. Around the wall hung white cardboard screens packed with lines of cuneiform glyphics and Kandinski's progressive breakdown of their meaning.

Ward held an enlargement of the original photograph of the Venusian tablet and listened to Kandinski's explanation.

'As you see from this,' Kandinski explained, 'in all probability there are not millions of Venusians, as everyone would expect, but only three or four of them altogether. Two are circling Venus, a third Uranus and possibly a fourth is in orbit around Neptune. This solves the difficulty that puzzled you and antagonizes everyone else. Why should the Prime have approached only one person out of several hundred million and selected him on a completely random basis? Now obviously he had seen the Russian and American satellite capsules and asssumed that our race, like his now, numbered no more than three or four, then concluded from the atmospheric H-bomb tests that we were in conflict and would soon destroy ourselves. This is one of the reasons why I think he will return shortly and why it is important to organize a world-wide reception for him on a governmental level.'

'Wait a minute,' Ward said. 'He must have known that the population of this planet numbered more than three or four. Even the weakest telescope would demonstrate that.'

'Of course, but he would naturally assume that the millions of inhabitants of the Earth belonged to an aboriginal sub-species, perhaps employed as work animals. After all, if he observed that despite this planet's immense resources the bulk of its population lived like animals, an alien visitor could only decide that they were considered as such.'

'But space vehicles are supposed to have been observing us since the Babylonian era, long before the development of satellite rockets. There have been thousands of recorded sightings.'

Kandinski shook his head. 'None of them has been authenticated.'

'What about the other landings that have been reported recently?' Ward asked. 'Any number of people have seen Venusians and Martians.'

'Have they?' Kandinski asked sceptically. 'I wish I could believe that. Some of the encounters reveal marvellous powers of invention, but no one can accept them as anything but fantasy.'

'The same criticism has been levelled at your spacecraft,' Ward reminded him.

Kandinski seemed to lose patience. 'I *saw* it,' he explained, impotently tossing his notebook on to the desk. 'I *spoke* to the Prime!'

Ward nodded non-committally and picked up the photograph again. Kandinski stepped over to him and took it out of his hands. 'Ward,' he said carefully. 'Believe me. You must. You know I am too big a man to waste myself on a senseless charade.' His massive hands squeezed Ward's shoulder, and almost lifted him off the seat. '*Believe* me. Together we can be ready for the next landings and alert the world. I am only Charles Kandinski, a waiter at a third-rate cafe, but you are Dr Andrew Ward of Mount Vernon Observatory. They will listen to you. Try to realize what this may mean for mankind.'

Ward pulled himself away from Kandinski and rubbed his shoulders.

'Ward, do you believe me? Ask yourself.'

Ward looked up pensively at Kandinski towering over him, his red beard like the burning, unconsumed bush.

'I think so,' he said quietly. 'Yes, I do.'

A week later the 23rd Congress of the International Geophysical Association opened at Mount Vernon Observatory. At 3.30 P.M., in the Hoyle Library amphitheatre, Professor Renthall was to deliver the inaugural address welcoming the 92 delegates and 25 newspaper and agency reporters to the fortnight's programme of lectures and discussions.

Shortly after 11 o'clock that morning Ward and Professor Cameron completed their final arrangements and escaped down to Vernon Gardens for an hour's relaxation.

'Well,' Cameron said as they walked over to the Site Tycho, 'I've got a pretty good idea of what it must be like to run the Waldorf-Astoria.' They picked one of the sidewalk tables and sat down. 'I haven't been here for weeks,' Cameron said. 'How are you getting on with the Man in the Moon?'

'Kandinski? I hardly ever see him,' Ward said.

'I was talking to the *Time* magazine stringer about Charles,' Cameron said, cleaning his sunglasses. 'He thought he might do a piece about him.'

'Hasn't Kandinski suffered enough of that sort of thing?' Ward asked moodily.

'Perhaps he has,' Cameron agreed. 'Is he still working on his crossword puzzle? The tablet thing, whatever he calls it.'

Casually, Ward said: 'He has a theory that it should be possible to see the lunar bases. Refuelling points established there by the Venusians over the centuries.'

'Interesting,' Cameron commented.

'They're sited near Copernicus,' Ward went on. 'I know Vandone at Milan is mapping Archimedes and the Imbrium. I thought I might mention it to him at his semester tomorrow.'

Professor Cameron took off his glasses and gazed quizzically at Ward. 'My dear Andrew, what has been going on? Don't tell me you've become one of Charles's converts?'

Ward laughed and shook his head. 'Of course not. Obviously there are no lunar bases or alien spacecraft. I don't for a moment believe a word Kandinski says.' He gestured helplessly. 'At the same time I admit I have become involved with him. There's something about Kandinski's personality. On the one hand I can't take him seriously—'

'Oh, I take him seriously,' Cameron cut in smoothly. 'Very seriously indeed, if not quite in the sense you mean.' Cameron turned his back on the sidewalk crowds. 'Jung's views on flying saucers are very illuminating, Andrew; they'd help you to understand Kandinski. Jung believes that civilization now stands at the conclusion of a Platonic Great Year, at the eclipse of the sign of Pisces which has dominated the Christian epoch, and that we are entering the sign of Aquarius, a period of confusion and psychic chaos. He remarks that throughout history, at all times of uncertainty and discord, cosmic space vehicles have been seen approaching Earth, and that in a few extreme cases actual meetings with their occupants are supposed to have taken place.'

As Cameron paused, Ward glanced across the tables for Kandinski, but a relief waiter served them and he assumed it was Kandinski's day off.

Cameron continued: 'Most people regard Charles Kandinski as a lunatic, but as a matter of fact he is performing one of the most important roles in the world today, the role of a prophet alerting people of this coming crisis. The real significance of his fantasies, like that of the ban-the-bomb movements, is to be found elsewhere than on the conscious plane, as an expression of the immense psychic forces stirring below the surface of rational life, like the isotactic movements of the continental tables which heralded the major geological transformations.'

Ward shook his head dubiously. 'I can accept that a man such as Freud was a prophet, but Charles Kandinski—?'

'Certainly. Far more than Freud. It's unfortunate for Kandinski, and for the writers of science fiction for that matter, that they have to perform their tasks of describing the symbols of transformation in a so-called rationalist society, where a scientific, or at least a pesudo-scientific explanation is required *a priori*. And because the true prophet never deals in what may be rationally deduced, people such as Charles are ignored or derided today.'

'It's interesting that Kandinski compared his meeting with the Venusian with Paul's conversion on the road to Damascus,' Ward said.

'He was quite right. In both encounters you see the same mechanism of blinding unconscious revelation. And you can see too that Charles feels the same overwelming need to spread the Pauline revelation to the world. The Anti-Apollo movement is only now getting under way, but within the next decade it will recruit millions, and men such as Charles Kandinski will be the fathers of its apocalypse.'

'You make him sound like a titanic figure,' Ward remarked quietly. 'I think he's just a lonely, tired man obsessed by something he can't understand. Perhaps he simply needs a few friends to confide in.'

Slowly shaking his head, Cameron tapped the table with his glasses. 'Be warned, Andrew, you'll burn your fingers if you play with Charles's brand of fire. The mana-personalities of history have no time for personal loyalties – the founder of the Christian church made that pretty plain.'

Shortly after seven o'clock that evening Charles Kandinski mounted his bicycle and set off out of Vernon Gardens. The small room in the seedy area where he lived always depressed him on his free days from the Tycho, and as he pedalled along he ignored the shouts from his neighbours sitting out on their balconies with their crates of beer. He knew that his beard and the high, ancient bicycle with its capacious wicker basket made him a grotesque, Quixotic figure, but he felt too preoccupied to care. That morning he had heard that the French translation of *The Landings from Outer Space*, printed at his own cost, had been completely ignored by the Paris press. In addition a jobbing printer in Santa Vera was pressing him for payment for 5,000 anti-Apollo leaflets that had been distributed the previous year.

Above all had come the news on the radio that the target date of the first manned moon flight had been advanced to 1969, and on the following day would take place the latest and most ambitious of the instrumented lunar flights. The anticipated budget for the Apollo programme (in a moment of grim humour he had calculated that it would pay for the printing of some 1,000 billion leaflets) seemed to double each year, but so far he had found little success in his attempt to alert people to the folly of venturing into space. All that day he had felt sick with frustration and anger.

At the end of the avenue he turned on to the highway which served the asparagus farms lying in the 20-mile strip between Vernon Gardens and the desert. It was a hot empty evening and few cars or trucks passed him. On either side of the road the great lemon-green terraces of asparagus lay seeping in their moist paddy beds, and occasionally a marsh-hen clacked overhead and dived out of sight.

Five miles along the road he reached the last farmhouse above the edge of the desert. He cycled on to where the road ended 200 yards ahead, dismounted and left the bicycle in a culvert. Slinging his camera over one shoulder, he walked off across the hard ground into the mouth of a small valley.

The boundary between the desert and the farm-strip was irregular. On his left, beyond the rocky slopes, he could hear a motor-reaper purring down one of the mile-long spits of fertile land running into the desert, but the barren terrain and the sense of isolation began to relax him and he forgot the irritations that had plagued him all day.

A keen naturalist, he saw a long-necked sand-crane perched on a spur of shale fifty feet from him and stopped and raised his camera. Peering through the finder he noticed that the light had faded too deeply for a photograph. Curiously, the sand-crane was clearly silhouetted against a circular glow of light which emanated from beyond a low ridge at the end of the valley. This apparently sourceless corona fitfully illuminated the darkening air, as if coming from a lighted mineshaft.

Putting away his camera, Kandinski walked forward, within a few minutes reached the ridge, and began to climb it. The face sloped steeply, and he pulled himself up by the hefts of brush and scrub, kicking away footholds in the rocky surface.

Just before he reached the crest he felt his heart surge painfully with the exertion, and he lay still for a moment, a sudden feeling of dizziness spinning in his head. He waited until the spasm subsided, shivering faintly in the cool air, an unfamiliar undertone of uneasiness in his mind. The air seemed to vibrate strangely with an intense inaudible music that pressed upon his temples. Rubbing his forehead, he lifted himself over the crest.

The ridge he had climbed was U-shaped and about 200 feet across, its open end away from him. Resting on the sandy floor in its centre was an enormous metal disc, over 100 feet in diameter and 30 feet high. It seemed to be balanced on a huge conical boss, half of which had already sunk into the sand. A fluted rim ran around the edge of the disc and separated the upper and lower curvatures, which were revolving rapidly in opposite directions, throwing off magnificent flashes of silver light.

Kandinski lay still, as his first feeling of fear retreated and his courage and presence of mind returned. The inaudible piercing music had faded, and his mind felt brilliantly clear. His eyes ran rapidly over the spaceship, and he estimated that it was over twice the size of the craft he had seen three years earlier. There were no markings or ports on the carapace, but he was certain it had not come from Venus.

Kandinski lay watching the spacecraft for ten minutes, trying to decide upon his best course of action. Unfortunately he had smashed the lens of his camera. Finally, pushing himself backwards, he slid slowly down the slope. When he reached the floor he could still hear the whine of the rotors. Hiding in the pools of shadow, he made his way up the valley, and two hundred yards from the ridge he broke into a run.

He returned the way he had come, his great legs carrying him across the ruts and boulders, seized his bicycle from the culvert and pedalled rapidly towards the farmhouse.

A single light shone in an upstairs room and he pressed one hand to the bell and pounded on the screen door with the other, nearly tearing it from its hinges. Eventually a young woman appeared. She came down the stairs reluctantly, uncertain what to make of Kandinski's beard and ragged, dusty clothes.

'Telephone!' Kandinski bellowed at her, gasping wildly, as he caught back his breath.

The girl at last unlatched the door and backed away from him nervously. Kandinski lurched past her and staggered blindly around the darkened hall. 'Where is it?' he roared.

The girl switched on the lights and pointed into the sitting room. Kandinski pushed past her and rushed over to it.

Ward played with his brandy glass and discreetly loosened the collar of his dress shirt, listening to Dr MacIntyre of Greenwich Observatory, four seats away on his right, make the third of the after-dinner speeches. Ward was to speak next, and he ran through the opening phrases of his speech, glancing down occasionally to con his notes. At 34 he was the youngest member to address the Congress banquet, and by no means unimpressed by the honour. He looked at the venerable figures to his left and right at the top table, their black jackets and white shirt fronts reflected in the table silver, and saw Professor Cameron wink at him reassuringly.

He was going through his notes for the last time when a steward bent over his shoulder. 'Telephone for you, Dr Ward.'

'I can't take it now,' Ward whispered. 'Tell them to call later.'

'The caller said it was extremely urgent, Doctor. Something about some people from the Neptune arriving.'

'The Neptune?'

'I think that's a hotel in Santa Vera. Maybe the Russian delegates have turned up after all.'

Ward pushed his chair back, made his apologies and slipped away.

Professor Cameron was waiting in the alcove outside the banqueting hall when Ward stepped out of the booth. 'Anything the trouble, Andrew? It's not your father, I hope—'

'It's Kandinski,' Ward said hurriedly. 'He's out in the desert, near the farm-strip. He says he's seen another space vehicle.'

'Oh, is that all?' Cameron shook his head. 'Come on, we'd better get back. The poor fool!'

'Hold on,' Ward said. 'He's got it under observation now. It's on the ground. He told me to call General Wayne at the air base and alert the Strategic Air Command.' Ward chewed his lip. 'I don't know what to do.'

Cameron took him by the arm. 'Andrew, come on. MacIntyre's winding up.'

'What can we do, though?' Ward asked. 'He seemed all right, but then he said that he thought they were hostile. That sounds a little sinister.'

'Andrew!' Cameron snapped. 'What's the matter with you? Leave Kandinski to himself. You can't go now. It would be unpardonable rudeness.'

'I've got to help Kandinski,' Ward insisted. 'I'm sure he needs it this time.' He wrenched himself away from Cameron.

'Ward!' Professor Cameron called. 'For God's sake, come back!' He followed Ward onto the balcony and watched him run down the steps and disappear across the lawn into the darkness.

As the wheels of the car thudded over the deep ruts, Ward cut the headlights and searched the dark hills which marked the desert's edge. The warm glitter of Vernon Gardens lay behind him and only a few isolated lights shone in the darkness on either side of the road. He passed the farmhouse from which he assumed Kandinski had telephoned, then drove on slowly until he saw the bicycle Kandinski had left for him.

It took him several minutes to mount the huge machine, his feet well clear of the pedals for most of their stroke. Laboriously he covered a hundred yards, and after careering helplessly into a clump of scrub was forced to dismount and continue on foot.

Kandinski had told him that the ridge was about a mile up the valley. It was almost night and the starlight reflected off the hills lit the valley with fleeting, vivid colours. He ran on heavily, the only sounds he could hear were those of a thresher rattling like a giant metal insect half a mile behind him. Filling his lungs, he pushed on across the last hundred yards.

Kandinski was still lying on the edge of the ridge, watching the spaceship and waiting impatiently for Ward. Below him in the hollow the upper and lower rotor sections swung around more slowly, at about one revolution per second. The space-ship had sunk a further ten feet into the desert floor and he was now on the same level as the observation dome. A single finger of light poked out into the darkness, circling the ridge walls in jerky sweeps.

Then out of the valley behind him he saw someone stumbling along towards the ridge at a broken run. Suddenly a feeling of triumph and exhilaration came over him, and he knew that at last he had his witness.

Ward climbed up the slope to where he could see Kandinski. Twice he lost his grip and slithered downwards helplessly, tearing his hands on the gritty surface. Kandinski was lying flat on his chest his head just above the ridge. Covered by dust, he was barely distinguishable from the slope itself.

'Are you all right?' Ward whispered. He pulled off his bow tie and ripped open his collar. When he had controlled his breathing he crawled up besides Kandinski.

'Where?' he asked.

Kandinski pointed down into the hollow.

Ward raised his head, levering himself up on his elbows. For a few seconds he peered out into the darkness, and then drew his head back.

'You see it?' Kandinski whispered. His voice was short and laboured. When Ward hesitated before replying he suddenly seized Ward's wrist in a vice-like grip. In the faint light reflected by the white dust on the ridge Ward could see plainly his bright inflamed eyes.

'Ward! Can you see it?'

The powerful fingers remained clamped to his wrist as he lay beside Kandinski and gazed down into the darkness.

*

Below the compartment window one of Ward's fellow passengers was being seen off by a group of friends, and the young women in bright hats and bandanas and the men in slacks and beach sandals made him feel that he was leaving a seaside resort at the end of a holiday. From the window he could see the observatory domes of Mount Vernon rising out of the trees, and he identified the white brickwork of the Hoyle Library a thousand feet below the summit. Edna Cameron had brought him to the station, but he had asked her not to come onto the platform, and she had said goodbye and driven off. Cameron himself he had seen only once, when he had collected his books from the Institute.

Trying to forget it all, Ward noted thankfully that the train would leave within five minutes. He took his bankbook out of his wallet and counted the last week's withdrawals. He winced at the largest item, 600 dollars which he had transferred to Kandinski's account to pay for the cablegrams.

Deciding to buy something to read, he left the car and walked back to the news-stand. Several of the magazines contained what could only be described as discouraging articles about himself, and he chose two or three newspapers.

Just then someone put a hand on his shoulder. He turned and saw Kandinski.

'Are you leaving?' Kandinsky asked quietly. He had trimmed his beard so that only a pale vestige of the original bloom remained, revealing his high bony cheekbones. His face seemed almost fifteen years younger, thinner and more drawn, but at the same time composed, like that of a man recovering slowly from the attack of some intermittent fever.

'I'm sorry, Charles,' Ward said as they walked back to the car. 'I should have said goodbye to you but I thought I'd better not.'

Kandinski's expression was subdued but puzzled. 'Why?' he asked. 'I don't understand.'

Ward shrugged. 'I'm afraid everything here has more or less come to an end for me, Charles. I'm going back to Princeton until the spring. Freshman physics.' He smiled ruefully at himself. 'Boyle's Law, Young's Modulus, getting right back to fundamentals. Not a bad idea, perhaps.'

'But why are you leaving?' Kandinski pressed.

'Well, Cameron thought it might be tactful of me to leave. After our statement to the Secretary-General was published in *The New York Times* I became very much *persona non grata* at the Hubble. The trustees were on to Professor Renthall again this morning.'

Kandinski smiled and seemed relieved. 'What does the Hubble matter?' he scoffed. 'We have more important work to do. You know, Ward, when Mrs Cameron told me just now that you were leaving I couldn't believe it.'

'I'm sorry, Charles, but it's true.'

'Ward,' Kandinski insisted. 'You can't leave. The Primes will be returning soon. We must prepare for them.'

'I know, Charles, and I wish I could stay.' They reached the car and Ward put his hand out. 'Thanks for coming to see me off.'

Kandinski held his hand tightly. 'Andrew, tell me the truth. Are you afraid of what people will think of you? Is that why you want to leave? Haven't you enough courage and faith in yourself?'

'Perhaps that's it,' Ward conceded, wishing the train would start. He reached for the rail and began to climb into the car but Kandinski held him.

'Ward, you can't drop your responsibilities like this!'

'Please, Charles,' Ward said, feeling his temper rising. He pulled his hand away but Kandinski seized him by the shoulder and almost dragged him off the car.

Ward wrenched himself away. 'Leave me alone!' he snapped fiercely. 'I saw your spaceship, didn't I?'

Kandinski watched him go, a hand picking at his vanished beard, completely perplexed.

Whistles sounded, and the train began to edge forward.

'Goodbye, Charles,' Ward called down. 'Let me know if you see anything else.'

He went into the car and took his seat. Only when the train was twenty miles from Mount Vernon did he look out of the window.

Title: Men Without Bones
Writer: *Gerald Kersh*

Briefing: *Gods from Space – alien visitors to Earth in prehistoric times, recorded in the hieroglyphics of ancient civilizations.* Doctor Goodbody is the only survivor of the Yeoward Expedition which went into the jungles of Nicaragua to investigate an old Indian folk legend about a race of gods said to have come down from the heavens centuries ago. He returns to the outside world with the story of the scientists' discovery of an awesome, pear-shaped machine on a high plateau and, close by, something *almost* human . . . horrifying in its implications.

Author: English writer Gerald Kersh deserves an accolade for having anticipated the theories of the Swiss author, Erich von Daniken, who, in the late Sixties and Seventies, in a series of books beginning with *Chariots of the Gods* (1968), set out to prove that aliens from space had influenced the great civilizations of the Ancient Egyptians and the Mayas of South America. 'Men Without Bones' is, in fact, just one of several 'scientific speculations' which Kersh, a soldier turned journalist and novelist, wrote during his prolific career. His novel, *The Weak and the Strong* (1945), for instance, features an underground world, while 'Voices in the Dust of Annan' (1947) speculates that only the little folk such as fairies will survive a nuclear holocaust and 'Whatever Happened to Corporal Cuckoo?' (1953) considers the consequences of immortality. 'Men Without Bones', first published in *Esquire* magazine in the fall of 1954, is also about some survivors in an alien world – but these are men with a significance that Kersh witholds until the very last line of his story. But do *not* be tempted to look first!

We were loading bananas into the *Claire Dodge* at Puerto Pobre, when a feverish little fellow came aboard. Everyone stepped aside to let him pass – even the soldiers who guard the port with nickel-plated Remington rifles, and who go barefoot but wear polished leather leggings. They stood back from him because they believed that he was afflicted-of-God, mad; harmless but dangerous; best left alone.

All the time the naphtha flares were hissing, and from the hold came the reverberation of the roaring voice of the foreman of the gang down below crying: 'Fruta! Fruta! *FRUTA!*' The leader of the dock gang bellowed the same cry, throwing down stem after stem of brilliant green bananas. The occasion would be memorable for this, if for nothing else – the magnificence of the night, the bronze of the Negro foreman shining under the flares, the jade green of that fruit, and the mixed odours of the waterfront. Out of one stem of bananas ran a hairy grey spider, which frightened the crew and broke the banana-chain, until a Nicaraguan boy, with a laugh, killed it with his foot. It was harmless, he said.

It was about then that the madman came aboard, unhindered, and asked me: 'Bound for where?'

He spoke quietly and in a carefully modulated voice; but there was a certain blank, lost look in his eyes that suggested to me that I keep within ducking distance of his restless hands which, now that I think of them, put me in mind of that grey, hairy, bird-eating spider.

'Mobile, Alabama,' I said.

'Take me along?' he asked.

'None of my affair. Sorry. Passenger myself,' I said. 'The skipper's ashore. Better wait for him on the wharf. He's the boss.'

'Would you happen, by any chance, to have a drink about you?'

Giving him some rum, I asked: 'How come they let you aboard?'

'I'm not crazy,' he said. 'Not actually . . . a little fever, nothing more. Malaria, dengue fever, jungle fever, rat-bite fever. Feverish country, this, and others of the same nature. Allow me to introduce myself. My name is Goodbody, Doctor of Science of Osbaldeston University. Does it convey nothing to you? No? Well then; I was assistant to Professor Yeoward. Does *that* convey anything to you?'

I said: 'Yeoward, Professor Yeoward? Oh, yes. He was lost, wasn't he, somewhere in the upland jungle beyond the source of the Amer River?'

'Correct!' cried the little man who called himself Goodbody. 'I saw him get lost.'

Fruta! – Fruta! – Fruta! – Fruta! came the voices of the men in the hold. There was rivalry between their leader and the big black stevedore ashore. The flares spluttered. The green bananas came down. And a kind of sickly sigh came out of the jungle, off the rotting river – not a wind, not a breeze – something like the foul breath of high fever.

Trembling with eagerness and, at the same time, shaking with fever chills, so that he had to use two hands to raise his glass to his lips – even so, he spilled most of the rum – Doctor Goodbody said: 'For God's sake, get me out of this country – take me to Mobile – hide me in your cabin!'

'I have no authority,' I said, 'but you are an American citizen; you can identify yourself; the consul will send you home.'

'No doubt. But that would take time. The consul thinks I am crazy too. And if I don't get away, I fear that I really will go out of my mind. Can't you help me? I'm afraid.'

'Come on, now,' I said. 'No one shall hurt you while I'm around. What are you afraid of?'

'Men without bones,' he said, and there was something in his voice that stirred the hairs on the back of my neck. 'Little fat men without bones!'

I wrapped him in a blanket, gave him some quinine, and let him sweat and shiver for a while, before I asked, humouring him: 'What men without bones?'

He talked in fits and starts in his fever, his reason staggering just this side of delirium:

'. . . What men without bones? . . . They are nothing to be afraid of, actually. It is they who are afraid of you. You can kill them with your boot, or with a stick . . . They are something like jelly. No, it is not really fear – it is the nausea, the disgust they inspire. It overwhelms. It paralyzes! I have seen a jaguar, I tell you – a full-grown jaguar – stand frozen, while they clung to him, in hundreds, and ate him up alive! Believe me, I saw it. Perhaps it is some oil they secrete, some odour they give out . . . I don't know . . .'

Then, weeping, Doctor Goodbody said: 'Oh, nightmare – nightmare – nightmare! To think of the depths to which a noble creature can be degraded by hunger! Horrible, horrible!'

'Some debased form of life that you found in the jungle above the source of the Amer?' I suggested. 'Some degenerate kind of anthropoid?'

'No, no, no. *Men*! Now surely you remember Professor Yeoward's technological expedition?'

'It was lost,' I said.

'All but me,' he said. '. . . We had bad luck. At the Anaña rapids we lost two canoes, half our supplies and most of our instruments. And also Doctor Terry, and Jack Lambert, and eight of our carriers . . .

'Then we were in Ahu territory where the Indians use poison darts, but we made friends with them and bribed them to carry our stuff westward through the jungle . . . because, you see, all science starts with a guess, a rumour, an old wives' tale; and the object of Professor Yeoward's expedition was to investigate a series of Indian folk tales that tallied. Legends of a race of gods that came down from the sky in a great flame when the world was very young . . .

'Line by crisscross line, and circle by concentric circle, Yeoward localized the place in which these tales had their root – an unexplored place that has no name because the Indians refuse to give it a name, it being what they call a "bad place".'

His chills subsiding and his fever abating, Doctor Goodbody spoke calmly and rationally now. He said, with a short laugh: 'I don't know why, whenever I get a touch of fever, the memory of those boneless men comes back in a nightmare to give me the horrors . . .

'So, we went to look for the place where the gods came down in flame out of the night. The little tattooed Indians took us to the edge of the Ahu territory and then put down their packs and asked for their pay, and no consideration would induce them to go further. We were going, they said, to a very bad place. Their chief, who had been a great man in his day, sign-writing with a twig, told us that he had strayed there once, and drew a picture of something with an oval body and four limbs, at which he spat before rubbing it out with his foot in the dirt. Spiders? we asked. Crabs? What?

'So we were forced to leave what we could not carry with the old chief against our return, and go on unaccompanied, Yeoward and I, through thirty miles of the rottenest jungle in the world. We made about a quarter of a mile in a day . . . a pestilential place! When that stinking wind blows out of the jungle, I smell nothing but death, and panic . . .

'But, at last, we cut our way to the plateau and climbed the slope, and there we saw something marvellous. It was something that had been a gigantic machine. Originally it must have been a pear-shaped thing, at least a thousand feet long and, in its widest part, six hundred feet in diameter. I don't know of what metal it had been made, because there was only a dusty outline of a hull and certain ghostly remains of unbelievably intricate mechanisms to prove that it had ever been. We could not guess from where it had come; but the impact of its landing had made a great valley in the middle of the plateau.

'It was the discovery of the age! It proved that, countless ages ago, this planet had been visited by people from the stars! Wild with excitement, Yeoward and I plunged into this fabulous ruin. But whatever we touched fell away to fine powder.

'At last, on the third day, Yeoward found a semicircular plate of some extraordinarily hard metal, which was covered with the most maddeningly familiar diagrams. We cleaned it, and for twenty-four hours, scarcely pausing to eat and drink, Yeoward studied it. And, then, before the dawn of the fifth day he awoke me, with a great cry, and said: "It's a map, a map of the heavens, and a chart of a course from Mars to Earth!"

'And he showed me how those ancient explorers of space had proceeded from Mars to Earth, via the moon ... To crash on this naked plateau in this green hell of a jungle? I wondered. "Ah, but was it a jungle then?" said Yeoward. "This may have happened five million years ago!"

'I said: "Oh, but surely! it took only a few hundred years to bury Rome. How could this thing have stayed above ground for five thousand years, let alone five million?" Yeoward said: "It didn't. The earth swallows things and regurgitates them. This is a volcanic region. One little upheaval can swallow a city, and one tiny peristalsis in the bowels of the earth can bring its remains to light again a million years later. So it must have been with the machine from Mars ..."

'"I wonder who was inside it," I said. Yeoward replied: "Very likely some utterly alien creatures that couldn't tolerate the Earth, and died, or else were killed in the crash. No skeleton could survive such a space of time."

'So, we built up the fire, and Yeoward went to sleep. Having slept, I watched. Watched for what? I didn't know. Jaguars, peccaries, snakes? None of these beasts climbed up to the plateau; there was nothing for them up there. Still, unaccountably, I was afraid.

'There was the weight of ages on the place. *Respect old age*, one is told ... The greater the age, the deeper the respect, you might say. But it is not respect; it is dread, it is fear of time and death, sir! ... I must have dozed, because the fire was burning low – I had been most careful to keep it alive and bright – when I caught my first glimpse of the boneless men.

'Starting up, I saw, at the rim of the plateau, a pair of eyes that picked up luminosity from the fading light of the fire. *A jaguar*, I thought, and took up my rifle. But it could not have been a jaguar because, when I looked left and right I saw that the plateau was ringed with pairs of shining eyes ... as it might be, a collar of opals; and there came to my nostrils an odour of God knows what.

'Fear has its smell as any animal-trainer will tell you. Sickness has its smell – ask any nurse. These smells compel healthy animals to fight or to run away. This was a combination of the two, plus a stink of vegetation gone bad. I fired at the pair of eyes I had first seen. Then, all the eyes disappeared while, from the jungle, there came a chattering and a twittering of monkeys and birds, as the echoes of the shot went flapping away.

'And then, thank God, the dawn came. I should not have liked to see by artificial light the thing I had shot between the eyes.

'It was grey and, in texture, tough and gelatinous. Yet, in form, externally, it was not unlike a human being. It had eyes, and there were either vestiges – or rudiments – of head, and neck, and a kind of limbs.

'Yeoward told me that I must pull myself together; overcome my "childish revulsion", as he called it; and look into the nature of the beast. I may say that he kept a long way away from it when I opened it. It was my job as zoologist of the expedition, and I had to do it. Microscopes and other delicate instruments had been lost with the canoes. I worked with a knife and forceps. And found? Nothing: a kind of digestive system enclosed in very tough jelly, a rudimentary nervous system, and a brain about the size of a walnut. The entire creature, stretched out, measured four feet.

'In a laboratory I could tell you, perhaps, something about it . . . with an assistant or two, to keep me company. As it was, I did what I could with a hunting-knife and forceps, without dyes or microscope, swallowing my nausea – it was a nauseating thing – memorizing what I found. But, as the sun rose higher, the thing liquefied, melted, until by nine o'clock there was nothing but a glutinous grey puddle, with two green eyes swimming in it . . . And those eyes – I can see them now – burst with a thick *pop*, making a detestable sticky ripple in that puddle of corruption . . .

'After that, I went away for a while. When I came back, the sun had burned it all away, and there was nothing but something like what you see after a dead jellyfish has evaporated on a hot beach. Slime. Yeoward had a white face when he asked me: "What the devil is it?" I told him that I didn't know, that it was something outside my experience, and that although I pretended to be a man of science with a detached mind, nothing would induce me ever to touch one of the things again.

'Yeoward said: "You're getting hysterical, Goodbody. Adopt the proper attitude. God knows, we are not here for the good of our health. Science, man, science! Not a day passes but some doctor pokes his fingers into fouler things than that!" I said: "Don't you believe it. Professor Yeoward, I have handled and dissected some pretty queer things in my time, but this is something repulsive. I have nerves? I dare say. Maybe we should have brought a psychiatrist . . . I notice, by the way, that you aren't too anxious to come close to me after I've tampered with that thing. I'll shoot one with pleasure, but if you want to investigate it, try it yourself and see!"

'Yeoward said that he was deeply occupied with his metal plate. There was no doubt, he told me, that this machine had come from Mars. But, evidently, he preferred to keep the fire between himself and me, after I had touched that abomination of hard jelly.

'Yeoward kept himself to himself, rummaging in the ruin. I went about my business, which was to investigate forms of animal life. I do not know what I might have found, if I had had – I don't say the courage, because I didn't lack that – if I had had some company. Alone, my nerve broke.

'It happened one morning. I went into the jungle that surrounded us, trying to swallow the fear that choked me, and drive away the sense of revulsion that not only made me want to turn and run, but made me afraid to turn my back even to get away. You may or may not know that, of all the beasts that live in that jungle, the most impregnable is the sloth. He finds a stout limb, climbs out on it, and hangs from it by his twelve steely claws; a tardigrade that lives on leaves. Your tardigrade is so tenacious that even in death, shot through the heart, it will hang on to its branch. It has an immensely tough hide covered by an impenetrable coat of coarse, matted hair. A panther or a jaguar is helpless against the passive resistance of such a creature. It finds itself a tree, which it does not leave until it has eaten every leaf, and chooses for a sleeping place a branch exactly strong enough to bear its weight.

'In this detestable jungle, on one of my brief expeditions – brief, because I was alone and afraid – I stopped to watch a giant sloth hanging motionless from the largest bough of a half-denuded tree, asleep, impervious, indifferent. Then, out of that stinking green twilight came a horde of those jellyfish things. They *poured up* the tree, and writhed along the branch.

'Even the sloth, which generally knows no fear, was afraid. It tried to run away, hooked itself on to a thinner part of the branch, which broke. It fell, and at once was covered with a shuddering mass of jelly. Those boneless men do not bite: they suck. And, as they suck, their colour changes from grey to pink and then to brown.

'But they are afraid of us. There is race-memory involved here. We repel them, and they repel us. When they became aware of my presence, they – I was going to say, ran away – they slid away, dissolved into the shadows that kept dancing and dancing and dancing under the trees. And the horror came upon me, so that I ran away, and arrived back at our camp, bloody about the face with thorns, and utterly exhausted.

'Yeoward was lancing a place in his ankle. A tourniquet was tied under his knee. Nearby lay a dead snake. He had broken its back with that same metal plate, but it had bitten him first. He said: 'What kind of a snake do you call this? I'm afraid it is venomous. I feel a numbness in my cheeks and around my heart, and I cannot feel my hands.'

'I said: "Oh, my God! You've been bitten by a jararacal!"

'"And we have lost our medical supplies," he said, with regret. "And there is so much work left to do. Oh, dear me, dear me! . . . Whatever happens, my dear fellow, take *this* and get back."

'And he gave me that semicircle of unknown metal as a sacred trust. Two hours later, he died. That night the circle of glowing eyes grew narrower. I emptied my rifle at it, time and again. At dawn, the boneless men disappeared.

'I heaped rocks on the body of Yeoward. I made a pylon, so that the men without bones could not get at him. Then – oh, so dreadfully lonely and afraid! – I shouldered my pack, and took my rifle and my machete, and ran away, down the trail we had covered. But I lost my way.

'Can by can of food, I shed weight. Then my rifle went, and my ammunition. After that, I threw away even my machete. A long time later, that semicircular plate became too heavy for me, so I tied it to a tree with liana vine, and went on.

'So I reached the Ahu territory, where the tattooed men nursed me and were kind to me. The women chewed my food for me, before they fed me, until I was strong again. Of the stores we had left there, I took only as much as I might need, leaving the rest as payment for guides and men to man the canoe down the river. And so I got back out of the jungle . . .

'Please give me a little more rum.' His hand was steady, now, as he drank, and his eyes were clear.

I said to him: 'Assuming that what you say is true: these "boneless men" – they were, I presume, the Martians? Yet it sounds unlikely, surely? Do invertebrates smelt hard metals and—'

'Who said anything about Martians?' cried Doctor Goodbody, 'No, no, no! The Martians came here, adapted themselves to new conditions of life. Poor fellows, they changed, sank low; went through a whole new process – a painful process of evolution. What I'm trying to tell you, you fool, is that Yeoward and I did *not* discover Martians. Idiot, don't you see? *Those boneless things are men. We are Martians!'*

File classification: Alien Abduction
Location: Hawaii, USA

Title: Goldfish Bowl
Writer: *Robert A. Heinlein*

Briefing: *Alien Abduction – conviction held by an increasing number of people that they have been forcibly captured by space travelling aliens for study and/or experimentation.* When a number of fishing vessels and their crews go missing without trace in an area just off the coast of Hawaii, Doctor Graves from the Navy Department is sent to investigate. He has a hunch that a phenomenon that looks like a giant fireball *might* be the cause. But when he and a colleague get too close to the source of the disappearances, they suddenly find themselves prisoners in a totally alien environment . . .

Author: The American Robert A. Heinlein was for many years one of the world's most important and innovative sf writers – an occupation he turned to after serving as an officer in the US Navy until ill-health forced him to quit. Hugely imaginative and ahead of his time in his ideas, Heinlein began writing what he later referred to as his 'Future History' series in the Forties, but earned his enduring reputation in the following decade with *Starship Troopers* (1959), *Stranger in a Strange Land* (1961) and *The Moon is a Harsh Mistress* (1966). Heinlein's interest in encounters between mankind and aliens became generally evident in his novel, *The Puppet Masters* (1951), but he had actually tackled the theme a decade earlier in 'Goldfish Bowl' which was published in *Astounding* in 1942. Heinlein's development of the story established a benchmark for many subsequent tales – and it is also interesting to note his use of the term 'X' in relation to the paranormal more than a quarter of a century before the phenomenal success of *The X Files*.

On the horizon lay the immobile cloud which capped the incredible waterspouts known as the Pillars of Hawaii.

Captain Blake lowered his binoculars. 'There they stand, gentlemen.'

In addition to the naval personnel of the watch, the bridge of the hydrographic survey ship U.S.S. *Mahan* held two civilians; the captain's words were addressed to them. The elder and smaller of the pair peered intently through a spyglass he had borrowed from the quartermaster. 'I can't make them out,' he complained.

'Here – try my glasses, doctor,' Blake suggested, passing over his binoculars. He turned to the officer of the deck and added, 'Have the forward range finger manned, if you please, Mr Mott.' Lieutenant Mott caught the eye of the bos'n's mate of the watch, listening from a discreet distance, and jerked a thumb upward. The petty officer stepped to the microphone, piped a shrill stand-by, and the metallic voice of the loudspeaker filled the ship, drowning out the next words of the captain:

'Raaaaange one! Maaaaaaaan and cast loose!'

'I asked,' the captain repeated, 'if that was any better.'

'I think I see them,' Jacobson Graves acknowledged. 'Two dark vertical stripes, from the cloud to the horizon.'

'That's it.'

The other civilian, Bill Eisenberg, had taken the telescope when Graves had surrendered it for the binoculars. 'I got 'em, too,' he announced. 'There's nothing wrong with this 'scope, Doc. But they don't look as big as I had expected,' he admitted.

'They are still beyond the horizon,' Blake explained. 'You see only the upper segments. But they stand just under eleven thousand feet from water line to cloud – if they are still running true to form.'

Graves looked up quickly. 'Why the mental reservation? Haven't they been?'

Captain Blake shrugged. 'Sure. Right on the nose. But they ought not to be there at all – four months ago they did not exist. How do I know what they will be doing today – or tomorrow?'

Graves nodded. 'I see your point – and agree with it. Can we estimate their height from the distance?'

'I'll see.' Blake stuck his head into the charthouse. 'Any reading, Archie?'

'Just a second, captain.' The navigator stuck his face against a voice tube and called out, 'Range!'

A muffled voice replied, 'Range one – no reading.'

'Something greater than twenty miles,' Blake told Graves cheerfully. 'You'll have to wait, doctor.'

Lieutenant Mott directed the quartermaster to make three bells; the captain left the bridge, leaving word that he was to be informed when the ship approached the critical limit of three miles from the Pillars. Somewhat reluctantly, Graves and Eisenberg followed him down; they had barely time enough to dress before dining with the captain.

Captain Blake's manners were old-fashioned; he did not permit the conversation to turn to shop talk until the dinner had reached the coffee and cigars stage. 'Well, gentlemen,' he began, as he lit up, 'just what is it you propose to do?'

'Didn't the Navy Department tell you?' Graves asked with a quick look.

'Not much. I have had one letter, directing me to place my ship and command at your disposal for research concerning the Pillars, and a dispatch two days ago telling me to take you aboard this morning. No details.'

Graves looked nervously at Eisenberg, then back to the captain. He cleared his throat. 'Uh – we propose, captain, to go up the Kanaka column and down the Wahini.'

Blake gave him a sharp look, started to speak, reconsidered, and started again. 'Doctor – you'll forgive me, I hope; I don't mean to be rude – but that sounds utterly crazy. A fancy way to commit suicide.'

'It may be a little dangerous—'

'Hummph!'

'—but we have the means to accomplish it, if, as we believe to be true, the Kanaka column supplies the water which becomes the Wahini column on the return trip.' He outlined the method. He and Eisenberg totalled between them nearly twenty-five years of bathysphere experience, eight for Eisenberg, seventeen for himself. They had brought aboard the *Mahan*, at present in an uncouth crate on the fantail, a modified bathysphere. Externally it was a bathysphere with its anchor weights removed; internally it much more nearly resembled some of the complicated barrels in which foolhardy exhibitionists have essayed the spectacular, useless trip over Niagara Falls. It would supply air, stuffy but breathable, for forty-eight hours; it held water and concentrated food for at least that period; there were even rude but adequate sanitary arrangements.

But its principal feature was an anti-shock harness, a glorified corset, a strait-jacket, in which a man could hang suspended clear of the walls by means of a network of Gideon cord and steel springs. In it, a man might reasonably hope to survive most violent pummelling. He could perhaps be shot from a cannon, bounced down a hillside, subjected to the sadistic mercy of a baggage smasher, and still survive with bones intact and viscera unruptured.

Blake poked a finger at a line sketch with which Graves had illustrated his description. 'You actually intend to try to ascend the Pillars in that?'

Eisenberg replied. 'Not him, captain. Me.'

Graves reddened. 'My damned doctor—'

'*And* your colleagues,' Eisenberg added. 'It's this way, captain: There's nothing wrong with Doc's nerve, but he has a leaky heart, a pair of submarine ears, and a set of not-so-good arteries. So the Institute has delegated me to kinda watch over him.'

'Now look here,' Graves protested, 'Bill, you're not going to be stuffy about this. I'm an old man; I'll never have another such chance.'

'No go,' Eisenberg denied. 'Captain, I wish to inform you that the Institute vested title of record to that gear we brought aboard in me, just to keep the old war horse from doing anything foolish.'

'That's your pidgin,' Blake answered testily. 'My instructions are to facilitate Dr Graves's research. Assuming that one or the other of you wish to commit suicide in that steel coffin, how do you propose to enter the Kanaka Pillar?'

'Why, that's your job, captain. You put the sphere into the up column and pick it up again when it comes down the down column.'

Blake pursed his lips, then slowly shook his head. 'I can't do that.'

'Huh? Why not?'

'I will not take my ship closer than three miles to the Pillars. The *Mahan* is a sound ship, but she is not built for speed. She can't make more than twelve knots. Some place inside that circle the surface current which feeds the Kanaka column will exceed twelve knots. I don't care to find out where, by losing my ship.

'There have been an unprecedented number of unreported fishing vessels out of the island lately. I don't care to have the *Mahan* listed.'

'You think they went up the column?'

'I do.'

'But look, captain,' suggested Bill Eisenberg, 'you wouldn't have to risk the ship. You could launch the sphere from a power boat.'

Blake shook his head. 'Out of the question,' he said grimly. 'Even if the ship's boats were built for the job, which they aren't, I will not risk naval personnel. This isn't war.'

'I wonder,' said Graves softly.

'What's that?'

Eisenberg chuckled. 'Doc has a romantic notion that all the odd phenomena turned up in the past few years can be hooked together into one smooth theory with a single, sinister cause – everything from the Pillars to LaGrange's fireballs.'

'LaGrange's fireballs? How could there be any connection there? They are simply static electricity, allee samee heat lightning. I know; I've seen 'em.'

The scientists were at once attentive, Graves's pique and Eisenberg's amusement alike buried in truth-tropism. 'You did? When? Where?'

'Golf course at Hilo. Last March. I was—'

'*That* case! That was one of the disappearance cases!'

'Yes, of course. I'm trying to tell you. I was standing in a sand trap near the thirteenth green, when I happened to look up—' A clear, balmy island day. No clouds, barometer normal, light breeze. Nothing to suggest atmospheric disturbance, no maxima of sunspots, no static on the radio. Without warning a half dozen, or more, giant fireballs – ball 'lightning' on an unprecedented scale – floated across the golf course in a sort of skirmish line, a line described by some observers as mathematically even – an assertion denied by others.

A woman player, a tourist from the mainland, screamed and began to run. The flanking ball nearest her left its place in line and danced after her. No one seemed sure that the ball touched her – Blake could not say although he had watched it happen – but when the ball had passed on, there she lay on the grass, dead.

A local medico of somewhat flamboyant reputation insisted that he found evidence in the cadaver of both coagulation and electrolysis, but the jury that sat on the case followed the coroner's advice in calling it heart failure, a verdict heartily approved by the local chamber of commerce and tourist bureau.

The man who disappeared did not try to run; his fate came to meet him. He was a caddy, a Japanese-Portygee-Kanaka mixed breed, with no known relatives, a fact which should have made it easy to leave his name out of the news reports had not a reporter smelled it out. 'He was standing on the green, not more than twenty-five yards away from me,' Blake recounted, 'when the fireballs approached. One passed on each side of me. My skin itched, and my hair stood up. I could smell ozone. I stood still—'

'That saved you,' observed Graves.

'Nuts,' said Eisenberg. 'Standing in the dry sand of the trap was what saved him.'

'Bill, you're a fool,' Graves said wearily. 'These fireball things perform with intelligent awareness.'

Blake checked his account. 'Why do you assume that, doctor?'

'Never mind, for the moment, please. Go on with your story.'

'Hm-m-m. Well, they passed on by me. The caddy fellow was directly in the course of one of them. I don't believe he saw it – back toward it, you see. It reached him, enveloped him, passed on – but the boy was gone.'

Graves nodded. 'That checks with the accounts I have seen. Odd that I did not recall your name from the reports.'

'I stayed in the background,' Blake said shortly. 'Don't like reporters.'

'Hm-m-m. Anything to add to the reports that did come out? Any errors in them?'

'None that I can recall. Did the reports mention the bag of golf clubs he was carrying?'

'I think not.'

'They were found on the beach, six miles away.'

Eisenberg sat up. 'That's news,' he said. 'Tell me: Was there anything to suggest how far they had fallen? Were they smashed or broken?'

Blake shook his head. 'They weren't even scratched, nor was the beach sand disturbed. But they were – ice-cold.'

Graves waited for him to go on; when the captain did not do so he inquired, 'What do you make of it?'

'Me? I make nothing of it.'

'How do you explain it?'

'I don't. Unclassified electrical phenomena. However, if you want a rough guess, I'll give you one. This fireball is a static field of high potential. It englobes the caddy and charges him, whereupon he bounces away like a pith ball – electrocuted, incidentally. When the charge dissipates, he falls into the sea.'

'So? There was a case like it in Kansas, rather too far from the sea.'

'The body might simply never have been found.'

'They never are. But even so – how do you account for the clubs being deposited so gently? And why were they cold?'

'Dammit, man, *I* don't know! I'm no theoretician; I'm a maritime engineer by profession, an empiricist by disposition. Suppose you tell me.'

'All right – but bear in mind that my hypothesis is merely tentative, a basis for investigation. I see in these several phenomena, the Pillars, the giant fireballs, a number of other assorted phenomena which should never have happened, but did – including the curious case of a small mountain peak south of Boulder, Colorado, which had its tip leveled off "spontaneously" – I see in these things evidence of intelligent direction, a single conscious cause.' He shrugged. 'Call it the "X" factor. I'm looking for X.'

Eisenberg assumed a look of mock sympathy. 'Poor old Doc,' he sighed. 'Sprung a leak at last.'

The other two ignored the crack. Blake inquired, 'You are primarily an ichthyologist, aren't you?'

'Yes.'

'How did you get started along this line?'

'I don't know. Curiosity, I suppose. My boisterous young friend here would tell you that ichthyology is derived from "icky".'

Blake turned to Eisenberg. 'But aren't *you* an ichthyologist?'

'Hell, no! I'm an oceanographer specialising in ecology.'

'He's quibbling,' observed Graves. 'Tell Captain Blake about Cleo and Pat.'

Eisenberg looked embarrassed. 'They're damned nice pets,' he said defensively.

Blake looked puzzled; Graves explained. 'He kids me, but *his* secret shame is a pair of goldfish. Goldfish! You'll find 'em in the washbasin in his stateroom this minute.'

'Scientific interest?' Blake inquired with a dead pan.

'Oh, no! He thinks they are devoted to him.'

'They're damned nice pets,' Eisenberg insisted. 'They don't bark, they don't scratch, they don't make messes. And Cleo does so have expression!'

In spite of his initial resistance to their plans Blake co-operated actively in trying to find a dodge whereby the proposed experiment could be performed without endangering naval personnel or matériel. He liked these two; he understood their curious mixture of selfless recklessness and extreme caution; it matched his own – it was professionalism, as distinguished from economic motivation.

He offered the services of his master diver, an elderly commissioned warrant officer, and his technical crew in checking their gear. 'You know,' he added, 'there is some reason to believe that your bathysphere could make the round trip, aside from the proposition that what goes up must come down. You know of the *VJ-14?'*

'Was that the naval plane lost in the early investigation?'

'Yes.' He buzzed for his orderly. 'Have my writer bring up the jacket on the *VJ-14,'* he directed.

Attempts to reconnoitre the strange 'permanent' cloud and its incredible waterspouts had been made by air soon after its discovery. Little was learned. A plane would penetrate the cloud. Its ignition would fail; out it would glide, unharmed, whereupon its engines would fire again. Back into the cloud – engine failure. The vertical reach of the cloud was greater than the ceiling of any plane.

'The *VJ-14*,' Blake stated, referring occasionally to the file jacket which had been fetched, 'made an air reconnaissance of the Pillars themselves on 12 May, attended by the U.S.S. *Pelican*. Besides the pilot and radioman she carried a cinematographer and a chief aerographer, Mm-m-m – only the last two entries seem to be pertinent: "Changing course. Will fly between the Pillars – *14*," and "0913 – Ship does not respond to controls – *14*," Telescopic observation from the *Pelican* shows that she made a tight upward spiral around the Kanaka Pillar, about one and a half turns, and was sucked into the column itself. Nothing was seen to fall.

'Incidentally the pilot, Lieutenant – m-m-m-m, yes – Mattson – Lieutenant Mattson was exonerated posthumously by the court of inquiry. Oh, yes, here's the point pertinent to our question: From the log of the *Pelican*: "1709 – Picked up wreckage identified as part of *VJ-14*. See additional sheet for itemised description." We needn't bother with that. Point is, they picked it up four miles from the base of the Wahini Pillar on the side away from the Kanaka. The inference is obvious and your scheme might work. Not that you'd live through it.'

'I'll chance it,' Eisenberg stated.

'Mm-m-m – yes. But I was going to suggest we send up a dead load, say a crate of eggs packed into a hogshead.' The buzzer from the bridge sounded; Captain Blake raised his voice toward the brass funnel of a voice tube in the overhead. 'Yes?'

'Eight o'clock, Captain. Eight o'clock lights and galley fires out; prisoners secured.'

'Thank you, sir.' Blake stood up. 'We can get together on the details in the morning.'

A fifty-foot motor launch bobbed listlessly astern the *Mahan*. A nine-inch coir line joined it to its mother ship; bound to it at fathom intervals was a telephone line ending in a pair of headphones worn by a signalman seated in the stern sheets of the launch. A pair of flags and a spyglass lay on the thwart beside him; his blouse had crawled up, exposing part of the lurid cover of a copy of *Dynamic Tales*, smuggled along as a precaution against boredom.

Already in the coat were the coxswain, the engineman, the boat officer, Graves and Eisenberg. With them, forward in the boat, was a breaker of water rations, two fifty-gallon drums of gasoline – and a hogshead. It contained not only a carefully packed crate of eggs but also a jury-rigged smoke-signal device, armed three ways – delayed action set for eight, nine, and ten hours; radio relay triggered from the ship; and simple salt-water penetration to complete an electrical circuit. The torpedo gunner in charge of diving hoped that one of them might work and thereby aid in locating the hogshead. He was busy trying to devise more nearly foolproof gear for the bathysphere.

The boat officer signalled ready to the bridge. A megaphoned bellow responded, 'Pay her out handsomely!' The boat drifted slowly away from the ship and directly toward the Kanaka Pillar, three miles away.

The Kanaka Pillar loomed above them, still nearly a mile away but loweringly impressive nevertheless. The place where it disappeared in cloud seemed almost overhead, falling toward them. Its five-hundred-foot-thick trunk gleamed purplish-black, more like polished steel than water.

'Try your engine again, coxswain.'

'Aye, aye, sir!' The engine coughed, took hold; the engine-man eased in the clutch, the screw bit in, and the boat surged forward, taking the strain off the towline. 'Slack line, sir.'

'Stop your engine.' The boat officer turned to his passengers. 'What's the trouble, Mr Eisenberg? Cold feet?'

'No, dammit – seasick. I *hate* a small boat.'

'Oh, that's too bad. I'll see if we haven't got a pickle in that chow up forward.'

'Thanks, but pickles don't help me. Never mind, I can stand it.'

The boat officer shrugged, turned and let his eye travel up the dizzy length of the column. He whistled, something which he had done every time he had looked at it. Eisenberg, made nervous by his nausea, was beginning to find it cause for homicide. '*Whew!* You really intend to try to go up that thing, Mr Eisenberg?'

'I do!'

The boat officer looked startled at the tone, laughed uneasily, and added, 'Well, you'll be worse than seasick, if you ask me.'

Nobody had. Graves knew his friend's temperament; he made conversation for the next few minutes.

'Try your engine, coxswain.' The petty officer acknowledged, and reported back quickly:

'Starter doesn't work, sir.'

'Help the engine-man get a line on the flywheel. I'll take the tiller.'

The two men cranked the engine over easily, but got no answering cough. 'Prime it!' Still no results.

The boat officer abandoned the useless tiller and jumped down into the engine space to lend his muscle to heaving on the cranking line. Over his shoulder he ordered the signalman to notify the ship.

'Launch Three, calling bridge. Launch Three, calling bridge. Bridge –

reply! Testing – testing.' The signalman slipped a phone off one ear. 'Phone's dead, sir.'

'Get busy with your flags. Tell 'em to haul us in!' The officer wiped sweat from his face and straightened up. He glanced nervously at the current *slap-slapping* against the boat's side.

Graves touched his arm. 'How about the barrel?'

'Put it over the side if you like. I'm busy. Can't you raise them, Sears?'

'I'm trying, sir.'

'Come on, Bill,' Graves said to Eisenberg. The two of them slipped forward in the boat, threading their way past the engine on the side away from the three men sweating over the flywheel. Graves cut the hogshead loose from its lashings, then the two attempted to get a purchase on the awkward, unhandy object. It and its light load weighed less than two hundred pounds, but it was hard to manage, especially on the uncertain footing of heaving floorboards.

They wrestled it outboard somehow, with one smashed finger for Eisenberg, a badly banged shin for Graves. It splashed heavily, drenching them with sticky salt water, and bobbed astern, carried rapidly toward the Kanaka Pillar by the current which fed it.

'Ship answers, sir!'

'Good! Tell them to haul us in – *carefully*.' The boat officer jumped out of the engine space and ran forward, where he checked again the secureness with which the towline was fastened.

Graves tapped him on the shoulder. 'Can't we stay here until we see the barrel enter the column?'

'No! Right now you had better pray that that line holds, instead of worrying about the barrel – or we go up the column, too. Sears, has the ship acknowledged?'

'Just now, sir.'

'Why a coir line, Mr Parker?' Eisenberg inquired, his nausea forgotten in the excitement. 'I'd rather depend on steel, or even good stout Manila.'

'Because coir floats, and the others don't,' the officer answered snappishly. 'Two miles of line would drag us to the bottom. *Sears*! Tell them to ease the strain. We're shipping water.'

'Aye, aye, sir!'

The hogshead took less than four minutes to reach the column, enter it, a fact which Graves ascertained by borrowing the signalman's glass to follow it on the last leg of its trip – which action won him a dirty look from the nervous boat officer. Some minutes later, when the boat was about five hundred yards farther from the Pillar than it had been at nearest approach, the telephone came suddenly to life. The starter of the engine was tested immediately; the engine roared into action.

The trip back was made with engine running to take the strain off the towline – at half speed and with some manoeuvring, in order to avoid fouling the screw with the slack bight of the line.

The smoke signal worked – one circuit or another. The plume of smoke was sighted two miles south of the Wahini Pillar, elapsed time from the moment the vessel had entered the Kanaka column just over eight hours.

Bill Eisenberg climbed into the saddle of the exerciser in which he was to receive antibends treatment – thirty minutes of hard work to stir up his circulation while breathing an atmosphere of hellum and oxygen, at the end of which time the nitrogen normally dissolved in his bloodstream would be largely replaced by helium. The exerciser itself was simply an old bicycle mounted on a stationary platform. Blake looked it over. 'You needn't have bothered to bring this,' he remarked. 'We've a better one aboard. Standard practice for diving operations these days.'

'We didn't know that,' Graves answered. 'Anyhow, this one will do. All set, Bill?'

'I guess so.' He glanced over his shoulder to where the steel bulk of the bathysphere lay, uncrated, checked, and equipped, ready to be swung outboard by the boat crane. 'Got the gasket-sealing compound?'

'Sure. The Iron Maiden is all right. The gunner and I will seal you in. Here's your mask.'

Eisenberg accepted the inhaling mask, started to strap it on, checked himself. Graves noticed the look on his face. 'What's the trouble, son?'

'Doc . . . uh—'

'Yes?'

'I say – you'll look out for Cleo and Pat, won't you?'

'Why, sure. But they won't need anything in the length of time you'll be gone.'

'Um-m-m, no, I suppose not. But you'll look out for 'em?'

'Sure.'

'OK.' Eisenberg slipped the inhaler over his face, waved his hand to the gunner waiting by the gas bottles. The gunner eased open the cut-off valves, the gas lines hissed, and Eisenberg began to pedal like a six-day racer.

With thirty minutes to kill, Blake invited Graves to go forward with him for a smoke and a stroll on the fo'c's'le. They had completed about twenty turns when Blake paused by the wildcat, took his cigar from his mouth and remarked, 'Do you know, I believe he has a good chance of completing the trip.'

'So? I'm glad to hear that.'

'Yes, I do, really. The success of the trial with the dead load convinced me. And whether the smoke gear works or not, if that globe comes back down the Wahini Pillar, *I'll find it.*'

'I know you will. It was a good idea of yours, to paint it yellow.'

'Help us to spot it, all right. I don't think he'll learn anything, however. He won't see a thing through those ports but blue water, from the time he enters the column to the time we pick him up.'

'Perhaps so.'

'What else *could* he see?'

'I don't know. Whatever it is that *made* those Pillars, perhaps.'

Blake dumped the ashes from his cigar carefully over the rail before replying. 'Doctor, I don't understand you. To my mind, those Pillars are a natural, even though strange, phenomenon.'

'And to me it's equally obvious that they are not "natural". They exhibit intelligent interference with the ordinary processes of nature as clearly as if they had a sign saying so hung on them.'

'I don't see how you can say that. Obviously, they are not man-made.'

'No.'

'Then who did make them – if they were made?'

'I don't know.'

Blake started to speak, shrugged, and held his tongue. They resumed their stroll. Graves turned aside to chuck his cigarette overboard, glancing outboard as he did so.

He stopped, stared, then called out: 'Captain Blake!'

'Eh?' The captain turned and looked where Graves pointed. 'Great God! Fireballs!'

'That's what I thought.'

'They're some distance away,' Blake observed, more to himself than to Graves. He turned decisively. 'Bridge!' he shouted. 'Bridge! Bridge ahoy!'

'Bridge, aye aye!'

'Mr Weems – pass the word: "All hands, below decks." Dog down all ports. Close all hatches. And close up the bridge itself! Sound the general alarm.'

'Aye aye, sir!'

'Move!' Turning to Graves, he added, 'Come inside.' Graves followed him; the captain himself stopped to dog down the door by which they entered. Blake pounded up the inner ladders to the bridge, Graves in his train. The ship was filled with whine of the bos'n pipe, the raucous voice of the loudspeaker, the clomp of hurrying feet, and the monotonous, menacing *cling-cling cling!* of the general alarm.

The watch on the bridge were still struggling with the last of the heavy glass shutters of the bridge when the captain burst into their midst. 'I'll take it, Mr Weems,' he snapped. In one continuous motion he moved from one side of the bridge to the other, letting his eye sweep the port side aft, the fo'c's'le, the starboard side aft, and finally rest on the fireballs – distinctly nearer and heading straight for the ship. He cursed. 'Your friend did not get the news,' he said to Graves. He grasped the crank which could open or close the after starboard shutter of the bridge.

Graves looked past his shoulder, saw that he meant – the afterdeck was empty, save for one lonely figure pedalling away on a stationary bicycle. The LaGrange fireballs were closing in.

The shutter stuck, jammed tight, would not open. Blake stopped trying, swung quickly to the loudspeaker control panel, and cut in the whole board without bothering to select the proper circuit. 'Eisenberg! *Get below!*'

Eisenberg must have heard his name called, for he turned his head and looked over his shoulder – Graves saw distinctly – just as the fireball reached him. It passed on, and the saddle of the exerciser was empty.

The exerciser was undamaged, they found, when they were able to examine it. The rubber hose to the inhaler mask had been cut smoothly. There was no blood, no marks. Bill Eisenberg was simply gone.

'I'm going up.'

'You are in no physical shape to do so, doctor.'

'You are in no way responsible, Captain Blake.'

'I know that. You may go it you like – after we have searched for your friend's body.'

'Search be damned! I'm going up to *look* for him. If you are right, he's dead, and there is no point in searching for his body. If I'm right, there is just an outside chance of finding him – up there!' He pointed toward the cloud cap of the Pillars.

Blake looked him over slowly, then turned to the master diver. 'Mr Hargreave, find an inhaler mask for Dr Graves.'

They gave him thirty minutes of conditioning against the caisson disease while Blake looked on with expressionless silence. The ship's company, bluejackets and officers alike, stood back and kept quiet; they walked on eggs when the Old Man had that look.

Exercise completed, the diver crew dressed Graves rapidly and strapped him into the bathysphere with dispatch, in order not to expose him too long to the nitrogen in the air. Just before the escape port was dogged down Graves spoke up. 'Captain Blake.'

'Yes, doctor?'

'Bill's goldfish – will you look out for them?'

'Certainly, doctor.'

'Thanks.'

'Not at all. Are you ready?'

'Ready.'

Blake stepped forward, stuck an arm through the port of the sphere and shook hands with Graves. 'Good luck.' He withdrew his arm. 'Seal it up.'

They lowered it over the side; two motor launches nosed it half a mile in the direction of the Kanaka Pillar where the current was strong enough to carry it along. There they left it and bucked the current back to the ship, were hoisted in.

Blake followed it with his glasses from the bridge. It drifted slowly at first, then with increased speed as it approached the base of the column. It whipped into rapid motion the last few hundred yards; Blake saw a flash of yellow just above the water line, then nothing more.

Eight hours – no plume of smoke. Nine hours, ten hours, nothing. After twenty-four hours of steady patrol in the vicinity of the Wahini Pillar, Blake radioed the Bureau.

Four days of vigilance – Blake knew that the bathysphere's passenger must be dead; whether by suffocation, drowning, implosion, or other means was not important. He so reported and received orders to proceed on duty assigned. The ship's company was called to quarters; Captain Blake read the service for the dead aloud in a harsh voice, dropped over the side some rather wilted hibiscus blooms – all that his steward could produce at the time – and went to the bridge to set his course for Pearl Harbor.

On the way to the bridge he stopped for a moment at his cabin and called to his steward. 'You'll find some goldfish in the stateroom occupied by Mr Eisenberg. Find an appropriate container and place them in my cabin.'

'Yes, suh, Cap'n.'

When Bill Eisenberg came to his senses he was in a Place.

Sorry, but no other description is suitable; it lacked features. Oh, not entirely, of course – it was not dark where he was, nor was it in a state of vacuum, nor was it cold, nor was it too small for comfort. But it did lack features to such a remarkable extent that he had difficulty in estimating the size of the place. Consider – stereo vision, by which we estimate the size of things *directly*, does not work beyond twenty feet or so. At greater distances we depend on previous knowledge of the true size of familiar objects, usually making our estimates subconsciously – a man *so high* is about *that far* away, and vice versa.

But the Place contained no familiar objects. The ceiling was a considerable distance over his head, too far to touch by jumping. The floor curved up to join the ceiling and thus prevented further lateral progress of more than a dozen paces or so. He would become aware of the obstacle by losing his balance. (He had no reference lines by which to judge the vertical; furthermore, his sense of innate balance was affected by the mistreatment his inner ears had undergone through years of diving. It was easier to sit than to walk, nor was there any reason to walk, after the first futile attempt at exploration.)

When he first woke up he stretched and opened his eyes, looked around. The lack of detail confused him. It was as if he were on the inside of a giant eggshell, illuminated from without by a soft, mellow, slightly amber light. The formless vagueness bothered him; he closed his eyes, shook his head, and opened them again – no better.

He was beginning to remember his last experience before losing consciousness – the fireball swooping down, his frenzied, useless attempt to duck, the 'Hold your hats, boys!' thought that flashed through his mind in the long-drawn-out split second before contact. His orderly mind began to look for explanations. Knocked cold, he thought, and my optic nerve paralysed. Wonder if I'm blind for good.

Anyhow, they ought not to leave him alone like this in his present helpless condition. 'Doc!' he shouted. 'Doc Graves!'

No answer, no echo – he became aware that there was *no* sound, save for his own voice, none of the random little sounds that fill completely the normal 'dead' silence. This place was as silent as the inside of a sack of flour. Were his ears shot, too?

No, he had heard his own voice. At that moment he realized that he was looking at his own hands. Why, there was nothing wrong with his eyes – he could see them plainly!

And the rest of himself, too. He was naked.

It might have been several hours later, it might have been moments, when he reached the conclusion that he was dead. It was the only hypothesis which seemed to cover the facts. A dogmatic agnostic by faith, he had expected no survival after death; he had expected to go out like a light, with a sudden termination of consciousness. However, he had been subjected in a charge of static electricity more than sufficient to kill a man; when he regained awareness, he found himself without all the usual experience which makes up living. Therefore – he was dead. Q.E.D.

To be sure, he seemed to have a body, but he was acquainted with the subjective-objective paradox. He still had memory, the strongest pattern in one's memory is body awareness. This was not his body, but his detailed sensation memory of it. So he reasoned. Probably, he thought, my dream-body will slough away as my memory of the object-body fades.

There was nothing to do, nothing to experience, nothing to distract his mind. He fell asleep at last, thinking that, if this were death, it was damned dull!

He awoke refreshed, but quite hungry and extremely thirsty. The matter of dead, or not-dead, no longer concerned him; he was interested in neither theology nor metaphysics. He was hungry.

Furthermore, he experienced on awakening a phenomenon which destroyed most of the basis for his intellectual belief in his own death – it had never reached the stage of emotional conviction. Present there with him in the Place he found material objects other than himself, objects which could be seen and touched.

And eaten.

Which last was not immediately evident, for they did not look like food. There were two sorts. The first was an amorphous lump of nothing in particular, resembling a greyish cheese in appearance, slightly greasy to the touch, and not appetizing. The second sort was a group of objects of uniform and delightful appearance. They were spheres, a couple of dozen; each one seemed to Bill Eisenberg to be a duplicate of a crystal ball he had once purchased – true Brazilian rock crystal the perfect beauty of which he had not been able to resist; he had bought it and smuggled it home to gloat over in private.

The little spheres were like that in appearance. He touched one. It was smooth as crystal and had the same chaste coolness, but it was soft as jelly. It quivered like jelly, causing the lights within it to dance delightfully, before resuming its perfect roundness.

Pleasant as they were, they did not look like food, whereas the cheesy, soapy lump might be. He broke off a small piece, sniffed it, and tasted it tentatively. It was sour, nauseating, unpleasant. He spat it out, made a wry face, and wished heartily that he could brush his teeth. If that was food, he would have to be much hungrier—

He turned his attention back to the delightful little spheres of crystallike jelly. He balanced them in his palms, savouring their soft, smooth touch. In the heart of each he saw his own reflection, imaged in miniature, made elfin and graceful. He became aware almost for the first time of the serene beauty of the human figure, almost any human figure, when viewed as a composition and not as a mass of colloidal detail.

But thirst became more pressing than narcissist admiration. It occurred to him that the smooth, cool spheres, if held in the mouth, might promote salivation, as pebbles will. He tried it; the sphere he selected struck against his lower teeth as he placed it in his mouth, and his lips and chin were suddenly wet, while drops trickled down his chest. The spheres were water, nothing but water, no cellophane skin, no container of any sort. Water had been delivered to him, neatly packaged, by some esoteric trick of surface tension.

He tried another, handling it more carefully to insure that it was not pricked by his teeth until he had it in his mouth. It worked; his mouth was filled with cool, pure water – too quickly; he choked. But he had caught on to the trick; he drank four of the spheres.

His thirst satisfied, he became interested in the strange trick whereby water became its own container. The spheres were tough; he could not squeeze them into breaking down, nor did smashing them hard against the floor disturb their precarious balance. They bounced like golf balls and came up for more. He managed to pinch the surface of one between thumb and fingernail. It broke down at once, and the water trickled between his fingers – water alone, no skin nor foreign substance. It seemed that a cut alone could disturb the balance of tensions; even wetting had no effect, for he could hold one carefully in his mouth, remove it, and dry it off on his own skin.

He decided that, since his supply was limited, and no more water was in prospect, it would be wise to conserve what he had and experiment no further.

The relief of thirst increased the demands of hunger. He turned his attention again to the other substance and found that he could force himself to chew and swallow. It might not be food, it might even be poison, but it filled his stomach and stayed the pangs. He even felt well fed, once he had cleared out the taste with another sphere of water.

After eating he rearranged his thoughts. He was not dead, or, if he were, the difference between living and being dead was imperceptible, verbal. OK, he was alive. But he was shut up alone. Somebody knew where he was and was aware of him, for he had been supplied with food and drink – mysteriously but cleverly. *Ergo* – he was a prisoner, a word which implies a warden.

Whose prisoner? He had been struck by a LaGrange fireball and had awakened in his cell. It looked, he was forced to admit, as if Doc Graves had been right; the fireballs were intelligently controlled. Furthermore, the person or persons behind them had novel ideas as to how to care for prisoners as well as strange ways of capturing them.

Eisenberg was a brave man, as brave as the ordinary run of the race from which he sprang – a race as foolhardy as Pekingese dogs. He had the high degree of courage so common in the human race, a race capable of conceiving death, yet able to face its probability daily, on the highway, on the obstetrics table, on the battlefield, in the air, in the subway – and to face lightheartedly the certainty of death in the end.

Eisenberg was apprehensive, but not panic-stricken. His situation was decidedly interesting; he was no longer bored. If he were a prisoner, it seemed likely that his captor would come to investigate him presently, perhaps to question him, perhaps to attempt to use him in some fashion.

The fact that he had been saved and not killed implied some sort of plans for his future. Very well, he would concentrate on meeting whatever exigency might come with a calm and resourceful mind. In the meantime, there was nothing he could do toward freeing himself; he had satisfied himself of that. This was a prison which would baffle Houdini – smooth continuous walls, no way to get a purchase.

He had thought once that he had a clue to escape; the cell had sanitary arrangements of some sort, for that which his body rejected went elsewhere. But he got no further with that lead; the cage was self-cleaning – and that was that. He could not tell how it was done. It baffled him.

Presently he slept again.

When he awoke, one element only was changed – the food and water had been replenished. The 'day' passed without incident, save for his own busy and fruitless thoughts.

And the next 'day.' And the next.

He determined to stay awake long enough to find out how food and water were placed in his cell. He made a colossal effort to do so, using drastic measures to stimulate his body into consciousness. He bit his lips, he bit his tongue. He nipped the lobes of his ears viciously with his nails. He concentrated on difficult mental feats.

Presently he dozed off; when he awoke, the food and water had been replenished.

The waking periods were followed by sleep, renewed hunger and thirst, the satisfying of same, and more sleep. It was after the sixth or seventh sleep that he decided that some sort of a calendar was necessary to his mental health. He had no means of measuring time except by his sleeps; he arbitrarily designated them as days. He had no means of keeping records, save his own body. He made that do. A thumbnail shred, torn off, made a rough tattooing needle. Continued scratching of the same area on his thigh produced a red welt which persisted for a day or two, and could be renewed. Seven welts made a week. The progression of such welts along ten fingers and ten toes gave him the means to measure twenty weeks – which was a much longer period than he anticipated any need to measure.

He had tallied the second set of seven thigh welts on the ring finger of his left hand when the next event occurred to disturb his solitude. When he awoke from the sleep following said tally, he became suddenly and overwhelmingly aware that he was not alone!

There was a human figure sleeping beside him. When he had convinced himself that he was truly wide awake – his dreams were thoroughly populated – he grasped the figure by the shoulder and shook it. 'Doc!' he yelled. 'Doc! Wake up!'

Graves opened his eyes, focused them, sat up, and put out his hand. 'Hi, Bill,' he remarked. 'I'm damned glad to see you.'

'Doc!' He pounded the older man on the back. 'Doc! For Criminy sake! You don't know how glad *I* am to see *you*.'

'I can guess.'

'Look, Doc – where have you been? How did you get here? Did the fireballs snag you, too?'

'One thing at a time, son. Let's have breakfast.' There was a double ration of food and water on the 'floor' near them. Graves picked up a sphere, nicked it expertly, and drank it without losing a drop. Eisenberg watched him knowingly.

'You've been here for some time.'

'That's right.'

'Did the fireballs get you the same time they got me?'

'No.' He reached for the food. 'I came up the Kanaka Pillar.'

'What!'

'That's right. Matter of fact, I was looking for you.'

'The hell you say!'

'But I do say. It looks as if my wild hypothesis was right; the Pillars and the fireballs are different manifestations of the same cause – X!'

It seemed almost possible to hear the wheels whir in Eisenberg's head. 'But, Doc . . . look here, Doc, that means your whole hypothesis was correct. Somebody *did* the whole thing. Somebody has us locked up here now.'

'That's right.' He munched slowly. He seemed tired, older and thinner than the way Eisenberg remembered him. 'Evidence of intelligent control. Always was. No other explanation.'

'But *who*?'

'Ah!'

'Some foreign power? Are we up against something utterly new in the way of an attack?'

'Hummph! Do you think the Russians, for instance, would bother to serve us water like *this*?' He held up one of the dainty little spheres.

'Who, then?'

'I wouldn't know. Call 'em Martians – that's a convenient way to think of them.'

'Why Martians?'

'No reason. I said that was a convenient way to think of them.'

'Convenient how?'

'Convenient because it keeps you from thinking of them as human beings – which they obviously aren't. Nor animals. Something very intelligent, but not animals, because they are smarter than we are. Martians.'

'But . . . but— Wait a minute. Why do you assume that your X people aren't human? Why not humans who have a lot of stuff on the ball that we don't have? New scientific advances?'

'That's a fair question,' Graves answered, picking his teeth with a forefinger. 'I'll give you a fair answer. Because in the present state of the world we know pretty near where all the best minds are and what they are doing. Advances like these couldn't be hidden and would be a long time in developing. X indicates evidence of a half a dozen different lines of development that are clear beyond our ken and which would require years of work by hundreds of researchers, to say the very least. *Ipso facto*, nonhuman science.

'Of course,' he continued, 'if you want to postulate a mad scientist and a secret laboratory, I can't argue with you. But I'm not writing Sunday supplements.'

Bill Eisenberg kept very quiet for some time, while he considered what Graves said in the light of his own experience. 'You're right, Doc,' he finally admitted. 'Shucks – you're usually right when we have an argument. It has to be Martians. Oh, I don't mean inhabitants of Mars; I mean some form of intelligent life from outside this planet.'

'Maybe.'

'But you just said so!'

'No, I said it was a convenient way to look at it.'

'But it has to be, by elimination.'

'Elimination is a tricky line of reasoning.'

'What else could it be?'

'Mm-m-m. I'm not prepared to say just what I do think – yet. But there are stronger reasons than we have mentioned for concluding that we are up against nonhumans. Psychological reasons.'

'What sort?'

'X doesn't treat prisoners in any fashion that arises out of human behaviour patterns. Think it over.'

They had a lot to talk about; much more than X, even though X was a subject they were bound to return to. Graves gave Bill a simple bald account of how he happened to go up the Pillar – an account which Bill found very moving for what was left out, rather than told. He felt suddenly very humble and unworthy as he looked at his elderly, frail friend. 'Doc, you don't look well.'

'I'll do.'

'That trip up the Pillar was hard on you. You shouldn't have tried it.'

Graves shrugged. 'I made out all right.' But he had not, and Bill could see that he had not. The old man was 'poorly'.

They slept and they ate and they talked and they slept again. The routine that Eisenberg had grown used to alone continued, save with company. But Graves grew no stronger.

'Doc, it's up to us to do something about it.'

'About what?'

'The whole situation. This thing that has happened to us is an intolerable menace to the whole human race. We don't know what may have happened down below—'

'Why do you say "down below"?'

'Why, you came up the Pillar.'

'Yes, true – but I don't know when or how I was taken out of the bathysphere, nor where they may have taken me. But go ahead. Let's have your idea.'

'Well, but – OK – we don't know what may have happened to the rest of the human race. The fireballs may be picking them off one at a time, with no chance to fight back and no way of guessing what has been going on. We have some idea of the answer. It's up to us to escape and warn them. There may be some way of fighting back. It's our duty; the whole future of the human race may depend on it.'

Graves was silent so long after Bill had finished his tocsin that Bill began to feel embarrassed, a bit foolish. But when he finally spoke it was to agree. 'I think you are right, Bill. I think it quite possible that you are right. Not necessarily, but distinctly possible. And that possibility does place an obligation on us to all mankind. I've known it. I knew it before we got into this mess, but I did not have enough data to justify shouting, "Wolf!"

'The question is,' he went on, 'how can we give such a warning – now?'

'We've got to escape!'

'Ah!'

'There *must* be some way.'

'Can you suggest one?'

'Maybe. We haven't been able to find any way in or out of this place, but there must be a way – has to be; we were brought in. Furthermore, our rations are put inside every day – somehow. I tried once to stay awake long enough to see how it was done, but I fell asleep—'

'So did I.'

'Uh-huh. I'm not surprised. But there are two of us now; we could take turns, watch on and watch off, until something happened.'

Graves nodded. 'It's worth trying.'

Since they had no way of measuring the watches, each kept the vigil until sleepiness became intolerable, then awakened the other. But nothing happened. Their food ran out, was not replaced. They conserved their water balls with care, were finally reduced to one, which was not drunk because each insisted on being noble about it – the other must drink it! But still no manifestation of any sort from their unseen captors.

After an unmeasured and unestimated length of time – but certainly long, almost intolerably long – at a time when Eisenberg was in a light, troubled sleep, he was suddenly awakened by a touch and the sound of his name. He sat up, blinking, disoriented. 'Who? What? Wha'sa matter?'

'I must have dozed off,' Graves said miserably. 'I'm sorry, Bill.' Eisenberg looked where Graves pointed. Their food and water had been renewed.

Eisenberg did not suggest a renewal of the experiment. In the first place, it seemed evident that their keepers did not intend for them to learn the combination to their cell and were quite intelligent enough to outmanoeuvre their necessarily feeble attempts. In the second place, Graves was an obviously sick man; Eisenberg did not have the heart to suggest another long, gruelling, half-starved vigil.

But, lacking knowledge of the combination, it appeared impossible to break jail. A naked man is a particularly helpless creature; lacking materials wherewith to fashion tools, he can do little. Eisenberg would have swapped his chances for eternal bliss for a diamond drill, an acetylene torch, or even a rusty, secondhand chisel. Without tools of some sort it was impressed on him that he stood about as much chance of breaking out of his cage as his goldfish, Cleo and Patra, had of chewing their way out of a glass bowl.

'Doc.'

'Yes, son.'

'We've tackled this the wrong way. We know that X is intelligent; instead of trying to escape, we should be trying to establish communication.'

'How?'

'I don't know. But there must be *some* way.'

But if there was, he could never conjure it up. Even if he assumed that his captors could see and hear him, how was he to convey intelligence to them by word or gesture? Was it theoretically possible for any nonhuman being, no matter how intelligent, to find a pattern of meaning in human speech symbols, if he encountered them without context, without background, without pictures, without *pointing*? It is certainly true that the human race, working under much more favourable circumstances, has failed almost utterly to learn the languages of the other races of animals.

What should he do to attract their attention, stimulate their interest?

Recite the 'Gettysburg Address'? Or the multiplication table? Or, if he used gestures, would deaf-and-dumb language mean any more, or any less, to his captors than the sailor's hornpipe?

'Doc.'

'What is it, Bill?' Graves was sinking; he rarely initiated a conversation these 'days'.

'Why are we here? I've had it in the back of my mind that *eventually* they would take us out and do something with us. Try to question us, maybe. But it doesn't look like they mean to.'

'No, it doesn't.'

'Then why are we here? Why do they take care of us?'

Graves paused quite a long time before answering: 'I think that they are expecting us to reproduce.'

'What!'

Graves shrugged.

'But that's ridiculous.'

'Surely. But would they know it?'

'But they are intelligent.'

Graves chuckled, the first time he had done so in many sleeps. 'Do you know Roland Young's little verse about the flea:

> *'A funny creature is the Flea*
> *You cannot tell the She from He.*
> *But He can tell – and so can She.'*

'After all, the visible differences between men and women are quite superficial and almost negligible – except to men and women!'

Eisenberg found the suggestion repugnant, almost revolting; he struggled against it. 'But look, Doc – even a little study would show them that the human race is divided up into sexes. After all, we aren't the first specimens they've studied.'

'Maybe they don't study us.'

'Huh?'

'Maybe we are just – pets.'

Pets! Bill Eisenberg's morale had stood up well in the face of danger and uncertainty. This attack on it was more subtle. Pets! He had thought of Graves and himself as prisoners of war, or, possibly, objects of scientific research. But pets!

'I know how you feel,' Graves went on, watching his face. 'It's . . . it's *humiliating* from an anthropocentric viewpoint. But I think it may be true. I may as well tell you my own private theory as to the possible nature of X, and the relation of X to the human race. I haven't up to now, as it is almost sheer conjecture, based on very little data. But it does cover the known facts.

'I conceive of the X creatures as being just barely aware of the existence of men, unconcerned by them, and almost completely uninterested in them.'

'But they hunt us!'

'Maybe. Or maybe they just pick us up occasionally by accident. A lot of men have dreamed about an impingement of nonhuman intelligences on the human race. Almost without exception the dream has taken one of two forms, invasion and war, or exploration and mutual social inter-course. Both concepts postulate that nonhumans are enough like us either to fight with us or talk to us – treat us as equals, one way or the other.

'I don't believe that X is sufficiently interested in human beings to want to enslave them, or even exterminate them. They may not even study us, even when we come under their notice. They may lack the scientific spirit in the sense of having a monkeylike curiosity about everything that moves. For that matter, how thoroughly do *we* study other life forms? Did you ever ask your goldfish for their views on goldfish poetry or politics? Does a termite think that a woman's place is in the home? Do beavers prefer blondes or brunettes?'

'You are joking.'

'No, I'm not. Maybe the life forms I mentioned don't have such involved ideas. My point is: if they did, or do, we'd never guess it. I don't think X conceives of the human race as intelligent.'

Bill chewed this for a while, then added: 'Where do you think they came from, Doc? Mars, maybe? Or clear out of the Solar System?'

'Not necessarily. Not even probably. It's my guess that they came from the same place we did – *from up out of the slime of this planet.*'

'Really, Doc—'

'I mean it. And don't give me that funny look. I may be sick, but, I'm not balmy. *Creation took eight days!*'

'Huh?'

'I'm using biblical language. "And God blessed them, and God said unto them, Be fruitful and multiply, and replenish the earth, and subdue it: and have dominion over the fish of the sea, and over the fowl of the air, and over every living thing that moveth upon the earth." And so it came to pass. But nobody mentioned the stratosphere.'

'Doc – are you sure you feel all right?'

'Dammit – quit trying to psychoanalyse me! I'll drop the allegory. What I mean is: We aren't the latest or the highest stage in evolution. First the oceans were populated. Then lungfish to amphibian, and so on up, until the continents were populated, and, in time, man ruled the surface of the earth – or thought he did. But did evolution stop there? I think not. Consider – from a fish's point of view air is a hard vacuum. From our point of view the upper reaches of the atmosphere, sixty, seventy, maybe a hundred thousand feet up, seem like a vacuum and unfit to sustain life. But it's not vacuum. It's thin, yes, but there is matter there and radiant energy. Why not life, intelligent life, highly evolved as it would have to be – but evolved from the same ancestry as ourselves and fish? We wouldn't see it happen; man hasn't been aware in a scientific sense, that long. When our grand-daddies were swinging in the trees, it had already happened.'

Eisenberg took a deep breath. 'Just wait a minute, Doc. I'm not disputing the theoretical possibility of your thesis, but it seems to me it is out on direct evidence alone. We've never seen them, had no direct evidence of them. At least, not until lately. And we *should* have seen them.'

'Not necessarily. Do ants see men? I doubt it.'

'Yes – but, consarn it, a man has better eyes than an ant.'

'Better eyes for what? For his own needs. Suppose the X creatures are too high up, or too tenuous, or too fast-moving for us to notice them. Even a thing as big and as solid and as slow as an airplane can go up high enough to pass out of sight, even on a clear day. If X is tenuous and even semitransparent, we never *would* see them – nor even as occultations of stars, or shadows against the moon – though as a matter of fact there have been some very strange stories of just that sort of thing.'

Eisenberg got up and stomped up and down. 'Do you mean to suggest,' he demanded, 'that creatures so insubstantial they can float in a soft vacuum built the Pillars?'

'Why not? Try explaining how a half-finished, naked embryo like *homo sapiens* built the Empire State Building.'

Bill shook his head. 'I don't get it.'

'You don't try. Where do you think *this* came from?' Graves held up one of the miraculous little water spheres. 'My guess is that life on this planet is split three ways, with almost no intercourse between the three. Ocean culture, land culture, and another – call it stratoculture. Maybe a fourth, down under the crust – but we don't know. We know a little about life under the sea, because we are curious. But how much do they know of us? Do a few dozen bathysphere descents constitute an invasion? A fish that sees our bathysphere might go home and take to his bed with a sick headache, but he wouldn't talk about it, and he wouldn't be believed if he did. If a lot of fish see us and swear out affidavits, along comes a fish-psychologist and explains it as mass hallucination.

'No, it takes something at least as large and solid and permanent as the Pillars to have any effects on orthodox conceptions. Casual visitations have no real effect.'

Eisenberg let his thoughts simmer for some time before commenting further. When he did, it was half to himself. 'I don't believe it. I won't believe it!'

'Believe what?'

'Your theory. Look, Doc – if you are right, don't you see what it means? We're helpless, we're outclassed.'

'I don't think they will bother much with human beings. They haven't, up till now.'

'But that isn't it. Don't you see? We've had some dignity as a race. We've striven and accomplished things. Even when we failed, we had the tragic satisfaction of knowing that we were, nevertheless, superior and more able than the other animals. We've had faith in the race – we would accomplish great things yet. But if we are just one of the lower animals ourselves, what does our great work amount to? Me, I couldn't go on pretending to be a "scientist" if I thought I was just a fish, mucking around in the bottom of a pool. My work wouldn't *signify* anything.'

'Maybe it doesn't.'

'No, maybe it doesn't.' Eisenberg got up and paced the constricted area of their prison. 'Maybe not. But I won't surrender to it. I *won't*! Maybe you're right. Maybe you're wrong. It doesn't seem to matter very much *where* the X people came from. One way or the other, they are a threat to our own kind. Doc, we've got to get out of here and warn them!'

'How?'

Graves was comatose a large part of the time before he died. Bill maintained an almost continuous watch over him, catching only occasional cat naps. There was little he could do for his friend, even though he did watch over him, but the spirit behind it was comfort to them both.

But he was dozing when Graves called his name. He woke at once, though the sound was a bare whisper. 'Yes, Doc?'

'I can't talk much more, son. Thanks for taking care of me.'

'Shucks, Doc.'

'Don't forget what you're here for. Some day you'll get a break. Be ready for it and don't muff it. People have to be warned.'

'I'll do it, Doc. I swear it.'

'Good boy.' And then, almost inaudibly, 'G'night, son.'

Eisenberg watched over the body until it was quite cold and had begun to stiffen. Then, exhausted by his long vigil and emotionally drained, he collapsed into a deep sleep. When he woke up the body was gone.

It was hard to maintain his morale, after Graves was gone. It was all very well to resolve to warn the rest of mankind at the first possible chance, but there was the endless monotony to contend with. He had not even the relief from boredom afforded the condemned prisoner – the checking off of limited days. Even his 'calendar' was nothing but a counting of his sleeps.

He was not quite sane much of the time, and it was the twice-tragic insanity of intelligence, aware of its own instability. He cycled between periods of elation and periods of extreme depression, in which he would have destroyed himself, had he the means.

During the periods of elation he made great plans for fighting against the X creatures – after he escaped. He was not sure how or when, but, momentarily, he was sure. He would lead the crusade himself; rockets could withstand the dead zone of the Pillars and the cloud; atomic bombs could destroy the dynamic balance of the Pillars. They would harry them and hunt them down; the globe would once again be the kingdom of man, to whom it belonged.

During the bitter periods of relapse he would realize clearly that the puny engineering of mankind would be of no force against the powers and knowledge of the creatures who built the Pillars, who kidnapped himself and Graves in such a casual and mysterious a fashion. They were outclassed. Could codfish plan a sortie against the city of Boston? Would it matter if the chattering monkeys in Guatemala passed a resolution to destroy the navy?

They were outclassed. The human race has reached its highest point – the point at which it began to be aware that it was not the highest race, and the knowledge was death to it, one way or the other – the mere knowledge alone, even as the knowledge was now destroying him, Bill Eisenberg, himself. Eisenberg – *homo piscis*. Poor fish!

His overstrained mind conceived a means by which he might possibly warn his fellow beings. He could not escape as long as his surroundings remained unchanged. That was established and he accepted it; he no longer paced his cage. But certain things *did* leave his cage: left-over food, refuse – and Graves's body. If he died, his own body would be removed, he felt sure. Some, at least, of the things which had gone up the Pillars had come down again – he knew that. Was it not likely that the X creatures disposed of any heavy mass for which they had no further use by dumping it down the Wahini Pillar? He convinced himself that it was so.

Very well, his body would be returned to the surface, eventually. How could he use it to give a message to his fellow men, if it were found? He had no writing materials, nothing but his own body.

But the same make-do means which served him as a calendar gave him a way to write a message. He could make welts on his skin with a shred of thumbnail. If the same spot were irritated over and over again, not permitted to heal, scar tissue would form. By such means he was able to create permanent tattooing.

The letters had to be large; he was limited to space to the fore part of his body; involved argument was impossible. He was limited to a fairly simple warning. If he had been quite right in his mind, perhaps he would have been able to devise a more cleverly worded warning – but then he was not.

In time, he had covered his chest and belly with cicatrix tattooing worthy of a bushman chief. He was thin by then and of an unhealthy colour; the welts stood out plainly.

His body was found floating in the Pacific, by Portuguese fishermen who could not read the message, but who turned it in to the harbour police of Honolulu. They, in turn, photographed the body, fingerprinted it, and disposed of it. The fingerprints were checked in Washington, and William Eisenberg, scientist, fellow of many distinguished societies, and high type of *homo sapiens*, was officially dead for the second time, with a new mystery attached to his name.

The cumbersome course of official correspondence unwound itself and the record of his reappearance reached the desk of Captain Blake, at a port in the South Atlantic. Photographs of the body were attached to the record, along with a short official letter telling the captain that, in view of his connection with the case, it was being provided for his information and recommendation.

Captain Blake looked at the photographs for the dozenth time. The message told in scar tissue was plain enough: 'BEWARE – CREATION TOOK EIGHT DAYS.' But what did it mean?

Of one thing he was sure – Eisenberg had not had those scars on his body when he disappeared from the *Mahan*.

The man had lived for a considerable period after he was grabbed up by the fireball – that was certain. And he had learned something. What? The reference to the first chapter of Genesis did not escape him; it was not such as to be useful.

He turned to his desk and resumed making a draft in painful longhand of his report to the bureau. '—the message in scar tissue adds to the mystery, rather than clarifying it. I am now forced to the opinion that the Pillars and the LaGrange fireballs are connected in some way. The patrol around the Pillars should not be relaxed. If new opportunities or methods for investigating the nature of the Pillars should develop, they should be pursued thoroughly. I regret to say that I have nothing of the sort to suggest—'

He got up from his desk and walked to a small aquarium supported by gimbals from the inboard bulkhead, and stirred up the two goldfish therein with a forefinger. Noticing the level of the water, he turned to the pantry door. 'Johnson, you've filled this bowl too full again. Pat's trying to jump out again!'

'I'll fix it, captain.' The steward came out of the pantry with a small pan. ('Don't know why the Old Man keeps these tarnation fish. He ain't interested in 'em – *that's certain.*') Aloud he added: 'That Pat fish don't want to stay in there, captain. Always trying to jump out. And he don't *like* me, captain.'

'What's that?' Captain Blake's thoughts had already left the fish; he was worrying over the mystery again.

'I say that fish don't *like* me, captain. Tries to bite my finger every time I clean out the bowl.'

'Don't be silly, Johnson.'

File classification: Extraterrestrial (ET)
Location: New Jersey, USA

Title: Mewhu's Jet
Writer: *Theodore Sturgeon*

Briefing: *Extraterrestrial – a normally intelligent creature said to originate from another world; often abreviated to ET.* Writer Jack Garry, his wife and daughter are on vacation near Normandy Beach, New Jersey when a comet-like object plummets across the sky and crash-lands, damaging their holiday home. But after the shock of the impact, the family soon discover something far stranger outside – and begin to realize they are face to face with an alien from *somewhere . . .*

Author: American fantasy writer Theodore Sturgeon wrote this remarkable story in 1946, a whole year *before* one of the most famous and still hotly debated UFO incidents when an occupied alien craft was said to have crashed in New Mexico, creating what is now referred to as the 'Roswell Incident'. Sturgeon is rightly acknowledged as one of the leading figures in that group of writers, including Robert A. Heinlein, A. E. Van Vogt and Isaac Asimov, who helped to create a new age of science fiction in the years immediately after the Second World War. A man of diverse abilities – he had previously been a trapeze artist, bulldozer driver and the manager of a hotel in the West Indies – Sturgeon brought an original and intensely curious imagination to the genre and was encouraged by John W. Campbell, the influential editor of *Astounding Science Fiction*. Encounters with UFOs were, in fact, a recurring theme in his short stories, and 'Mewhu's Jet', originally published in *Astounding* in November 1946, has been held up by Arthur C. Clarke, among others, as one of the earliest tales of an encounter between a child and a friendly ET and, as such, a forerunner of Steven Spielberg's classic 1982 movie.

'*We interrupt this programme to announce—*'

'Jack! Don't jump like that! And you've dropped ashes all over your—'

'Aw, Iris, honey, let me listen to—'

'*—at first identified as a comet, the object is pursuing an erratic course through the stratosphere occasionally dipping as low as—*'

'You make me nervous, Jack! You're an absolute slave to the radio. I wish you paid that much attention to me.'

'Darling, I'll argue the point, or pay attention to you, or anything in the wide world you like when I've heard this announcement; but please, *please* LET ME LISTEN!'

'*—dents of the East Coast are warned to watch for the approach of this ob—*'

'Iris, don't—'

Click!

'Well, of all the selfish, inconsiderate, discourteous—'

'That will do, Jack Garry! It's my radio as much as yours, and I have a right to turn it off when I want to!'

'Might I ask why you find it necessary to turn it off at this moment?'

'Because I know the announcement will be repeated any number of times if it's important, and you'll shush me every time. Because I'm not interested in that kind of thing and don't see why I should have it rammed down my throat. Because the only thing you ever want to listen to is something which couldn't possibly affect us. But mostly because you YELLED at me!'

'I did NOT yell at you!'

'You *did*! And you're yelling NOW!'

'*MOM!* DADDY!'

'Oh, Molly, darling, we woke you up!'

'Poor bratlet. Hey – what about your slippers?'

'It isn't cold tonight, Daddy. What was that on the radio?'

'Something buzzing around in the sky, darling, I didn't hear it all.'

'A spaceship, I betcha.'

'You see? You and your so-called science-fiction!'

'Call us a science-faction. The kid's got more judgement than you have.'

'You have as little judgement as a seven-year-old child, you mean. And b-besides, you're turning her a-against me!'

'Aw, for Pete's sake, Mom, don't cry!'

At which point, something like a giant's fist clouted off the two-room top storey of the seaside cottage and scattered it down the beach. The lights winked out, and outside, the whole waterfront lit up with a brief, shattering blue glare.

'Jacky darling, are you hurt?'

'Mom, he's bleedin'!'

'Jack, honey, say something. *Please* say something.'

'Urrrrgh,' said Jack Garry obediently, sitting up with a soft clatter of pieces of falling lath and plaster. He put his hands gently on the sides of his head and whistled. 'Something hit the house.'

His red-headed wife laughed half-hysterically. 'Not really, darling.' She put her arms around him, whisked some dust out of his hair, and began stroking his neck. 'I'm ... frightened, Jack.'

'You're frightened!' He looked around, shakily, in the dim moonlight that filtered in. Radiance from an unfamiliar place caught his bleary gaze, and he clutched Iris's arm. 'Upstairs ... it's gone!' he said hoarsely, struggling to his feet. 'Molly's room ... Molly—'

'I'm here, Daddy. Hey! You're squeezin'!'

'Happy little family,' said Iris, her voice trembling. 'Vacationing in a quiet little cottage by the sea, so Daddy can write technical articles while Mummy regains her good disposition – without a phone, without movies within miles, and living in a place where the roof flies away. Jack – what hit us?'

'One of those things you were talking about,' said Jack sardonically. 'One of the things you refuse to be interested in, that couldn't possibly affect us. Remember?'

'The thing the radio was talking about?'

'I wouldn't be surprised. We'd better get out of here. This place may fall in on us, or burn, or something.'

'An' we'll all be kilt,' crooned Molly.

'Shut up, Molly! Iris, I'm going to poke around. Better go on out and pick us a place to pitch the tent – if I can find the tent.'

'Tent?' Iris gasped.

'Boy oh boy,' said Molly.

'Jack Garry, I'm not going to go to bed in a tent. Do you realize that this place will be swarming with people in no time flat?'

'OK – OK. Only get out from under what's left of the house. Go for a swim. Take a walk. Or g'wan to bed in Molly's room, if you can find it. Iris, you can pick the oddest times to argue!'

'I'm not going out there by myself!'

Jack sighed. 'I should've asked you to stay in here,' he muttered. 'If you're not the contrariest woman ever to— Be quiet, Molly!'

'I didn't say anything.'

Meeew-w-w!

'Aren't you doing that caterwauling?'

'No, Daddy, truly.'

Iris said, 'I'd say a cat was caught in the wreckage except that cats are smart and no cat would ever come near this place.'

Wuh-wuh-muh-meeee-ew-w-w!

'What a dismal sound!'

'Jack, that isn't a cat.'

'Well, stop shaking like the well-known aspen leaf.'

Molly said, 'Not without aspen Daddy's leaf to do it.'

'Molly! You're too young to make bad puns!'

'Sorry, Daddy. I fergot.'

Mmmmmew. Mmm – m-m-m.

'Whatever it is,' Jack said, 'it can't be big enough to be afraid of and make a funny little noise like that.' He squeezed Iris's arm and, stepping carefully over the rubble, began peering in and around it. Molly scrambled beside him. He was about to caution her against making so much noise, and then thought better of it. What difference would a little racket make?

The noise was not repeated, and five minutes' searching elicited nothing. Garry went back to his wife, who was fumbling around the shambles of a living room, pointlessly setting chairs and coffee tables back on their legs.

'I didn't find anyth—'

'YIPE!'

'Molly! What is it?'

Molly was just outside, in the shrubbery. 'Oh . . . oh— Daddy, you better come quick!'

Spurred by the urgency of her tone, he went crashing outside. He found Molly standing rigid, trying to cram both her fists in her mouth at the same time. And at her feet was a man with, silver-grey skin and a broken arm, who mewed at him.

'—Guard and Navy Department have withdrawn their warnings. The pilot of a Pan American transport has reported that the object disappeared into the zenith. It was last seen eighteen miles east of Normandy Beach, New Jersey. Reports from the vicinity describe it as travelling very slowly, with a hissing noise.

*Although it reached within a few feet of the ground several times, no damage has
been reported. Inves—'*

'Think of that,' said Iris, switching off the little three-way portable. 'No
damage.'

'Yeah. And if no one saw the thing hit, no one will be out here to
investigate. So you can retire to your downy couch in the tent without fear
of being interviewed.'

'Go to sleep? Are you mad? Sleep in that flimsy tent with that mewing
monster lying there?'

'Oh heck, Mom, he's sick! He wouldn't hurt anybody.'

They sat around a cheerful fire, fed by roof shingles. Jack had set up the
tent without much trouble. The silver-grey man was stretched out in the
shadows, sleeping lightly and emitting an occasional moan.

Jack smiled at Iris. 'Y'know, I love your silly chatter, darling. The way
you turned to and set his arm was a pleasure to watch. You didn't think of
him as a monster while you were tending to him.'

'Didn't I, though? Maybe "monster" was the wrong word to use. Jack, he
has only one bone in his forearm!'

'He has what? Oh, nonsense, honey! 'Tain't scientific. He'd have to have
a ball-and-socket joint in his wrist.'

'He *has* a ball and socket joint in his wrist.'

'This I have to see,' Jack muttered. He picked up a flash lantern and went
over to the long prone figure.

Silver eyes blinked up at the light. There was something queer about
them. He turned the beam closer. The pupils were not black in that light,
but dark-green. They all but closed – from the sides, like a cat's. Jack's
breath wheezed out. He ran the light over the man's body. It was clad in a
bright-blue roomy bathroom effect, with a yellow sash. The sash had a
buckle which apparently consisted of two pieces of yellow metal placed
together; there seemed to be nothing to keep them together. They just
stayed. When the man had fainted, just as they found him, it had taken
almost all Jack's strength to pull them apart.

'Iris.'

She got up and came over to him. 'Let the poor devil sleep.'

'Iris – what color was his robe?'

'Red, with a . . . but it's *blue!*'

'Is now. Iris, what on earth have we got here?'

'I don't know. I don't know. Some poor thing that escaped from an
institution for . . . for—'

'For what?'

'How should I know?' she snapped. 'There must be some place where
they send creatures that get born like that.'

'Creatures don't get born like that. Iris, he isn't deformed. He's just different.'

'I see what you mean. I don't know why I see what you mean, but I'll tell you something.' She stopped, and was quiet for so long that he turned to her, surprised. She said slowly, 'I ought to be afraid of him, because he's strange, and ugly, but – I'm not.'

'Me, too.'

'Molly, go back to bed!'

'He's a leprechaun.'

'Maybe you're right. Go on to bed, chicken, and in the morning you can ask him where he keeps his crock of gold.'

'Gee.' She went off a little way then stood on one foot, drawing a small circle in the sand with the other. 'Daddy.'

'Yes, Molly-m'love.'

'Can I sleep in the tent tomorrow, too?'

'If you're good.'

'Daddy obviously means,' said Iris acidly, 'that if you're *not* good he'll have a roof on the house by tomorrow night.'

'I'll be good.' She disappeared into the tent.

'For kids,' Jack said admiringly, 'it never rains tomorrow.'

The grey man mewed.

'Well, old guy, what is it?'

The man reached over and fumbled at his splinted arm.

'It hurts him,' said Iris. She knelt beside him and, taking the wrist of his good arm, lifted it away from the splint, where he was clawing. The man did not resist, but lay and looked at her with pain-filled, slitted eyes.

'He has six fingers,' Jack said. 'See?' He knelt beside his wife and gently took the man's wrist. He whistled. 'It *is* a ball and socket.'

'Give him some aspirin.'

'That's a good . . . wait.' Jack stood pulling his lip in puzzlement. 'Do you think we should?'

'Why not?'

'We don't know where he comes from. We know nothing of his body chemistry, or what any of our medicines might do to him.'

'He . . . what do you mean, where he comes from?'

'Iris, will you open up your mind just a little? In the face of evidence like this, are you going to even attempt to cling to the idea that this man comes from anywhere on this earth?' Jack said with annoyance. 'You know your anatomy. Don't tell me you ever saw a human freak with skin and bones like that! That belt buckle – that material in his clothes . . .

come on, now. Drop your prejudices and give your brains a chance, will you?'

'You're suggesting things that simply don't *happen!*'

'That's what the man in the street said – in Hiroshima. That's what the old-time aeronaut said from the basket of his balloon when they told him about heavier-than-air craft. That's what—'

'All right, all right, Jack! I know the rest of the speech. If you want dialectics instead of what's left of a night's sleep, I might point out that the things you have mentioned have all concerned human endeavours. Show me any new plastic, a new metal, a new kind of engine, and though I may not begin to understand it, I can accept it because it is of human origin. But this . . . this man, or whatever he is—'

'I know,' said Jack, more gently. 'It's frightening because it's strange, and away down underneath we feel that anything strange is necessarily dangerous. That's why we wear our best manners for strangers and not for our friends – but I still don't think we should give this character any aspirin.'

'He seems to breathe the same air we do. He perspires, he talks . . . I think he talks—'

'You have a point. Well, if it'll ease his pain at all, it may be worth trying. Give him just one.'

Iris went to the pump with a collapsible cup from her first-aid kit, and filled it. Kneeling by the silver-skinned man, she propped up his head, gently put the aspirin between his lips, and brought the cup to his mouth. He sucked the water in greedily, and then went completely limp.

'Oh, oh. I was afraid of that.'

Iris put her hand over the man's heart. '*Jack!*'

'Is he . . . what is it, Iris?'

'Not dead, if that's what you mean. Will you feel this?'

Jack put his hand beside Iris's. The heart was beating with massive, slow blows, about eight to the minute. Under it, out of phase completely with the main beat, was another, an extremely fast, sharp beat, which felt as if it were going about three hundred.

'He's having some sort of palpitation,' Jack said.

'And in two hearts at once!'

Suddenly the man raised his head and uttered a series of ululating shrieks and howls. His eyes opened wide, and across them fluttered a translucent nicitating membrane. He lay perfectly still with his mouth open, shrieking and gargling. Then, with a lightning movement, he snatched Jack's hand to his mouth. A pointed tongue, light-orange and four inches longer than it had any right to be, flicked out and licked Jack's hand. Then the strange eyes closed, the shrieks died to a whimper and faded out, and the man relaxed.

'Sleeping now,' said Iris. 'Oh, I hope we haven't done anything to him!'

'We've done something. I just hope it isn't serious. Anyhow, his arm isn't bothering him any. That's all we were worried about in the first place.'

Iris put a cushion under the man's oddly planed head, touched the beach mattress he was lying on to see that he would be comfortable. 'He has a beautiful moustache,' she said. 'Like silver. He looks very old and wise, doesn't he?'

'So does an owl. Let's go to bed.'

Jack woke early, from a dream in which he had bailed out of a flying motorcycle with an umbrella that turned into a candy cane as he fell. He landed in the middle of some sharp-toothed crags which gave like sponge rubber. He was immediately surrounded by mermaids who looked like Iris and who had hands shaped like spur gears. But nothing frightened him. He awoke smiling, inordinately happy.

Iris was still asleep. Outside, somewhere, he heard the tinkle of Molly's laugh. He sat up, looked at Molly's camp cot. It was empty.

Moving quietly, so as not to disturb his wife, he slid his feet into moccasins and went out.

Molly was on her knees beside their strange visitor, who was squatting on his haunches and—

They were playing patty-cake.

'*Molly!*'

'Yes, Daddy.'

'What are you trying to do? Don't you realize that that man has a broken arm?'

'Oh gosh, I'm sorry. Do you s'pose I hurt him?'

'I don't know. It's very possible,' said Jack Garry testily. He went to the alien, took his good hand.

The man looked up at him and smiled. His smile was peculiarly engaging. All of his teeth were pointed, and they were very widely spaced. 'Eeee-yu mow madibu Mewhu,' he said.

'That's his name,' Molly said excitedly. She leaned forward and tugged at the man's sleeve. 'Mewhu. Hey, Mewhu!' And she pointed at her chest.

'Mooly,' said Mewhu. 'Mooly – Geery.'

'See. Daddy?' Molly said ecstatically. 'See?' She pointed at her father. 'Daddy. Dah—dee.'

'Deedy,' said Mewhu.

'No, silly! Daddy.'

'Dewdy.'

'*Dah*-dy!'

Jack, quite entranced, pointed at himself and said, 'Jack'.

'Jeek.'

'Good enough. Molly, the man can't say "ah". He can say "oo" or "ee" but not "ah". That's good enough.'

Jack examined the splints. Iris had done a very competent job. When she realized that instead of the radius-ulna development of a true human, Mewhu had only one bone in his forearm, she had set the arm and laid on two splints instead of one. Jack grinned. Intellectually, Iris would not accept Mewhu's existence even as a possibility; but as a nurse, she not only accepted his body structure but skilfully compensated for its differences.

'I guess he wants to be polite,' said Jack to his repentant daughter, 'and if you want to play patty-cake, he'll go along with you, even if it hurts. Don't take advantage of him, chicken.'

'I won't, Daddy.'

Jack started up the fire and had a green-stick crane built and hot water bubbling by the time Iris emerged. 'Takes a cataclysm to get you to start breakfast,' she grumbled through a pleased smile. 'When were you a boy scout?'

'Matter of fact,' said Garry, 'I was once. Will modom now take over?'

'Modom will. How's the patient?'

'Thriving. He and Molly had a patty-cake tournament this morning. His clothes, by the way, are red again.'

'Jack – where does he come from?'

'I haven't asked him yet. When I learn to caterwaul, or he learns to talk, perhaps we'll find out. Molly has already elicited the information that his name's Mewhu.' Garry grinned. 'And he calls me "Jeek".'

'Can't pronounce an "r", hm?'

'That'll do, woman. Get on with the breakfast.'

While Iris busied herself over breakfast, Jack went to look at the house. It wasn't as bad as he had thought – a credit to poor construction. Apparently the upper two rooms were a late addition and had just been perched onto the older, comparatively flat-topped lower section. The frame of Molly's bed was bent beyond repair, but the box spring and mattress were intact. The old roof seemed fairly sound, where the removal of the jerry-built little top storey had exposed it. The living room would be big enough for him and Iris, and Molly's bed could be set up in the study. There were tools and lumber in the garage, the weather was warm and clear, and like any other writer, Jack Garry was very much attracted by the prospect of hard work for which he would not get paid, as long as it wasn't writing. By the time Iris called him for breakfast, he had most of the debris cleared from the roof and a plan of action mapped out. It would only be necessary to cover the hole where the stairway landing had been, and go over the roof for potential leaks. A good rain, he reflected, would search those out for him quickly enough.

'What about Mewhu?' Iris asked as she handed him an aromatic plate of eggs and bacon. 'If we feed him any of this, do you think he'll throw another fit?'

Jack looked at their visitor, who sat on the other side of the fire very close to Molly, gazing big-eyed at their breakfasts.

'I don't know. We could give him a little, I suppose.'

Mewhu inhaled his sample, and wailed for more. He ate a second helping, and when Iris refused to fry more eggs, he gobbled toast and jam. Each new thing he tasted he would nibble at, blink twice, and then bolt down. The only exception was the coffee. One taste was sufficient. He put it down on the ground and very carefully, very delicately overturned it.

'Can you talk to him?' Iris asked suddenly.

'He can talk to me,' declared Molly.

'I've heard him,' Jack said.

'Oh, no. I don't mean *that*,' Molly denied vehemently. 'I can't make any sense out of that stuff.'

'What do you mean, then?'

'I . . . I dunno, Mommy. He just – talks to me, that's all.'

Jack and Iris looked at each other. 'Must be a game,' said Iris. Jack shook his head, looking at his daughter carefully as if he had not really seen her before. He could think of nothing to say, and rose.

'Think the house can be patched up?'

'Oh sure.' He laughed. 'You never did like the colour of the upstairs rooms, anyway.'

'I don't know what's gotten into me,' said Iris thoughtfully. 'I'd have kicked like a mule at any part of this. I'd have packed up and gone home if, say, just a wall was gone upstairs, or if there were just a hole in the roof, or if this . . . this android phenomenon arrived suddenly. But when it all happens at once – I can take it all!'

'Question of perspective. Show me a nagging woman and I'll show you one who hasn't enough to worry about.'

'You'll get out of my sight or you'll have this frying pan bounced off your yammering skull,' said Iris steadily. Jack got.

Molly and Mewhu trailed after him as he returned to the house, stood side by side goggling at him as he mounted the ladder.

'Whatsha doing, Daddy?'

'Marking off the edges of this hole where the stairway hits the place where the roof isn't, so I can clean up the edges with a saw.'

'Oh.'

Jack roughed out the area with a piece of charcoal, lopped off the more manageable rough edges with a hatchet, cast about for his saw. It was still in the garage. He climbed down, got it, climbed up again, and began to saw. Twenty minutes of this, and sweat was streaming down his face. He knocked off, climbed down, doused his head at the pump, lit a cigarette, climbed back up on the roof.

'Why don't you jump off and back?'

The roofing job was looking larger and the day seemed warmer than it had. Jack's enthusiasm was in inverse proportion to these factors. 'Don't be funny, Molly.'

'Yes, but Mewhu wants to know.'

'Oh, he does. Ask him to try it.'

He went back to work. A few minutes later, when he paused for a breath, Mewhu and Molly were nowhere to be seen. Probably over by the tent, in Iris's hair, he thought, and went on sawing.

'Daddy!'

Daddy's unaccustomed arm and shoulder were, by this time, yelling for help. The dry soft-wood alternately cheesed the saw out of line and bound it. He answered impatiently, 'Well, what?'

'Mewhu says to come. He wants to show you something.'

'Show me what? I haven't time to play now, Molly. I'll attend to Mewhu when we get a roof over our heads again.'

'But it's for you!'

'What is?'

'The thing in the tree.'

'Oh, all right.' Prompted more by laziness than by curiosity, Jack climbed back down the ladder. Molly was waiting. Mewhu was not in sight.

'Where is he?'

'By the tree,' she said with exaggerated patience, taking his hand. 'Come on. It's not far.'

She led him around the house and across the bumpy track that was euphemistically known as a road. There was a tree down on the other side. He looked from it to the house, saw that in line with the felled tree and his damaged roof were more broken trees, where something had come down out of the sky, skimmed the tops of the trees, angling closer to the ground until it wiped the top off his house and had then risen up and up – to where?

They went deeper into the woods for ten minutes, skirting an occasional branch or fallen treetop, until they came to Mewhu, who was leaning against a young maple. He smiled, pointed up into the tree, pointed to his arm, to the ground. Jack looked at him in puzzlement.

'He fell out of the tree and broke his arm,' said Molly.

'How do you know?'

'Well, he just did, Daddy.'

'Nice to know. Now can I get back to work?'

'He wants you to get the thing in the tree!'

Jack looked upward. Hung on a fork two-thirds of the way up the tree was a gleaming object, a stick about five feet long with a streamlined shape on each end, rather like the wingtip tanks of a P-80. 'What on earth is that?'

'I dunno. I can't— He tol' me, but I dunno. Anyway, it's for you, so you don't . . . so you don't—' She looked at Mewhu for a moment. The alien's silver moustache seemed to swell a little. '—so you don't have to climb the ladder so much.'

'Molly – how did you know that?'

'He *told* me, that's all. Gosh, Daddy, don't be mad. I don't know how, honest; he just did, that's all.'

'I don't get it,' muttered Jack. 'Anyhow – what's this about that thing in the tree? I'm supposed to break my arm too?'

'It isn't dark.'

'What do you mean by that?'

Molly shrugged. 'Ask him.'

'Oh. I think I catch that. He fell out of the tree because it was dark. He thinks I can get up there and get the whatzit without hurting myself because I can see what I am doing. He also flatters me. Or is it flattery? How close to the apes does he think we are?'

'What are you talking about, Daddy?'

'Never mind . . . why am I supposed to get that thing, anyway?'

'Uh – so's you can jump off the roof.'

'That is just silly. However, I do want a look at that thing. Since his ship is gone, that object up there seems to be the only artifact he brought with him except his clothes.'

'What's an artifact?'

'Second cousin to an artichoke. Here goes nothin',' and he swung up into the tree. He had not climbed a tree for years, and as he carefully chose his way, it occurred to him that there were probably more efficient ways of gaining altitude. An escalator, for example. Why didn't escalators grow on trees?

The tree began to shiver and sway with his weight. He looked down once and decided instantly not to do it again. He looked up and was gratified to see how close he was to the object he was after. He pulled himself up another three feet and was horrified at how far away it was, for the branches were very small up here. He squirmed upward, reached, and his fingers just brushed against the shank of the thing. It had two rings fastened to it, he noticed, one each side of the centre, large enough to get an arm through. It was one these which was hung up on a branch. He chinned himself, then, with his unpractised muscles cracking, took one hand off and reached.

The one-hand chinning didn't come off so well. His arm began to sag. The ring broke off its branch as his weight came on it. He was immediately surrounded by the enthusiastic crackling of breaking shrubbery. He folded his tongue over and got his teeth on it. Since he had a grip on Mewhu's artifact, he held on . . . even when it came free. He began to fall, tensed himself for the bone-breaking jolt he would get at the bottom.

He didn't get it.

He fell quite fast at first, and then the stick he was holding began to bear him up. He thought that it must have caught on a branch, by some miracle – but it hadn't! He was drifting down like a thistle seed, hanging from the rod, which in some impossible fashion was supporting itself in midair. There was a shrill, faint *whooshing* sound from the two streamlined fixtures at the ends of the rod. He looked down, blinked sweat out of his eyes, looked again. Mewhu was grinning a broad and happy grin, and Molly was slack-jawed with astonishment.

The closer he came to the ground the slower he went. When, after what seemed an eternity, he felt the blessed pressure of earth under his feet, he had to stand and *pull* the rod down. It yielded slowly, like an eddy current brake. Dry leaves danced and whirled under the end pieces.

'Gee, Daddy, that was wonderful!'

He swallowed twice to wet down his dry oesophagus, and pulled his eyes back in. 'Yeah. Fun,' he said weakly.

Mewhu came and took the rod out of his hand, and dropped it. It stayed perfectly horizontal, and sank slowly down to the ground, where it lay. Mewhu pointed at it, at the tree, and grinned.

'Just like a parachute. Oh, *gee*, Daddy!'

'You keep away from it,' said Jack, familiar with youthful intonation. 'Heaven knows what it is. It might go off, or something.'

He looked fearfully at the object. It lay quietly, the hissing of the end pieces stilled. Mewhu bent suddenly and picked it up, held it over his head with one hand. Then he calmly lifted his feet and hung from it. It lowered him gently, butt first, until he sat on the ground, in a welter of dead leaves; for as soon as he picked it up, the streamlined end pieces had begun to blast again.

'That's the silliest thing I ever saw. Here – let me see it.' It was hovering about waist-high. He leaned over one of the ends. It had a fine round grille over it. He put out a hand. Mewhu reached out and caught his wrist shaking his head. Apparently it was dangerous to go too near those ends. Garry suddenly saw why. They were tiny, powerful jet motors of some kind. If the jet was powerful enough to support a man's weight, the intake must be drawing like mad – probably enough to snap a hole through a man's hand like a giant ticket-puncher.

But what controlled it? How was the jet strength adjusted to the weight borne by the device, and to the altitude? He remembered without pleasure that when he had fallen with it from the treetop, he had dropped quite fast, and that he went slower and slower as he approached the ground. And yet when Mewhu had held it over his head, it had borne his weight instantly and lowered him very slowly. And besides – how was it so stable? Why didn't it turn upside down and blast itself and passenger down to earth?

He looked at Mewhu with some increase of awe. Obviously he came from a place where the science was really advanced. He wondered if he would ever be able to get any technical information from his visitor – and if he would be able to understand it. Of course, Molly seemed to be able to—

'He wants you to take it back and try it on the roof,' said Molly.

'How can that refugee from a Kuttner opus help me?'

Immediately Mewhu took the rod, lifted it, ducked under it, and slipped his arms through the two rings, so that it crossed his back like a water-bucket yoke. Peering around, he turned to face a clearing in the trees, and before their startled eyes, he leaped thirty feet in the air, drifted away in a great arc, and came gently to rest twenty yards away.

Molly jumped up and down and clapped her hands, speechless with delight. The only words Garry could find were a reiterated, 'Ah, no!'

Mewhu stood where he was smiling his engaging smile, waiting for them. They walked toward him, and when they were close, he leaped again and soared out toward the road.

'What do you do with a thing like this?' breathed Jack. 'Who do you go to, and what do you say to him?'

'Le's just keep him for a pet, Daddy.'

Jack took her hand, and they followed the bounding, soaring silver man. A pet! A member of some alien race, from some unthinkable civilization – and obviously a highly trained individual, too, for no 'man in the street' would have made such a trip. What was his story? Was he an advance guard? Or – was he the sole survivor of his people? How far had he come? Mars? Venus?

They caught up with him at the house. He was standing by the ladder. His strange rod was lying quiet on the ground. He was fascinatedly operating Molly's yo-yo. When he saw them, he threw down the yo-yo, picked up his device, and slipping it across his shoulders, sprang high in the air and drifted down to the roof. 'Eee-yu!' he said, with emphasis, and jumped off backward. So stable was the rod that, as he sank through the air, his long body swung to and fro.

'Very nice,' said Jack. 'Also spectacular. And I have to go back to work.' He went to the ladder.

Mewhu bounded over to him, caught his arm, whimpering and whistling in his peculiar speech. He took the rod and extended it toward Jack.

'He wants you to use it,' said Molly.

'No, thanks,' said Jack, a trace of his tree-climbing vertigo returning to him. 'I'd just as soon use the ladder.' And he put his hand out to it.

Mewhu, hopping with frustration, reached past him and toppled the ladder. It levered over a box as it fell and struck Jack painfully on the shin.

'I guess you better use the flyin' belt, Daddy.'

Jack looked at Mewhu. The silver man was looking as pleasant as he could with that kind of a face; on the other hand, it might just possibly be wise to humour him a little. Being safely on the ground to begin with, Jack felt that it might not matter if the fantastic thing wouldn't work for him. And if it failed him over the roof – well, the house wasn't *very* tall.

He shrugged his arms through the two rings. Mewhu pointed to the roof, to Jack, made a jumping motion. Jack took a deep breath, aimed carefully, and, hoping the gadget wouldn't work – jumped.

He shot up close to the house – too close. The eave caught him a resounding thwack on precisely the spot where the ladder had just hit him. The impact barely checked him. He went sailing up over the roof, hovered for a breathless second, and then began to come down. For a moment he thought his flailing legs would find purchase on the far edge of the roof. He just missed it. All he managed to do was to crack the same shin, in the same place, mightily on the other eave. Trailing clouds of profanity, he landed standing – in Iris's wash basket. Iris, just turning from the clothes line, confronted him.

'Jack! What on earth are you . . . get out of that! You're standing right on my wash with your dirty . . . *oh!*'

'Oh oh!' said Jack, and stepped backward out of the wash basket. His foot went into Molly's express wagon, which Iris used to carry the heavy basket. To get his balance, he leaped – and immediately rose high in the air. This time his luck was better. He soared completely over the kitchen wing of the house and came to earth near Molly and Mewhu.

'Daddy, you were just like a bird!'

'I'm going to be just like a corpse if your mother's expression means what I think it does.' He shucked off the 'flyin' belt' and dove into the house just as Iris rounded the corner. He heard Molly's delighted 'He went *that* way' as he ploughed through the shambles of the living room and out the front door. As the kitchen door slammed he was rounding the house. He charged up to Mewhu, snatched the gadget from him, slipped it on and jumped. This time his judgement was faultless. He cleared the house easily although he came very near landing astride the clothesline. When Iris, panting and furious, stormed out of the house, he was busily hanging sheets.

'Just what,' said Iris, her voice crackling at the seams, 'do you think you're doing?'

'Just giving you a hand with the laundry, m'love,' said Jack.

'What is that . . . that object on your back?'

'Another evidence of the ubiquity of the devices of science-fiction,' said Jack blandly. 'This is a multilateral, three-dimensional mass adjuster, or pogo-chute. With it I can fly like a gull, evading the cares of the world and the advances of beautiful redheads, at such times as their passions are distasteful to me.'

'Sometime in the very near future, you gangling hatrack, I am going to pull the tongue out of your juke box of a head and tie a bowknot in it.' Then she laughed.

He heaved a sigh of relief, went and kissed her. 'Darling, I am sorry. I was scared silly, dangling from this thing. I didn't see your clothes basket, and if I had I don't know how I'd have steered clear.'

'What is it, Jack? How does it work?'

'I dunno. Jets on the ends. They blast hard when there's a lot of weight pushing them toward the earth. They blast harder near the earth then up high. When the weight on them slacks off a bit, they throttle down. What makes them do it, what they are using for power – I just wouldn't know. As far as I can see, they suck in air at the top and blow it out through the jets. And, oh yes – they point directly downward no matter which way the rod is turned.'

'Where did you get it?'

'Off a tree. It's Mewhu's. Apparently he used it for a parachute. On the way down, a tree branch, speared through one of these rings and he slipped out of it and fell and broke his arm.'

'What are we going to do with him, Jack?'

'I've been worrying about that myself. We can't sell him to a sideshow.' He paused, thoughtfully. 'There's no doubt that he has a lot that would be of value to humanity. Why – this thing alone would change the face of the earth! Listen – I weigh a hundred and seventy. I *fell* on this thing, suddenly, when I lost my grip on a tree, and it bore my weight immediately. Mewhu weighs more than I do, judging from his build. It took his weight when he lifted his feet off the ground while holding it over his head. If it can do that, it or a larger version should be able, not only to drive, but to support an aircraft. If for some reason that isn't possible, the power of those little jets certainly could turn a turbine.'

'Will it wash clothes?' Iris was glum.

'That's exactly what I mean! Light, portable, and more power than it has any right to have – of *course* it'll wash clothes. And drive generators, and cars, and . . . Iris, what do you *do* when you have something as big as this?'

'Call a newspaper, I guess.'

'And have a hundred thousand people peeking and prying all over the place, and Congressional investigations, and what all? Uh . . . *uh!*'

'Why not ask Harry Zinsser?'

'Harry? I thought you didn't like him.'

'I never said that. It's just that you and he go off in the corner and chatter about multitude amputation and debilities of reactance and things like that, and I have to sit, knit – and spit when I want someone's attention. Harry's all right.'

'Gosh, honey, you've got it! Harry'll know what to do. I'll go right away.'

'You'll do nothing of the kind! With that hole in the roof? I thought you said you could have it patched up for the night at least. By the time you get back here it'll be dark.'

The prospect of sawing out the ragged hole in the roof was suddenly the least appealing thing in the world. But there was logic and an 'or else' tone to what she said. He sighed and went off mumbling something about the greatest single advance in history awaiting the whim of a woman. He forgot he was wearing Mewhu's armpit altitudinizer, and only his first two paces were on the ground. Iris hooted with laughter at his clumsy walking on air. When he reached the ground, he set his jaw and leaped lightly up to the roof. 'Catch me now, you and your piano legs,' he taunted cheerfully, ducked the lancelike clothes prop she hurled at him, and went back to work.

As he sawed, he was conscious of a hubbub down below.

'Dah – dee! Mr-r-roo ellue—'

He sighed and put down the saw. 'What is it?'

'Mewhu wants his flyin' belt!'

Jack looked at the roof, at the lower shed, and decided that his old bones could stand it if he had to get down without a ladder. He took the jet-tipped rod and dropped it. It stayed perfectly horizontal, falling no slower and no faster than it had when he had ridden it down. Mewhu caught it, deftly slipped his splinted arm through it – it was astonishing how careful he was of the arm, and yet how little it inconvenienced him – then the other arm, and sprang up to join Jack on the roof.

'What do you say, fella?'

'Woopen yew weep.'

'I know how you feel.' He knew that the silver man wanted to tell him something, but couldn't help him out. He grinned and picked up the saw. Mewhu took it out of his hand and tossed it off the roof, being careful to miss Molly, who was dancing back to get a point of vantage.

'What's the big idea?'

'Dellihew hidden,' said Mewhu. 'Pento deh numinew heh,' and he pointed at the flyin' belt and at the hole in the roof.

'You mean I'd rather fly off in that thing than work? Brother, you got it. But I'm afraid I have to—'

Mewhu circled his arm, pointing all around the hole in the roof, and pointed again to the pogo-chute, indicating one of the jet motors.

'I don't get it,' said Jack.

Mewhu apparently understood, and an expression of amazement crossed his mobile face. Kneeling, he placed his good hand around one of the little jet motors, pressed two tiny studs, and the casing popped open. Inside was a compact, sealed, and simple-looking device, the core of the motor itself, apparently. There seemed to be no other fastening. Mewhu lifted it out and handed it to Jack. It was about the size and shape of an electric razor. There was a button on the side. Mewhu pointed at it, pressed the back; and then moved Jack's hand so that the device was pointed away from them both. Jack, expecting anything, from nothing at all to the 'blinding bolt of searing, raw energy' so dear to the science-fiction world, pressed the button.

The gadget hissed, and snuggled back into his palm in an easy recoil.

'That's fine,' said Jack, 'but what do I do with it?'

Mewhu pointed at Jack's saw cut, then at the device.

'Oh,' said Jack. He bent close, aimed the thing at the end of the saw cut, and pressed the button. Again the hiss, and the slight, steady recoil; and a fine line appeared in the wood. It was a cut, about half as thick as the saw cut, clean and even and, as long as he kept his hand steady, very straight. A fine cloud of pulverized wood rose out of the hole in the roof, carried on a swirl of air.

Jack experimented, holding the jet close to the wood and away from it. He found that it cut finer the closer he got to it. As he drew it away from the wood, the slot got wider and the device cut slower until at about eighteen inches it would not cut at all. Delighted, Jack quickly cut and trimmed the hole. Mewhu watched grinning. Jack grinned back, knowing how he would feel if he introduced a saw to some primitive who was trying to work wood with a machete.

When he was finished, he handed the jet back to the silver man, and slapped his shoulder. 'Thanks a million, Mewhu.'

'Jeek,' said Mewhu, and reached for Jack's neck. One of his thumbs lay on Jack's collarbone, the other on his back, over the scapula. Mewhu squeezed twice, firmly.

'That the way you shake hands back home?' smiled Jack. He thought it likely. Any civilized race was likely to have a manual greeting. The handshake evolved from a raised palm, indicating that the saluter was unarmed. It was quite possible that this was an extension, in a slightly different direction, of the same sign. It would indeed be an indication of friendliness to have two individuals present their throats, each to the other.

Mewhu, with three deft motions, slipped the tiny jet back into its casing, and holding the rod with one hand, stepped off the roof, letting himself be lowered in that amazing thistledown fashion to the ground. Once there, he tossed the rod back. Jack was startled to see it hurtle upward like any earthly object. He grabbed it and missed. It reached the top of its arc, and as soon as it started down again the jets cut in, and it sank easily to him. He put it on and floated down to join Mewhu.

The silver man followed him to the garage, where he kept a few pieces of milled lumber. He selected some one-inch pine boards and dragged them out, to measure them and mark them off to the size he wanted to knock together a simple trapdoor covering for the useless stair well; a process which Mewhu watched with great interest.

Jack took up the flying belt and tried to open the streamlined shell to remove the cutter. It absolutely defied him. He pressed, twisted, wrenched, and pulled. All it did was to hiss gently when he moved it toward the floor.

'Eek, Jeek,' said Mewhu. He took the jet from Jack, pressed it. Jack watched closely. Then he grinned and took the cutter.

He swiftly cut the lumber up with it, sneering gayly at the ripsaw which hung on the wall. Then he put the whole trap together with a Z-brace, trimmed off the few rough corners, and stood back to admire it. He realized instantly that it was too heavy to carry by himself, let alone lift to the roof. If Mewhu had two good hands, now, or if— He scratched his head.

'Carry it on the flyin' belt, Daddy.'

'Molly! What made you think of that?'

'Mewhu tol' . . . I mean, I sort of—'

'Let's get this straight once and for all. How does Mewhu talk to you?'

'I dunno, Daddy. It's sort of like I remembered something he said, but not the . . . the words he said. I jus' . . . jus'—' she faltered, and then said vehemently, 'I don' *know*, Daddy. Truly I don't!'

'What'd he say this time?'

She looked at Mewhu. Again Jack noticed the peculiar swelling of Mewhu's silver moustache. She said, 'Put the door you jus' made on the flyin' belt and lift it. The flyin' belt'll make it fall slow, and you can push it along while . . . it's . . . fallin'.'

Jack looked at the door, at the jet device, and got the idea. When he had slipped the jet-rod under the door, Mewhu gave him a lift. Up it came; and then Mewhu, steadying it, towed it well outside the garage before it finally sank to the ground. Another lift, another easy tow, and they covered thirty more feet. In this manner they covered the distance to the house, with Molly skipping and laughing behind, pleading for a ride and handing the grinning Mewhu a terrific brag.

At the house, Jack said, 'Well, Einstein Junior, how do we get it up on the roof?'

Mewhu picked up Molly's yo-yo and began to operate it deftly. Doing so, he walked around the corner of the house.

'Hey!'

'He don't know, Daddy. You'll have to figger it out.'

'You mean he could dream up that slick trick for carrying it out here and now his brains give out?'

'I guess so, Daddy.'

Jack Garry looked after the retreating form of the silver man, and shook his head. He was already prepared to expect better than human reasoning from Mewhu, even if it was a little different. He couldn't quite phase this with Mewhu's shrugging off a problem in basic logic. Certainly a man with his capabilities would not have reasoned out such an ingenious method of bringing the door out here without realizing that that was only half the problem.

Shrugging, he went back to the garage and got a small block and tackle. He had to put up a big screw hook on the eave, and another on the new trapdoor; and once he had laboriously hauled the door up until the tackle was two-blocked, it was a little more than arduous to work it over the edge and drag it into position. Mewhu had apparently quite lost interest. It was two hours later, just as he put the last screw in the tower bolt on the trapdoor and was calling the job finished, that he heard Mewhu begin to shriek again. He dropped his tools, shrugged into the jet stick, and sailed off the roof.

'Iris! Iris! What's the matter?'

'I don't know, Jack. He's . . . he's—'

Jack pounded around the house to the front. Mewhu was lying on the ground in the midst of some violent kind of convulsion. He lay on his back, arching it high, digging his heels into the turf; and his head was bent back at an impossible angle, so that his weight was on his heels and his forehead. His good arm pounded the ground, though the splinted one lay limp. His lips writhed and he uttered an edgy, gasping series of ululations quite horrible to listen to. He seemed to be able to scream as loudly when inhaling as when exhaling.

Molly stood beside him, watching him hypnotically. She was smiling. Jack knelt beside the writhing form and tried to steady it. 'Molly, stop grinning at the poor fellow!'

'But – he's happy, Daddy.'

'He's what?'

'Can't you see, silly? He feels – good, that's all. He's laughing!'

'Iris, what's the matter with him? Do you know?'

'He's been into the aspirin again, that's all I can tell you.'

'He ate four,' said Molly. 'He loves 'em.'

'What can we do, Jack?'

'I don't know, honey,' said Jack worriedly. 'Better just let him work it out. Any emetic or sedative we give him might be harmful.'

The attack slackened and ceased suddenly, and Mewhu went quite limp. Again, with his hand over the man's chest, Jack felt the strange double pulsing.

'Out cold,' he said.

Molly said in a strange, quiet voice, 'No, Daddy. He's lookin' at dreams.'

'Dreams?'

'A place with a or'nge sky,' said Molly. He looked up sharply. Her eyes were closed. 'Lots of Mewhus. Hunderds an' hunderds – big ones. As big as Mr Thorndyke.' (Thorndyke was an editor whom they knew in the city. He was six feet seven.) 'Round houses, an' big airplanes with . . . sticks fer wings.'

'Molly, you're talking nonsense!' said her mother worriedly. Jack shushed her. 'Go on, baby.'

'A place, a room. It's a . . . Mewhu is there and a bunch more. They're in . . . in lines. Rows. There's a big one with a yella hat. He – keeps them in rows. Here's Mewhu. He's outa the line. He's jumpin' out th' windy with a flyin' belt.' There was a long silence. Mewhu moaned.

'Well?'

'Nothin', Daddy – wait! It's . . . all . . . fuzzy. Now there's a thing, a kinda summerine. Only on the ground, not in the water. The door's open.

Mewhu is . . . is inside. Knobs, and clocks. Pull on the knobs. Push a— Oh. *Oh*! It hurts!' She put her fists to her temples.

'Molly!'

Molly opened her eyes and said, quite calmly, 'Oh, *I'm* all right, Mommy. It was a thing in the dream that hurt, but it didn't hurt *me*. It was all a bunch of fire an' . . . an' a sleepy feeling, only bigger. An' it hurt.'

'Jack, he'll harm the child!'

'I doubt it,' said Jack.

'So do I,' said Iris, wonderingly, and then, almost inaudibly, 'Now, why did I say that?'

'Mewhu's asleep,' said Molly suddenly.

'No more dreams?'

'No more dreams. Gee. That was – funny.'

'Come and have some lunch,' said Iris. Her voice shook a little. They went into the house. Jack looked down at Mewhu, who was smiling peacefully in his sleep. He thought of putting the strange creature to bed, but the day was warm and the grass was thick and soft where he lay. He shook his head and went into the house.

'Sit down and feed,' Iris said.

He looked around. 'You've done wonders in here,' he said. The litter of lath and plaster was gone, and Iris's triumphant antimacassars blossomed from the upholstery. She curtsied. 'Thank you, m'lord.'

They sat around the card table and began to do damage to tongue sandwiches. 'Jack.'

'Mm-m?'

'What was that – telepathy?'

'Think so. Something like that. Oh, wait'll I tell Zinsser! He'll never believe it.'

'Are you going down to the airfield this afternoon?'

'You bet. Maybe I'll take Mewhu with me.'

'That would be a little rough on the populace, wouldn't it? Mewhu isn't the kind of fellow you can pass off as your cousin Julius.'

'Heck, he'd be all right. He could sit in the back seat with Molly while I talked Zinsser into coming out to have a look at him.'

'Why not get Zinsser out here?'

'You know that's silly. When we see him in town, he's got time off. Out here he's tied to that airport almost every minute.'

'Jack – do you think Molly's quite safe with that creature?'

'Of course! Are you worried?'

'I . . . I am, Jack. But not about Mewhu. About me. I'm worried because I think I should worry more, if you see what I mean.'

Jack leaned over and kissed her. 'The good old maternal instinct at work,' he chuckled. 'Mewhu's new and strange and might be dangerous. At the same time Mewhu's helpless and inoffensive, and something in you wants to mother him, too.'

'There you really have something,' said Iris, thoughtfully. 'He's as big and ugly as you are, and unquestionably more intelligent. Yet I don't mother you.'

Jack grinned. 'You're not kiddin'.' He gulped his coffee and stood up. 'Eat it up, Molly, and go wash your hands and face. I'm going to have a look at Mewhu.'

'You're going in to the airport, then?' asked Iris.

'If Mewhu's up to it. There's too much I want to know, too much I haven't the brains to figure out. I don't think I'll get all the answers from Zinsser, by any means; but between us we'll figure out what to do about this thing. Iris, it's *big*!'

Full of wild, induced speculation, he stepped out on the lawn. Mewhu was sitting up, happily contemplating a caterpillar.

'Mewhu.'

'Dew?'

'How'd you like to take a ride?'

'Hubilly grees. Jeck?'

'I guess you don't get the idea. C'mon,' said Jack, motioning toward the garage. Mewhu very, very carefully set the caterpillar down on a blade of grass and rose to follow; and just then the most unearthly crash issued from the garage. For a frozen moment no one moved, and then Molly's voice set up a hair-raising reiterated screech. Jack was pounding toward the garage before he knew he had moved.

'Molly! what is it?'

At the sound of his voice the child shut up as if she were switch-operated.

'Molly!'

'Here I am, Daddy,' she said in an extremely small voice. She was standing by the car her entire being concentrated in her protruding, faintly quivering lower lip. The car was nose-foremost through the back wall of the garage.

'Daddy, I didn't mean to do it: I just wanted to help you get the car out. Are you going to spank me? Please, Daddy, I didn't—'

'*Quiet!*'

She was quiet, but immediately. 'Molly, what on earth possessed you to do a thing like that? You know you're not supposed to touch the starter!'

'I was pretending, Daddy, like it was a summerine that could fly the way Mewhu did.'

Jack threaded his way through this extraordinary shambles of syntax. 'Come here,' he said sternly. She came, her paces half-size, her feet dragging, her hands behind her where her imagination told her they would do the most good. 'I ought to whack you you know.'

'Yeah,' she answered tremulously. 'I guess you oughta. Not more'n a couple of times, huh Daddy?'

Jack bit the insides of his cheeks for control, but couldn't make it. He grinned. *You little minx*, he thought. 'Tell you what,' he said gruffly, looking at the car. The garage was fortunately flimsy, and the few new dents on hood and fenders would blend well with the old ones. 'You've got three good whacks coming to you. I'm going to add those on to your next spanking.'

'Yes, Daddy,' said Molly, her eyes big and chastened. She climbed into the back seat and sat, very straight and small, away back out of sight. Jack cleared away what wreckage he could, and then climbed in, started the old puddle-vaulter and carefully backed out of the damaged shed.

Mewhu was standing well clear, watching the groaning automobile with startled silver eyes. 'Come on in,' said Jack, beckoning. Mewhu backed off.

'Mewhu!' cried Molly, putting her head out the rear door. Mewhu said 'Yowk,' and came instantly. Molly opened the door and he climbed in, and Molly shouted with laughter when he crouched down on the floor, and made him get up on the seat. Jack pulled around the house, stopped, picked up Mewhu's jet rod, blew a kiss through the window to Iris, and they were off.

Forty minutes later they wheeled up to the airport after an ecstatic ride during which Molly had kept up a running fire of descriptive commentary on the wonders of a terrestrial countryside. Mewhu had goggled and ogled in a most satisfactory fashion, listening spellbound to the child – sometimes Jack would have sworn that the silver man understood everything she said – and uttering little shrieks, exclamatory mewings, and interrogative peeps.

'Now,' said Jack, when he had parked at the field boundary, 'you two stay in the car for a while. I'm going to speak to Mr Zinsser and see if he'll come out and meet Mewhu. Molly, do you think that you can make Mewhu understand that he's to stay in the car, and out of sight? You see, if other people see him, they'll want to ask a lot of silly questions, and we don't want to embarrass him, do we?'

'No, Daddy. Mewhu'll be good. Mewhu,' she said, turning to the silver man. She held his eyes with hers. His moustache swelled, rippled. 'You'll be good, won't you, and stay out of sight?'

'Jeek,' said Mewhu. 'Jeek mereedy.'

'He says you're the boss.'

Jack laughed, climbing out. 'He does, eh?' Did the child really know or was it mostly a game? 'Be good, then. See you soon.' Carrying the jet rod, he walked into the building.

Zinsser, as usual, was busy. The field was not large, but did a great deal of private-plane business, and as traffic manager, Zinsser had his hands full. He wrapped one of his pudgy, flexible hands around the phone he was using. 'Hi, Garry! What's new out of this world?' he grated cheerfully. 'Siddown. With you in a minute.' He bumbled cheerfully into the telephone, grinning at Jack as he talked. Jack made himself as comfortable as patience permitted and waited until Zinsser hung up.

'Well now,' said Zinsser, and the phone rang again.

Jack closed his open mouth in annoyance. Zinsser hung up and another bell rang. He picked up a field telephone from its hook on the side of his desk. 'Zinsser. Yes—'

'Now that's enough,' said Jack to himself. He rose, went to the door, closed it softly so that he was alone with the manager. He took the jet rod, and to Zinsser's vast astonishment, stood up on his desk, raised the rod high over his head, and stepped off. A hurricane screamed out of the jets. Jack, hanging by his hands from the rod as it lowered him gently through the air, looked over his shoulder. Zinsser's face looked like a red moon in a snow flurry, surrounded as it was by every interoffice memo for the past two weeks.

Anyway, the first thing he did when he could draw a breath was to hang up the phone.

'Thought that would do it,' said Jack, grinning.

'You . . . you . . . what *is* that thing?'

'It's a dialectical polarizer,' said Jack, alighting. 'That is, it makes conversations possible with airport managers who won't get off the phone.'

Zinsser was out of his chair and around the desk, remarkably light on his feet for a man his size. 'Let me see that.'

Jack handed it over.

'Look, Mewhu! Here comes a plane!'

Together they watched the Cub slide in for a landing, and squeaked at the little puffs of dust that were thrown up by the tyres and flicked away by the slipstream.

'And there goes another one. It's gonna take off!' The little blue low-wing coupé taxied across the field, braked one wheel, swung in its own length and roared down toward them, lifting to howl away into the sky far over their heads.

'Eeeeeyow,' droned Molly, imitating the sound of the motor as it passed overhead.

'S-s-s-s-sweeeeee!' hissed Mewhu, exactly duplicating the whine of control surfaces in the problast.

Molly clapped her hands and shrieked with delight. Another plane began to circle the field. They watched it avidly.

'Come on out and have a look at him,' said Jack.

Zinsser looked at his watch. I can't. All kidding aside, I got to stick by the phone for another half hour at the very least. Will he be all right out there? There's hardly anyone around.'

'I think so. Molly's with him and as I told you, they get along beautifully together. That's one of the things I want to have investigated – that telepathy angle. He laughed suddenly. 'That Molly . . . know what she did this afternoon?' He told Zinsser about Molly's driving the car through the wrong end of the garage.

'The little hellion,' chuckled Zinsser. 'They'll all do it, bless 'em. At some time or other in, his life, I think every kid climbs aboard something he doesn't know anything about and runs it wrong. My brother's kid went to work on the front lawn with his mother's vacuum cleaner the other day.' He laughed. 'To get back to what's-his-name – Mewhu, and this gadget of his. Jack, we've got to hang on to it. Do you realize that he and his clothes and this thing are the only clues we have as to as to what he is and where he came from?'

'I sure do. But listen – he's very intelligent. I'm sure he'll be able to tell us plenty.'

'You can bet he's intelligent,' said Zinsser. 'He's probably above average on his planet. They wouldn't send just anyone on a trip like that. Jack, what a pity we don't have his ship!'

'Maybe it'll be back. What's your guess as to where he comes from?'

'Mars, maybe.'

'Now, you know better than that. We know Mars has an atmosphere, but it's mighty tenuous. An organism the size of Mewhu would have to have enormous lungs to keep him going. No; Mewhu's used to an atmosphere pretty much like ours.'

'That would rule Venus out.'

'He wears clothes quite comfortably here. His planet must have not only pretty much the same atmosphere, but the same climate. He seems to be able to take most of our foods, though he is revolted by some of them – and aspirin sends him high as a kite. He gets what looks like a laughing drunk on when he takes it.'

'You don't say. Let's see; it wouldn't be Jupiter, because he isn't built to take a gravity like that. And the outer planets are too cold, and Mercury is too hot.' Zinsser leaned back in his chair and absently mopped his bald head. 'Jack, this guy doesn't even come from this solar system!'

'Gosh. I guess you're right. Harry, what do you make of this jet gadget?'

'From the way you say it cuts wood . . . can I see that, by the way?' Zinsser asked.

'Sure,' Garry went to work on the jet. He found the right studs to press simultaneously. The casing opened smoothly. He lifted out the active core of the device, and, handling it gingerly, sliced a small corner off Zinsser's desk top.

'That is the strangest thing I have ever seen,' said Zinsser. 'May I see it?'

He took it and turned it over in his hands. 'There doesn't seem to be any fuel for it,' he said, musingly.

'I think it uses air,' said Jack.

'But what pushes the air?'

'Air,' said Jack. 'No – I'm not kidding. I think that in some way it disintegrates part of the air, and uses the energy released to activate a small jet. If you had a shell around this jet, with an intake at one end and a blast tube at the other, it would operate like a high-vacuum pump, dragging more air through.'

'Or like an athodyd,' said Zinsser. Garry's blood went cold as the manager sighted down into the jet orifice. 'For heaven's sake don't push that button.'

'I won't. Say – you're right. The tube's concentric. Now, how on earth could a disruption unit be as small and light as that?'

Jack Garry said, 'I've been chewing on that all day. I have one answer. Can you take something that sounds really fantastic, so long as it's logical?'

'You know me,' grinned Zinsser waving at a long shelf of back number science-fiction magazines. 'Go ahead.'

'Well,' said Jack carefully. 'You know what binding energy is. The stuff that holds the nucleus of an atom together. If I understand my smattering of nuclear theory properly, it seems possible to me that a sphere of binding energy could be produced that would be stable.'

'A sphere? With what inside it?'

'Binding energy – or maybe just nothing . . . space. Anyhow, if you surround that sphere with another, this one a force-field which is capable of penetrating the inner one, or of allowing matter to penetrate it, it seems to me that anything entering that balance of force would be disrupted. An explosive pressure would be bottled up inside the inner sphere. Now if you bring your penetrating field in contact with the binding-energy sphere, the pressures inside will come blasting out. Incase the whole rig in a device which controls the amount of matter going in one side of the sphere and the amount of orifide allowed for the escape of energy and incase that further in an outside shell which will give you a stream of air induced violently through it – like the vacuum pump you mentioned – and you have this,' and he rapped on the little jet motor.

'Most ingenious,' said Zinsser, wagging his head. 'Even if you're wrong, it's an ingenious theory. What you're saying, you know, is that all we have to do to duplicate this device is to discover the nature of binding energy and then find a way to make it stay stably in spherical form. After which we figure out the nature of a field which can penetrate binding energy and allow any matter to do likewise – one way.' He spread his hands. 'That's all. Just learn to actually use the stuff that the long-hair boys haven't thought of theorizing about yet, and we're all set.'

'Shucks,' said Garry, 'Mewhu will give us all the dope.'

'I hope so, Jack, this can revolutionize the entire industrial world!'

'You're understanding,' grinned Jack.

The phone rang. Zinsser looked at his watch again. 'There's my call.' He sat down, answered the phone, and while he went on at great length to some high-powered character at the other end of the line, about bills of lading and charter service and interstate commerce restrictions, Jack lounged against the cut-off corner of the desk and dreamed. Mewhu – a superior member of a superior race, come to earth to lead struggling humanity out of its struggling, wasteful ways. He wondered what Mewhu was like at home among his strange people. Young, but very mature, he decided, and gifted in many ways – the pick of the crop, fit to be ambassador to a new and dynamic civilization like Earth's. And what about the ship? Having dropped Mewhu, had it and its pilot returned to the mysterious corner of the universe from which they had come? Or was it circling about somewhere in space, anxiously awaiting word from the adventurous ambassador?

Zinsser cradled his instrument and stood up with a sigh. 'A credit to my will power,' he said. 'The greatest thing that has ever happened to me, and I stuck by the day's work in spite of it. I feel like a kid on Christmas Eve. Let's go have a look at him.'

'*Wheeeeyouwow!*' screamed Mewhu as another rising plane passed over their heads. Molly bounced joyfully up and down on the cushions, for Mewhu was an excellent mimic.

The silver man slipped over the back of the driver's seat in a lithe movement, to see a little better around the corner of a nearby hangar. One of the Cubs had been wheeled into it, and was standing not far away, its prop ticking over.

Molly leaned her elbows on the edge of the seat and stretched her little neck so she could see, too. Mewhu brushed against her head and her hat fell off. He bent to pick it up and bumped his own head on the dashboard, and the glove compartment flew open. His strange pupils narrowed, and the nictitating membranes flickered over his eyes as he reached inside. The next thing Molly knew, he was out of the car and running over the parking area, leaping high in the air, mouthing strange noises, and stopping every few jumps to roll and beat with his good hand on the ground.

Horrified, Molly Garry left the car and ran after him. 'Mewhu!' she cried. 'Mewhu, come *back!*'

He cavorted toward her, his arms outspread. 'W-r-r-row-w!' he shouted, rushing past her. Lowering one arm a little and raising the other like an airplane banking, he ran in a wide arc, leaped the little tarmac retaining wall and bounded out onto the hangar area.

Molly, panting and sobbing, stopped and stamped her foot. 'Mewhu!' she croaked helplessly. 'Daddy said—'

Two mechanics standing near the idling Cub looked around at a sound like a civet-cat imitating an Onondaga war whoop. What they saw was a long-legged, silver-grey apparition with a silver-white moustache, and slotted eyes, dressed in a scarlet robe that turned to indigo. Without a sound, moving as one man, they cut and ran. And Mewhu with one last terrible shriek of joy, leaped to the plane and disappeared inside.

Molly put her hands to her mouth and her eyes bugged. 'Oh, Mewhu,' she breathed. 'Now you've done it.' She heard pounding feet, turned. Her father was racing toward her, with Mr Zinsser waddling behind. 'Molly! Where's Mewhu?'

Wordlessly, she pointed at the Cub; and as if it were a signal, the little ship throttled up and began to crawl away from the hangars.

'Hey! Wait! Wait!' screamed Jack Garry uselessly, sprinting after the plane. He leaped the wall but misjudged it because of his speed. His toe hooked it and he sprawled slithering, jarringly on the tarmac. Zinsser and Molly ran to him, helped him up. Jack's nose was bleeding. He whipped out a handkerchief, looked out at the dwindling plane. 'Mewhu!'

The little plane waddled across the field, bellowed suddenly with power. The tail came up, and it scooted away from them – cross-wind, cross the runway. Jack turned to speak to Zinsser and saw the fat man's face absolutely stricken. He followed Zinsser's eyes and saw the other plane, the big six-place cabin job, coming in.

He had never felt so helpless in all his life. Those planes were going to collide. There was nothing anyone could do about it. He watched them, unblinking, almost detachedly. They were hurtling but they seemed to creep; the moment lasted for ever. Then, with twenty feet altitude, Mewhu cut his gun and dropped a wing. The Cub slowed, leaned into the wind, and *side-slipped* so close under the cabin ship that another coat of paint on either craft would have meant disaster.

Jack didn't know how long he had been holding that breath, but it was agony when he let it out.

'Anyway, he can fly,' breathed Zinsser.

'Of course he can fly,' snapped Jack. 'A prehistoric thing like an airplane would be child's play for him. Child's play.'

'Oh, Daddy, I'm scared.'

'I'm not,' said Jack hollowly.

'Me, too,' said Zinsser with an unconvincing laugh. 'The plane's insured.'

The Cub arrowed upward. At a hundred feet it went into a skiding turn, harrowing to watch, suddenly winged over and came shouting down at them. Mewhu buzzed them so close that Zinsser went flat on his face. Jack and Molly simply stood there, wall-eyed. An enormous cloud of dust obscured everything for ninety interminable seconds. When they next saw the plane it was wobbling crazily at a hundred and fifty.

Suddenly Molly screamed piercingly and put her hands over her face.

'Molly! Kiddo, what is it?'

She flung her arms around his neck and sobbed so violently that he knew it was hurting her throat. 'Stop it!' He yelled; and then, very gently, he asked, 'What's the matter, darling?'

'He's scared. Mewhu's terrible, terrible scared,' she said brokenly.

Jack looked up at the plane. It yawed, fell away on one wing. Zinsser shouted, his voice cracking, 'Gun her! Gun her! Throttle up, you idiot!'

Mewhu cut the gun.

Dead stick, the plane winged over and plunged to the ground. The impact was crushing.

Molly said, quite calmly, 'All Mewhu's pictures have gone out now,' and slumped unconscious to the ground.

They got him to the hospital. It was messy – all of it; picking him up, carrying him to the ambulance—

Jack wished fervently that Molly had not seen; but she had sat up and cried as they carried him past. He thought worriedly as he and Zinsser crossed and recrossed in their pacing of the waiting room, that he would have his hands full with the child when this thing was all over.

The resident physician came in, wiping his hands. He was a small man with a nose like a walnut meat. 'Who brought that plane-crash case in here – you?'

'Both of us,' said Zinsser.

'What . . . who is he?'

'A friend of mine. Is he . . . will he live?'

'How should I know?' snapped the doctor impatiently. 'I have never in my experience—' He exhaled through his nostrils. 'The man has two circulatory systems. Two *closed* circulatory systems, and a heart for each. All his arterial blood looks veinous – it's purple. How'd he happen to get hurt?'

'He ate half a box of aspirin out of my car,' said Jack. 'Aspirin makes him drunk. He swiped a plane and piled it up.'

'Aspirin makes him—' The doctor looked at each of them in turn, 'I won't ask if you're kidding me. Just to see that . . . that thing in there is enough to kid any doctor. How long has that splint been on his arm?'

Zinsser looked at Jack and Jack said, 'About eighteen hours.'

'Eighteen *hours*?' The doctor shook his head. 'It's so well knitted that I'd say eighteen days.' Before Jack could say anything he added. 'He needs a transfusion.'

'But you can't! I mean . . . his blood—'

'I know. Took a sample to type it. I have two technicians trying to blend chemicals into plasma so we can approximate it. Both of 'em called me a liar. But he's got to have the transfusion. I'll let you know.' He strode out of the room.

'There goes one bewildered medico.'

'He's OK,' said Zinsser. 'I know him well. Can you blame him?'

'For feeling that way? Gosh, no. Harry, I don't know what I'll do if Mewhu checks out.'

'That fond of him?'

'Oh, it isn't only that. But to come so close to meeting a new culture, and then have it slip from our fingers like this – it's too much.'

'That jet . . . Jack, without Mewhu to explain it, I don't think any scientist will be able to build another. It would be like . . . like giving a Damascus sword-smith some tungsten and asking him to draw it into filaments. There the jet would be, hissing when you shove it toward the ground, sneering at you.'

'And that telepathy – what J. B. Rhine wouldn't give to be able to study it!'

'Yeah, and what about his origin?' Zinsser asked excitedly. 'He isn't from this system. It means that he used an interstellar drive of some kind, or even that space-time warp the boys write about.'

'He's got to live,' said Jack. 'He's got to, or there ain't no justice. There are too many things we've got to know, Harry! Look – he's here. That must mean that some more of his people will come some day.'

'Yeah. Why haven't they come before now?'

'Maybe they have. Charles Forte—'

'Aw, look,' said Zinsser, 'don't let's get this thing out of hand.'

The doctor came back. 'I think he'll make it.'

'Really?'

'Not really. Nothing real about that character. But from all indications, he'll be OK. Responds very strongly. What does he eat?'

'Pretty much the same as we do, I think.'

'You think. You don't seem to know much about him.'

'I don't. He only just got here. No – don't ask me where from,' said Jack. 'You'll have to ask him.'

The doctor scratched his head. 'He's out of this world. I can tell you that. Obviously adult, but every fracture but one is a green-stick break; kind of thing you get on a three-year-old. Transparent membranes over his . . . what are you laughing at?' he asked suddenly.

Jack had started easily, with a chuckle, but it got out of control. He roared.

Zinsser said, 'Jack! Cut it out. This is a hosp—'

Jack shoved his hand away. 'I . . . I got to,' he said helplessly and went off on another peal.

'You've got to what?'

'Laugh,' said Jack, gasping. He sobered – he more than sobered. 'It has to be funny, Harry. I won't let it be anything else.'

'What the devil do you—'

'Look, Harry. We assumed a lot about Mewhu, his culture, his technology, his origin . . . we'll never know anything about it!'

'Why?' You mean he won't tell us—'

'He won't tell us. I'm wrong. He'll tell us plenty. But it won't do any good. Here's what I mean. Because he's our size, because he obviously arrived in a spaceship, because he brought a gadget or two that's obviously the product of a highly advanced civilization, we believe that *he* produced the civilization; that he's a superior individual in his own place.'

'Well, he must be.'

'He must be? Harry, did Molly invent the automobile?'

'No, but—'

'But she drove one through the back of the garage.'

Light began to dawn on Zinsser's moon face. 'You mean—'

'It all fits! Remember when Mewhu figured out how to carry that heavy trapdoor of mine on the jet stick, and then left the problem half-finished? Remember his fascination with Molly's yo-yo? What about that peculiar rapport he has with Molly that he has with no one else? Doesn't that begin to look reasonable? Look at Iris's reaction to him – almost maternal, though she didn't know why.'

'The poor little fellow,' breathed Zinsser. 'I wonder if he thought he was home when he landed?'

'Poor little fellow – sure,' said Jack, and began to laugh again. 'Can Molly tell you how an internal combustion engine works? Can she explain laminar flow on an airfoil?' He shook his head. 'You wait and see. Mewhu will be able to tell us the equivalent of Molly's "I rode in the car with Daddy and we went sixty miles an hour."'

'But how did he get here?'

'How did Molly get through the back of my garage?'

The doctor shrugged his shoulders helplessly. 'About that I don't know. But his biological reactions do look like those of a child – and if he is a child, then his rate of tissue restoration will be high, and I'll guarantee he'll live.'

Zinsser groaned. 'Much good will it do us – and him, poor kid. With a kid's inherent faith in any intelligent adult anywhere, he's probably been feeling happily sure we'd get him home somehow. Well – we haven't got what it takes, and won't have for a long, long time. We don't know enough to start duplicating that jet of his – and that was just a little kid's toy on his world.'

archive 4
time warps

File classification: Mythology
Location: New Mexico, USA

Title: Unicorn Variation
Writer: *Roger Zelazny*

Briefing: *Mythology – ancient mystery tales about fabulous heroes and legendary creatures with timeless symbolic meaning.* Martin is a backpacker holed up in a New Mexico shanty town. He's a keen chessplayer and seven years ago reached the world preliminaries. Now, in the unlikely setting of the deserted bar, he finds himself playing a match with a mythical opponent and a lot more than honour at stake.

Author: American Roger Zelazny has frequently drawn on mythology in his stories ever since the Sixties when he emerged as one of the leading figures in the New Wave of US sf writers. Originally from Ohio, Roger studied at Western Reserve University and worked for the US Government Social Security Administratation before two of his stories won Nebula awards in the same year: 1966. One was for 'He Who Shapes', focusing on dream analysis, and the other, 'The Doors of His Face, the Lamps of His Mouth', about the hunting of an immense sea-monster. His novel, *Lord of Light* (1967) brilliantly combined Hindu legends and sf, and it heralded the books and short stories which have since assured his reputation, including the 'Amber' series about Prince Corbin and his son, Merlin (widely compared to C. S. Lewis's classic tales of Narnia) and *The Last Defender of Camelot* (1980) with its wonderful mythic resonances. 'Unicorn Variation' also won a Hugo when it was published in 1980 and brilliantly combines the New Mexico terrain around Sante Fe where Zelazny lived for years, along with his enduring fascination for, and deep understanding of, mythology.

A bizarrerie of fires, cunabulum of light, it moved with a deft, almost dainty deliberation, phasing into and out of existence like a storm-shot piece of evening; or perhaps the darkness between the flares was more akin to its truest nature – swirl of black ashes assembled in prancing cadence to the lowing note of desert wind down the arroyo behind buildings as empty yet filled as the pages of unread books or stillnesses between the notes of a song.

Gone again. Back again. Again.

Power, you said? Yes. It takes considerable force of identity to manifest before or after one's time. Or both.

As it faded and gained it also advanced, moving through the warm afternoon, its tracks erased by the wind. That is, on those occasions when there were tracks.

A reason. There should always be a reason. Or reasons.

It knew why it was there – but not why it was *there*, in that particular locale.

It anticipated learning this shortly, as it approached the desolation-bound line of the old street. However, it knew that the reason may also come before, or after. Yet again, the pull was there and the force of its being was such that it had to be close to something.

The buildings were worn and decayed and some of them fallen and all of them drafty and dusty and empty. Weeds grew among floorboards. Birds nested upon rafters. The droppings of wild things were everywhere; and it knew them all as they would have known it, were they to meet face to face.

It froze, for there had come the tiniest unanticipated sound from somewhere ahead and to the left. At that moment, it was again phasing into existence and it released its outline which faded as quickly as a rainbow in hell, but the naked presence remained beyond subtraction.

Invisible, yet existing, strong, it moved again. The clue. The cue. Ahead. *A gauche.* Beyond the faded word SALOON on weathered board above. Through the swinging doors. (One of them pinned alop.)

Pause and assess.

Bar to the right, dusty. Cracked mirror behind it. Empty bottles. Broken bottles. Brass rail, black, encrusted. Tables to the left and rear. In various states of repair.

Man seated at the best of the lot. His back to the door. Levis. Hiking boots. Faded blue shirt. Green backpack leaning against the wall to his left.

Before him, on the tabletop, is the faint, painted outline of a chessboard, stained, scratched, almost obliterated.

The drawer in which he had found the chessmen is still partly open.

He could no more have passed up a chess set without working out a problem or replaying one of his better games than he could have gone without breathing, circulating his blood or maintaining a relatively stable body temperature.

It moved nearer, and perhaps there were fresh prints in the dust behind it, but none noted them.

It, too, played chess.

It watched as the man replayed what had perhaps been his finest game, from the world preliminaries of seven years past. He had blown up after that – surprised to have gotten even as far as he had – for he never could perform well under pressure. But he had always been proud of that one game, and he relived it as all sensitive beings do certain turning points in their lives. For perhaps twenty minutes, no one could have touched him. He had been shining and pure and hard and clear. He had felt like the best.

It took up a position across the board from him and stared. The man completed the game, smiling. Then he set up the board again, rose and fetched a can of beer from his pack. He popped the top.

When he returned, he discovered that White's King's Pawn had been advanced to K4. His brow furrowed. He turned his head, searching the bar, meeting his own puzzled gaze in the grimy mirror. He looked under the table. He took a drink of beer and seated himself.

He reached out and moved his Pawn to K4. A moment later, he saw White's King's Knight rise slowly into the air and drift forward to settle upon KB3. He stared for a long while into the emptiness across the table before he advanced his own Knight to his KB3.

White's Knight moved to take his Pawn. He dismissed the novelty of the situation and moved his Pawn to Q3. He all but forgot the absence of a tangible opponent as the White Knight dropped back to its KB3. He paused to take a sip of beer, but no sooner had he placed the can upon the tabletop than it rose again, passed across the board and was upended. A gurgling noise followed. Then the can fell to the floor, bouncing, ringing with an empty sound.

'I'm sorry,' he said, rising and returning to his pack. 'I'd have offered you one if I'd thought you were something that might like it.'

He opened two more cans, returned with them, placed one near the far edge of the table, one at his own right hand.

'Thank you,' came a soft, precise voice from a point beyond it.

The can was raised, tilted slightly, returned to the tabletop.

'My name is Martin,' the man said.

'Call me Tlingel,' said the other. 'I had thought that perhaps your kind was extinct. I am pleased that you at least have survived to afford me this game.'

'Huh?' Martin said. 'We were all still around the last time that I looked – a couple of days ago.'

'No matter. I can take care of that later,' Tlingel replied. 'I was misled by the appearance of this place.'

'Oh. It's a ghost town. I backpack a lot.'

'Not important. I am near the proper point in your career as a species. I can feel that much.'

'I am afraid that I do not follow you.'

'I am not at all certain that you would wish to. I assume that you intend to capture that pawn?'

'Perhaps. Yes, I do wish to. What are you talking about?'

The beer can rose. The invisible entity took another drink.

'Well,' said Tlingel, 'to put it simply, your – successors – grow anxious. Your place in the scheme of things being such an important one, I had sufficient power to come and check things out.'

'"Successors"? I do not understand.'

'Have you seen any griffins recently?'

Martin chuckled.

'I've heard the stories,' he said, 'seen the photos of the one supposedly shot in the Rockies. A hoax, of course.'

'Of course it must seem so. That is the way with mythical beasts.'

'You're trying to say that it was real?'

'Certainly. Your world is in bad shape. When the last grizzly bear died recently, the way was opened for the griffins – just as the death of the last aepyornis brought in the yeti, the dodo the Loch Ness creature, the passenger pigeon the sasquatch, the blue whale the kraken, the American eagle the cockatrice—'

'You can't prove it by me.'

'Have another drink.'

Martin began to reach for the can, halted his hand and stared.

A creature approximately two inches in length, with a human face, a lion-like body and feathered wings was crouched next to the beer can.

'A mini-sphinx,' the voice continued. 'They came when you killed off the last smallpox virus.'

'Are you trying to say that whenever a natural species dies out a mythical one takes its place?' he asked.

'In a word – yes. Now. It was not always so, but you have destroyed the mechanisms of evolution. The balance is now redressed by those others of us from the morning land – we, who have never truly been endangered. We return, in our time.'

'And you – whatever you are, Tlingel – you say that humanity is now endangered?'

'Very much so. But there is nothing that you can do about it, is there? Let us get on with the game.'

The sphinx flew off. Martin took a sip of beer and captured the pawn.

'Who,' he asked then, 'are to be our successors?'

'Modesty almost forbids,' Tlingel replied. 'In the case of a species as prominent as your own, it naturally has to be the loveliest, most intelligent, most important of us all.'

'And what are you? Is there any way that I can have a look?'

'Well – yes. If I exert myself a trifle.'

The beer can rose, was drained, fell to the floor. There followed a series of rapid rattling sounds retreating from the table. The air began to flicker over a large area opposite Martin, darkening within the growing flame-work. The outline continued to brighten, its interior growing jet black. The form moved, prancing about the saloon, multitudes of tiny, cloven hoof-prints scoring and cracking the floorboards. With a final, near-blinding flash it came into full view and Martin gasped to behold it.

A black unicorn with mocking, yellow eyes sported before him, rising for a moment onto its hind legs to strike a heraldic pose. The fires flared about it a second longer, then vanished.

Martin had drawn back, raising one hand defensively.

'Regard me!' Tlingel announced. 'Ancient symbol of wisdom, valour, and beauty, I stand before you!'

'I thought your typical unicorn was white,' Martin finally said.

'I am archetypical,' Tlingel responded, dropping to all fours, 'and possessed of virtues beyond the ordinary.'

'Such as?'

'Let us continue our game.'

'What about the fate of the human race? You said—'

' . . . And save the small talk for later.'

'I hardly consider the destruction of humanity to be small talk.'

'And if you've any more beer . . .'

'All right,' Martin said, retreating to his pack as the creature advanced, its eyes like a pair of pale suns. 'There's some lager.'

Something had gone out of the game. As Martin sat before the ebon horn on Tlingel's bowed head, like an insect about to be pinned, he realized that his playing was off. He had felt the pressure the moment he had seen the beast – and there was all that talk about an imminent doomsday. Any run-of-the-mill pessimist could say it without troubling him, but coming from a source as peculiar as this . . .

His earlier elation had fled. He was no longer in top form. And Tlingel was good. Very good. Martin found himself wondering whether he could manage a stalemate.

After a time, he saw that he could not and resigned.

The unicorn looked at him and smiled.

'You don't really play badly – for a human,' it said.

'I've done a lot better.'

'It is no shame to lose to me, mortal. Even among mythical creatures there are very few who can give a unicorn a good game.'

'I am pleased that you were not wholly bored,' Martin said. 'Now will you tell me what you were talking about concerning the destruction of my species?'

'Oh, that,' Tlingel replied. 'In the morning land where those such as I dwell, I felt the possibility of your passing come like a gentle wind to my nostrils, with the promise of clearing the way for us—'

'How is it supposed to happen?'

Tlingel shrugged, horn writing on the air with a toss of the head.

'I really couldn't say. Premonitions are seldom specific. In fact, that is what I came to discover. I should have been about it already, but you diverted me with beer and good sport.'

'Could you be wrong about this?'

'I doubt it. That is the other reason I am here.'

'Please explain.'

'Are there any beers left?'

'Two, I think.'

'Please.'

Martin rose and fetched them.

'Damn! The tab broke off this one,' he said.

'Place it upon the table and hold it firmly.'

'All right.'

Tlingel's horn dipped forward quickly, piercing the can's top.

' . . . Useful for all sorts of things,' Tlingel observed, withdrawing it.

'The other reason you're here . . .' Martin prompted.

'It is just that I am special. I can do things that the others cannot.'

'Such as?'

'Find your weak spot and influence events to exploit it, to – hasten matters. To turn the possibility into a probability, and then—'

'*You* are going to destroy us? Personally?'

'That is the wrong way to look at it. It is more like a game of chess. It is as much a matter of exploiting your opponent's weaknesses as of exercising your own strengths. If you had not already laid the groundwork I would be powerless. I can only influence that which already exists.'

'So what will it be? World War III? An ecological disaster? A mutated disease?'

'I do not really know yet, so I wish you wouldn't ask me in that fashion. I repeat that at the moment I am only observing. I am only an agent—'

'It doesn't sound that way to me.'

Tlingel was silent. Martin began gathering up the chessmen.

'Aren't you going to set up the board again?'

'To amuse my destroyer a little more? No thanks.'

'That's hardly the way to look at it—'

'Besides, those are the last beers.'

'Oh.' Tlingel stared wistfully at the vanishing pieces, then remarked, 'I would be willing to play you again without additional refreshment . . .'

'No thanks.'

'You are angry.'

'Wouldn't you be, if our situations were reversed?'

'You are anthropomorphizing.'

'Well?'

'Oh, I suppose I would.'

'You could give us a break, you know – at least, let us make our own mistakes.'

'You've hardly done that yourself, though, with all the creatures my fellows have succeeded.'

Martin reddened.

'Okay. You just scored one. But I don't have to like it.'

'You are a good player. I know that . . .'

'Tlingel, if I were capable of playing at my best again, I think I could beat you.'

The unicorn snorted two tiny wisps of smoke.

'Not *that* good,' Tlingel said.

'I guess you'll never know.'

'Do I detect a proposal?'

'Possibly. What's another game worth to you?'

Tlingel made a chuckling noise.

'Let me guess: You are going to say that if you beat me you want my promise not to lay my will upon the weakest link in mankind's existence and shatter it.'

'Of course.'

'And what do I get for winning?'

'The pleasure of the game. That's what you want, isn't it?'

'The terms sound a little lopsided.'

'Not if you are going to win anyway. You keep insisting that you will.'

'All right. Set up the board.'

'There is something else that you have to know about me first.'

'Yes?'

'I don't play well under pressure, and this game is going to be a terrific strain. You want my best game, don't you?'

'Yes, but I'm afraid I've no way of adjusting your own reactions to the play.'

'I believe I could do that myself if I had more than the usual amount of time between moves.'

'Agreed.'

'I mean a lot of time.'

'Just what do you have in mind?'

'I'll need time to get my mind off it, to relax, to come back to the positions as if they were only problems . . .'

'You mean to go away from here between moves?'

'Yes.'

'All right. How long?'

'I don't know. A few weeks, maybe.'

'Take a month. Consult your experts, put your computers onto it. It may make for a slightly more interesting game.'

'I really didn't have that in mind.'

'Then it's time that you're trying to buy.'

'I can't deny that. On the other hand, I will need it.'

'In that case, I have some terms. I'd like this place cleaned up, fixed up, more lively. It's a mess. I also want beer on tap.'

'Okay. I'll see to that.'

'Then I agree. Let's see who goes first.'

Martin switched a black and a white pawn from hand to hand beneath the table. He raised his fists then and extended them. Tlingel leaned forward and tapped. The black horn's tip touched Martin's left hand.

'Well, it matches my sleek and glossy hide,' the unicorn announced.

Martin smiled, setting up the white for himself, the black pieces for his opponent. As soon as he had finished, he pushed his Pawn to K4.

Tlingel's delicate, ebon hoof moved to advance the Black King's Pawn to K4.

'I take it that you want a month now, to consider your next move?'

Martin did not reply but moved his Knight to KB3. Tlingel immediately moved a Knight to QB3.

Martin took a swallow of beer and then moved his Bishop to N5. The unicorn moved the other Knight to B3. Martin immediately castled and Tlingel moved the Knight to take his Pawn.

'I think we'll make it,' Martin said suddenly, 'if you'll just let us alone. We do learn from our mistakes, in time.'

'Mythical beings do not exactly exist in time. Your world is a special case.'

'Don't you people ever make mistakes?'

'Whenever we do they're sort of poetic.'

Martin snarled and advanced his Pawn to Q4. Tlingel immediately countered by moving the Knight to Q3.

'I've got to stop,' Martin said, standing. 'I'm getting mad, and it will affect my game.'

'You will be going, then?'

'Yes.'

He moved to fetch his pack.

'I will see you here in one month's time?'

'Yes.'

'Very well.'

The unicorn rose and stamped upon the floor and lights began to play across its dark coat. Suddenly, they blazed and shot outward in all directions like a silent explosion. A wave of blackness followed.

Martin found himself leaning against the wall, shaking. When he lowered his hand from his eyes, he saw that he was alone, save for the knights, the bishops, the kings, the queens, their castles and both the kings' men.

He went away.

Three days later Martin returned in a small truck, with a generator, lumber, windows, power tools, paint, stain, cleaning compounds, wax. He dusted and vacuumed and replaced rotted wood. He installed the windows. He polished the old brass until it shone. He stained and rubbed. He waxed the floors and buffed them. He plugged holes and washed glass. He hauled all the trash away.

It took him the better part of a week to turn the old place from a wreck back into a saloon in appearance. Then he drove off, returned all of the equipment he had rented and bought a ticket for the Northwest.

The big, damp forest was another of his favourite places for hiking, for thinking. And he was seeking a complete change of scene, a total revision of outlook. Not that his next move did not seem obvious, standard even. Yet, something nagged . . .

He knew that it was more than just the game. Before that he had been ready to get away again, to walk drowsing among shadows, breathing clean air.

Resting his back against the bulging root of a giant tree, he withdrew a small chess set from his pack, set it up on a rock he'd moved into position nearby. A fine, mist-like rain was settling, but the tree sheltered him, so far. He reconstructed the opening through Tlingel's withdrawal of the Knight to Q3. The simplest thing would be to take the Knight with the Bishop. But he did not move to do it.

He watched the board for a time, felt his eyelids drooping, closed them and drowsed. It may only have been for a few minutes. He was never certain afterwards.

Something aroused him. He did not know what. He blinked several times and closed his eyes again. Then he reopened them hurriedly.

In his nodded position, eyes directed downward, his gaze was fixed upon an enormous pair of hairy, unshod feet – the largest pair of feet that he had ever beheld. They stood unmoving before him, pointed toward his right.

Slowly – very slowly – he raised his eyes. Not very far, as it turned out. The creature was only about four and a half feet in height. As it was looking at the chessboard rather than at him, he took the opportunity to study it.

It was unclothed but very hairy, with a dark brown pelt, obviously masculine, possessed of low brow ridges, deep-set eyes that matched its hair, heavy shoulders, five-fingered hands that sported opposing thumbs.

It turned suddenly and regarded him, flashing a large number of shining teeth.

'White's pawn should take the pawn,' it said in a soft, nasal voice.

'Huh? Come on,' Martin said. 'Bishop takes knight.'

'You want to give me black and play it that way? I'll walk all over you.' Martin glanced again at its feet.

'. . . Or give me white and let me take that pawn. I'll still do it.'

'Take white,' Martin said, straightening. 'Let's see if you know what you're talking about.' He reached for his pack. 'Have a beer?'

'What's a beer?'

'A recreational aid. Wait a minute.'

Before they had finished the six-pack, the sasquatch – whose name, he had learned, was Grend – had finished Martin. Grend had quickly entered a ferocious midgame, backed him into a position of dwindling security and pushed him to the point where he had seen the end and resigned.

'That was one hell of a game,' Martin declared, leaning back and considering the ape-like countenance before him.

'Yes, we Bigfeet are pretty good, if I do say it. It's our one big recreation, and we're so damned primitive we don't have much in the way of boards and chessmen. Most of the time, we just play it in our heads. There're not many can come close to us.'

'How about unicorns?' Martin asked.

Grend nodded slowly.

'They're about the only ones can really give us a good game. A little dainty, but they're subtle. Awfully sure of themselves, though, I must say. Even when they're wrong. Haven't seen any since we left the morning land, of course. Too bad. Got any more of that beer left?'

'I'm afraid not. But listen, I'll be back this way in a month. I'll bring some more if you'll meet me here and play again.'

'Martin, you've got a deal. Sorry. Didn't mean to step on your toes.'

He cleaned the saloon again and brought in a keg of beer which he installed under the bar and packed with ice. He moved in some bar stools, chairs and tables which he had obtained at a Goodwill store. He hung red curtains. By then it was evening. He set up the board, ate a light meal, unrolled his sleeping bag behind the bar and camped there that night.

The following day passed quickly. Since Tlingel might show up at any time, he did not leave the vicinity, but took his meals there and sat about working chess problems. When it began to grow dark, he lit a number of oil lamps and candles.

He looked at his watch with increasing-frequency. He began to pace. He couldn't have made a mistake. This was the proper day. He—

He heard a chuckle.

Turning about, he saw a black unicorn head floating in the air above the chessboard. As he watched, the rest of Tlingel's body materialized.

'Good evening, Martin.' Tlingel turned away from the board. 'The place looks a little better. Could use some music . . .'

Martin stepped behind the bar and switched on the transistor radio he had brought along. The sounds of a string quartet filled the air. Tlingel winced.

'Hardly in keeping with the atmosphere of the place.'

He changed stations, located a Country & Western show.

'I think not,' Tlingel said. 'It loses something in transmission.'

He turned it off.

'Have we a good supply of beverage?'

Martin drew a gallon stein of beer – the largest mug that he could locate, from a novelty store – and set it upon the bar. He filled a much smaller one for himself. He was determined to get the beast drunk if it were at all possible.

'Ah! Much better than those little cans,' said Tlingel, whose muzzle dipped for but a moment. 'Very good.'

The mug was empty. Martin refilled it.

'Will you move it to the table for me?'

'Certainly.'

'Have an interesting month?'

'I suppose I did.'

'You've decided upon your next move?'

'Yes.'

'Then let's get on with it.'

Martin seated himself and captured the Pawn.

'Hm. Interesting.'

Tlingel stared at the board for a long while, then raised a cloven hoof which parted in reaching for the piece.

'I'll just take that bishop with this little knight. Now I suppose you'll be wanting another month to decide what to do next.'

Tlingel leaned to the side and drained the mug.

'Let me consider it,' Martin said, 'while I get you a refill.'

Martin sat and stared at the board through three more refills. Actually, he was not planning. He was waiting. His response to Grend had been Knight takes Bishop, and he had Grend's next move ready.

'Well?' Tlingel finally said. 'What do you think?'

Martin took a small sip of beer.

'Almost ready,' he said. 'You hold your beer awfully well.'

Tlingel laughed.

'A unicorn's horn is a detoxicant. Its possession is a universal remedy. I wait until I reach the warm-glow stage, then I use my horn to burn off any excess and keep me right there.'

'Oh,' said Martin. 'Neat trick, that.'

' . . . If you've had too much, just touch my horn for a moment and I'll put you back in business.'

'No, thanks. That's all right. I'll just push this little pawn in front of the queen's rook two steps ahead.'

'Really . . .' said Tlingel. 'That's interesting. You know, what this place really needs is a piano – rinkytink, funky . . . Think you could manage it?'

'I don't play.'

'Too bad.'

'I suppose I could hire a piano player.'

'No. I do not care to be seen by other humans.'

'If he's really good, I suppose he could play blindfolded.'

'Never mind.'

'I'm sorry.'

'You are also ingenious. I am certain that you will figure something out by next time.'

Martin nodded.

'Also, didn't these old places used to have sawdust all over the floors?'

'I believe so.'

'That would be nice.'

'Check.'

Tlingel searched the board frantically for a moment.

'Yes. I meant "yes". I said "check". It means "yes" sometimes, too.'

'Oh. Rather. Well, while we're here . . .'

Tlingel advanced the Pawn to Q3.

Martin stared. That was not what Grend had done. For a moment, he considered continuing on his own from here. He had tried to think of Grend as a coach up until this point. He had forced away the notion of crudely and crassly pitting one of them against the other. Until P-Q3. Then he recalled the game he had lost to the sasquatch.

'I'll draw the line here,' he said, 'and take my month.'

'All right. Let's have another drink before we say good night. Okay?'

'Sure. Why not?'

They sat for a time and Tlingel told him of the morning land, of primeval forests and rolling plains, of high craggy mountains and purple seas, of magic and mythic beasts.

Martin shook his head.

'I can't quite see why you're so anxious to come here,' he said, 'with a place like that to call home.'

Tlingel sighed.

'I suppose you'd call it keeping up with the griffins. It's the thing to do these days. Well. Till next month . . .'

Tlingel rose and turned away.

'I've got complete control now. Watch!'

The unicorn form faded, jerked out of shape, grew white, faded again, was gone, like an afterimage.

Martin moved to the bar and drew himself another mug. It was a shame to waste what was left. In the morning, he wished the unicorn were there again. Or at least the horn.

It was a grey day in the forest and he held an umbrella over the chessboard upon the rock. The droplets fell from the leaves and made dull, plopping noises as they struck the fabric. The board was set up again through Tlingel's P-Q3. Martin wondered whether Grend had remembered, had kept proper track of the days . . .

'Hello,' came the nasal voice from somewhere behind him and to the left.

He turned to see Grend moving about the tree, stepping over the massive roots with massive feet.

'You remembered,' Grend said. 'How good! I trust you also remembered the beer?'

'I've lugged up a whole case. We can set up the bar right here.'

'What's a bar?'

'Well, it's a place where people go to drink – in out of the rain – a bit dark, for atmosphere – and they sit up on stools before a big counter, or else at little tables – and they talk to each other – and sometimes there's music – and they drink.'

'We're going to have all that here?'

'No. Just the dark and the drinks. Unless you count the rain as music. I was speaking figuratively.'

'Oh. It does sound like a very good place to visit, though.'

'Yes. If you will hold this umbrella over the board, I'll set up the best equivalent we can have here.'

'All right. Say, this looks like a version of that game we played last time.'

'It is. I got to wondering what would happen if it had gone this way rather than the way that it went.'

'Hmm. Let me see . . .'

Martin removed four six-packs from his pack and opened the first.

'Here you go.'

'Thanks.'

Grend accepted the beer, squatted, passed the umbrella back to Martin.

'I'm still white?'

'Yeah.'

'Pawn to King six.'

'Really?'

'Yep.'

'About the best thing for me to do would be to take this pawn with this one.'

'I'd say. Then I'll just knock off your knight with this one.'

'I guess I'll just pull this knight back to K2.'

' . . . And I'll take this one over to B3. May I have another beer?'

An hour and a quarter later, Martin resigned. The rain had let up and he had folded the umbrella.

'Another game?' Grend asked.

The afternoon wore on. The pressure was off. This one was just for fun. Martin tried wild combinations, seeing ahead with great clarity, as he had that one day . . .

'Stalemate,' Grend announced much later. 'That was a good one, though. You picked up considerably.'

'I was more relaxed. Want another?'

'Maybe in a little while. Tell me more about bars now.'

So he did. Finally, 'How is all that beer affecting you?' he asked.

'I'm a bit dizzy. But that's all right. I'll still cream you the third game.'

And he did.

'Not bad for a human, though. Not bad at all. You coming back next month?'

'Yes.'

'Good. You'll bring more beer?'

'So long as my money holds out.'

'Oh. Bring some plaster of Paris then. I'll make you some nice footprints and you can take casts of them. I understand they're going for quite a bit.'

'I'll remember that.'

Martin lurched to his feet and collected the chess set.

'Till then.'

'Ciao.'

Martin dusted and polished again, moved in the player piano and scattered sawdust upon the floor. He installed a fresh keg. He hung some reproductions of period posters and some atrocious old paintings he had located in a junk shop. He placed cuspidors in strategic locations. When he was finished, he seated himself at the bar and opened a bottle of mineral water. He listened to the New Mexico wind moaning as it passed, to grains of sand striking against the windowpanes. He wondered whether the whole world would have that dry, mournful sound to it if Tlingel found a means for doing away with humanity, or – disturbing thought – whether the successors to his own kind might turn things into something resembling the mythical morning land.

This troubled him for a time. Then he went and set up the board through Black's P-Q3. When he turned back to clear the bar he saw a line of cloven hoofprints advancing across the sawdust.

'Good evening, Tlingel,' he said. 'What is your pleasure?'

Suddenly, the unicorn was there, without preliminary pyrotechnics. It moved to the bar and placed one hoof upon the brass rail.

'The usual.'

As Martin drew the beer, Tlingel looked about.

'The place has improved, a bit.'

'Glad you think so. Would you care for some music?'

'Yes.'

Martin fumbled at the back of the piano, locating the switch for the small, battery-operated computer which controlled the pumping mechanism and substituted its own memory for rolls. The keyboard immediately came to life.

'Very good,' Tlingel stated. 'Have you found your move?'

'I have.'

'Then let us be about it.'

He refilled the unicorn's mug and moved it to the table.

'Pawn to King six,' he said, executing it.

'What?'

'Just that.'

'Give me a minute. I want to study this.'

'Take your time.'

'I'll take the pawn,' Tlingel said, after a long pause and another mug.

'Then I'll take this knight.'

Later, 'Knight to K2,' Tlingel said.

'Knight to B3.'

An extremely long pause ensued before Tlingel moved the Knight to N3.

The hell with asking Grend, Martin suddenly decided. He'd been through this part any number of times already. He moved his Knight to N5.

'Change the tune on that thing!' Tlingel snapped.

Martin rose and obliged.

'I don't like that one either. Find a better one or shut it off!'

After three more tries, Martin shut it off.

'And get me another beer!'

He refilled their mugs.

'All right.'

Tlingel moved the Bishop to K2.

Keeping the unicorn from castling had to be the most important thing at the moment. So Martin moved his Queen to R5. Tlingel made a tiny, strangling noise, and when Martin looked up smoke was curling from the unicorn's nostrils.

'More beer?'

'If you please.'

As he returned with it, he saw Tlingel move the Bishop to capture the Knight. There seemed no choice for him at that moment, but he studied the position for a long while anyhow.

Finally, 'Bishop takes bishop,' he said.

'Of course.'

'How's the warm glow?'

Tlingel chuckled.

'You'll see.'

The wind rose again, began to howl. The building creaked.

'Okay,' Tlingel finally said, and moved the Queen to Q2.

Martin stared. What was he doing? So far, it had gone all right, but— He listened again to the wind and thought of the risk he was taking.

'That's all, folks,' he said, leaning back in his chair. 'Continued next month.'

Tlingel sighed.

'Don't run off. Fetch me another. Let me tell you of my wanderings in your world this past month.'

'Looking for weak links?'

'You're lousy with them. How do you stand it?'

'They're harder to strengthen than you might think. Any advice?'

'Get the beer.'

They talked until the sky paled in the east, and Martin found himself taking surreptitious notes. His admiration for the unicorn's analytical abilities increased as the evening advanced.

When they finally rose, Tlingel staggered.

'You all right?'

'Forgot to detox, that's all. Just a second. Then I'll be fading.'

'Wait!'

'Whazzat?'

'I could use one, too.'

'Oh. Grab hold, then.'

Tlingel's head descended and Martin took the tip of the horn between his fingertips. Immediately, a delicious, warm sensation flowed through him. He closed his eyes to enjoy it. His head cleared. An ache which had been growing within his frontal sinus vanished. The tiredness went out of his muscles. He opened his eyes again.

'Thank—'

Tlingel had vanished. He held but a handful of air.

'—you.'

'Rael here is my friend,' Grend stated. 'He's a griffin.'

'I'd noticed.'

Martin nodded at the beaked, golden-winged creature.

'Pleased to meet you, Rael.'

'The same,' cried the other in a high-pitched voice. 'Have you got the beer?'

'Why – uh – yes.'

'I've been telling him about beer,' Grend explained, half-apologetically. 'He can have some of mine. He won't kibitz or anything like that.'

'Sure. All right. Any friend of yours—'

'The beer!' Rael cried. 'Bars!'

'He's not real bright,' Grend whispered. 'But he's good company. I'd appreciate your humouring him.'

Martin opened the first six-pack and passed the griffin and the sasquatch a beer apiece. Rael immediately punctured the can with his beak, chugged it, belched and held out his claw.

'Beer!' he shrieked. 'More beer!'

Martin handed him another.

'Say, you're still into that first game, aren't you?' Grend observed, studying the board. 'Now, *that* is an interesting position.'

Grend drank and studied the board.

'Good thing it's not raining,' Martin commented.

'Oh, it will. Just wait a while.'

'More beer!' Rael screamed.

Martin passed him another without looking.

'I'll move my pawn to N6,' Grend said.

'You're kidding.'

'Nope. Then you'll take that pawn with your bishop's pawn. Right?'

'Yes . . .'

Martin reached out and did it.

'Okay. Now I'll just swing this knight to Q5.'

Martin took it with the Pawn.

Grend moved his Rook to K1.

'Check,' he announced.

'Yes. That *is* the way to go,' Martin observed.

Grend chuckled.

'I'm going to win this game another time,' he said.

'I wouldn't put it past you.'

'More beer?' Rael said softly.

'Sure.'

As Martin passed him another, he noticed that the griffin was now leaning against the tree trunk.

After several minutes, Martin pushed his King to B1.

'Yeah, that's what I thought you'd do,' Grend said. 'You know something?'

'What?'

'You play a lot like a unicorn.'

'Hm.'

Grend moved his Rook to R3.

Later, as the rain descended gently about them and Grend beat him again, Martin realized that a prolonged period of silence had prevailed. He glanced over at the griffin. Rael had tucked his head beneath his left wing, balanced upon one leg, leaned heavily against the tree and gone to sleep.

'I told you he wouldn't be much trouble,' Grend remarked.

Two games later, the beer was gone, the shadows were lengthening, and Rael was stirring.

'See you next month?'

'Yeah.'

'You bring any plaster of Paris?'

'Yes, I did.'

'Come on, then. I know a good place pretty far from here. We don't want people beating about *these* bushes. Let's go make you some money.'

'To buy beer?' Rael said, looking out from under his wing.

'Next month,' Grend said.

'You ride?'

'I don't think you could carry both of us,' said Grend, 'and I'm not sure I'd want to right now if you could.'

'Bye-bye then,' Rael shrieked, and he leaped into the air, crashing into branches and tree trunks, finally breaking through the overhead cover and vanishing.

'There goes a really decent guy,' said Grend. 'He sees everything and he never forgets. Knows how everything works – in the woods, in the air – even in the water. Generous, too, whenever he has anything.'

'Hm,' Martin observed.

'Let's make tracks,' Grend said.

'Pawn to N6? Really?' Tlingel said. 'All right. The bishop's pawn will just knock off the pawn.'

Tlingel's eyes narrowed as Martin moved the Knight to Q5.

'At least this is an interesting game,' the unicorn remarked. 'Pawn takes knight.'

Martin moved the rook.

'Check.'

'Yes, it is. This next one is going to be a three-flagon move. Kindly bring me the first.'

Martin thought back as he watched Tlingel drink and ponder. He almost felt guilty for hitting it with a powerhouse like the sasquatch behind its back. He was convinced now that the unicorn was going to lose. In every variation of this game that he'd played with Black against Grend, he'd been beaten. Tlingel was very good, but the sasquatch was a wizard with not much else to do but mental chess. It was unfair. But it was not a

matter of personal honour, he kept telling himself. He was playing to
protect his species against a supernatural force which might well be able to
precipitate World War III by some arcane mind-manipulation or magically
induced computer foul up. He didn't dare give the creature a break.

'Flagon number two, please.'

He brought it another. He studied it as it studied the board. It was
beautiful, he realized for the first time. It was the loveliest living thing he
had ever seen. Now that the pressure was on the verge of evaporating and
he could regard it without the overlay of fear which had always been there
in the past, he could pause to admire it. If something *had* to succeed the
human race, he could think of worse choices . . .

'Number three now.'

'Coming up.'

Tlingel drained it and moved the King to B1.

Martin leaned forward immediately and pushed the Rook to R3.

Tlingel looked up, stared at him.

'Not bad.'

Martin wanted to squirm. He was struck by the nobility of the creature.
He wanted so badly to play and beat the unicorn on his own, fairly. Not
this way.

Tlingel looked back at the board, then almost carelessly moved the
Knight to K4.

'Go ahead. Or will it take you another month?'

Martin growled softly, advanced the Rook, and captured the Knight.

'Of course.'

Tlingel captured the Rook with the Pawn. This was not the way that the
last variation with Grend had run. Still . . .

He moved his Rook to KB3. As he did, the wind seemed to commence a
peculiar shrieking, above, amid the ruined buildings.

'Check,' he announced.

The hell with it! he decided. I'm good enough to manage my own
endgame. Let's play this out.

He watched and waited and finally saw Tlingel move the King to N1.

He moved his Bishop to R6. Tlingel moved the Queen to K2. The
shrieking came again, sounding nearer now. Martin took the Pawn with
the Bishop.

The unicorn's head came up and it seemed to listen for a moment. Then
Tlingel lowered it and captured the Bishop with the King.

Martin moved his Rook to KN3.

'Check.'

Tlingel returned the King to B1.

Martin moved the Rook to KB3.

'Check.'

Tlingel pushed the King to N2.

Martin moved the Rook back to KN3.

'Check.'

Tlingel returned the King to B1, looked up and stared at him, showing teeth.

'Looks as if we've got a drawn game,' the unicorn stated. 'Care for another one?'

'Yes, but not for the fate of humanity.'

'Forget it. I'd given up on that a long time ago. I decided that I wouldn't care to live here after all. I'm a little more discriminating than that.

'Except for this bar.' Tlingel turned away as another shriek sounded just beyond the door, followed by strange voices. 'What is that?'

'I don't know,' Martin answered, rising.

The doors opened and a golden griffin entered.

'Martin!' it cried. 'Beer! Beer!'

'Uh – Tlingel, this is Rael, and, and—'

Three more griffins followed him in. Then came Grend, and three others of his own kind.

'—and that one's Grend,' Martin said lamely. 'I don't know the others.'

They all halted when they beheld the unicorn.

'Tlingel,' one of the sasquatches said. 'I thought you were still in the morning land.'

'I still am, in a way. Martin, how is it that you are acquainted with my former countrymen?'

'Well – uh – Grend here is my chess coach.'

'Aha! I begin to understand.'

'I am not sure that you really do. But let me get everyone a drink first.'

Martin turned on the piano and set everyone up.

'How did you find this place?' he asked Grend as he was doing it. 'And how did you get here?'

'Well . . .' Grend looked embarrassed. 'Rael followed you back.'

'Followed a jet?'

'Griffins are supernaturally fast.'

'Oh.'

'Anyway, he told his relatives and some of my folks about it. When we saw that the griffins were determined to visit you, we decided that we had better come along to keep them out of trouble. They brought us.'

'—see. Interesting . . .'

'No wonder you played like a unicorn, that one game with all the variations.'

'Uh – yes.'

Martin turned away, moved to the end of the bar.

'Welcome, all of you,' he said. 'I have a small announcement. Tlingel, a while back you had a number of observations concerning possible ecological and urban disasters and lesser dangers. Also, some ideas as to possible safeguards against some of them.'

'I recall,' said the unicorn.

'I passed them along to a friend of mine in Washington who used to be a member of my old chess club. I told him that the work was not entirely my own.'

'I should hope so.'

'He has since suggested that I turn whatever group was involved into a think tank. He will then see about paying something for its efforts.'

'I didn't come here to save the world,' Tlingel said.

'No, but you've been very helpful. And Grend tells me that the griffins, even if their vocabulary is a bit limited, know almost all that there is to know about ecology.'

'That is probably true.'

'Since they have inherited a part of the Earth, it would be to their benefit as well to help preserve the place. Inasmuch as this many of us are already here, I can save myself some travel and suggest right now that we find a meeting place – say here, once a month – and that you let me have your unique viewpoints. You must know more about how species become extinct than anyone else in the business.'

'Of course,' said Grend, waving his mug, 'but we really should ask the yeti, also. I'll do it, if you'd like. Is that stuff coming out of the big box music?'

'Yes.'

'I like it. If we do this think-tank thing, you'll make enough to keep this place going?'

'I'll buy the whole town.'

Grend conversed in quick gutturals with the griffins, who shrieked back at him.

'You've got a think tank,' he said, 'and they want more beer.'

Martin turned toward Tlingel.

'They were your observations. What do you think?'

'It may be amusing,' said the unicorn, 'to stop by occasionally.' Then, 'So much for saving the world. Did you say you wanted another game?'

'I've nothing to lose.'

Grend took over the tending of the bar while Tlingel and Martin returned to the table.

He beat the unicorn in thirty-one moves and touched the extended horn.

The piano keys went up and down. Tiny sphinxes buzzed about the bar, drinking the spillage.

File classification: Lost Continent
Location: Pacific Ocean

Title: The New Atlantis
Writer: *Ursula K. Le Guin*

Briefing: *Atlantis – an island continent which according to legend sank as a result of fire and tidal waves, c. 9,600 BC.* Bella has got her problems. Her husband is about to be released from a rehabilitation centre and the FBI are bugging their apartment. So does she really need to hear from the mysterious stranger on the bus that pollution and the greenhouse effect are causing America to *sink*? And if that isn't crazy enough, some of the older, lost continents are going to reappear in the Atlantic and Pacific Oceans . . .

Author: Prize-winning American writer Ursula Le Guin was the daughter of two academics and grew up with a passion for ancient Romantic Literature which has not surprisingly found its way into her work. Ursula's stature as a major writer of sf became evident with the publication of the first titles in the 'Hainish' series about a future universe and the people living on its habitable worlds. She won both the Hugo and Nebula awards for her novel, *The Left Hand of Darkness* in 1969, while two years later, *The Lathe of Heaven* (1971) was also highly praised by a number of leading mainstream literary critics. This novel was dramatized for television in 1980 starring Bruce Davison and Margaret Avery and has subsequently been described as 'perhaps the best sf TV movie ever made'. Le Guin's story 'The New Atlantis' is unique among the many tales on this theme in both its concept and execution.

Coming back from my Wilderness Week I sat by an odd sort of man in the bus. For a long time we didn't talk; I was mending stockings, and he was reading. Then the bus broke down a few miles outside Gresham. Boiler trouble, the way it generally is when the driver insists on trying to go over thirty. It was a Supersonic Superscenic Deluxe Long Distance coal-burner, with Home Comfort, that means a toilet, and the seats were pretty comfortable, at least those that hadn't yet worked loose on their bolts, so everybody waited inside the bus; besides, it was raining. We began talking, the way people do when there's a breakdown and a wait. He held up his pamphlet and tapped it – he was a dry-looking man with a schoolteacher-ish way of using his hands – and said, 'This is interesting. I've been reading that a new continent is rising from the depths of the sea.'

The blue stockings were hopeless. You have to have something besides holes to darn onto. 'Which sea?'

'They're not sure yet. Most specialists think the Atlantic. But there's evidence it may be happening in the Pacific too.'

'Won't the oceans get a little crowded?' I said, not taking it seriously. I was a bit snappish, because of the breakdown, and because those blue stockings had been good warm ones.

He tapped the pamphlet again and shook his head, quite serious, 'No,' he said. 'The old continents are sinking, to make room for the new. You can see that that is happening.'

You certainly can. Manhattan Island is now under eleven feet of water at low tide, and there are oyster beds in Ghirardelli Square.

'I thought that was because the oceans are rising from polar melt.'

He shook his head again. 'That is a factor. Due to the greenhouse effect of pollution, indeed Antarctica may become inhabitable. But climatic factors will not explain the emergence of the new – or, possibly, very old – continents in the Atlantic and Pacific.' He went on explaining about continental drift, but I liked the idea of inhabiting Antarctica, and daydreamed about it for a while. I thought of it as very empty, very quiet, all white and blue, with a faint golden glow northward from the unrising sun behind the long peak of Mount Erebus. There were a few people there;

they were very quiet, too, and wore white tie and tails. Some of them carried oboes and violas. Southward the white land went up in a long silence towards the pole.

Just the opposite, in fact, of the Mount Hood Wilderness Area. It had been a tiresome vacation. The other women in the dormitory were all right, but it was macaroni for breakfast, and there were so many organised sports. I had looked forward to the hike up to the National Forest Preserve, the largest forest left in the United States, but the trees didn't look at all the way they do in the postcards and brochures and Federal Beautification Bureau advertisements. They were spindly, and they all had little signs on, saying which union they had been planted by. There were actually a lot more green picnic tables and cement Men's and Women's than there were trees. There was an electrified fence all around the forest to keep out unauthorised persons. The Forest Ranger talked about mountain jays, 'bold little robbers,' he said, 'who will come and snatch the sandwich from your very hand,' but I didn't see any. Perhaps because it was the weekly Watch Those Surplus Calories! Day for all the women, and so we didn't have any sandwiches. If I'd seen a mountain jay I might have snatched the sandwich from his very hand, who knows. Anyhow it was an exhausting week, and I wished I'd stayed home and practised, even though I'd have lost a week's pay because staying home and practising the viola doesn't count as planned implementation of recreational leisure as defined by the Federal Union of Unions.

When I came back from my Antarctic expedition the man was reading again, and I got a look at his pamphlet; and that was the odd part of it. The pamphlet was called 'Increasing Efficiency in Public Accountant Training Schools,' and I could see from the one paragraph I got a glance at that there was nothing about new continents emerging from the ocean depths in it – nothing at all.

Then we had to get out and walk on into Gresham, because they had decided that the best thing for us all to do was get onto the Greater Portland Area Rapid Public Transit Lines, since there had been so many breakdowns that the charter bus company didn't have any more buses to send out to pick us up. The walk was wet, and rather dull, except when we passed the Cold Mountain Commune. They have a wall around it to keep out unauthorized persons, and a big neon sign out front saying 'Cold Mountain Commune' – and there were some people in authentic jeans and ponchos by the highway selling macrame belts and sand-cast candles and soybean bread to the tourists. In Gresham, I took the 4:40 GPARTL Superjet Flyer train to Burnside and East 230th, and then walked to 217th and got the bus to the Goldschmidt Overpass, and transferred to the shuttlebus, but it had boiler trouble too, so I didn't reach the downtown transfer point until 8:10, and the buses go on a once-an-hour schedule at eight, so I got a meatless hamburger at the Long-horn Inch-Thick Steak House Dinerette and caught the nine o'clock bus and got home about ten. When I let myself into the apartment I turned on the lights, but there still weren't any. There had been a power outage in West Portland for three weeks. So I went feeling about for the candles in the dark, and it was a minute or so before I noticed that somebody was lying on my bed.

I panicked, and tried again to turn the lights on.

It was a man, lying there in a long thin heap. I thought a burglar had got in somehow while I was away, and died. I opened the door so I could get out quick or at least my yells could be heard, and then I managed not to shake long enough to strike a match, and lighted the candle, and came a little closer to the bed.

The light disturbed him. He made a sort of snoring in his throat, and turned his head. I saw it was a stranger, but I knew his eyebrows, then the breadth of his closed eyelids, then I saw my husband.

He woke up while I was standing there over him with the candle in my hand. He laughed and said still half asleep, 'Ah, Psyche! from the regions which are holy land.'

Neither of us made much fuss. It was unexpected, but it did seem so natural for him to be there, after all, much more natural than for him not to be there; and he was too tired to be very emotional. We lay there together in the dark, and he explained that they had released him from the Rehabilitation Camp early because he had injured his back in an accident in the gravel quarry, and they were afraid it might get worse. If he died there it wouldn't be good publicity abroad, since there have been some nasty rumours about deaths from illness in the Rehabilitation Camps and the Federal Medical Association Hospitals; and there are scientists abroad who have heard of Simon, since somebody published his proof of Goldbach's Hypothesis in Peking. So they let him out early, with eight dollars in his pocket, which is what he had in his pocket when they arrested him, which made it, of course, fair. He had walked and hitched home from Coeur D'Alene, Idaho, with a couple of days in jail in Walla Walla for being caught hitchhiking. He almost fell asleep telling me this, and when he had told me, he did fall asleep. He needed a change of clothes and a bath but I didn't want to wake him. Besides, I was tired too. We lay side by side and his head was on my arm. I don't suppose that I have ever been so happy. No; was it happiness? Something wider and darker, more like knowledge, more like the night: joy.

It was dark for so long, so very long. We were all blind. And there was the cold, a vast, unmoving, heavy cold. We could not move at all. We did not move. We did not speak. Our mouths were closed, pressed shut by the cold and by the weight. Our eyes were pressed shut. Our limbs were held still. Our minds were held still. For how long? There was no length of time; how long is death? And is one dead only after living, or before life as well? Certainly we thought, if we thought anything, that we were dead; but if we had ever been alive, we had forgotten it.

There was a change. It must have been the pressure that changed first, although we did not know it. The eyelids are sensitive to touch. They must have been weary of being shut. When the pressure upon them weakened a little, they opened. But there was no way for us to know that. It was too cold for us to feel anything. There was nothing to be seen. There was black.

But then – 'then', for the event created time, created before and after, near and far, now and then – 'then' there was the light. One light. One small, strange light that passed slowly, at what distance we could not tell. A small, greenish-white, slightly blurred point of radiance, passing.

Our eyes were certainly open, 'then', for we saw it. We saw the moment. The moment is a point of light. Whether in darkness or in the field of all light, the moment is small, and moves, but not quickly. And 'then' it is gone.

It did not occur to us that there might be another moment. There was no reason to assume that there might be more than one. One was marvel enough: that in all the field of the dark, in the cold, heavy, dense, moveless, timeless, placeless, boundless black, there should have occurred, once, a small, slightly blurred, moving light! Time need be created only once, we thought.

But we were mistaken. The difference between one and more-than-one is all the difference in the world. Indeed, that difference is the world.

The light returned.

The same light, or another one? There was no telling.

But, 'this time', we wondered about the light: was it small and near to us, or large and far away? Again there was no telling; but there was something about the way it moved, a trace of hesitation, a tentative quality, that did not seem proper to anything large and remote. The stars, for instance. We began to remember the stars.

The stars had never hesitated.

Perhaps the noble certainty of their gait had been a mere effect of distance. Perhaps in fact they had hurtled wildly, enormous furnace fragments of a primal bomb thrown through the cosmic dark; but time and distance soften all agony. If the universe, as seems likely, began with an act of destruction, the stars we had used to see told no tales of it. They had been implacably serene.

The planets, however ... We began to remember the planets. They had suffered certain changes of appearance and course. At certain times of the year Mars would reverse its direction and go backwards through the stars. Venus had been brighter and less bright as she went through her phases of crescent, full, and wane. Mercury had shuddered like a skidding drop of rain on the sky flushed with daybreak. The light we now watched had that erratic, trembling quality. We saw it, unmistakably, change direction and go backwards. It then grew smaller and fainter; blinked – an eclipse? – and slowly disappeared.

Slowly, but not slowly enough for a planet.

Then – the third 'then' – arrived the indubitable and positive Wonder of the World, the Magic Trick, watch now, watch, you will not believe your eyes, mama, mama, look what I can do —

Seven lights in a row, proceeding fairly rapidly, with a darting movement, from left to right. Proceeding less rapidly from right to left, two dimmer, greenish lights. Two-lights halt, blink, reverse course, proceed hastily and in a wavering manner from left to right. Seven-lights increase speed, and catch up. Two-lights flash desperately, flicker, and are gone.

Seven-lights hang still for some while, then merge gradually into one streak, veering away, and little by little vanish into the immensity of the dark.

But in the dark now are growing other lights, many of them: lamps, dots, rows, scintillations: some near at hand, some far. Like the stars, yes, but not stars. It is not the great Existences we are seeing, but only the little lives.

In the morning Simon told me something about the Camp, but not until after he had had me check the apartment for bugs. I thought at first he had been given behaviour mod and gone paranoid. We never had been infested. And I'd been living alone for a year and a half; surely they didn't want to hear me talking to myself? But he said, 'They may have been expecting me to come here.'

'But they let you go free!'

He just lay there and laughed at me. So I checked everywhere we could think of. I didn't find any bugs, but it did look as if somebody had gone through the bureau drawers while I was away in the Wilderness. Simon's papers were all at Max's, so that didn't matter. I made tea on the Primus, and washed and shaved Simon with the extra hot water in the kettle – he had a thick beard and wanted to get rid of it because of the lice he had brought from Camp – and while we were doing that he told me about the Camp. In fact he told me very little, but not much was necessary.

He had lost about twenty pounds. As he only weighed 140 to start with, this left little to go on with. His knees and wrist bones stuck out like rocks under the skin. His feet were all swollen and chewed-looking from the Camp boots; he hadn't dared take the boots off, the last three days of walking, because he was afraid he wouldn't be able to get them back on. When he had to move or sit up so I could wash him, he shut his eyes.

'Am I really here?' he asked. 'Am I here?'

'Yes,' I said. 'You are here. What I don't understand is how you got here.'

'Oh, it wasn't bad so long as I kept moving. All you need is to know where you're going – to have some place to go. You know, some of the people in Camp, if they'd let them go, they wouldn't have had that. They couldn't have gone anywhere. Keeping moving was the main thing. It's just that my back's seized up, now.'

When he had to get up to go to the bathroom he moved liked a ninety-year-old. He couldn't stand straight, but was all bent out of shape, and shuffled. I helped him put on clean clothes. When he lay down on the bed again a sound of pain came out of him, like tearing thick paper. I went around the room putting things away. He asked me to come sit by him, and said I was going to drown him if I went on crying. 'You'll submerge the entire North American continent,' he said. I can't remember what else he said, but he made me laugh finally. It is hard to remember things Simon says, and hard not to laugh when he says them. This is not merely the partiality of affection: he makes everybody laugh. I doubt that he intends to. It is just that a mathematician's mind works differently from other people's. Then when they laugh, that pleases him.

It was strange, and it is strange, to be thinking about 'him', the man I have known for ten years, the same man, while 'he' lay there changed out of recognition, a different man. It is enough to make you understand why most languages have a word like 'soul'. There are various degrees of death, and time spares us none of them. Yet something endures, for which a word is needed.

I said what I had not been able to say for a year and a half: 'I was afraid they'd brainwash you.'

He said, 'Behaviour mod is expensive. Even just with drugs. They save it mostly for the V.I.P.s. But I'm afraid they got a notion I might be important after all. I got questioned a lot the last couple of months. About my "foreign contacts".' He snorted. 'The stuff that got published abroad, I suppose. So I want to be careful and make sure it's just a Camp again next time, and not a Federal Hospital.'

'Simon, were they . . . are they cruel, or just righteous?'

He did not answer for a while. He did not want to answer. He knew what I was asking. He knew what thread hangs hope, the sword, above our heads.

'Some of them . . . ,' he said at last, mumbling.

Some of them had been cruel. Some of them had enjoyed their work. You cannot blame everything on society.

'Prisoners, as well as guards,' he said.

You cannot blame everything on the enemy.

'Some of them, Belle,' he said with energy, touching my hand – 'some of them, there were men like gold there—'

The thread is tough; you cannot cut it with one stroke.

'What have you been playing?' he asked.

'Forrest, Schubert.'

'With the quartet?'

'Trio, now. Janet went to Oakland with a new lover.'

'Ah, poor Max.'

'It's just as well, really. She isn't a good pianist.'

I make Simon laugh, too, though I don't intend to. We talked until it was past time for me to go to work. My shift since the Full Employment Act last year is ten to two. I am an inspector in a recycled paper bag factory. I have never rejected a bag yet; the electronic inspector catches all the defective ones first. It is a rather depressing job. But it's only four hours a day, and it takes more time than that to go through all the lines and physical and mental examinations, and fill out all the forms, and talk to all the welfare counsellors and inspectors every week in order to qualify as Unemployed, and then line up every day for the ration stamps and the dole. Simon thought I ought to go to work as usual. I tried to, but I couldn't. He had felt very hot to the touch when I kissed him goodbye. I went instead and got a black-market doctor. A girl at the factory had recommended her, for an abortion, if I ever wanted one without going through the regulation two years of sex-depressant drugs the fed-meds make you take after they give you an abortion. She was a jeweller's assistant in a shop on Alder Street, and the girl said she was convenient because if you didn't have enough cash you could leave something in pawn at the jeweller's as payment. Nobody ever does have enough cash, and of course credit cards aren't worth much on the black market.

The doctor was willing to come at once, so we rode home on the bus together. She gathered very soon that Simon and I were married, and it was funny to see her look at us and smile like a cat. Some people love illegality for its own sake. Men, more often than women. It's men who make laws, and enforce them, and break them, and think the whole performance is wonderful: Most women would rather just ignore them. You could see that this woman, like a man, actually enjoyed breaking them. That may have been what put her into an illegal business in the first place, a preference for the shady side. But there was more to it than that. No doubt she'd wanted to be a doctor, too; and the Federal Medical Association doesn't admit women into the medical schools. She probably got her training as some other doctor's private pupil, under the counter. Very much as Simon learned mathematics, since the universities don't teach much but Business Administration and Advertising and Media Skills any more. However she learned it, she seemed to know her stuff. She fixed up a kind of homemade traction device for Simon very handily, and informed him that if he did much more walking for two months he'd be crippled the rest of his life, but if he behaved himself he'd just be more or less lame. It isn't the kind of thing you'd expect to be grateful for being told, but we both were. Leaving, she gave me a bottle of about two hundred plain white pills, unlabelled. 'Aspirin,' she said. 'He'll be in a good deal of pain off and on for weeks.'

I looked at the bottle. I had never seen aspirin before, only the Super-Buffered Pane-Gon and the Triple Power N-L-G-Zic and the Extra Strength Apansprin with the miracle ingredient more doctors recommend, which the fed-meds always give you prescriptions for, to be filled at your FMA-approved private-enterprise friendly drugstore at the low, low prices established by the Pure Food and Drug Administration in order to inspire competitive research.

'Aspirin,' the doctor repeated. 'The miracle ingredient more doctors recommend.' She cat-grinned again. I think she liked us because we were living in sin. That bottle of black-market aspirin was probably worth more than the old Navajo bracelet I pawned for her fee.

I went out again to register Simon as temporarily domiciled at my address, and to apply for Temporary Unemployment Compensation ration stamps for him. They only give them to you for two weeks and you have to come every day; but to register him as Temporarily Disabled meant getting the signatures of two fed-meds, and I thought I'd rather put that off for a while. It took three hours to go through the lines and get the forms he would have to fill out, and to answer the crats' questions about why he wasn't there in person. They smelled something fishy. Of course it's hard for them to prove that two people are married, if you move now and then, and your friends help out by sometimes registering one of you as living at their address; but they had all the back files on both of us and it was obvious that we had been around each other for a suspiciously long time. The State really does make things awfully hard for itself. It must have been simpler to enforce the laws, back when marriage was legal and adultery was what got you into trouble. They only had to catch you once. But I'll bet people broke the law just as often then as they do now.

The lantern creatures came close enough at last that we could see not only their light, but their bodies in the illumination of the light. They were not pretty. They were dark-coloured, most often a dark red, and they were all mouth. They ate one another whole. Light swallowed light all swallowed together in the vaster mouth of the darkness. They moved slowly, for nothing, however small and hungry, could move fast under that weight, in that cold. Their eyes, round with fear, were never closed. Their bodies were tiny and bony, behind the gaping jaws. They wore queer, ugly decorations on their lips and skulls: fringes, serrated wattles, featherlike fronds, gauds, bangles, lures. Poor little sheep of the deep pastures! Poor ragged, hunch-jawed dwarfs squeezed to the bone by the weight of the darkness, chilled to the bone by the cold of the darkness, tiny monsters burning with bright hunger, who brought us back to life!

Occasionally, in the wan, sparse illumination of one of the lantern creatures, we caught a momentary glimpse of other large, unmoving shapes: the barest suggestion, off in the distance, not of a wall, nothing so solid and certain as a wall, but of a surface, an angle ... Was it there?

Or something would glitter, faint, far off, far down. There was no use trying to make out what it might be. Probably it was only a fleck of sediment, mud or mica, disturbed by a struggle between the lantern creatures, flickering like a bit of diamond dust as it rose and settled slowly. In any case, we could not move to go see what it was. We had not even the cold, narrow freedom of the lantern creatures. We were immobilized, borne down, still shadows among the half-guessed shadow walls. Were we there?

The lantern creatures showed no awareness of us. They passed before us, among us, perhaps even through us – it was impossible to be sure. They were not afraid, or curious.

Once something a little larger than a hand came crawling near, and for a moment we saw quite distinctly the clean angle where the foot of a wall rose from the pavement, in the glow cast by the crawling creature, which was covered with a foliage of plumes, each plume dotted with many tiny, bluish points of light. We saw the pavement beneath the creature and the wall beside it, heartbreaking in its exact, clear linearity, its opposition to all that was fluid, random, vast, and void. We saw the creature's claws, slowly reaching out and retracting like small stiff fingers, touch the wall. Its plumage of light quivering, it dragged itself along and vanished behind the corner.

So we knew that the wall was there; and that it was an outer wall, a housefront, perhaps, or the side of one of the towers of the city.

We remembered the towers. We remembered the city. We had forgotten it. We had forgotten who we were; but we remembered the city, now.

When I got home, the FBI had already been there. The computer at the police precinct where I registered Simon's address must have flashed it right over to the computer at the FBI building. They had questioned Simon for about an hour, mostly about what he had been doing during the twelve days it took him to get from the Camp to Portland. I suppose they thought he had flown to Peking or something. Having a police record in Walla Walla for hitchhiking helped him establish his story. He told me that one of them had gone to the bathroom. Sure enough I found a bug stuck on the top of the bathroom doorframe. I left it, as we figured it's really better to leave it when you know you have one, than to take it off and then never be sure they haven't planted another one you don't know about. As Simon said, if we felt we had to say something unpatriotic we could always flush the toilet at the same time.

I have a battery radio – there are so many stoppages because of power failures, and days the water has to be boiled, and so on, that you really have to have a radio to save wasting time and dying of typhoid – and he turned it on while I was making supper on the Primus. The six-o'clock All American Broadcasting Company news announcer announced that peace was at hand in Uruguay, the President's confidential aide having been seen to smile at a passing blonde as he left the 613th day of the secret negotiations in a villa outside Katmandu. The war in Liberia was going well; the enemy said they had shot down 17 American planes but the Pentagon said we had shot down 22 enemy planes, and the capital city – I forget its name, but it hasn't been inhabitable for seven years anyway – was on the verge of being recaptured by the forces of freedom. The police action in Arizona was also successful. The Neo-Birch insurgents in Phoenix could not hold out much longer against the massed might of the American Army and Air Force, since their underground supply of small tactical nukes from the Weatherpeople in Los Angeles had been cut off. Then there was an advertisement for Fed-Cred cards, and a commercial for the Supreme Court – 'Take your legal troubles to the Nine Wise Men!' Then there was something about why tariffs had gone up, and a report from the stock market which had just closed at over 2000, and a commercial for U.S. Government canned water, with a catchy little tune: 'Don't be sorry when you drink – It's not as healthy as you think – Don't you think you really ought to – Drink coo-ool, puu-uure U.S.G. Water?' – with three sopranos in close harmony on the last line. Then, just as the battery began to give out and his voice was dying away into a faraway tiny whisper, the announcer seemed to be saying something about a new continent emerging.

'What was that?'

'I didn't hear,' Simon said, lying with his eyes shut and his face pale and sweaty. I gave him two aspirins before we ate. He ate little, and fell asleep while I was washing the dishes in the bathroom. I had been going to practise, but a viola is fairly wakeful in a one-room apartment. I read for a while instead. It was a bestseller Janet had given me when she left. She thought it was very good, but then she likes Franz Liszt too. I don't read much since the libraries were closed down, it's too hard to get books; all you can buy is bestsellers. I don't remember the title of this one, the cover just said Ninety Million Copies in Print!!! It was about small-town sex life in the last century, the dear old 1970s when there weren't any problems and life was so simple and nostalgic. The author squeezed all the naughty thrills he could out of the fact that all the main characters were married. I looked at the end and saw that all the married couples shot each other after all their children became schizophrenic hookers, except for one brave pair that divorced and then leapt into bed together with a clear-eyed pair of Government-employed lovers for eight pages of healthy group sex as a brighter future dawned. I went to bed then, too. Simon was hot, but sleeping quietly. His breathing was like the sound of soft waves far away, and I went out to the dark sea on the sound of them.

I used to go out to the dark sea, often, as a child, falling asleep. I had almost forgotten it with my waking mind. As a child all I had to do was stretch out and think, 'the dark sea . . . the dark sea . . . ' and soon enough I'd be there, in the great depths, rocking. But after I grew up it only happened rarely, and a great gift. To know the abyss of the darkness and not to fear it, to entrust oneself to it and whatever may arise from it – what greater gift?

We watched the tiny lights come and go around us, and doing so, we gained a sense of space and of direction – near and far, at least, and higher and lower. It was that sense of space that allowed us to become aware of the currents. Space was no longer entirely still around us, suppressed by the enormous pressure of its own weight. Very dimly we were aware that the cold darkness moved, slowly, softly, pressing against us a little for a long time, then ceasing, in a vast oscillation. The empty darkness flowed slowly along our unmoving unseen bodies; along them, past them; perhaps through them; we could not tell.

Where did they come from, those dim, slow, vast tides? What pressure or attraction stirred the deeps to these slow drifting movements? We could not understand that; we could only feel their touch against us, but in straining our sense to guess their origin or end, we became aware of something else: something out there in the darkness of the great currents: sounds. We listened. We heard.

So our sense of space sharpened and localized to a sense of place. For sound is local, as sight is not. Sound is delimited by silence; and it does not rise out of the silence unless it is fairly close, both in space and in time. Though we stand where once the singer stood we cannot hear the voice singing; the years have carried it off on their tides, submerged it. Sound is a fragile thing, a tremor, as delicate as life itself. We may see the stars, but we cannot hear them. Even were the hollowness of outer space an atmosphere, an ether that transmitted the waves of sound, we could not hear the stars; they are too far away. At most if we listened we might hear our own sun, all the mighty roiling, exploding storm of its burning, as a whisper at the edge of hearing.

A sea wave laps one's feet: it is the shock wave of a volcanic eruption on the far side of the world. But one hears nothing.

A red light flickers on the horizon: it is the reflection in smoke of a city on the distant mainland, burning. But one hears nothing.

Only on the slopes of the volcano, in the suburbs of the city, does one begin to hear the deep thunder, and the high voices crying.

Thus, when we became aware that we were hearing, we were sure that the sounds we heard were fairly close to us. And yet we may have been quite wrong. For we were in a strange place, a deep place. Sound travels fast and far in the deep places, and the silence there is perfect, letting the least noise be heard for hundreds of miles.

And these were not small noises. The lights were tiny, but the sounds were vast: not loud, but very large. Often they were below the range of hearing, long slow vibrations rather than sounds. The first we heard seemed to us to rise up through the currents from beneath us: immense groans, sighs felt along the bone, a rumbling, a deep uneasy whispering.

Later, certain sounds came down to us from above, or borne along the endless levels of the darkness, and these were stranger yet, for they were music. A huge, calling, yearning music from far away in the darkness, calling not to us. *Where are you? I am here.*

Not to us.

They were the voices of the great souls, the great lives, the lonely ones, the voyagers. Calling. Not often answered. *Where are you? Where have you gone?*

But the bones, the keels and girders of white bones on icy isles of the South, the shores of bones did not reply.

Nor could we reply. But we listened, and the tears rose in our eyes, salt, not so salt as the oceans, the world-girdling deep bereaved currents, the abandoned roadways of the great lives; not so salt, but warmer.

I am here. Where have you gone?

No answer.

Only the whispering thunder from below.

But we knew now, though we could not answer, we knew because we heard, because we felt, because we wept, we knew that we were; and we remembered other voices.

Max came the next night. I sat on the toilet lid to practise, with the bathroom door shut. The FBI men on the other end of the bug got a solid half hour of scales and double stops, and then a quite good performance of the Hindemith unaccompanied viola sonata. The bathroom being very small and all hard surfaces, the noise I made was really tremendous. Not a good sound, far too much echo, but the sheer volume was contagious, and I played louder as I went on. The man up above knocked on the floor once; but if I have to listen to the weekly All-American Olympic Games at full blast every Sunday morning from his TV set, then he has to accept Paul Hindemith coming up out of his toilet now and then.

When I got tired I put a big wad of cotton over the bug, and came out of the bathroom half deaf. Simon and Max were on fire. Burning, unconsumed. Simon was scribbling formulae in traction, and Max was pumping his elbows up and down the way he does, like a boxer, and saying, 'The e-lec-tron emission . . .' through his nose, with his eyes narrowed, and his mind evidently going light-years per second faster than his tongue, because he kept beginning over and saying, 'The e-lec-tron emis-sion . . .' and pumping his elbows.

Intellectuals at work are very strange to look at. As strange as artists. I never could understand how an audience can sit there and *look* at a fiddler rolling his eyes and biting his tongue, or a horn player collecting spit, or a pianist like a black cat strapped to an electrified bench, as if what they *saw* had anything to do with the music.

I damped the fires with a quart of black-market beer – the legal kind is better, but I never have enough ration stamps for beer, I'm not thirsty enough to go without eating – and gradually Max and Simon cooled down. Max would have stayed talking all night, but I drove him out, because Simon was looking tired.

I put a new battery in the radio and left it playing in the bathroom, and blew out the candle and lay and talked with Simon; he was too excited to sleep. He said that Max had solved the problems that were bothering them before Simon was sent to Camp, and had fitted Simon's equations to (as Simon put it) the bare facts: which means they have achieved 'direct energy conversion'. Ten or twelve people have worked on it at different times since Simon published the theoretical part of it when he was twenty-two. The physicist Ann Jones had pointed out right away that the simplest practical application of the theory would be to build a 'sun tap', a device for collecting and storing solar energy, only much cheaper and better than the U.S.G. Sola-Heetas that some rich people have on their houses. And it would have been simple only they kept hitting the same snag. Now Max has got around the snag.

I said that Simon published the theory, but that is inaccurate. Of course he's never been able to publish any of his papers, in print; he's not a Federal employee and doesn't have a Government clearance. But it did get circulated in what the scientists and poets call Sammy's-dot, that is, just handwritten or hectographed. It's an old joke that the FBI arrests everybody with purple fingers, because they have either been hectographing Sammy's-dots, or they have impetigo.

Anyhow, Simon was on top of the mountain that night. His true joy is in the pure math; but he had been working with Clara and Max and the others in this effort to materialize the theory for ten years, and a taste of material victory is a good thing, once in a lifetime.

I asked him to explain what the sun tap would mean to the masses, with me as a representative mass. He explained that it means we can tap solar energy for power, using a device that's easier to build than a jar battery. The efficiency and storage capacity are such that about ten minutes of sunlight will power an apartment complex like ours, heat and lights and elevators and all, for twenty-four hours; and no pollution, particulate or thermal or radioactive. 'There isn't any danger of using up the sun?' I asked. He took it soberly – it was a stupid question, but after all not so long ago people thought there wasn't any danger of using up the earth – and said no, because we wouldn't be pulling out energy, as we did when we mined and forested and split atoms, but just using the energy that comes to us anyhow: as the plants, the trees and grass and rosebushes, always have done. 'You could call it Flower Power,' he said. He was high, high up on the mountain, ski jumping in the sunlight.

'The State owns us,' he said, 'because the corporative State has a monopoly on power sources, and there's not enough power to go round. But now, anybody could build a generator on their roof that would furnish enough power to light a city.'

I looked out the window at the dark city.

'We could completely decentralize industry and agriculture. Technology could serve life instead of serving capital. We could each run our own life. Power is power! . . . The State is a machine. We could unplug the machine, now. Power corrupts; absolute power corrupts absolutely. But that's true only when there's a price on power. When groups can keep the power to themselves; when they can use physical power-to in order to exert spiritual power-over; when might makes right. But if power is free? If everybody is equally mighty? Then everybody's got to find a better way of showing that he's right . . .'

'That's what Mr Nobel thought when he invented dynamite,' I said. 'Peace on earth.'

He slid down the sunlit slope a couple of thousand feet and stopped beside me in a spray of snow, smiling. 'Skull at the banquet,' he said, 'finger writing on the wall. Be still! Look, don't you see the sun shining on the Pentagon, all the roofs are off, the sun shines at last into the corridors of power . . . And they shrivel up, they wither away. The green grass grows through the carpets of the Oval Room, the Hotline is disconnected for non-payment of the bill. The first thing we'll do is build an electrified fence outside the electrified fence around the White House. The inner one prevents unauthorized persons from getting in. The outer one will prevent authorized persons from getting out . . .'

Of course he was bitter. Not many people come out of prison sweet.

But it was cruel, to be shown this great hope, and to know that there was no hope for it. He did know that. He knew it right along. He knew that there was no mountain, that he was skiing on the wind.

The tiny lights of the lantern creatures died out one by one, sank away. The distant lonely voices were silent. The cold, slow currents flowed, vacant, only shaken from time to time by a shifting in the abyss.

It was dark again, and no voice spoke. All dark, dumb, cold.

Then the sun rose.

It was not like the dawns we had begun to remember: the change, manifold and subtle, in the smell and touch of the air; the hush that, instead of sleeping, wakes, holds still, and waits; the appearance of objects, looking grey, vague, and new, as if just created – distant mountains against the eastern sky, one's own hands, the hoary grass full of dew and shadow, the fold in the edge of a curtain hanging by the window – and then, before one is quite sure that one is indeed seeing again, that the light has returned, that day is breaking, the first abrupt, sweet stammer of a waking bird. And after that the chorus, voice by voice: This is my nest, this is my tree, this is my egg, this is my day, this is my life, here I am, here I am, hurray for me! I'm here!— No, it wasn't like that at all, this dawn. It was completely silent, and it was blue.

In the dawns that we had begun to remember, one did not become aware of the light itself, but of the separate objects touched by the light, the things, the world. They were there, visible again, as if visibility were their own property, not a gift from the rising sun.

In this dawn, there was nothing but the light itself. Indeed there was not even light, we would have said, but only colour: blue.

There was no compass bearing to it. It was not brighter in the east. There was no east or west. There was only up and down, below and above. Below was dark. The blue light came from above. Brightness fell. Beneath, where the shaking thunder had stilled, the brightness died away through violet into blindness.

We, arising, watched light fall.

In a way it was more like an ethereal snowfall than like a sunrise. The light seemed to be in discrete particles, infinitesimal flecks, slowly descending, faint, fainter than flakes of fine snow on a dark night, and tinier; but blue. A soft, penetrating blue tending to the violet, the colour of the shadows in an iceberg, the colour of a streak of sky between grey clouds on a winter afternoon before snow: faint in intensity but vivid in hue: the colour of the remote, the colour of the cold, the colour farthest from the sun.

On Saturday night they held a scientific congress in our room. Clara and Max came, of course, and the engineer Phil Drum, and three others who had worked on the sun tap. Phil Drum was very pleased with himself because he had actually built one of the things, a solar cell, and brought it along. I don't think it had occurred to either Max or Simon to build one. Once they knew it could be done, they were satisfied and wanted to get on with something else. But Phil unwrapped his baby with a lot of flourish, and people made remarks like, 'Mr Watson, will you come here a minute,' and 'Hey, Wilbur, you're off the ground!' and 'I say, nasty mould you've got there, Alec, why don't you throw it out?' and 'Ugh, ugh, burns, burns, wow, ow,' the latter from Max, who does look a little Pre-Mousterian. Phil explained that he had exposed the cell for one minute at four in the afternoon up in Washington Park during a light rain. The lights were back on on the West Side since Thursday, so we could test it without being conspicuous.

We turned off the lights, after Phil had wired the table-lamp cord to the cell. He turned on the lamp switch. The bulb came on, about twice as bright as before, at its full 40 watts – city power of course was never full strength. We all looked at it. It was a dime-store table-lamp with a metallized gold base and a white plasticloth shade.

'Brighter than a thousand suns,' Simon murmured from the bed.

'Could it be,' said Clara Edmonds, 'that we physicists have known sin – and have come out the other side?'

'It really wouldn't be any good at all for making bombs with,' Max said dreamily.

'Bombs,' Phil Drum said with scorn. 'Bombs are obsolete. Don't you realize that we could move a mountain with this kind of power? I mean pick up Mount Hood, move it, and set it down. We could thaw Antarctica, we could freeze the Congo. We could sink a continent. "Give me a fulcrum and I'll move the world." Well, Archimedes, you've got your fulcrum. The sun.'

'Christ,' Simon said, 'the radio, Belle!'

The bathroom door was shut and I had put cotton over the bug, but he was right; if they were going to go ahead at this rate there had better be some added static. And though I liked watching their faces in the clear light of the lamp – they all had good, interesting faces, well worn, like the handles of wooden tools or the rocks in a running stream – I did not much want to listen to them talk tonight. Not because I wasn't a scientist; that made no difference. And not because I disagreed or disapproved or disbelieved anything they said. Only because it grieved me terribly, their talking. Because they couldn't rejoice aloud over a job done and a discovery made, but had to hide there and whisper about it. Because they couldn't go out into the sun.

I went into the bathroom with my viola and sat on the toilet lid and did a long set of sautillé exercises. Then I tried to work at the Forrest trio, but it was too assertive. I played the solo part from *Harold in Italy*, which is beautiful, but wasn't quite the right mood either. They were still going strong in the other room. I began to improvise.

After a few minutes in E minor the light over the shaving mirror began to flicker and dim; then it died. Another outage. The table-lamp in the other room did not go out, being connected with the sun, not with the twenty-three atomic fission plants that power the Greater Portland Area. Within two seconds somebody had switched it off too, so that we shouldn't be the only window in the West Hills left alight; and I could hear them rooting for candles and rattling matches. I went on improvising in the dark. Without light, when you couldn't see all the hard shiny surfaces of things, the sound seemed softer and less muddled. I went on, and it began to shape up. All the laws of harmonics sang together when the bow came down. The strings of the viola were the cords of my own voice, tightened by sorrow, tuned to the pitch of joy. The melody created itself out of air and energy; it raised up the valleys, and the mountains and hills were made low, and the crooked straight, and the rough places plain. And the music went out to the dark sea and sang in the darkness, over the abyss.

When I came out they were all sitting there and none of them was talking. Max had been crying. I could see little candle flames in the tears around his eyes. Simon lay flat on the bed in the shadows, his eyes closed. Phil Drum sat hunched over, holding the solar cell in his hands.

I loosened the pegs, and put the bow and the viola in the case, and cleared my throat. It was embarrassing. I finally said, 'I'm sorry.'

One of the women spoke: Rose Abramski, a private student of Simon's, a big shy woman who could hardly speak at all unless it was in mathematical symbols. 'I saw it,' she said. 'I saw it. I saw the white towers, and the water streaming down their sides, and running back down to the sea. And the sunlight shining in the streets, after ten thousand years of darkness.'

'I heard them,' Simon said, very low, from the shadow. 'I heard their voices.'

'Oh, Christ! Stop it!' Max cried out, and got up and went blundering out into the unlit hall, without his coat. We heard him running down the stairs.

'Phil,' said Simon, lying there, 'could we raise up the white towers, with our lever and our fulcrum?'

After a long silence Phil Drum answered, 'We have the power to do it.'

'What else do we need?' Simon said. 'What else do we need, besides power?'

Nobody answered him.

The blue changed. It became brighter, lighter, and at the same time thicker: impure. The ethereal luminosity of blue-violet turned to turquoise, intense and opaque. Still we could not have said that everything was now turquoise-coloured, for there were still no things. There was nothing, except the colour of turquoise.

The change continued. The opacity became veined and thinned. The dense, solid colour began to appear translucent transparent. Then it seemed as if we were in the heart of a sacred Jade, or the brilliant crystal of a sapphire or an emerald.

As at the inner structure of a crystal, there was no motion. But there was something, now, to see. It was as if we saw the motionless, elegant inward structure of the molecules of a precious stone. Planes and angles appeared about us, shadowless and clear in that even, glowing, blue-green light.

These were the walls and towers of the city, the streets, the windows, the gates.

We knew them, but we did not recognize them. We did not dare to recognize them. It had been so long. And it was so strange. We had used to dream, when we lived in this city. We had lain down, nights, in the rooms behind the windows, and slept, and dreamed. We had all dreamed of the ocean, of the deep sea. Were we not dreaming now?

Sometimes the thunder and tremor deep below us rolled again, but it was faint now, far away; as far away as our memory of the thunder and the tremor and the fire and the towers falling, long ago. Neither the sound nor the memory frightened us. We knew them.

The sapphire light brightened overhead to green, almost green-gold. We looked up. The tops of the highest towers were hard to see, glowing in the radiance of light. The streets and doorways were darker, more clearly defined.

In one of those long, jewel-dark streets something was moving: something not composed of planes and angles, but of curves and arcs. We all turned to look at it, slowly, wondering as we did so at the slow ease of our own motion, our freedom. Sinuous, with a beautiful flowing, gathering, rolling movement, now rapid and now tentative, the thing drifted across the street from a blank garden wall to the recess of a door. There, in the dark blue shadow, it was hard to see for a while. We watched. A pale blue curve appeared at the top of the doorway. A second followed, and a third. The moving thing clung or hovered there, above the door, like a swaying knot of silvery cords or a boneless hand, one arched finger pointing carelessly to something above the lintel of the door, something like itself, but motionless – a carving. A carving in jade light. A carving in stone.

Delicately and easily the long curving tentacle followed the curves of the carved figure, the eight petal limbs, the round eyes. Did it recognize its image?

The living one swung suddenly, gathered its curves in a loose knot, and darted away down the street, swift and sinuous. Behind it a faint cloud of darker blue hung for a minute and dispersed, revealing again the carved figure above the door: the sea flower, the cuttlefish, quick, great-eyed, graceful, evasive, the cherished sign, carved on a thousand walls, worked into the design-of cornices, pavements, handles, lids of jewel boxes, canopies, tapestries, tabletops, gateways.

Down another street, at about the level of the first-floor windows, came a flickering drift of hundreds of motes of silver. With a single motion all turned towards the cross street, and glittered off into the dark blue shadows.

There were shadows, now.

We looked up, up from the flight of silver fish, up from the streets where the jade-green currents flowed and the blue shadows fell. We moved and looked up, yearning, to the high towers of our city. They stood, the fallen towers. They glowed in the ever-brightening radiance, not blue or blue-green, up there, but gold. Far above them lay a vast, circular, trembling brightness: the sun's light on the surface of the sea.

We are here. When we break through the bright circle into life, the water will break and stream white down the white sides of the towers, and run down the steep streets back into the sea. The water will glitter in dark hair, on the eyelids of dark eyes, and dry to a thin white film of salt.

We are here.

Whose voice? Who called to us?

He was with me for twelve days. On 28 January the crats came from the Bureau of Health Education and Welfare and said that since he was receiving unemployment compensation while suffering from an untreated illness, the Government must look after him and restore him to health, because health is the inalienable right of the citizens of a democracy. He refused to sign the consent forms, so the chief Health Officer signed them. He refused to get up, so two of the policemen pulled him up off the bed. He started to try to fight them. The chief Health Officer pulled his gun and said that if he continued to struggle he would shoot him for resisting welfare, and arrest me for conspiracy to defraud the Government. The man who was holding my arms behind my back said they could always arrest me for unreported pregnancy with intent to form a nuclear family. At that Simon stopped trying to get free. It was really all he was trying to do, not to fight them, just to get his arms free. He looked at me, and they took him out.

He is in the Federal Hospital in Salem. I have not been able to find out whether he is in the regular hospital or the mental wards.

It was on the radio again yesterday, about the rising land masses in the South Atlantic and the Western Pacific. At Max's the other night I saw a TV special explaining about geophysical stresses, and subsidence, and faults. The U.S. Geodetic Service is doing a lot of advertising around town; the commonest one is a big billboard that says 'It's Not Our Fault!' with a picture of a beaver pointing to a schematic map that shows how even if Oregon has a major earthquake and subsidence as California did last month, it will not affect Portland, or only the western suburbs perhaps. The news also said that they plan to halt the tidal waves in Florida by dropping nuclear bombs where Miami was. Then they will re-attach Florida to the mainland with landfill. They are already advertising real estate for housing developments on the landfill. The President is staying at the Mile High White House in Aspen, Colorado. I don't think it will do him much good. Houseboats down on the Willamette are selling for $500,000. There are no trains or buses running south from Portland, because all the highways were badly damaged by the tremors and landslides last week, so I will have to see if I can get to Salem on foot. I still have the rucksack I bought for the Mount Hood Wilderness Week. I got some dry lima beans and raisins with my Federal Fair Share Super Value Green Stamp minimal ration book for February – it took the whole book – and Phil Drum made me a tiny camp stove powered with the solar cell. I didn't want to take the Primus, it's too bulky, and I did want to be able to carry the viola. Max gave me a half pint of brandy. When the brandy is gone I expect I will stuff this notebook into the bottle and put the cap on tight and leave it on a hillside somewhere between here and Salem. I like to think of it being lifted up little by little by the water, and rocking, and going out to the dark sea.

Where are you?
We are here. Where have you gone?

Title: The Shining Pyramid
Writer: *Arthur Machen*

Briefing: *The Little People – ancient name for fairies; believed to be the prehistoric, cave-dwelling Turanian inhabitants of the country.* Local beauty Annie Trevor has gone missing, believed murdered. But there are darker rumours among the superstitious local people that she has been 'taken by the fairies'. When a number of flint stones arranged in a pyramid pattern are discovered, followed by some drawings of peculiar shaped eyes, the resourceful occult investigator Dyson forsakes the comforts of London for the wild Welsh countryside to solve the mystery . . .

Author: Arthur Machen was born at Caerleon-on-Usk in Wales amidst ancient ruins and a rich store of curious folklore that was to shape his writing. After a period as a clerk, teacher, actor and journalist, Machen began to produce the series of weird and macabre books which have earned him comparison to M. R. James and Algernon Blackwood, as well as attracting a wide circle of admirers including Julian Lloyd Webber and Barry Humphries. Among his most acclaimed works are *The Inmost Light* (1894), dealing with the dangers of occultism; *Black Crusade* (1895) which hints at man's non-human origin; and *The Hill of Dreams* (1907) about a man lost in his own dream-world. Machen became the centre of an enduring controversy in 1914 when he wrote 'The Bowmen' which related how some ghostly archers came to the rescue of British soldiers at the Battle of Mons. Despite his insistence that the tale was pure fiction, a number of soldiers became convinced they *had* actually seen phantoms and Machen's invention became part of the mythology of the war. However, his research into British folk legend convinced him of the continuing existence of the 'little people' still leading secret lives in certain remote areas of the countryside. 'The Shining Pyramid' illustrates this belief as well as being one of Machen's finest tales of the unexplained.

1. The Arrow-head Character

'Haunted, you said?'

'Yes, haunted. Don't you remember, when I saw you three years ago, you told me about your place in the west with the ancient woods hanging all about it, and the wild, domed hills, and the ragged land? It has always remained a sort of enchanted picture in my mind as I sit at my desk and hear the traffic rattling in the street in the midst of whirling London. But when did you come up?'

'The fact is, Dyson, I have only just got out of the train. I drove to the station early this morning and caught the 10.45.'

'Well, I am very glad you looked in on me. How have you been getting on since we last met? There is no Mrs Vaughan, I suppose?'

'No,' said Vaughan, 'I am still a hermit, like yourself. I have done nothing but loaf about.'

Vaughan had lit his pipe and sat in the elbow chair, fidgeting and glancing about him in a somewhat dazed and restless manner. Dyson had wheeled round his chair when his visitor entered and sat with one arm fondly reclining on the desk of his bureau, and touching the litter of manuscript.

'And you are still engaged in the old task?' said Vaughan, pointing to the pile of papers and the teeming pigeon-holes.

'Yes, the vain pursuit of literature, as idle as alchemy, and as entrancing. But you have come to town for some time, I suppose; what shall we do tonight?'

'Well, I rather wanted you to try a few days with me down in the west. It would do you a lot of good, I'm sure.'

'You are very kind, Vaughan, but London in September is hard to leave. Doré could not have designed anything more wonderful and mystic than Oxford Street as I saw it the other evening; the sunset flaming, the blue haze transmuting the plain street into a road "far in the spiritual city".'

'I should like you to come down, though. You would enjoy roaming over our hills. Does this racket go on all day and all night? It quite bewilders me; I wonder how you can work through it. I am sure you would revel in the great peace of my old home among the woods.'

Vaughan lit his pipe again, and looked anxiously at Dyson to see if his inducements had had any effect, but the man of letters shook his head, smiling, and vowed in his heart a firm allegiance to the streets.

'You cannot tempt me,' he said.

'Well, you may be right. Perhaps, after all, I was wrong to speak of the peace of the country. There, when a tragedy does occur, it is like a stone thrown into a pond; the circles of disturbance keep on widening, and it seems as if the water would never be still again.'

'Have you ever any tragedies where you are?'

'I can hardly say that. But I was a good deal disturbed about a month ago by something that happened; it may or may not have been a tragedy in the usual sense of the word.'

'What was the occurrence?'

'Well, the fact is a girl disappeared in a way which seems highly mysterious. Her parents, people of the name of Trevor, are well-to-do farmers, and their eldest daughter Annie was a sort of village beauty; she was really remarkably handsome. One afternoon she thought she would go and see her aunt, a widow who farms her own land, and as the two houses are only about five or six miles apart, she started off, telling her parents she would take the short cut over the hills. She never got to her aunt's, and she never was seen again. That's putting it in a few words.'

'What an extraordinary thing! I suppose there are no disused mines, are there, on the hills? I don't think you quite run to anything so formidable as a precipice?'

'No; the path the girl must have taken had no pitfalls of any description; it is just a track over wild, bare hillside, far, even, from a byroad. One may walk for miles without meeting a soul, but it is all perfectly safe.'

'And what do people say about it?'

'Oh, they talk nonsense – among themselves. You have no notion as to how superstitious English cottagers are in out-of-the-way parts like mine. They are as bad as the Irish, every whit, and even more secretive.'

'But what do they say?'

'Oh, the poor girl is supposed to have "gone with the fairies", or to have been "taken by the fairies". Such stuff!' he went on. 'One would laugh if it were not for the real tragedy of the case.'

Dyson looked somewhat interested.

'Yes,' he said, ' "fairies" certainly strike a little curiously on the ear in these days. But what do the police say? I presume they do not accept the fairy-tale hypothesis?'

'No; but they seem quite as fault. What I am afraid of is that Annie Trevor must have fallen in with some scoundrels on her way. Castletown is a large seaport, you know, and some of the worst of the foreign sailors occasionally desert their ships and go on the tramp up and down the country. Not many years ago a Spanish sailor named Garcia murdered a whole family for the sake of plunder that was not worth sixpence. They are hardly human, some of these fellows, and I am dreadfully afraid the poor girl must have come to an awful end.'

'But no foreign sailor was seen by anyone about the country?'

'No; there is certainly that; and of course country people are quick to notice anyone whose appearance and dress are a little out of the common. Still, it seems as if my theory were the only possible explanation.'

'There are no data to go upon,' said Dyson, thoughtfully. 'There was no question of a love affair, or anything of the kind, I suppose?'

'Oh, no, not a hint of such a thing. I am sure if Annie were alive she would have contrived to let her mother know of her safety.'

'No doubt, no doubt. Still it is barely possible that she is alive and yet unable to communicate with her friends. But all this must have disturbed you a good deal.'

'Yes, it did; I hate a mystery, and especially a mystery which is probably the veil of horror. But frankly, Dyson, I want to make a clean breast of it; I did not come here to tell you all this.'

'Of course not,' said Dyson, a little surprised at Vaughan's uneasy manner. 'You came to have a chat on more cheerful topics.'

'No, I did not. What I have been telling you about happened a month ago, but something which seems likely to affect me more personally has taken place within the last few days, and to be quite plain, I came up to town with the idea that you might be able to help me. You recollect that curious case you spoke to me about at our last meeting; something about a spectacle-maker.'

'Oh, yes, I remember that I know I was quite proud of my acumen at the time; even to this day the police have no idea why those peculiar yellow spectacles were wanted. But, Vaughan, you really look quite put out; I hope there is nothing serious?'

'No, I think I have been exaggerating, and I want you to reassure me. But what has happened is very odd.'

'And what has happened?'

'I am sure that you will laugh at me, but this is the story. You must know there is a path, a right of way, that goes through my land, and to be precise, close to the wall of the kitchen garden. It is not used by many people; a woodman now and again finds it useful, and five or six children who go to school in the village pass twice a day. Well, a few days ago I was taking a walk about the place before breakfast, and I happened to stop to fill my pipe just by the large doors in the garden wall. The wood, I must tell you, comes to within a few feet of the wall, and the track I spoke of runs right in the shadow of the trees. I thought the shelter from a brisk wind that was blowing rather pleasant, and I stood there smoking with my eyes on the ground. Then something caught my attention. Just under the wall, on the short grass, a number of small flints were arranged in a pattern; something like this' – and Mr Vaughan caught at a pencil and piece of paper, and dotted down a few strokes.

'You see,' he went on, 'there were, I should think, twelve little stones neatly arranged in lines, and spaced at equal distances, as I have shown it on the paper. They were pointed stones, and the points were very carefully directed one way.'

'Yes,' said Dyson, without much interest, 'no doubt the children you have mentioned had been playing there on their way from school. Children, as you know, are very fond of making such devices with oyster shells or flints or flowers, or with whatever comes in their way.'

'So I thought; I just noticed these flints were arranged in a sort of pattern and then went on. But the next morning I was taking the same round, which, as a matter of fact, is habitual with me, and again I saw at the same spot a device in flints. This time it was really a curious pattern; something like the spokes of a wheel, all meeting at a common centre, and this centre formed by a device which looked like a bowl; all, you understand, done in flints.'

'You are right,' said Dyson, 'that seems odd enough. Still it is reasonable that your half-a-dozen school children are responsible for these fantasies in stone.'

'Well, I thought I would set the matter at rest. The children pass the gate every evening at half-past five, and I walked by at six, and found the device just as I had left it in the morning. The next day I was up and about at a quarter to seven, and I found the whole thing had been changed. There was a pyramid outlined in flints upon the grass. The children I saw going by an hour and a half later, and they ran past the spot without glancing to right or left. In the evening I watched them going home, and this morning when I got to the gate at six o'clock there was a thing like a half moon waiting for me.'

'So then the series runs thus: firstly ordered lines, then the device of the spokes and the bowl, then the pyramid, and finally, this morning, the half moon. That is the order, isn't it?'

'Yes; that is right. But do you know it has made me feel very uneasy? I suppose it seems absurd, but I can't help thinking that some kind of signalling is going on under my nose, and that sort of thing is disquieting.'

'But what have you to dread? You have no enemies?'

'No; but I have some very valuable old plate.'

'You are thinking of burglars then?' said Dyson, with an accent of considerable interest, 'but you must know your neighbours. Are there any suspicious characters about?'

'Not that I am aware of. But you remember what I told you of the sailors.'

'Can you trust your servants?'

'Oh, perfectly. The plate is preserved in a strong room; the butler, an old family servant, alone knows where the key is kept. There is nothing wrong there. Still, everybody is aware that I have a lot of old silver, and all country folks are given to gossip. In that way information may have got abroad in very undesirable quarters.'

'Yes, but I confess there seems something a little unsatisfactory in the burglar theory. Who is signalling to whom? I cannot see my way to accepting such an explanation. What put the plate into your head in connection with these flint signs, or whatever one may call them?'

'It was the figure of the Bowl,' said Vaughan. 'I happen to possess a very large and very valuable Charles II punch-bowl. The chasing is really exquisite, and the thing is worth a lot of money. The sign I described to you was exactly the same shape as my punch-bowl.'

'A queer coincidence certainly. But the other figures or devices: you have nothing shaped like a pyramid?'

'Ah, you will think that queerer. As it happens, this punch-bowl of mine, together with a set of rare old ladles, is kept in a mahogany chest of a pyramidal shape. The four sides slope upwards, the narrow towards the top.'

'I confess all this interests me a good deal,' said Dyson. 'Let us go on then. What about the other figures; how about the Army, as we may call the first sign, and the Crescent or Half Moon?'

'Ah, there is no reference that I can make out of these two. Still, you see I have some excuse for curiosity at all events. I should be very vexed to lose any of the old plate; nearly all the pieces have been in the family for generations. And I cannot get it out of my head that some scoundrels mean to rob me, and are communicating with one another every night.'

'Frankly,' said Dyson, 'I can make nothing of it; I am as much in the dark as yourself. Your theory seems certainly the only possible explanation, and yet the difficulties are immense.'

He leaned back in his chair, and the two men faced each other, frowning, and perplexed by so bizarre a problem.

'By the way,' said Dyson, after a long pause, 'what is your geological formation down there?'

Mr Vaughan looked up, a good deal surprised by the question.

'Old red sandstone and limestone, I believe,' he said. 'We are just beyond the coal measures, you know.'

'But surely there are no flints either in the sandstone or the limestone?'

'No, I never see any flints in the fields. I confess that did strike me as a little curious.'

'I should think so! It is very important. By the way, what size were the flints used in making these devices?'

'I happen to have brought one with me; I took it this morning.'

'From the Half Moon?'

'Exactly. Here it is.'

He handed over a small flint, tapering to a point, and about three inches in length.

Dyson's face blazed up with excitement as he took the thing from Vaughan.

'Certainly,' he said, after a moment's pause, 'you have some curious neighbours in your country. I hardly think they can harbour any designs on your punch-bowl. Do you know this is a flint arrow-head of vast antiquity, and not only that, but an arrow-head of a unique kind? I have seen specimens from all parts of the world, but there are features about this thing that are quite peculiar.'

He laid down his pipe, and took out a book from a drawer.

'We shall just have time to catch the 5.45 to Castletown,' he said.

2. The Eyes on the Wall

Mr Dyson drew in a long breath of the air of the hills and felt all the enchantment of the scene about him. It was very early morning, and he stood on the terrace in the front of the house. Vaughan's ancestor had built on the lower slope of a great hill, in the shelter of a deep and ancient wood that gathered on three sides about the house, and on the fourth side, the south-west, the land fell gently away and sank to the valley, where a brook wound in and out in mystic esses, and the dark and gleaming alders tracked the stream's course to the eye. On the terrace in that sheltered place no wind blew, and far beyond, the trees were still. Only one sound broke in upon the silence, and Dyson heard the noise of the brook singing far below, the song of clear and shining water rippling over the stones, whispering and murmuring as it sank to dark deep pools. Across the stream, just below the house, rose a grey stone bridge, vaulted and buttressed, a fragment of the Middle Ages, and then beyond the bridge the hills rose again, vast and rounded like bastions, covered here and there with dark woods and thickets of undergrowth, but the heights were all bare of trees, showing only grey turf and patches of bracken, touched here and there with the gold of fading fronds. Dyson looked to the north and south, and still he saw the wall of the hills, and the ancient woods, and the steam drawn in and out between them; all grey and dim with morning mist beneath a grey sky in a hushed and haunted air.

Mr Vaughan's voice broke in upon the silence.

'I thought you would be too tired to be about so early,' he said. 'I see you are admiring the view. It is very pretty, isn't it, though I suppose old Meyrick Vaughan didn't think much about the scenery when he built the house. A queer grey, old place, isn't it?'

'Yes, and how it fits into the surroundings; it seems of a piece with the grey hills and the grey bridge below.'

'I am afraid I have brought you down on false pretences, Dyson,' said Vaughan, as they began to walk up and down the terrace. 'I have been to the place, and there is not a sign of anything this morning.'

'Ah, indeed. Well, suppose we go round together.'

They walked across the lawn and went by a path through the ilex shrubbery to the back of the house. There Vaughan pointed out the track leading down to the valley and up to the heights above the wood, and presently they stood beneath the garden wall, by the door.

'Here, you see, it was,' said Vaughan, pointing to a spot on the turf. 'I was standing just where you are now that morning I first saw the flints.'

'Yes, quite so. That morning it was the Army, as I call it; then the Bowl, then the Pyramid, and, yesterday, the Half Moon. What a queer old stone that is,' he went on, pointing to a block of limestone rising out of the turf just beneath the wall. 'It looks like a sort of dwarf pillar, but I suppose it is natural.'

'Oh, yes, I think so. I imagine it was brought here, though, as we stand on the red sandstone. No doubt it was used as a foundation stone for some older building.'

'Very likely.' Dyson was peering about him attentively, looking from the ground to the wall, and from the wall to the deep wood that hung almost over the garden and made the place dark even in the morning.

'Look here,' said Dyson at length, 'it is certainly a case of children this time. Look at that.'

He was bending down and staring at the dull red surface of the mellowed bricks of the wall. Vaughan came up and looked hard where Dyson's finger was pointing, and could scarcely distinguish a faint mark in deeper red.

'What is it?' he said. 'I can make nothing of it.'

'Look a little more closely. Don't you see it is an attempt to draw the human eye?'

'Ah, now I see what you mean. My sight is not very sharp. Yes, so it is, it is meant for an eye, no doubt, as you say. I thought the children learnt drawing at school.'

'Well, it is an odd eye enough. Do you notice the peculiar almond shape; almost like the eye of a Chinaman?'

Dyson looked meditatively at the work of the undeveloped artist, and scanned the wall again, going down on his knees in the minuteness of his inquisition.

'I should like very much,' he said at length, 'to know how a child in this out of the way place could have any idea of the shape of the Mongolian eye. You see the average child has a very distinct impression of the subject; he draws a circle, or something like a circle, and puts a dot in the centre. I don't think any child imagines that the eye is really made like that; it's just a convention of infantile art. But this almond-shaped thing puzzles me extremely. Perhaps it may be derived from a gilt Chinaman on a tea-canister in the grocer's shop. Still that's hardly likely.'

'But why are you so sure it was done by a child?'

'Why! Look at the height. These old-fashioned bricks are little more than two inches thick; there are twenty courses from the ground to the sketch if we call it so; that gives a height of three and a half feet. Now, just imagine you are going to draw something on this wall. Exactly; your pencil, if you had one, would touch the wall somewhere on the level with your eyes, that is, more than five feet from the ground. It seems, therefore, a very simple deduction to conclude that this eye on the wall was drawn by a child about ten years old.'

'Yes, I had not thought of that. Of course one of the children must have done it.'

'I suppose so; and yet as I said, there is something singularly unchildlike about those two lines, and the eyeball itself, you see, is almost an oval. To my mind, the thing has an odd, ancient air; and a touch that is not altogether pleasant. I cannot help fancying that if we could see a whole face from the same hand it would not be altogether agreeable. However, that is nonsense, after all, and we are not getting farther in our investigations. It is odd that the flint series has come to such an abrupt end.'

The two men walked away towards the house, and as they went in at the porch there was a break in the grey sky, and a gleam of sunshine on the grey hill before them.

All the day Dyson prowled meditatively about the fields and woods surrounding the house. He was thoroughly and completely puzzled by the trivial circumstances he proposed to elucidate, and now he again took the flint arrow-head from his pocket, turning it over and examining it with deep attention. There was something about the thing that was altogether different from the specimens he had seen at the museums and private collections; the shape was of a distinct type, and around the edge there was a line of little punctured dots, apparently a suggestion of ornament. Who, thought Dyson, could possess such things in so remote a place; and who, possessing the flints, could have put them to the fantastic use of designing meaningless figures under Vaughan's garden wall? The rank absurdity of the whole affair offended him unutterably; and as one theory after another rose in his mind, only to be rejected, he felt strongly tempted to take the next train back to town. He had seen the silver plate which Vaughan treasured, and had inspected the punch-bowl, the gem of the collection, with close attention; and what he saw and his interview with the butler convinced him that a plot to rob the strong box was out of the limits of enquiry. The chest in which the bowl was kept, a heavy piece of mahogany, evidently dating from the beginning of the century, was certainly strongly suggestive of a pyramid, and Dyson was at first inclined to the inept manoeuvres of the detective, but a little sober thought convinced him of the impossibility of the burglary hypothesis, and he cast wildly about for something more satisfying. He asked Vaughan if there were any gipsies in the neighbourhood, and heard that the Romany had not been seen for years. This dashed him a good deal, as he knew the gipsy habit of leaving queer hieroglyphics on the line of march, and had been much elated when the thought occurred to him. He was facing Vaughan by the old-fashioned hearth when he put the question, and leaned back in his chair in disgust at the destruction of his theory.

'It is odd,' said Vaughan, 'but the gipsies never trouble us here. Now and then the farmers find traces of fires in the wildest part of the hills, but nobody seems to know who the fire-lighters are.'

'Surely that looks like gipsies?'

'No, not in such places as those. Tinkers and gipsies and wanderers of all sorts stick to the roads and don't go very far from the farmhouses.'

'Well, I can make nothing of it. I saw the children going by this afternoon, and, as you say, they ran straight on. So we shall have no more eyes on the wall at all events.'

'No, I must waylay them one of these days and find out who is the artist.'

The next morning when Vaughan strolled in his usual course from the lawn to the back of the house he found Dyson already awaiting him by the garden door, and evidently in a state of high excitement, for he beckoned furiously with his hand, and gesticulated violently.

'What is it?' asked Vaughan. 'The flints again?'

'No; but look here, look at the wall. There; don't you see it?'

'There's another of those eyes!'

'Exactly. Drawn, you see, at a little distance from the first, almost on the same level, but slightly lower.'

'What on earth is one to make of it? It couldn't have been done by the children; it wasn't there last night, and they won't pass for another hour. What can it mean?'

'I think the very devil is at the bottom of all this,' said Dyson. 'Of course, one cannot resist the conclusion that these infernal almond eyes are to be set down to the same agency as the devices in the arrow-heads; and where that conclusion is to lead us is more than I can tell. For my part, I have to put a strong check on my imagination, or it would run wild.'

'Vaughan,' he said, as they turned away from the wall, 'has it struck you that there is one point – a very curious point – in common between the figures done in flints and the eyes drawn on the wall?'

'What is that?' asked Vaughan, on whose face there had fallen a certain shadow of indefinite dread.

'It is this. We know that the signs of the Army, the Bowl, the Pyramid, and the Half Moon must have been done at night. Presumably they were meant to be seen at night. Well, precisely the same reasoning applies to those eyes on the wall.'

'I do not quite see your point.'

'Oh, surely. The nights are dark just now, and have been very cloudy, I know, since I came down. Moreover, those overhanging trees would throw that wall into deep shadow even on a clear night.'

'Well?'

'What struck me was this. What very peculiarly sharp eyesight, they, whoever "they" are, must have to be able to arrange arrow-heads in intricate order in the blackest shadow of the wood, and then draw the eyes on the wall without a trace of bungling, or a false line.'

'I have read of persons confined in dungeons for many years who have been able to see quite well in the dark,' said Vaughan.

'Yes,' said Dyson, 'there was the abbé in *Monte Cristo*. But it is a singular point.'

3. The Search for the Bowl

'Who was that old man that touched his hat to you just now?' said Dyson, as they came to the bend of the lane near the house.

'Oh, that was old Trevor. He looks very broken, poor old fellow.'

'Who is Trevor?'

'Don't you remember? I told you the story that afternoon I came to your rooms – about a girl named Annie Trevor, who disappeared in the most inexplicable manner about five weeks ago. That was her father.'

'Yes, yes, I recollect now. To tell the truth, I had forgotten all about it. And nothing has been heard of the girl?'

'Nothing whatever. The police are quite at fault.'

'I am afraid I did not pay very much attention to the details you gave me. Which way did the girl go?'

'Her path would take her right across those wild hills above the house; the nearest point in the track must be about two miles from here.'

'Is it near that little hamlet I saw yesterday?'

'You mean Croesyceiliog, where the children came from? No; it goes more to the north.'

'Ah, I have never been that way.'

They went into the house, and Dyson shut himself up in his room, sunk deep in doubtful thought, but yet with the shadow of a suspicion growing within him that for a while haunted his brain, all vague and fantastic, refusing to take definite form. He was sitting by the open window and looking out on the valley and saw, as if in a picture, the intricate winding of the brook, the grey bridge, and the vast hills rising beyond; all still and without a breath of wind to stir the mystic hanging woods, and the evening sunshine glowed warm on the bracken, and down below a faint mist, pure white, began to rise from the stream. Dyson sat by the window as the day darkened and the huge bastioned hills loomed vast and vague, and the woods became dim and more shadowy; and the fancy that had seized him no longer appeared altogether impossible. He passed the rest of the evening in a reverie, hardly hearing what Vaughan said; and when he took his candle in the hall, he paused a moment before bidding his friend goodnight.

'I want a good rest,' he said. 'I have got some work to do tomorrow.'

'Some writing, you mean?'

'No. I am going to look for the Bowl.'

'The Bowl! If you mean my punch-bowl, that is safe in the chest.'

'I don't mean the punch-bowl. You may take my word for it that your plate has never been threatened. No; I will not bother you with any suppositions. We shall in all probability have something much stronger than suppositions before long. Goodnight, Vaughan.'

The next morning Dyson set off after breakfast. He took the path by the garden wall, and noted that there were now eight of the weird almond eyes dimly outlined on the brick.

'Six days more,' he said to himself, but as he thought over the theory he had formed, he shrank, in spite of strong conviction, from such a wildly incredible fancy. He struck up through the dense shadows of the wood, and at length came out on the bare hillside, and climbed higher and higher over the slippery turf, keeping well to the north, and following the indications given him by Vaughan. As he went on, he seemed to mount ever higher above the world of human life and customary things; to his right he looked at a fringe of orchard and saw a faint blue smoke rising like a pillar; there was the hamlet from which the children came to school, and there the only sign of life, for the woods embowered and concealed Vaughan's old grey house. As he reached what seemed the summit of the hill, he realized for the first time the desolate loneliness and strangeness of the land; there was nothing but grey sky and grey hill, a high, vast plain that seemed to stretch on for ever and ever, and a faint glimpse of a blue-peaked mountain far away and to the north. At length he came to the path, a slight track scarcely noticeable, and from its position and by what Vaughan had told him he knew that it was the way the lost girl, Annie Trevor, must have taken. He followed the path on the bare hill-top, noticing the great limestone rocks that cropped out of the turf, grim and hideous, and of an aspect as forbidding as an idol of the South Seas; and suddenly he halted, astonished, although he had found what he searched for. Almost without warning the ground shelved suddenly away on all sides, and Dyson looked down into a circular depression, which might well have been a Roman amphitheatre, and the ugly crags of limestone rimmed it round as if with a broken wall. Dyson walked round the hollow, and noted the position of the stones, and then turned on his way home.

'This,' he thought to himself, 'is more than curious. The Bowl is discovered, but where is the Pyramid?'

'My dear Vaughan,' he said, when he got back, 'I may tell you that I have found the Bowl, and that is all I shall tell you for the present. We have six days of absolute inaction before us; there is really nothing to be done.'

4. The Secret of the Pyramid

'I have just been round the garden,' said Vaughan one morning. 'I have been counting those infernal eyes, and I find there are fourteen of them. For heaven's sake, Dyson, tell me what the meaning of it all is.'

'I should be very sorry to attempt to do so. I may have guessed this or that, but I always make it a principle to keep my guesses to myself. Besides, it is really not worth while anticipating events; you will remember my telling you that we had six days of inaction before us? Well, this is the sixth day, and the last of idleness. Tonight I propose we take a stroll.'

'A stroll! Is that all the action you mean to take?'

'Well, it may show you some very curious things. To be plain, I want you to start with me at nine o'clock this evening for the hills. We may have to be out all night, so you had better wrap up well, and bring some of that brandy.'

'Is it a joke?' asked Vaughan, who was bewildered with strange events and strange surmises.

'No, I don't think there is much joke in it. Unless I am much mistaken we shall find a very serious explanation of the puzzle. You will come with me, I am sure?'

'Very good. Which way to do you want to go?'

'By the path you told me of; the path Annie Trevor is supposed to have taken.'

Vaughan looked white at the mention of the girl's name.

'I did not think you were on that track,' he said. 'I thought it was the affair of those devices in flint and of the eyes on the wall that you were engaged on. It's no good saying any more, but I will go with you.'

At a quarter to nine that evening the two men set out, taking the path through the wood, and up the hillside. It was a dark and heavy night, the sky was thick with clouds, and the valley full of mist, and all the way they seemed to walk in a world of shadow and gloom, hardly speaking, and afraid to break the haunted silence. They came out at last on the steep hillside, and instead of the oppression of the wood there was the long, dim sweep of the turf, and higher, the fantastic limestone rocks hinted horror through the darkness, and the wind sighed as it passed across the mountain to the sea, and in its passage beat chill about their hearts. They seemed to walk on and on for hours, and the dim outline of the hill still stretched before them, and the haggard rocks still loomed through the darkness, when suddenly Dyson whispered, drawing his breath quickly, and coming close to his companion:

'Here,' he said, 'we will lie down. I do not think there is anything yet.'

'I know the place,' said Vaughan, after a moment. 'I have often been by in the daytime. The country people are afraid to come here, I believe; it is supposed to be a fairies' castle, or something of the kind. But why on earth have we come here?'

'Speak a little lower,' said Dyson. 'It might not do us any good if we are overheard.'

'Overheard here! There is not a soul within three miles of us.'

'Possibly not; indeed, I should say certainly not. But there might be a body somewhat nearer.'

'I don't understand you in the least,' said Vaughan, whispering to humour Dyson, 'but why have we come here?'

'Well, you see this hollow before us is the Bowl. I think we had better not talk even in whispers.'

They lay full length upon the turf; the rock between their faces and the Bowl, and now and again, Dyson, slouching his dark, soft hat over his forehead, put out the glint of an eye, and in a moment drew back, not daring to take a prolonged view. Again he laid an ear to the ground and listened, and the hours went by, and the darkness seemed to blacken, and the faint sigh of the wind was the only sound.

Vaughan grew impatient with this heaviness of silence, this watching for indefinite terror; for to him there was no shape or form of apprehension, and he began to think the whole vigil a dreary farce.

'How much longer is this to last?' he whispered to Dyson, and Dyson, who had been holding his breath in the agony of attention, put his mouth to Vaughan's ear and said:

'Will you listen?' with pauses between each syllable, and in the voice with which the priest pronounces the awful words.

Vaughan caught the ground with his hands, and stretched forward, wondering what he was to hear. At first there was nothing, and then a low and gentle noise came very softly from the Bowl, a faint sound, almost indescribable, but as if one held the tongue against the roof of the mouth and expelled the breath. He listened eagerly and presently the noise grew louder, and became a strident and horrible hissing as if the pit beneath boiled with fervent heat, and Vaughan, unable to remain in suspense any longer, drew his cap half over his face in imitation of Dyson, and looked down to the hollow below.

It did, in truth, stir and seethe like an infernal caldron. The whole of the sides and bottom tossed and writhed with vague and restless forms that passed to and fro without the sound of feet, and gathered thick here and there and seemed to speak to one another in those tones of horrible sibilance, like the hissing of snakes, that he had heard. It was as if the sweet turf and the cleanly earth had suddenly become quickened with some foul writhing growth. Vaughan could not draw back his face, though he felt Dyson's finger touch him, but he peered into the quaking mass and saw faintly that there were things like faces and human limbs, and yet he felt his inmost soul chill with the sure belief that no fellow soul or human thing stirred in all that tossing and hissing host. He looked aghast, choking back sobs of horror, and at length the loathsome forms gathered thickest about some vague object in the middle of the hollow, and the hissing of their speech grew more venomous, and he saw in the uncertain light the abominable limbs, vague and yet too plainly seen, writhe and intertwine, and he thought he heard, very faint, a low human moan striking through the noise of speech that was not of man. At his heart something seemed to whisper ever 'the worm of corruption, the worm that dieth not', and grotesquely the image was pictured to his imagination of a piece of putrid offal stirring through and through with bloated and horrible creeping things. The writhing of the dusky limbs continued, they seemed clustered round the dark form in the middle of the hollow, and the sweat dripped and poured off Vaughan's forehead, and fell cold on his hand beneath his face.

Then, it seemed done in an instant, the loathsome mass melted and fell away to the sides of the Bowl, and for a moment Vaughan saw in the middle of the hollow the tossing of human arms. But a spark gleamed beneath, a fire kindled, and as the voice of a woman cried out loud in a shrill scream of utter anguish and terror, a great pyramid of flame spired up like a bursting of a pent fountain, and threw a blaze of light upon the whole mountain. In that instant Vaughan saw the myriads beneath; the things made in the form of men but stunted like children hideously deformed, the faces with the almond eyes burning with evil and unspeakable lusts; the ghastly yellow of the mass of naked flesh and then as if by magic the place was empty, while the fire roared and crackled, and the flames shone abroad.

'You have seen the Pyramid,' said Dyson in his ear, 'the Pyramid of fire.'

5. The Little People

'Then you recognize the thing?'

'Certainly. It is a brooch that Annie Trevor used to wear on Sundays; I remember the pattern. But where did you find it? You don't mean to say that you have discovered the girl?'

'My dear Vaughan, I wonder you have not guessed where I found the brooch. You have not forgotten last night already?'

'Dyson,' said the other, speaking very seriously, 'I have been turning it over in my mind this morning while you have been out. I have thought about what I saw, or perhaps I should say about what I thought I saw, and the only conclusion I can come to is this, that the thing won't bear recollection. As men live, I have lived soberly and honestly, in the fear of God, all my days, and all I can do is believe that I suffered from some monstrous delusion, from some phantasmagoria of the bewildered senses. You know we went home together in silence, not a word passed between us as to what I fancied I saw; had we not better agree to keep silence on the subject? When I took my walk in the peaceful morning sunshine, I thought all the earth seemed full of praise, and passing by that wall I noticed there were no more signs recorded, and I blotted out those that remained. The mystery is over, and we can live quietly again. I think some poison has been working for the last few weeks; I have trod on the verge of madness, but I am sane now.'

Mr Vaughan had spoken earnestly, and bent forward in his chair and glanced at Dyson with something of entreaty.

'My dear Vaughan,' said the other, after a pause, 'what's the use of this? It is much too late to take that tone; we have gone too deep. Besides you know as well as I that there is no delusion in the case; I wish there were with all my heart. No, in justice to myself I must tell you the whole story, so far as I know it.'

'Very good,' said Vaughan with a sigh, 'if you must, you must.'

'Then,' said Dyson, 'we will begin with the end, if you please. I found this brooch you have just identified in the place we have called the Bowl. There was a heap of grey ashes, as if a fire had been burning, indeed, the embers were still hot, and this brooch was lying on the ground, just outside the range of the flame. It must have dropped accidentally from the dress of the person who was wearing it. No, don't interrupt me; we can pass now to the beginning, as we have had the end. Let us go back to that day you came to see me in my rooms in London. So far as I can remember, soon after you came in you mentioned, in a somewhat casual manner, that an unfortunate and mysterious incident had occurred in your part of the country; a girl named Annie Trevor had gone to see a relative, and had disappeared. I confess freely that what you said did not greatly interest me; there are so many reasons which may make it extremely convenient for a man and more especially a woman to vanish from the circle of their relations and friends. I suppose, if we were to consult the police, one would find that in London somebody disappears mysteriously every other week, and the officers would, no doubt, shrug their shoulders, and tell you that by the law of averages it could not be otherwise. So I was very culpably careless to your story, and besides, there is another reason for my lack of interest; your tale was inexplicable. You could only suggest a blackguard sailor on the tramp, but I discarded the explanation immediately. For many reasons, but chiefly because the occasional criminal, the amateur in brutal crime, is always found out, especially if he selects the country as the scene of his operations. You will remember the case of that Garcia you mentioned; he strolled into a railway station the day after the murder, his trousers covered with blood, and the works of the Dutch clock, his loot, tied in a neat parcel. So rejecting this, your only suggestion, the whole tale became, as I say, inexplicable, and, therefore, profoundly uninteresting. Yes, *therefore*, it is a perfectly valid conclusion. Do you ever trouble your head about problems which you know to be in soluble? Did you ever bestow much thought on the old puzzle of Achilles and the tortoise? Of course not, because you knew it was a hopeless quest, and so when you told me the story of a country girl who had disappeared I simply placed the whole thing down in the category of the insoluble, and thought no more about the matter. I was mistaken, so it has turned out; but if you remember, you immediately passed on to an affair which interested you more intensely, because personally. I need not go over the very singular narrative of the flint signs; at first I thought it all trivial, probably some children's game, and if not that a hoax of some sort; but your showing me the arrow-head awoke my acute interest. Here, I saw, there was something widely removed from the commonplace, and matter of real curiosity; and as soon as I came here I set to work to find the solution, repeating to myself again and again the signs you had described. First came the sign we have agreed to call the Army; a number of serried lines of flints, all pointing in the same way. Then the lines, like the spokes of a wheel, all converging towards the figure of a Bowl, then the triangle or Pyramid, and last of all the Half Moon. I confess that I exhausted conjecture in my efforts to unveil this mystery, and as you will understand it was a duplex or rather triplex problem. For I had not merely to ask myself: what do these figures mean? but also, who can possibly be responsible for the designing of them? And again, who can possibly possess such valuable things, and knowing their value thus throw them down by the wayside? This line of thought led me to suppose that the person or persons in question did not know the value of unique flint arrow-heads, and yet this did not lead me far, for a well-educated man might easily be ignorant on such a subject. Then came the complication of the eye on the wall, and you remember that we could not avoid the conclusion that in the two cases the same agency was at work. The peculiar position of these eyes on the wall made me inquire if there was such a thing as a dwarf anywhere in the neighbourhood, but I found that there was not, and I knew that the children who pass by every day had nothing to do with the matter. Yet I felt convinced that whoever drew the eyes must be from three and a half to four feet high, since, as I pointed out at the time, anyone who draws on a perpendicular surface chooses by instinct a spot about level with his face. Then again, there was the question of the peculiar shape of the eyes; that marked Mongolian character of which the English country man could have no conception, and for a final cause of confusion the obvious fact that the designer or designers must be able practically to see in the dark. As you remarked, a man who has been confined for many years in an extremely dark cell or dungeon might acquire that power; but since the days of Edmond Dantès, where would such a prison be found in Europe? A sailor, who had been immured for a considerable period in some horrible Chinese oubliette, seemed the individual I was in search of, and though it looked improbable, it was not absolutely impossible that a sailor or, let us say, a man employed on shipboard, should be a dwarf. But how to account for my imaginary sailor being in possession of prehistoric arrow-heads? And the possession granted, what was the meaning and object of these mysterious signs of flint, and the almond-shaped eyes? Your theory of a contemplated burglary I saw, nearly from the first, to be quite untenable, and I confess I was utterly at a loss for a working hypothesis. It was a mere accident which put me on the track; we passed poor old Trevor, and your mention of his name and of the disappearance of his daughter, recalled the story which I had forgotten, or which remained unheeded. Here, then, I said to myself, is another problem, uninteresting, it is true, by itself; but what if it prove to be in relation with all these enigmas which torture me? I shut myself in my room, and endeavoured to dismiss all prejudice from my mind, and I went over everything *de novo*, assuming for theory's sake that the disappearance of Annie Trevor had some connection with the flint signs and the eyes on the wall. This assumption did not lead me very far, and I was on the point of giving the whole problem up in despair, when a possible significance of the Bowl struck me. As you know there is a 'Devil's Punch-bowl' in Surrey, and I saw that the symbol might refer to some feature in the country. Putting the two extremes together, I determined to look for the Bowl near the path which the lost girl had taken, and you know how I found it. I interpreted the sign by what I knew, and read the first, the Army, thus: 'there is to be a gathering or assembly at the Bowl in a fortnight (that is the Half Moon) to see the Pyramid, or to build the Pyramid.' The eyes, drawn one by one, day by day, evidently checked off the days, and I knew that there would be fourteen and no more. Thus far the way seemed pretty plain; I would not trouble myself to inquire as to the nature of the assembly, or as to who was to assemble in the loneliest and most dreaded place among these lonely hills. In Ireland or China or the West of America the question would have been easily answered: a muster of the disaffected, the meeting of a secret society, vigilantes summoned to report: the thing would be simplicity itself; but in this quiet corner of England, inhabited by quiet folk, no such suppositions were possible for a moment. But I knew that I should have an opportunity of seeing and watching the assembly, and I did not care to perplex myself with hopeless research; and in place of reasoning a wild fancy entered into judgement: I remembered what people had said about Annie Trevor's disappearance, that she had been 'taken by the fairies'. I tell you, Vaughan, I am a sane man as you are, my brain is not, I trust, mere vacant space to let any wild improbability, and I tried my best to thrust the fantasy away. And the hint came of the old name of fairies, 'the little people', and the very probable belief that they represent a tradition of the prehistoric Turanian inhabitants of the country, who were cave dwellers: and then I realized with a shock that I was looking for a being under four feet in height, accustomed to live in darkness, possessing stone instruments, and familiar with the Mongolian cast of features! I say this, Vaughan, that I should be ashamed to hint at such visionary stuff to you, if it were not for that which you saw with your very eyes last night, and I say that I might doubt the evidence of my senses, if they were not confirmed by yours. But you and I cannot look each other in the face and pretend delusion; as you lay on the turf beside me I felt your flesh shrink and quiver, and I saw your eyes in the light of the flame. And so I tell you without any shame what was in my mind last night as we went through the wood and climbed the hill, and lay hidden beneath the rock.

'There was one thing that should have been most evident that puzzled me to the very last. I told you how I read the sign of the Pyramid; the assembly was to see a pyramid, and the true meaning of the symbol escaped me to the last moment. The old derivation from πυρ, fire, though false, should have set me on the track, but it never occurred to me.

'I think I need say very little more. You know we were quite helpless, even if we had foreseen what was to come. Ah, the particular place where these signs were displayed? Yes, that is a curious question. But this house is, so far as I can judge, in a pretty central situation amongst the hills; and possibly, who can say yes or no, that queer, old limestone pillar by your garden wall was a place of meeting before the Celt set foot in Britain. But there is one thing I must add: I don't regret our inability to rescue the wretched girl. You saw the appearance of those things that gathered thick and writhed in the Bowl; you may be sure that what lay bound in the midst of them was no longer fit for earth.'

'So?' said Vaughan.

'So she passed in the Pyramid of Fire,' said Dyson, 'and they passed again to the underworld, to the places beneath the hills.'

File classification: Sasquatch
Location: Northwest USA

Title: The Bride of Bigfoot
Writer: *Kit Reed*

Briefing: *Sasquatch – large, hairy, humanoid said to have lived in remote areas of North America for centuries; referred to in folklore as 'Bigfoot'.* Susie lives on the edge of a forest where rumours abound about a creature that lurks in the dense tracts of undergrowth. A shy, elusive giant, blurred in even the few snatched photographs of it, local people also believe the creature is an omen for mankind. However, when some items of Susie's underwear disappear from the washing line, and then a bunch of flowers and a dead bird appear *inside* the house, she sees her own future beginning to unravel in a wholly unexpected way . . .

Author: American Kit Reed has produced an acclaimed body of work ranging across a wide spectrum from sharp little domestic fables to harsh pictures of future worlds riven by conflict and death. She first began to win her large circle of admirers in the pages of *Fantasy and Science Fiction Magazine*, to which she contributed short stories in the Fifties, and then followed these with several major novels including the mystery story, *Mother Isn't Dead She's Only Sleeping* (1961), *Magic Time* (1980), about a sinister theme park, and *Fort Privilege* (1985), a highly topical drama about the residents of a New York apartment block under virtual siege from the massed ranks of homeless people living on the streets below. 'The Bride of Bigfoot', with its picture of a rural community also living in the thrall of an ancient, almost supernormal force, was written for *Isaac Asimov's Science Fiction Magazine* in 1984.

Imagine the two of us together, the sound of our flesh colliding: the smell of him. The smell of me.

At first I was afraid. Who would not be frightened by stirring shadows, leaves that shiver inexplicably, the suspicion that just outside the circle of bug lamps and firelight something huge has passed? If there was a thing at all, it was reported to be shy; the best photographs are blurred and of questionable origin; hunters said it would not attack even if provoked, but still . . . The silence it left behind was enormous; I could feel my heart shudder in my chest. With gross figures roaming, who would not be afraid?

We did not see or hear it; there was only the intimation. It had been there. It was gone. Thomas, whom I married six months ago, said, Listen. I said, I don't hear anything. Roberta said, I'm cold. Thomas persisted: I thought I heard something. Did you hear anything? I did not speak, but Malcolm, who was torturing steaks on our behalf, spoke politely: Everybody's so quiet, it must be twenty of or twenty after. Then Roberta said, Something just walked over my grave. I tried to laugh, but I was cold.

This was the night of our first cookout of the summer, shortly before I found certain pieces of my underwear missing from the line.

Our house is on the outer ring of streets here, so that instead of backing up to our neighbours' carports and barbecues, we look out at a wooded hillside, dense undergrowth and slender trees marching up the slope.

If it weren't for dust and attrition and human failure our house would be picture perfect. I used to want to go to live in one of our arrangements; the future would find me among the plant stands, splayfooted and supporting a begonia; I would be both beautiful and functional, a true work of art. Or I would be discovered on the sofa among the pillows, my permanent face fixed in a perpetual smile. I would face the future with no worries and no obligations, just one more pretty, blameless thing. It's a long road that knows no turning but an even longer one we women go. Each night even as I surveyed my creation I could see fresh dust settling on my polished surfaces, crumbs collecting on my kitchen floor, and I knew soon the light would change and leaves drop from my plants no matter what I did. Each night I knew I had to turn from my creations and start dinner because although Thomas and I both worked, it was I who must prepare the food. Because women are free and we are in the new society I was not forced to do these things; I had to do them by choice.

But it was summer, we opened all the windows and went in the yard without coats. We had that first cookout and maybe it was the curling smoke that wakened it, or maybe it saw me in my bathing suit . . . All I can tell you is that I lost certain underthings: my satin panties, my gossamer-sheen bra. When I came home from work at night I went directly into the back yard. I tried to penetrate the woods, staring at the screen of leaves for so long that I was certain I had seen something move. The summer air was already dense with its scent, but what it was I did not know; I could not be sure whether that was a tuft of hair caught in the wild honeysuckle or only fur. Every night I lingered and therefore had to apologize to Thomas because dinner was late.

Something dragged a flowering bush to our door. Outside our bedroom the flowers were flattened mysteriously. I got up at dawn and listened to the woods. Did I imagine the sound of soft breath? Did I catch a flash of gold among the leaves, the pattern of shadows dappling a naked flank?

In midsummer something left a dead bird with some flowers on my kitchen table and I stopped going outside. I stopped leaving the windows open, too; I told Thomas we would sleep better with the air conditioning. I should have known none of our arrangements are permanent. Even with the house sealed and the air conditioner whirring I could hear something crashing in the woods. I ran to the back door to see and when I found nothing I stood a moment longer so that even though I could not see it, it would see me. When we went to bed that night it was not Thomas I imagined next to me, but something else.

In August I retreated to the kitchen; with the oven fan going and the radio on, the blender whizzing and all my whips and ladles and spatulas laid out I could pretend there was nothing funny happening. We had seafood soufflé one night and the next we had veal medallions, one of my best efforts. When we went to bed Thomas turned to me and I tried to be attentive but I was already torn. I was as uneasy as a girl waiting for something new to come to the high school party – one of those strange, tough boys that shows up unexpectedly, with a black T-shirt and the long, slick hair, who stands there with his pelvis on the slant and the slightly dangerous look that lets you know your mother would never approve.

On Friday I made salmon mayonnaise, which I decorated with cress and dill, and for dessert I made a raspberry fool, after which I put on my lavender shift and opened the back door. In spite of the heat I stood there until Thomas came in the front door. Then I touched the corners of the mats and napkins on my pretty table and aligned the wine glasses and the water tumblers because Thomas and I had pretty arrangements and we set store by them.

Honey, why such a big kiss?

I missed you, I said. How was your day?

Much the same.

So we sat down at the little table with all our precious objects: the crystal candle holders, the wedding china, the Waterford, him, me. I asked if he liked his dinner.

Mmmm.

All right; I tried to slip it in. Am I doing something wrong?

I'm just a little tired.

Tell me about your day, you never do.

Mmm.

Outside, the thing in the woods was stirring. Thomas, love is to man a thing apart, it's woman's whole existence.

Mmmmm.

In the woods there was the thunder of air curdling: something stopping in mid-rush.

I love you, Thomas.

I love you.

Honey, are you sure?

Mmmmm.

I put out a dish of milk for it.

No, lieutenant, there were no signs of a struggle, one reason I didn't think to call you right away. I thought she had just stepped out and was coming back. When I got home from work Monday she was gone. Nothing out of order, nothing to raise your suspicions, no broken windows or torn screens. The house was shining clean. She had even left a chicken pie for me. But there was this strange, wild stink in the bedroom, plus which later I found *this* stuck in the ornamental palm tree on our screen door; your lab could tell if it's hair, or fur.

I wish I could give you more details, like whether the thing knocked my wife out or tied her up or what, but I wasn't too careful looking for clues because I didn't even know there was a Thing. For all I knew she had run over to a neighbour's, or down to the store to pick up some wine, which is what I thought in spite of the heap of clothes by the bed, thought even after it got dark.

By midnight when I hadn't heard I called her folks. You can imagine. Then I checked the closet with my heart going clunk, clunk. Nothing gone. Her bankbook and wallet were in her purse. All right, I should have called you but to tell the truth I thought it was something I could handle by myself. Ought to handle. A man has a right to protect what's his, *droit de seigneur*, OK? Besides, I didn't think it was kidnappers. That grey fur. The smell. It had to be some kind of wild animal, an element with which I am equipped to cope. I used to hunt with my father, and I know what animals do when they're spooked. Your cordon of men or police helicopter could panic it into doing something we would all be sorry for. I figured if it was a bear or wolf or something that got in, and it didn't kill her right here, it had probably carried her off to its lair, which meant it was a job for one man alone.

Now, I have my share of trophies. You might as well know back home I was an Eagle Scout and furthermore I am a paid-up member of the N.R.A. Plus which, this is not exactly the wilds. This is suburban living enhanced by proximity to the woods. If something carried off my wife I would stalk it to its lair and lie in wait. Then when it fell asleep or went off hunting, I would swarm in and carry her out.

All right, it did cross my mind that we might get an exclusive. Also it was marginally possible that if I rescued her we might lure the creature into the open. I could booby trap the terrace and snare it on the hoof. Right, I had guessed what it was. Imagine the publicity! The North American serial rights alone . . . after which we could take our sweet time deciding which publisher, holding the paperback auction, choosing between the major motion picture and an exclusive on TV. I personally would opt for the movie, we could sell backward to television and follow up with a series pilot and spinoff, the possibilities are astronomical, and if we could get the thing to agree to star . . .

But my Sue is a sentimental girl and I couldn't spring this on her all at once. First I had to get her home and then I was going to have to walk her through it, one step at a time, how I was going to make it clear to the public that she was an unwilling prisoner, so nobody would think she was easy, or cheap. You know how girls are. I was going to have to promise not to take advantage of her privileged relationship with the thing. But what if we could train it to do what we wanted? What if we taught it to talk? I was going to lay it out to her in terms of fitting recompense. I mean, there is no point being a victim when you can cash in on a slice of your life.

Lord, if that was all I had to worry about! But what did I know? That was in another country, and besides . . . Right, T. S. Eliot. I don't want you to think of me as an uncultivated man.

I got up before dawn and dressed for the hunt: long-sleeved shirt and long trousers, against the insects; boots, against the snakes. I tied up my head for personal reasons and smeared insect repellent on my hands and face. Then I got the rest of my equipment: hunting knife, with sheath; a pint of rye, to lure it; tape recorder, don't ask; my rifle, in case. A coil of rope.

It took less time to track it than I thought. You might not even know there was anything in the woods because you're not attuned to these things, but I can tell you they left a trail a mile wide. Broken twigs, twisted leaves, that kind of thing. So I closed in on their arrangement while it was still light; I came over the last rise and down into a thicket and there it was. I had expected to have a hard time locating her once I got to the lair; the thing would have tied her in a tree, say, or concealed her under a mass of brush or behind a pile of rocks.

This was not the case. She was right out in the open, sitting on a ledge in front of its lair just as nice as you please. Except for the one thing, you would think she was out sunning in the park. Right. Except for the dirt and flowers in her hair, she was *au naturel*. There was my wife Susie sitting with a pile of fruits in season, she was not tied up and she was not screaming, she wasn't even writing a note. She was – good lord, she was combing her hair. I went to earth. I had to be careful in case the thing was using her for bait. It could be in its cave lying in wait, or circling behind me, ready to attack. I lay still for an hour while she combed and hummed and nothing happened. There was nothing, not even a trace. I got up and showed myself.

I guess I startled her. She jumped three feet. I said, Don't be frightened, it's me.

Oh, it's you. Where did you come from?

Never mind that now. We have to hurry.

What are you doing?

Suze, I have come to take you home.

Imagine my surprise. All this way to rescue my darling helpmate, the equipment, the precautions, the expense, and all she could find to say was: You can't do that.

What do you mean?

So she was trying to spare my feelings, but that would take me some time to figure out. You have to go for your own good, Thomas. He'll tear you limb from limb.

Just let him try. I shook my rifle.

Thomas, no!

I did not like the way this was going. Not only was she not thrilled to see me but she showed signs of wanting to stay put. I was not sure what we had here, whether she was playing a game I had not learned the rules to or whether she had been unhinged by the experience. You should only have to court a woman once. What I did at this point was assert my rights. Any husband would have done the same. I said, Enough is enough, honey, now let's get home before it gets dark. Listen, this is for your own good. Susie, what are you doing with that rock?

To make a long story short I had to bop her on the head and drag her out.

I don't know how we made it back to the house. Halfway down the hill she woke up and started struggling so I had to throw her on the ground and tie her up, in addition to which the woods were filled with what I would have to call intimations of the creature. There was always your getting pounced upon from the shadows, or jumped out of a tree onto, to say nothing of your getting grabbed from behind and shaken, your neck snapped with one pop. I kept thinking I heard the thing sneaking up behind me, I imagined its foul breath on my neck. As a matter of fact I never saw hide nor hair of it, and it crossed my mind that there might never have been a thing, a thought I quickly banished. Of course there had. Then I figured out that it was afraid to run after what it believed in, which meant that it was craven indeed, to let her go without a fight.

As soon as we got inside I locked all the doors and windows and put Susie in the tub with a hooker of gin and a pint of bubble bath, after which, together, we washed all that stuff out of her hair, including the smell. I guess the gin opened the floodgates; she just sat there with the tears running down her cheeks while I picked the flowers out of her hair. Somehow I knew this was not the time to bring up the major motion picture. What we had here might turn out to be private and not interesting to anybody but us.

There, there, Suze, I said. Don't feel bad.

She only cried louder.

Now we know who loves you the most.

She just kept on crying.

I tried to cheer her up by making a joke. Maybe it found a cheap date.

She howled and wouldn't speak to me.

So I looked at her naked, heaving shoulders and I thought: *Aren't you going to apologize?* I was afraid to ask but I had to say something; after all, she was my wife.

Don't be ashamed, Suze. We all get carried away at least once in our life.

When she would not stop crying I thought it must have been one of those one-night stands; if the thing cared about her at all it would be tearing the house down to get to her. She would get over it, I thought. But she would not be consoled. There, there, I said, there there. When this blows over I'll buy you a car.

Fat lot I knew. It was a tactic. All the thing had to do was lay back and wait for her to get loose. Which I discovered shortly before dawn when I woke to an unusual sound. I sat up and saw her moving among the bedroom curtains, trying to unlock the sliding door. Was the thing in the bushes, waiting? Would she run outside with cries of delight? I was afraid to find out. I sprang up and tackled her, after which I laid down the law. She didn't argue, she only wept and languished. It was terrible. I had tried to arm against the enemy outside and all the time I had this enemy within. I called us both in sick at work after which I marched her with me to the hardware store and surveilled her the whole time I was buying locks. Then I barred the doors and put extra locks on all the windows. The thing was so smart it wasn't going to show itself. It was just going to sit tight and wait. Well, two could play at that game, I thought. When it got tired of waiting and showed itself I would blow it apart.

I suppose I was counting too much on her. I thought sooner or later she would clean herself up and apologize and we could go back to our life. Not so. We went from vacation time into leave without pay and she was still a mess. She would not stop crying and she wouldn't speak to me. She just kept plastering herself to the windows with this awful look of hope. In addition to which, there was the smell. In spite of everything we still had this strange and fearsome smell. It would fill the room when I least expected it. My Susie would lift her head and sniff and grin and if I tried to lay a hand on her, look out! It was enough to make a grown man weep.

I had to act.

So what I did was put her in the cellar and lock her up, after which I put on my hunting clothes and located the equipment: rifle, knife, rope. The tape recorder, she had smashed. I didn't know how far I would have to stalk the thing or what I would have to do to make it show itself but I was sick of the waiting game.

Damn right I was scared. I took the double bar off the back door and went down the steps. I tiptoed across the night garden, and over to the trees. I know you're in there, I said in a reasonable tone. If you don't come out I'm coming in after you.

There was nothing, only the smell. I thought I would pass out.

Homewrecker. Bastard, come on. Right, I was getting mad. I cocked the rifle. In another minute I was going to spray the trees.

Then it showed itself. It just parted the maples like swinging doors and walked out.

Huge. Yes, and that foetor, wow! The hair that covered it, the teeth . . . You've heard tales brought back by hunters. You can imagine the rest. The thing stood there in the moonlight with its yellow teeth bared while I kept my rifle trained on its chest. It just stood there snuffling. I was . . . all right, I was overconfident.

I yelled: Are you going to leave Susie and me alone or what?

At which point it sprang. Before I could even squeeze the trigger this great big monstrous thing sprang right on top of me after which I don't remember much except the explosion of my rifle, the kick. So it must be wounded, at least, which I suppose means it has left a trail of blood, but Lieutenant, I don't want to press charges. The thing is, my Susie left me of her own free will and now that all is said and done I understand.

No, I can't explain, not exactly, except it has to do with the thing: the stench, the roar, the smack of its prodigious flesh. It must have squeezed the daylights out of me after which it threw me into Malcolm's grape arbour, which is where I woke up. They were gone, together, and Malcolm was calling the police.

So I'm letting her go, Lieutenant, and with my blessings, because in the grip of the monster I understood. For those few seconds I was disassembled, helpless in the power of a force I could not withstand. I learned something extraordinary in that terrible embrace. Susie didn't want this thing; it just carried her away. So I saw that there are things we don't *want* to lust after, but we desire them even as we beg forgiveness of those we love. We lay out these straight lines to walk along, and we walk on them in an orderly way until something wild happens that parts or bends them so we can see what's waiting just underneath: the chasm we are skating over, how close chaos is. If this could happen to my Susie, it could happen to you. To me. How can I not forgive her? Who am I to say the next time something big comes along, I won't get carried away?

archive 5

urban legends

Title: Tulips From Amsterdam
Writer: *Ian Watson*

Briefing: *The Hitchhiker – archetypal urban legend; story of unlikely occurrence which is often told as being true.* Richard Kershaw is a professor of sociology and social anthropology at the University of Blanchester. He has a special interest in urban legends and has been collecting and classifying material for ten years when a beautiful young student comes to him with what, at first, sounds like another classic hitchhiker story of being picked up by a mysterious motorist. But as Richard listens to her account, he begins to sense he may be about to understand just *how* such legends are created . . .

Author: English author Ian Watson has been described as perhaps the leading synthesizer in modern sf. Aside from his reputation as one of the most popular of today's writers, he has the distinction of having taught one of the first academic courses in sf in the UK when for six years he lectured on Future Studies at Birmingham Polytechnic. His early career as a lecturer in Tanzania and Japan was followed by the development of his remarkable talent as a writer of sf short stories and novels when he returned to England and took up his position at Birmingham. Since 1976 Watson has been a full-time writer and is already being spoken of as the natural successor to H. G. Wells. His novel, *The Embedding* (1973) won the Prix Apollo, and he scored another *succès d'estime* with *The Jonah Kit* which won the British Science Fiction Award in 1978. Ian Watson's short stories range widely for their themes: not a few inspired by historical and contemporary legends, such as 'Tulips from Amsterdam', written in 1996, and here making its first book appearance.

'So,' said Tulip to me, uncrossing her long legs, 'I climbed into the car with this fellow, and we cruised on to the motorway . . .'

Tulip was what her friends called her, so she said. In her olive-green jeans and tight chartreuse sweater she was certainly long-stemmed. She wore her short dyed hair in upright gelled petals of orange and yellow and apricot. A tiny golden tulip adorned her pierced right nostril. Quite a glorious and exotic creation she'd made of herself. Not garish. The punk hair was chic rather than brazen. The nose trinket was a perfect grace-note. How I desired her, though first I must carefully assess her.

As soon as Tulip had come into my office I had abandoned my cluttered desk and shown her to one of the two cosy chairs beside the low interview table. She had demurred at being recorded on cassette. I respected her wish. I cradled a notepad on my lap.

Slim nose, high cheek bones. Opaline eyes: green within cream. Gold subtly shadowed the orbits and brows, like a dust of pollen.

'On the last day of last term,' she said, 'which was a Friday, of course, we were all given an art history test to take away with us.' Her voice was surprisingly sweet, with a hint of Scots. There were no raucous or shrill notes such as often spoil a first impression of grace and intelligence.

'Our test took the form of a photo in a sealed envelope. Printed on the front was the instruction: *Don't open till Saturday morning.* Most of us would be travelling miles the next day, but by the evening of the same day we were supposed to write a page of comment about whatever painting the photo showed and post our page back in the stamped addressed envelope provided. By that time the college library was already shut, so I didn't sneak a look at the photo right away. Too much else to do.'

'This sounds more like an initiative test for secret agents,' I said. 'Who dreamed it up?'

'Roger Weeks. He hoped we'd be spontaneous and ingenious.'

I didn't know Weeks very well, but I was aware that he was innovative.

'Well now,' said Tulip, 'I was sitting with this stranger in his BMW doing about eighty in the slow lane, because the motorway was fairly empty—'

I must have pursed my lips. She nodded briefly.

'I know I shouldn't hitch on my own! Rapists, murderers, and molesters. It saves *money*, and I was skint. Deep in the red. Still am, in fact.'

'I'm sorry.' I never offered even a token fee in exchange for stories in case my subjects invented accounts in the hope of earning some cash. What I needed were genuine volunteers. There were always enough of those. Subsequently I might invite Tulip out for a drink and a meal. I couldn't be sure yet. Her arrival in my office at four o'clock put us conveniently close to such a possibility.

'So I opened my envelope and I started looking at *this*—'

From her suede patchwork bag she took a colour photograph, which she laid on the table and angled to face me.

In the painting the bearded faces of half a dozen peering men were illuminated by golden light. Black clothes with big white ornamental ruffs around the necks. Background: dark grey and black.

'A Rembrandt, isn't it?'

She laughed. 'You pass the test. Who else paints so dark and so bright?'

In the foreground lay a chalky corpse, naked but for a cloth across the loins. The only person who was wearing a hat – big-brimmed and black – was probing with slim silver forceps at the left arm of the corpse. A flayed, blood-red arm. A dissection was commencing.

'Mister BMW glanced at the photo on my knee and he said to me, "That's *The Anatomy Lesson*. Painted in 1632, or thereabouts." Wow, he recognized it!—'

The driver, as Tulip described him, was both dishy and dusty. Dishy, as regards craggy features and a moderately athletic body attired in an expensive grey suit, blue silk shirt and arty tie with pastel butterfly motifs. Dusty (in her parlance) as regards thinning wayward grey hair and a certain pallor to his skin, not unlike that of the corpse laid out for dissection. The man must have been about 50. Tulip couldn't decide whether a small mulberry birthmark on his forehead, in the shape of a mushroom, was fascinating or icky.

He was, so he said, a publisher's representative. Name of Tony. He travelled a lot. Stayed in motels mainly. He liked motels. He would curl up with a book if no finer entertainment offered itself.

What did this hint mean? Did Tony sometimes pick girls up at motorway service stations? Tulip suspected so. This sort of come-on was definitely dusty – if it really was a come-on.

Tony had grinned at her expression. Oh, but books are best, my dear, especially artistic books! Can't be too careful nowadays . . .

Was this meant to be reassuring? Maybe Tony was nervous. Tulip began to peg him as someone who liked to talk a bit dirty and experienced, so as to impress; but who didn't actually do much about whatever fantasies he harboured – one of which was now tantalizing him in the person of herself.

'Why didn't you tell him to stop and let you off?'

'What, on a motorway at eighty? Anyway, he knew about the Rembrandt. I didn't know a thing about this particular painting.'

Nor was I her moral counsellor. She was there in my office to tell me her story. I was about to collect it.

The weird thing was that this story was being recounted as having happened to *herself* – not to a friend, or to a friend of a friend. Could Tulip have misunderstood my interests, as outlined on a notice permanently pinned in the students' union?

For the past ten years I'd been collecting and classifying urban legends. Principally I taught sociology and social anthropology to a wide range of students at this so-called University of Blanchester. The university was an amalgamation of technical and higher-education colleges and an art school. These days, every place worth its salt must be a full-blown university so as to emulate mainland European educational standards (at least on paper).

The reality is overcrowding and scant resources and student poverty, along with a fudging of the unemployment statistics. Rejoice, nowadays we have three million young people in higher education!

Some of my students applied to study sociology because the subject seemed inherently interesting and they knew that realistically they had few job prospects on graduation, whatever humanities course they chose to study. Others were being 'humanized' as a sideline to their main degree work in computer studies or graphic design or whatever. They were a rich source of urban myths – though the Tale of the Starving Student Who Sold a Kidney Because his Student Loan was Three Months Late was rather close to the knuckle of truth, at least as regards the straitened circumstances of the young and the scandalous sloth of the Student Loan Company.

Events in urban legends never happen to the person from whom you hear the story. They happen to someone more distant – to an acquaintance of an acquaintance. The mysterious hitchhiker never rides with your informant, but with a friend of a friend of the informant. It is in that other person's car that the hitchhiker leaves the blood-stained hatchet. Your informant swears to the total truth of the tale. If you manage to track down the person to whom the incident supposedly occurred, why, actually it befell a friend of theirs. Or a friend of a friend.

Welcome to modern mythology – which concerns not Gods and Goddesses but homicidal hitchhikers and baby-sitters in peril and microwave ovens.

The Kidney Transplant? A favourite story of mine! And how symptomatic.

The person who wants the kidney is the owner of a lucrative Indian restaurant. The illegal operation will be carried out secretly by his brother, who is actually a vet, a graduate of Calcutta Veterinary School (exact details may vary) and a competent animal surgeon. In the clinic adjoining the vet's home there's an operating theatre, normally used for cats and dogs and rabbits. Some dogs are huge, thus the table is full size.

No sooner is the kidney successfully removed from the student than a lorry skids into the utility pole outside the clinic. This brings down the power line. Byebye to the electricity supply for at least the next 24 hours. Woe to the refrigerator which would have chilled the kidney till the following evening when the organ would be inserted into the brother.

The brother rushes back to his restaurant with the kidney in a container labelled with the student's name, to pop it in one of his own fridges. None of the waiters nor the chef know about the secret arrangement. The boss tells them sternly to *keep this box safe*.

The starving student recovers with remarkable speed. In fact, the very next day, to celebrate his new prosperity, he goes to the Indian restaurant for lunch and orders its Special Meat Curry. A waiter knows the student by name. The waiter knows that the container in the fridge is labelled with this customer's name. Consequently he hands the kidney to the chef . . .

Naturally there are gaping holes in the story. If the student is so destitute, how is he a habitué of a restaurant in the first place? (But if he isn't, how else would he know the manager well enough to make a clandestine bargain with him?) Most so-called Indian restaurants are actually run by Bangladeshis or Pakistanis, not by Indians. Kidneys play no noticeable role in the cuisine of the subcontinent, at least in the versions tailored for Britain – the macho Madrases and Vindaloos and other milder Tandoori concoctions. And as for the need to match donor with recipient, ho ho! No matter. The story speaks eloquently.

And Tulip spoke on, while outside on this February afternoon the sun was already low but blindingly bright, a trembling glaring ball of molten brass amidst a haze of richly pink and orange chiffon.

The dome of the sky was icily blue. Clouds were few and frail and unmoved by any breath of wind. Asthmatics, beware. For the past two days the chilly atmosphere had been motionless, trapping smoke and car fumes.

Beyond the low-slung engineering block and the town's rooftops and a church steeple, the horizon wore a frieze of pollution haze which that sun was tinting gloriously. Above that frieze floated long interweaving brown strands. While I was away from my office earlier, holding forth in a lecture room, jet fighters had been practising low-level flying over the farmland beyond the town. Those loose plaits of brown smoke mapped how the jets had hugged the contours of the land. What filthy fuel those planes must have burned, full of additives to supercharge the engines.

The glaring sunlight revealed all the dirt on the outside of my long office window, as though simultaneously providing illumination and also paradoxically a veil of privacy. Presiding over the heaped desk and thronged bookshelves and a grey steel filing cabinet (as well as over Tulip and myself, companionably close to one another) was an enlarged colour photograph of a wizened West African, taken by yours truly years ago. That old chap was a *griot*, a tribal storyteller. I had long since glided away from third-world social anthropology into the anthropology of industrial society – rather as Elizabeth, my sly African ex-wife, had glided away from me soon after she accomplished her transition from Africa to the Northern World. I'd been little more than her passport provider, so it seemed!

One new book which had recently captured Tony the traveller's attention – so that it was still at the top of his mind – was a volume of famous medical paintings. The book included such masterpieces as Hieronymus Bosch's *The Cure for Folly*, in which a quack drills into the head of a lugubrious melancholic, performing a misplaced medieval lobotomy. Particularly fascinating to Tony, for some reason, was Rembrandt's *Anatomy Lesson*. Maybe this was because he drove a lot, and feared ending up on a slab in a morgue.

'So Tony said to me, "I can tell you all about it—"'

Such coincidence is the very essence of urban legend.

'"For instance,"' he hinted to me, what would you say about the clothes those men are wearing—?'

Sombre and sober clothes.

Oh yes. But costly too. Those big posh white ruffs. These people are dignitaries. Burghers; members of the guild of doctors. The dissection is an important social as well as scientific occasion.

Come on, Tulip, cudgel your brains, what else about the clothes?

Um . . .

Why, the clothes are heavy and warm. Consequently it's wintertime. Before fridges were invented, dissections could only take place during the winter months. Otherwise, halfway through the procedure, the cadaver would have begun to rot. A thorough dissection could last a week or more. We aren't talking about quick butchery.

At this point Tony veered on to the matter of student poverty – which was obviously why Tulip was hitchhiking, despite the number of horrible incidents these days.

Tony had heard that some female students were turning to prostitution to pay for their fees and food and lodgings. Who would blame them, when a fellow might pay £80, the going rate, so he understood, for an hour of harmless fun?

The hint lay heavy. The BMW purred along at eighty, with cruise control engaged. Tony was fond of motorway motels, such bland anonymous rooms. He would be delighted to give Tulip an anatomy lesson. An art lesson. A profitable lesson, intellectually and physically and financially. Fun and money and no harm to anyone.

There: he had said his piece. Some beads of fidgety sweat sat on his brow. Anxiety and desire.

'Did you say no?' I asked. 'Or yes?'

'I *was* skint,' was Tulip's answer. 'I still am, Dr Kershaw. Can I call you Richard? Or Dick?'

'I prefer Rich.'

'Ah, Rich . . .' Compared with a student! Was the true purpose of her visit to solicit me?

Some people might have called me a philanderer because I had enjoyed a number of discreet affairs with students. I knew the itch of what one might call erotic frenzy, and I felt no shame about this, only caution. In these times of political correctness on campus, discretion and subtlety must be the watchword.

Our University of Blanchester had never gone so far as to employ an actual sexual-harassment officer. Some other universities did so for a while, until witchhunts ensued – secret files on male lecturers, over-zealous 'processing' units interrogating staff because of mischievous or spiteful tip-offs. At Blanchester we relied on an anti-harassment code.

Hitherto I had avoided pitfalls by choosing my young bed-partners wisely. In the last few years I'd restricted myself to students whom I didn't actually teach but who came in response to my notice to tell me an urban legend. An exception had been one of my foreign intake of students – a German *fraulein* – but continentals are open-minded. Despite Tulip's nickname (and the coincidental Rembrandt connection) she couldn't possibly be Dutch. Her trace of accent was surely Scottish . . .

So far there had been no repercussions from my romances. Had Tulip heard a rumour about me? In a roundabout way was she propositioning me? Was she proposing that I should pay for my pleasure? Pay her, specifically, £80?

Or might she be an agent provocateur, one of the clique of feminists? My gut instinct said *no* to this.

Since the ride in the BMW had supposedly happened to Tulip herself the tale was *not* a legitimate urban legend. What's more, she *herself* was the hitchhiker. Urban myths frequently feature mysterious passengers who turn out to be ghosts or serial killers or Jesus Christ. Few indeed are the tales from the viewpoint of the actual hitchhiker!

'You know *my* full name,' I said to Tulip, pen poised over the notepad. 'May I not know yours?'

At this point I imagined that she might abandon her story. The story was a mere pretext for proposing an anatomy lesson – not in this office, to be sure, but in my flat that same evening after a few drinks and a meal, for £80 to fund her overdraft. Yet no. She plunged on, ignoring my desire to know her real name.

'I agreed, Rich. I agreed to Tony's proposal. And didn't that make him buoyant! Along we zoomed to the next service area complete with its travellers' lodge. I waited in the car while he booked a bedroom. He took the ignition key with him after smiling a sloppy apology. No hard feelings. It was always conceivable that I might drive off in his nice BMW. While he was away I looked in the glove compartment and found a pack of condoms. What do you know? They were within a year of their expiry date. Tony mustn't have had much luck lately. Maybe he kept those as a symbol of hope.'

Likewise I always kept a packet in my pocket, though my luck was better than Tony's.

'We had lunch and a few drinks' – it was as if Tulip read my mind – 'then we adjourned to this double room in the travel lodge. Tony shut the curtains. The bedspread was as red as that dissected arm in the photo. On the wall was a print—'

'Of a Rembrandt?' I asked mischievously.

'Hardly! That would have been much too gloomy. Lonely travellers might kill themselves in the room. It was a print of jolly yachts at Cannes or somewhere flying lots of colourful flags. A Dufy. We undressed—'

She was provoking me.

'—and the anatomy lesson began, not at all hastily. While he was touching me all over, exploring me with fingertips and tongue, true to his word he told me all about the painting—'

In her eyes was I exempt from the desires and anxieties enshrined in legends, incapable of arousal, a man of clinical objectivity? How could she imagine so?

'Dissections didn't actually proceed as in the painting, Rich,' she explained. 'The surgeon never began by flaying an arm.' (I was imagining Tony's hands roving freely – as mine might later rove . . . if I chose, on this occasion, to pay for sex with her.) 'First, you would remove the internal organs and dissect those, because they're soft and would rot soonest.' (Despite this talk of soft decaying entrails, I was hard, as she must surely realize.) 'You only deal with arms and legs towards the end. But if the painting had been accurate it wouldn't have been beautiful. It would have shown a mess of guts.

'There's another important reason why Rembrandt concentrated on the arm. You see, Rich, the first accurate illustrated volume about anatomy based on dissection was published by a Flemish genius working in Italy. Vesalius, that was his name—'

She seemed determined to give me a lesson in art history.

According to Tulip, during his own lifetime Vesalius had not prospered as he deserved. Blinkered colleagues resolutely believed ancient Greek anatomy texts based on guesswork. They refused to accept the evidence of his hands-on approach. Disillusioned, Vesalius moved to Spain. There he performed an autopsy, and unfortunately found that the heart was still beating. Because of this, the Inquisition prosecuted him. If the King had not intervened, Vesalius would have been hanged. Instead, he was sentenced to make a pilgrimage to Jerusalem. On his way back, he was shipwrecked and died on a Greek island.

By the year when *The Anatomy Lesson* was painted, it was widely recognized that Vesalius had revolutionized our understanding of the human body. In the painting the man performing the dissection is a certain Dr Nicolaas Tulp. Tulp was a notable Amsterdam surgeon and several times mayor of the city. What the painting asserts is that Tulp is putting Amsterdam on the map of modern science.

The frontispiece of Vesalius' famous volume depicts the great man as holding a dissected hand and arm. Aesthetic criteria aside, this is the major reason why Rembrandt shows the dissection as beginning with the hand and arm. Here in the person of Tulp is the contemporary Vesalius, equal to or greater than the original founder of anatomy.

Oh yes, and the man on the slab was a condemned felon who had been hanged for stealing clothes. His nakedness is in ironic juxtaposition to his crime – and to the well-dressed spectators. His skin is being unpeeled like a suit of clothes.

Tulp. Tulp. The name nagged at me. It was so like Tulip.

Tulips from Amsterdam . . .

'I know it's dangerous to hitchhike,' she said. She patted her patchwork bag. 'That's why I was carrying a scalpel for protection. And a little pistol too.'

Panic surged through me. How could she possibly own a pistol? Did she have that pistol with her in that bag right now? Ought I to lunge at her?

'Don't you want to hear the rest of the story?' she asked with such a sweet smile.

'Look,' I said. I didn't know what to say next. A scalpel, from the Art School – yes indeed. But a gun?

'It isn't so hard to buy a pistol nowadays, Rich.' Her tone seemed very reasonable. 'Not in the area where I live. You don't need to be a big-time villain involved in bank robberies. People even use pistols to rob newsagents' shops.'

What would a pistol cost? Two hundred pounds in a pub? How could she afford to spend so much if she was skint'? This didn't make sense. Terrifyingly, it didn't.

'After a while,' she continued, 'still naked of course, I took the pistol out of my bag and I pointed it at Tony. Tony was very scared. He went quite limp. I said to him, "Now the true anatomy lesson begins, Tony-Daddy! I'm going to flay your right arm. I'm going to peel off some skin in payment—" '

Was she insane? Maybe she merely said those words to her exploiter to shock and appal him. I was certainly horror-stricken. Was her main intention in telling me her story to appal me? The story might be a total concoction especially tailored for me!

How could this tale be true? It ought to be the salesman (no, a friend of his) who was relating this account of the lovely and terrible hitchhiker. *So he took her to a motel. He gave the anatomy lesson as promised. However, when they finished having sex and talking about Rembrandt, she pulled a pistol out of her bag and she said to him, 'Now I'll give you an anatomy lesson.'* Yes, this ought to have been the pattern.

But I was being told the story from the viewpoint of the ghost hitchhiker or serial murderer, and by that very person, that urban-legendary person, none other.

Maybe Tulip was a performance artist. Maybe I was being set up – being sent the mischievous or malicious equivalent of a strippergram!

Alternatively, Tulip might indeed be an *angry woman*, a politically correct virago whose aim was to punish me on behalf of her sisters for my seductions.

I realized that her description of Tony was an inverted description of myself. My own 50-year-old body had retreated – or rather, expanded away from athleticism. Unlike Tony, I boasted a fine tan. I used the sunbeds at the leisure centre. I also had a small birthmark which was shaped more like a banana than a mushroom. The birthmark wasn't on my brow but on the left cheek of my bum. Could she have learned about this from one of my previous young bed-partners?

Did she possess some kind of *inherent* knowledge?

The structural inversion of themes is a perennial feature of myth, as analysed by Lévi-Strauss. A more bizarre inversion seemed now to be occurring: not merely the substitution of the phantom hitchhiker for the driver-victim, but a replacement of reality by myth itself, so that I – the observer – was becoming entrapped in the direct experience of a legend. This was at once exhilarating and deeply scary.

How much more likely that Tulip was either a performance artist or a virago! And she might still be one of the new breed of part-time whores of academe, selling her flesh to pay for a course of study which would probably be useless. And ingeniously set upon manipulating me.

She toyed with her bag.

'So I said to him, Rich, if you scream or shout I'll shoot you dead. You can whimper or moan quietly. Or bite on a towel. I'll put some colour into you. Our world's so dusty these days. All the concrete and exhaust fumes. I need more colour—'

What insanity! *Tulip, Tulp* . . . Something about these two names taunted me, and suddenly I thought I knew why.

'Excuse me—' Her hand promptly slid inside her bag. 'No, it's all right, Tulip, I'm not intending to leave the room. I need to look at a book.'

'Go ahead,' she allowed.

I rose. Was this when I should leap at her? When she would either shoot me, or shriek out that I was assaulting her? If I threw myself upon her, her bag might well prove to be empty of any weapon. My own account of what she had told me would seem incredible. If only I had been recording what she said!

I stepped to a bookcase. *Tibet's Myths and Mysteries*: this was the book I wanted. I took it out, flipped to the index and found the reference.

According to Tibetan myths a *tulpa* is the name for an illusory creature born from one's own mind in a hectic, obsessive state. A tulpa is a tangible apparition which achieves an independent existence, wilful and wild. Said a lama: 'Beware of these children of the mind, these tigers to which you give birth . . .'

I had thought for so long about the phantom hitchhiker. I had thought about young women's bodies. Here was the hitchhiker, equipped with her own autonomous motivation. On yes, the hitcher and the serial killer and the phantom and the bed-partner all rolled into one.

'Rembrandt's anatomist wasn't really called Tulp, was he?' I asked.

'Of course he was, Rich,' she said. 'Later, I checked up on what Tony told me. *The Anatomy Lesson of Dr Nicolaas Tulp*: that's the name of the painting.'

If only I had some book about Rembrandt on the shelves.

Here was a punk angel of urban myth, come to me. A messenger from the realm of modern legend. An incarnation. How desperately, yet fearfully, I wished in one part of myself to possess this flower endowed with consciousness. What would I give to do so?

'It's getting quite late,' she hinted. 'Should we continue this over a drink and then a meal in town?'

Oh she knew, she knew. I did desire this outcome. How long must we enact the pretence that she was simply a student known to her friends as Tulip?

'The eclipse of reason is here,' asserts Richard Kershaw.

A sunny print of daffodils hangs on the white-washed wall. There's no glass in the frame. Glass might break into dangerous daggers. The glass of the window near the bed is faintly meshed with fine wire for safety and security; and the slim bars on the inside divide lawn from woodland and ground from sky very neatly. Richard's hand and forearm are pink from the plastic surgery he underwent. The glossy artificial hue suggests that part of him was remade in plastic.

Sitting upon the bed, he leans towards me as if convinced that his own collapse of reason has brought enlightenment.

'Because of this eclipse,' he insists, 'myths are moving closer to us. Myths are become people. People are becoming myths. Consider the million alien abduction stories in America – told in the contactees' own words as an experience which happened to themselves and not to somebody else! Isn't this proof? When I leave here, I intend to work on experiencing this abduction syndrome myself – as a participant.'

'That painting by Rembrandt,' I remind him, 'really *is* of a man called Nicolaas Tulp.'

Richard waves a pink hand dismissively. 'That makes no difference, don't you see? Here's proof of a coming together, a new amalgam of mind. New connections in the psyche of the world.'

'The world doesn't have a psyche,' I tell him. 'There are simply millions of separate individuals. Most of us have fundamentally similar mental patterns.'

'No!' He thumps his patched hand upon the bedside table and splays his fingers painfully. 'That's the old Thatcherite lie that society doesn't exist! It's the lie which led to so much selfishness and self-interest and to the cutting of state funding for transport and the elderly and—'

'—for students and suchlike.' I can complete his sentence.

Wistfully he gazes at the daffodils.

'May I have a print of tulips on my wall instead?'

While I ponder, he adopts a tone of sham menace. If wheedling will not serve, a threat might persuade me.

'One day *you* might pick up a hitchhiker,' he says sternly.

'I wouldn't dream of doing any such thing, Richard,' I assure him.

'That's exactly what I mean about selfishness! Well, she may pick *you* up. An alien intruder not from some fanciful distant star, but from out of the mythic psyche of the world. An evolutionary crescendo is under way.'

'To surrender reason,' I insist, 'is to forsake civilization.'

I can predict his answer.

'Reason,' he says, 'is the dream from which we shall awake, just as prehumans once awoke to self-awareness and a form of logic.' This conviction, at any rate, gives him an air of serenity and patience. Some of the time.

It's all too true that delusions of imminent transcendence are becoming far more common, often in dramatically violent fashion. Members of cults commit group suicide or die in gunfights with police. Jihads are proclaimed. At times I dearly wish I could peer 200 years ahead. Generally such a prospect terrifies me. Will my own rational and liberal mind-set remain in tune with what awaits? Or will religions ravish a depleted world which will never again launch itself moonwards or dissect the secrets of life and mind?

By therapeutic custody of such as Richard, I serve as an anxious jailer on behalf of the past and its struggles for progress. The plastic pink of Richard's arm validates yet ridicules my efforts, and those of rational scientists such as Vesalius and his successors in whatever discipline.

In this hospital I confront my fears daily and I control them. Here's the essential difference between myself and Richard. A dark side of his psyche accosted him and he was unable to regulate it. A person can actively cultivate madness in themselves. Madness will sprout and flower. How precious sanity is; and how precarious.

Beyond the oasis of controlled insanity which this hospital is, how many other wild blooms are burgeoning in people's minds, luminous and poisonous, as the calendar sheds its leaves day by day, approaching the millennium? Day by day, due to meagre funds, we release patients too early into the community, as though our real task is to pollinate the world with delusions.

I can never let Richard be released. His account of the incarnation of urban myth is far too potent – similar, as he himself points out, to the alien abduction fantasies, yet far worse.

If what he says happened is true – and I do believe it to be so – then because of his obsessions Richard acted as a magnet (or should I say a seed crystal?) which attracted a creature of the mind into existence, into physical reality. To release Richard back into the community would be to encourage Tulip and similar beings to roam in our midst.

When I do replace the print of daffodils with one of tulips, I shall leave a scalpel somewhere in this room for Richard to find. Where will the scalpel have come from? Patients quite often steal things if they have a chance.

This gives them a sense of petty power. Poor Richard could have been given the blade by another inmate. Every afternoon he joins in a session of group therapy. We can hardly keep him in solitary confinement, can we? I tried to oppose this liberal attitude, but I was overruled.

Until now, I have regarded this hospital as a bastion. Yet essentially all along I have only been passive in my response to the death of reason. Reactive, not proactive.

Others in the past have behaved more positively. Right now I'm thinking of the way Jack the Ripper (much maligned) set out to purge London of whores. He was undoubtedly a doctor. That was about a century ago. The cycle of time has come round. Only, more so because now is a millennium. Richard himself must cleanse the infection that he represents. Logic dictates this.

'A tulip,' I tell him. 'A single cut tulip in a vase. I'll find you a print if I have to search high and low.'

How he smiles.

File classification: Jack the Ripper
Location: Islington, London

Title: Out of the Fog
Writer: *Basil Copper*

Briefing: *Jack the Ripper – Victorian serial killer whose victims were all prostitutes and whose identity has been the subject of innumerable legends.* It is the year 1888 and Dr Marion Lazenby has just become one of the first of her sex to qualify as a medical practitioner. Her happiness is about to be completed by marriage to another brilliant young doctor, Gerald Forster, when his body with a shotgun beside it is found in woodland near Islington. But *is* it a case of suicide, Marion wonders, or does his past hint at a darker side to the man she loved?

Author: Londoner Basil Copper has combined the careers of newspaper-man and writer and deservedly earned himself the reputation of being among the foremost contemporary horror writers. Colin Wilson recently referred to him as 'one of the last of the great traditionalists of English fiction'. Copper's interest in crime has ranged from a series of novels featuring a hard-boiled Los Angeles private eye, Mike Faraday, to the continuation of the exploits of Solar Pons, a Holmesian detective, created by the late American writer, August Derleth. In the horror genre, Copper has written several major novels including *The Great White Space* (1974) which earned him the accolade, 'best writer in the genre since H. P. Lovecraft', and the highly praised Gothic trio, *Necropolis* (1977), *The House of the Wolf* (1983) and *The Black Death* (1991). His short stories have been gathered in several collections, and a number have been adapted for radio and television. 'Out of the Fog' is one of the most thought-provoking 'solutions' to the best-known of all urban legends.

Four O'clock

The woman sat at a small satinwood desk in the room, which was simply equipped. She had been sitting in the same position for hours. The only sound was the occasional rumble made by the wheels of a passing carriage and the loud tick of a clock which marked the equally inevitable passage of the minutes. A single gas jet by the surgery door gave a harsh yellow light which fell upon the frosted panels. It was late summer yet the curtains had already been drawn for almost an hour. A small fire blazed in the hearth with its heavy firedogs and brass accoutrements. Outside, unseasonable yellow fog hung in acrid folds and an occasional streamer penetrated the dark green curtains.

The woman at the desk noted none of these things. She was slimly built, with strong, finely shaped hands. About thirty years of age, she would have been handsome except for her red-rimmed eyes and the deathly whiteness of her face. She had been weeping quietly to herself for some hours. Now she was quite calm to the outward eye, but a mental furnace within. Presently there came a tapping at the surgery door and the woman stirred herself and blinked about her. But she made no move to answer the knock until it was repeated, deferentially but a little louder than before.

She called out softly for the knocker to enter. He was a strong, heavy-framed man in his mid-fifties with a black beard flecked with grey. His eyes flashed mildly behind steel-framed lenses and drops of moisture glinted on the folds of the ulster he wore. He shook a broad-brimmed hat against his knee to get rid of the moisture. The woman finally rose from the desk and came towards him. She felt as though years had passed since the morning.

'It was good of you to come, Dr Morton.'

'It was the least I could do, dear lady,' said the doctor, stooping to the heat of the fire. Steam came up from his heavy coat into the oppressive warmth of the room.

'You are quite sure you want to go through with this? It is not at all necessary, you know. I can deal with all the details if you wish.'

He broke off as the slim woman caught him by the arm.

'I know you mean well, Dr Morton,' she said fiercely, 'but this is something I have to do. Is it far?'

'Quite a long way,' said the doctor, holding his hat out to the blaze. The firelight made a carmine mask of his face. 'Islington Mortuary. I have made all the arrangements. There is a cab outside.'

He looked curiously at the young woman whose white, handsome face showed nothing of the feelings she must be experiencing. He felt he ought to prescribe a sedative. Yet it might be presumptuous; after all, she was a doctor herself and a very distinguished one, among the first women in England to qualify for the profession and a subject of admiration to her patients. She would best know how to take care of herself; she was perfectly capable of prescribing her own remedies. He felt a flash of pity as he looked at her face in profile. The whole thing was a great tragedy; both she and Forster were at the beginning of brilliant careers. Now this had to happen. He could still hardly believe it. Even in an age of such progress it was astonishing that such inexplicable events could still happen in well-ordered Victorian society.

'Would you like a drink, doctor? It is a raw day for the time of year.'

'Thank you, yes,' said Morton, holding out his hand for the goblet of brandy the girl pressed on him. 'It is a little early for me, but as you say, the day ... If you will forgive me, Dr Lazenby, will you not partake yourself? You might find it helpful under the circumstances.'

The white-faced woman shook her head primly. 'I am quite all right now.'

She led the way out of the surgery and turned down the gas jets behind them with an assurance she was far from feeling; she was glad of the solid support of the doctor's arm as they went into the raw, yellow blanket that hung over the city. A wretched horse with a nosebag stood steaming miserably in the cold air; the cab itself smelt of dampness and leather as the driver let down the steps and helped them in. Morton had already told the man their destination. There were few people about in the murk to see them as the wheels grated across the cobbles. Dr Lazenby sank back against the cushions and watched the oil wick in the big driving lamp next to the opposite window rise, splutter and fall again in the fog.

Morton sat with his hands folded against the knob of his cane and looked down at the cab floor which was littered by the cast-off debris of many fares; he too seemed overwhelmed by the sombreness of the errand on which they were engaged. She felt a momentary stab of gratitude for his sturdy presence. Apart from the doctor who shared Gerald's rooms, she supposed this man was one of his closest colleagues. She looked again at the yellow lamp which flared and bobbed as the cab lurched on its way; it seemed to epitomize so many lives in this great city which burned up so full of brilliant promise, only to splutter out so dismally a short while afterwards.

Five O'clock

It was a long drive and the fog seemed thicker than ever when they rattled over a tarmacadam roadway and eventually drew up in a high brick yard; they were evidently expected, for a man in a dark smock opened the big wooden gates and drew them back for the hansom to pass within. The horse steamed and stamped impatiently, as though anxious to be away from this dismal place. Somewhere a clock struck the hour of five and the strokes, muffled by the fog, fell like blows on her own already overburdened heart. Morton asked the cabman to wait and bolts were already grating in front of them as they followed the man in the smock across the damp flags of the yard.

They passed within the building which seemed, if anything, even colder than the air outside. Naked gas jets cast blue shadows on the bare stone floors of the corridors and there was a raw smell of carbolic. Presently the attendant, after leading them down a succession of long passages, tapped deferentially at a thick oak door. The Medical Director, Dr Pruner, a stout, jovial person whose face now wore an appropriately solemn expression, was not a man to waste time on ceremony. He asked Dr Lazenby to sign a paper and to identify certain objects he took from a drawer; there was a gold hunter which she recognized, a crocodile-skin notecase and an engraved ring which she had herself presented to Gerald. She signed for these too.

Pruner cleared his throat and looked fixedly at Morton.

'There is no real necessity,' he began. 'If Dr Lazenby would agree . . .'

'The lady has already made up her mind,' said Morton. 'I shall accompany her myself, of course.'

'As you wish,' said Pruner, with an expressive gesture of hand and shoulder together, as though mentally absolving himself of all responsibility. 'Come back afterwards and if I can help, let me know. Biggins will show you the way.'

The attendant led them to a large green-painted door which had Mortuary painted on it in black letters; a dim light burned at the entrance.

'The Registrar is waiting,' he said softly to Morton as the doctor passed him.

There were six tables in the great white-washed barn of a place; sinks and marble-topped benches stood along one wall. Canvas shutters controlled by cords covered the vast skylights which lit the room by day; gas jets with conical reflectors threw brilliant plates of light down on to the sheeted shapes on the tables. The Registrar was a sandy-bearded young man with a dry cough and a wary eye. He seemed anxious to get off to his tea but he was kind enough. Introductions were awkward and brief, the tables and their burdens seeming an intrusion.

'This is Dr Marion Lazenby,' said Morton. 'Dr Forster was her fiancé.'

The Registrar coughed. 'Quite so,' he said, looking around him as though the sheeted forms might overhear. 'I am indeed sorry that we should meet under these melancholy circumstances. Number five, over here by the window.'

The two visitors were drawn inexorably to the position indicated by the Registrar, their reluctant feet seeming to take them automatically without conscious effort. The awkwardness of the moment was dissolved by the Registrar, who simply lifted the sheet from the dead face and recited a stream of technical details. Contrary to Morton's expectations, the dead man exhibited none of those signs often the occasion of violent death and which are so distressing to relatives; he merely looked as though he were asleep. It was a strong, determined face; the thick moustache and black curly hair well kept. The face of a young man of thirty-five used to making decisions and Morton wondered for the hundredth time what induced him to take such a step.

'A shotgun wound, you say?' he heard himself reciting. 'The autopsy report is with Dr Pruner. We will look at it on our way out.'

It was a short, simple story, except for the motive. Dr Forster's body had been found in thick woodland about two miles from the building where it now lay, late in the afternoon of the previous day. He had used a double-barrelled shotgun, which he had brought by canvas holdall to the spot; it was found beside his body by a sewerman who was taking a short cut across the open ground. There was no note. Dr Forster had apparently taken a long tram ride to the remote suburb and had then walked to the point where his body was found. Morton was grateful for the Registrar's sing-song chant which gave them so much information without painful prompting by Dr Lazenby; she had said nothing, merely stared fixedly at the table. But even the Registrar was startled when she drew down the sheet still further and examined the gaping wounds in the side, made even more ugly and monstrous by the police surgeon's rough incisions.

They were back in the Director's office before Dr Lazenby spoke again.

'You have, I believe, Dr Pruner, a copy of the post-mortem findings?'

Dr Pruner turned helplessly to Morton, as though seeking moral support. 'We have the records here, of course, my dear Dr Lazenby. But I could not imagine . . .'

'I would like to see it,' the slim woman said quietly. Her voice was soft and low but there was such authority in it that the substantial form of the Medical Director seemed momentarily to melt before her. He turned again to the impassive figure of Morton and gave a hopeless shrug.

'I see no objection, doctor,' said Morton stiffly.

Pruner laid his hand on the other's arm. 'One moment, if you please. These are exceptional circumstances.'

He drew the other to the end of the office; Dr Lazenby stood looking out at the yellow bank of fog. The voices of the two men came to her like the low mumble of the sea. She did not understand what they were saying, neither did she care. She felt no impatience or anger; just a great weariness. She would have liked to have stood looking at the fog for the rest of her life; but even that soothing occupation could not erase the ugly questions that were burning at the edges of her mind. She turned at last, as she felt the soft tread of Morton on the carpet behind her. The doctor's face was white and a thin trickle of perspiration rolled slowly down his left cheek.

'I think Dr Pruner is right, my dear lady,' he said, motioning her towards the door. 'I feel this has been enough for one day. Perhaps another time . . .'

There was rising anger in Dr Lazenby's voice as she broke impatiently away from him.

'I have no intention of leaving until I have read the findings,' she said.

Dr Pruner looked aghast, Morton merely distressed. But all he said was, 'There is a very good reason why you should not know the contents of the report, my dear. But if you wish we will call on Allardyce. He was Gerald's closest friend. He knows of the autopsy. And if he consents to tell you its findings, then I will have no objections.'

He waved his hand to indicate the rigid form of the Director in the background. 'And it would save Dr Pruner unnecessary embarrassment.'

Dr Lazenby stood hesitating for a moment. The fog seemed to roll forward and engulf the room. She shivered suddenly. Her great weariness took the decision from her.

'As you please,' she said. 'But it must be settled tonight.'

The door closed heavily behind them as they walked in silence down the long, damp corridor.

Six O'clock

The hooves of the cabhorse struck sparks from the cobbles as the hansom turned down Queensway; the gas lamps bloomed like glowworms in the fog. They had traversed several more streets before Morton broke the long silence.

'I feel it would be better if you saw Dr Allardyce alone. This is a delicate matter and best settled between the two of you. But if you need help or advice you know where to reach me. Don't hesitate to call, either day or night.'

Dr Lazenby leaned forward and pressed her companion's hand in grateful silence as Morton tapped with the head of his cane on the hatch above them. The driver turned into the kerb and stopped. Morton got out and stood with his hand on the door as he gave the cabman Allardyce's address.

His face was strained and serious as he said goodbye. 'I wish you wouldn't go on with this, my dear. No good can come of it. Gerald would not have wished it.'

'We have been all through that, Dr Morton,' the slim woman said, with a slight return of her old manner. 'Please do not mention it again. My mind is quite made up.'

'As you will,' said Morton slowly. 'I hope you will not live to regret it.'

He brushed her fingers with his lips and was then gone, a blurred figure among the passers-by in the fog. Dr Lazenby drove on, lost in her thoughts, until she was aroused by the stopping of the cab in a narrow thoroughfare of respectable, flat-chested houses, each identical to the other. The cabman ran lightly up a flight of steps in front of a door whose fanlight shone faint rays of gaslight through the mist. He rang at the bell and then ran back to help her down.

'Wait,' she said. 'I may need you again before the evening is over.'

Allardyce was more than six feet tall and with a craggy face from which two deep-set grey eyes looked at her with a troubled gaze. His sitting room was stacked with books and papers and he had to clear a chair for her.

'I'll ring for some tea,' he said and went off. While he was away she looked round curiously, conscious that this was a side of Gerald's life that she had never known. A side that she would never know. They drank the hot sweet tea and ate the little buttered scones in silence. The fog crouched at the window and muffled the passing noises of the street. Dr Lazenby was not conscious of what she was eating; it might have been sawdust and cardboard for all the impression it made on her palate but she knew it would please her companion.

Half an hour had passed before she broached the subject of her visit;

Allardyce went pale as her purpose became clear. He stammered in his explanations, grew embarrassed and red in the face and eventually fell silent before the intensity of her eyes.

'What you are asking is impossible,' he said awkwardly. 'Cannot you see that?'

'I can only see that my life has been ruined to no purpose,' the woman burst out passionately. 'There can be no rest for me until I discover why Gerald shot himself. He had everything to live for. As you know, we were to have been married quite soon.'

Allardyce's face was like a mask of stone as he answered.

'Gerald was my patient as well as my friend,' he said. 'I had been treating him for the last two years. May God forgive me for breaking a confidence. And are you sure you are prepared to forgo your peace of mind for perhaps a lifetime?'

'My peace of mind has already gone,' said the woman inflexibly. 'What could be worse than not knowing?'

Allardyce got heavily to his feet. His face was enigmatic in the semi-gloom.

'I will get the report,' he said. He came back with a two-page document. The lines of the printed sheets were covered in crabbed handwriting. Against the entry, Deceased, she saw the name Gerald Forster, followed by: Adult male. Allardyce went to the window and stared out at the fog as she read on. He was aroused by the crumpling of paper. He returned to her side. The crackling of the sheets sounded fiercely in the silent room. They floated unnoticed to the ground. Dr Lazenby sat with livid face, her eyes fixed on the wallpaper before her.

'Syphilis . . .' she murmured. 'Dear God, this is worse than one could have imagined. How was this possible? Could I have been so close to this man without knowing? And yet I did not know him.'

Her voice had risen slightly in her agitation and she was suddenly conscious that she was clutching at Dr Allardyce's shirt-front. She allowed him to force her back in the chair; she choked once or twice as the raw brandy burnt its way down her throat.

'Don't blame him, Marion,' said Allardyce, his words coming out in an uncontrolled flood. 'It happened a long time ago. He was a wild young man, like most medical students. And we thought he had been cured. He met you and all seemed set fair for his happiness. But some while ago it returned. In a more virulent form. He tried all sorts of specialist advice. We could do nothing. You understand, Marion, medical science is just at the threshold in these matters. And he could not bear to tell you or to hurt you in any way.'

The woman was calm again now. She sat staring in front of her, listening quietly to Allardyce's explanations. There were many bitter things she could have said in answer to his apologia for a friend, but she knew it would be pointless. There were only one or two more facts she had to know.

'Did you guess what he was going to do?'

Allardyce hesitated for the merest fraction of a second but she knew he was speaking the truth when he replied.

'As God is my witness, I had no idea, or I would have stopped him. I found the gun missing from the rack too late. He left me a short note.'

Dr Lazenby stood up with an abrupt movement. Her voice was quite calm when she spoke.

'Did he mention me?'

'Yes, he did,' said Allardyce. 'It was in a postscript. He simply said, "Don't tell Marion".'

Dr Lazenby drew on her gloves. 'Why did you break that promise?' she asked.

Allardyce opened the door of the sitting room. 'Because I knew you had the character to survive it. You could not have lived your life without knowing it.'

Dr Lazenby knew this was true as soon as the words were out.

'You are quite right, doctor,' she said. 'I am proud Gerald had you for a friend and colleague. Now I have only one last favour to ask you. Who was the woman?'

Allardyce started back against the doorpost. His lips moved but he could not seem to enunciate.

'What are you going to do?' he said huskily at last.

'Be calm,' said the slim woman. 'I just wanted to know.'

Allardyce stood motionless for what appeared an interminable time. 'I always believed it to be a woman called Mary Clarke,' he said at length. 'She was known as Red Meg because of her fiery hair. She was a fine figure of a girl in those days. But she's probably died of drink long ago if she hasn't come to a worse end.'

Dr Lazenby had one final question.

'Where did they meet?' she wanted to know.

Dr Allardyce sighed. He felt tired and he knew that this implacable woman would have the information from him if they stood there all night. 'It was in the East End,' he said. 'A place where no lady could go alone.'

'I asked you where it was,' said Dr Lazenby.

Dr Allardyce sighed again.

'A tavern called The Crippled Sailor,' he said.

Eight O'Clock

The lamps of The Crippled Sailor blazed through the fog and cast a lurid glow on the smeared window panes and the damp pavements of the street. The noises of passing cabs were drowned not only in the curling tendrils which swayed in oily dance but by the raucous laughter of the raddled women half-seen through the smoky interior and the jangling discord of an inexpertly played piano up at the end of the long bar.

Dr Marion Lazenby sat at a side-bench, appearing not to notice the habituées who sang or shouted at their companions as the fancy took them, but in reality her searching glances examined minutely every human being who passed before her in the dingy room. The red velvet stage curtains were drawn and the profiles of men could be seen through the frosted glass partitioning of the four-ale bar next door. She had sat for nearly an hour in the same position, her glass of gin, purchased of necessity, almost untasted before her. The nervous-looking waiter with handlebar moustache, slicked-back hair and wearing a dirty white apron over his black-and-white-striped waitcoat, had at first greeted her dubiously, as her expensive clothing and aristocratic air were obviously at odds with the atmosphere of his establishment. But the passing of some silver during a muffled conversation had mellowed his attitude amazingly and he fed her a constant stream of information as he passed to and fro with his trays of tankards.

'She mightn't be in tonight, madame,' he said, shooting the words jerkily out of the corner of his mouth. 'She's usually in long afore this.'

He had made the same remark at least a dozen times in the past hour but, as on the previous occasion, the woman ignored him. 'I'm in no hurry,' she said, finishing the drink. 'Bring me another. And this time put some more gin in it.'

The waiter picked up the glass, pretending offence at the reflection on his honesty. He was soon back, slopping the drink on to the oak settle in front of her in his anxiety to set it down.

'Keep the change,' said Dr Lazenby, her eyes fixed over the waiter's shoulder, to where a new group of drably dressed artisans had just entered the main doors.

She did not need the almost imperceptible narrowing of the waiter's eyelids to know that the woman she sought was among the newcomers. The flaming red hair, obviously dyed and entwined with cheap ornaments, would have been enough to tell her. That and the wreckage of a once strikingly beautiful face.

But now the eyes were glazed; the face, lined and shrunken, was a mask which only animation kept alive; drink, drugs and dissipation had turned the youth and vibrancy it had once possessed into a parody of its former self and even the still magnificent teeth could not disguise the rictus of the smile. This was a woman whose age should have placed her within the full flower of maturity but the features before the watcher at the table were those of an ancient puppet sustained alone by some unknown galvanic energy.

The creature known as Red Meg must have become aware of the silent onlooker for she stopped in the middle of a laugh and turned her head. Dr Marion Lazenby had made no sign but her stillness and the implacable hostility in her eyes seemed to draw the street-walker to her. She sidled through the crowd which pressed upon the bar and came towards the doctor's table; a feather boa vainly tried to hide the ruin of a splendid throat and the rouge on her cheeks made incongruous splashes of scarlet, so that her face resembled that of a wax doll.

She stopped in front of the doctor and stood swaying slightly, oblivious of the waiter's frowns.

'Seen enough, dearie?' she croaked.

There was a long silence and the menace in the seated figure began to penetrate even the sodden brain of the poor husk which was Mary Clarke.

'Enough,' said Dr Lazenby when an age had passed. 'You will be dead quite soon. I know these things. I am a doctor.'

The words took some time to distil their meaning; then the cheeks of Mary Clarke began to drain into a chalky hue, leaving the two crimson spots like the mark of a hideous plague on her face. She sprang forward screeching, reaching out for the girl whose eyes burned with hatred into her own. But the waiter was too quick for her. Aided by two burly customers he dragged the shrieking women away and into a side bar. He re-appeared after some minutes. He looked pale and wiped a thin trickle of blood from his face.

'I'd best got out, miss, if I were you,' he mumbled. 'No telling what she might do when she's in that mood. Never seen her with such a bad turn. She didn't know you, did she?'

The doctor shook her head. She put some more silver into the waiter's hand. She glanced at her reflection in the gilt mirror set along the side of the bar. To her somewhat overheated imagination she looked like death at the feast. She got up, a trim figure that drew glances from all corners; a young woman quite out of place in that milieu. She passed out into the fog so quickly that her going was almost unnoticed. Two pairs of eyes only had more than a passing glance for her. The waiter's were puzzled. But Mary Clarke's, watching from behind the glass screen, held the knowledge of death.

Ten O'Clock

Dr Marion Lazenby sat alone in the surgery. She had been there, she supposed, for more than an hour, but she was scarcely conscious of time today. She sat as she had sat earlier that afternoon. Her hands were held tightly together in front of her and her body was quite rigid on the chair. The gas was turned low and the fire had almost burnt out; the harsh, clinical atmosphere of the consulting room was transformed into something softer. Few sounds penetrated the green curtains; only the faint scrape of a distant cab and now and then the beat of a pedestrian's footfall over the setts.

Through a chink in the curtains she could sense the fog, curled and sentient in the damp night; as though waiting for her. It had been an abominable summer and promised to be a harsh winter. She smiled a little to herself. It would have been a terrible thing if anyone had been near to see. Now, with the events of the morning, it was all one to her whether it were winter or summer. There was an intolerable pain round her heart and a dull rage that seemed to mount to her brain. She did not know why she was there and was barely conscious of what she was doing. Dr Morton had been right; she did need looking after and she missed his comforting presence that night.

She was aware too that she had eaten little all day and with this physical need manifesting itself came a reminder that she had much to do in the time to come. One image alone danced before her; the raddled face of Mary Clarke, a woman with a thousand years of foul knowledge in her sagging features, beneath the dyed red hair of a young girl. Dr Lazenby's raging thoughts impelled her to action at this vision; she cried aloud with pain and then realized that she had bitten her tongue. The sharp stab made her rise to her feet. Then she turned up the gas and examined her mouth in the surgery mirror. She did not expect that her experiences of the past twelve hours could have improved her looks but she was shocked at her appearance. Absently, she patted her hair into position.

Then she lifted an oil lamp which still burned on her desk and took it through into her partner's consulting room; she made up her mind and knew what she was going to do. A dull rage had replaced her previous indecision and all the events of the day crystallized and became clear to her. She put down the lamp on a table in Dr Marsh's surgery and picked up her own medical bag; she emptied its contents out and put them in the drawer of her desk.

She went back into Marsh's surgery and unlocked the glass-fronted cupboard; instruments winked at her in the dim light of the lamp. There were scalpels, various kinds of knives, saws, clamps and wedges. She made a careful selection, her firm, strong hands taking only those which she knew to be essential to her purposes. She put some bandage and gauze in last of all, together with a bottle of disinfectant.

She turned out the lamp and put it back on the desk. She paused at the mirror by the door and for the first time that day gave her reflected image a brief, genuine smile. She stood by the threshold, her hand on the doorknob, and took a deep breath.

She glanced round the surgery once again, making sure she had forgotten nothing, noting the clock and the desk calendar. It was exactly 10.15 p.m. on the evening of August 6th, 1888. It was a Bank Holiday. She smiled again at the irony. Then Dr Marion Lazenby turned out the gas. The case of instruments weighed heavily on her hand as she opened the door and stepped out into the fog and into history as Jack the Ripper.

File classification: The Hook
Location: Spector Street Estate, England

Title: The Forbidden
Writer: *Clive Barker*

Briefing: *The Hook – one of the most infamous figures in contemporary urban legends; a bogeyman reported on both sides of the Atlantic.* Helen is writing a treatise on 'Graffiti: the semiotics of urban despair' and this has brought her into intimate contact with the grim realities of life on the run-down Spector Street Estate. She has already heard stories of brutal murder and mutilation when she stumbles onto the even darker rumours of 'The Candyman', a killer with a hook instead of a hand. It's not long before Helen begins to realize that in today's urban legends the line between fact and fiction is horrifyingly thin.

Author: Liverpool-born Clive Barker has been called the UK's answer to Stephen King – although he has now settled in Beverley Hills, California and added the careers of screenwriter and film director to his achievements as a best-selling novelist. Barker made a huge impression on the genre with his debut work, a collection of short stories, *The Books of Blood*, published in 1984, and the following year showed himself to be equally at home novel-writing with the terrifying *Damnation Game*. He has subsequently scripted several hit movies including *Underworld* (1987) and *Hellraiser* (1988) which was based on his own novelette, 'The Hellbound Heart'. In 'The Forbidden', Barker draws on his own background for the story of a hook-handed killer who is accompanied everywhere by a swarm of deadly bees. There can be few more horrifying urban legends in fiction.

Like a flawless tragedy, the elegance of which structure is lost upon those suffering in it, the perfect geometry of the Spector Street Estate was only visible from the air. Walking in its drear canyons, passing through its grimy corridors from one grey concrete rectangle to the next, there was little to seduce the eye or stimulate the imagination. What few saplings had been planted in the quadrangles had long since been mutilated or uprooted; the grass, though tall, resolutely refused a healthy green.

No doubt the estate and its two companion developments had once been an architect's dream. No doubt the city-planners had wept with pleasure at a design which housed three hundred and thirty-six persons per hectare, and still boasted space for a children's playground. Doubtless fortunes and reputations had been built upon Spector Street, and at its opening fine words had been spoken of it being a yardstick by which all future developments would be measured. But the planners – tears wept, words spoken – had left the estate to its own devices; the architects occupied restored Georgian houses at the other end of the city, and probably never set foot here.

They would not have been shamed by the deterioration of the estate even if they had. Their brain-child (they would doubtless argue) was as brilliant as ever: its geometries as precise, its ratios as calculated; it was *people* who had spoiled Spector Street. Nor would they have been wrong in such an accusation. Helen had seldom seen an inner city environment so comprehensively vandalized. Lamps had been shattered and back-yard fences overthrown; cars, whose wheels and engines had been removed and chassis then burned, blocked garage facilities. In one courtyard three or four ground-floor maisonettes had been entirely gutted by fire, their windows and doors boarded up with planks and corrugated iron.

More startling still was the graffiti. That was what she had come here to see, encouraged by Archie's talk of the place, and she was not disappointed. It was difficult to believe, staring at the multiple layers of designs, names, obscenities and dogmas that were scrawled and sprayed on every available brick, that Spector Street was barely three and a half years old. The walls, so recently virgin, were now so profoundly defaced that the

Council Cleaning Department could never hope to return them to their former condition. A layer of whitewash to cancel this visual cacophony would only offer the scribes a fresh and yet more tempting surface on which to make their mark.

Helen was in seventh heaven. Every corner she turned offered some fresh material for her thesis: 'Graffiti: the semiotics of urban despair'. It was a subject which married her two favourite disciplines – sociology and aesthetics – and as she wandered around the estate she began to wonder if there wasn't a book, in addition to her thesis, in the subject. She walked from courtyard to courtyard, copying down a large number of the more interesting scrawlings, and noting their location. Then she went back to the car to collect her camera and tripod and returned to the most fertile of the areas, to make a thorough visual record of the walls.

It was a chilly business. She was not an expert photographer, and the late October sky was in full flight, shifting the light on the bricks from one moment to the next. As she adjusted and re-adjusted the exposure to compensate for the light changes her fingers steadily became clumsier, her temper correspondingly thinner. But she struggled on, the idle curiosity of passers-by notwithstanding. There were so many designs to document. She reminded herself that her present discomfort would be amply repaid when she showed the slides to Trevor, whose doubt of the project's validity had been perfectly apparent from the beginning.

'The writing on the wall?' he'd said, half smiling in that irritating fashion of his. 'It's been done a hundred times.'

This was true, of course; and yet not. There certainly were learned works on graffiti, chock-full of sociological jargon: *cultural disenfranchisement; urban alienation*. But she flattered herself that *she* might find something amongst this litter of scrawlings that previous analysts had not: some unifying convention perhaps, that she could use as the lynchpin of her thesis. Only a vigorous cataloguing and cross-referencing of the phrases and images before her would reveal such a correspondence; hence the importance of the photographic study. So many hands had worked here: so many minds left their mark, however casually. If she could find some pattern, some predominant motive, or *motif*, the thesis would be guaranteed some serious attention, and so, in turn, would she.

'What are you doing?' a voice from behind her asked.

She turned from her calculations to see a young woman with a pushchair on the pavement behind her. She looked weary, Helen thought, and pinched by the cold. The child in the pushchair was mewling, his grimy fingers clutching an orange lollipop and the wrapping from a chocolate bar. The bulk of the chocolate, and the remains of previous jujubes, was displayed down the front of his coat.

Helen offered a thin smile to the woman; she looked in need of it.

'I'm photographing the walls,' she said in answer to the initial enquiry, though surely this was perfectly apparent.

The woman – Helen judged she could barely be twenty – said: 'You mean the filth?'

'The writing and the pictures,' Helen said. Then: 'Yes. The filth.'

'You from the Council?'

'No, the University.'

'It's bloody disgusting,' the woman said. 'The way they do that. It's not just kids, either.'

'No?'

'Grown men. Grown men, too. They don't give a damn. Do it in broad daylight. You see 'em . . . broad daylight.' She glanced down at the child, who was sharpening his lollipop on the ground. 'Kerry!' she snapped, but the boy took no notice. 'Are they going to wipe it off?' she asked Helen.

'I don't know,' Helen said, and reiterated: 'I'm from the University.'

'Oh,' the woman replied, as if this was new information, 'so you're nothing to do with the Council?'

'No.'

'Some of it's obscene, isn't it? Really dirty. Makes me embarrassed to see some of the things they draw.'

Helen nodded, casting an eye at the boy in the pushchair. Kerry had decided to put his sweet in his ear for safekeeping.

'Don't do that!' his mother told him, and leaned over to slap the child's hand. The blow, which was negligible, began the child bawling. Helen took the opportunity to return to her camera. But the woman still desired to talk. 'It's not just on the outside, neither,' she commented.

'I beg your pardon?' Helen said.

'They break into the flats when they go empty. The Council tried to board them up, but it does no good. They break in anyway. Use them as toilets, and write more filth on the walls. They light fires too. Then nobody can move back in.'

The description piqued Helen's curiosity. Would the graffiti on the *inside* walls be substantially different from the public displays? It was certainly worth an investigation.

'Are there any places you know of around here like that?'

'Empty flats, you mean?'

'With graffiti.'

'Just by us, there's one or two,' the woman volunteered. 'I'm in Butts' Court.'

'Maybe you could show me?' Helen asked.

The woman shrugged.

'By the way, my name's Helen Buchanan.'

'Anne-Marie,' the mother replied.

'I'd be very grateful if you could point me to one of those empty flats.'

Anne-Marie was baffled by Helen's enthusiasm, and made no attempt to disguise it, but she shrugged again and said: 'There's nothing much to see. Only more of the same stuff.'

Helen gathered up her equipment and they walked side by side through the intersecting corridors between one square and the next. Though the estate was low-rise, each court only five storeys high, the effect of each quadrangle was horribly claustrophobic. The walkways and staircases were a thief's dream, rife with blind corners and ill-lit tunnels. The rubbish-dumping facilities – chutes from the upper floors down which bags of refuse could be pitched – had long since been sealed up, thanks to their efficiency as fire-traps. Now plastic bags of refuse were piled high in the corridors, many torn open by roaming dogs, their contents strewn across the ground. The smell, even in the cold weather, was unpleasant. In high summer it must have been overpowering.

'I'm over the other side,' Anne-Marie said, pointing across the quadrangle. 'The one with the yellow door.' She then pointed along the opposite side of the court. 'Five or six maisonettes from the far end,' she said. 'There's two of them been emptied out. Few weeks now. One of the family's moved into Ruskin Court; the other did a bunk in the middle of the night.'

With that, she turned her back on Helen and wheeled Kerry, who had taken to trailing spittle from the side of his pushchair, around the side of the square.

'Thank you,' Helen called after her. Anne-Marie glanced over her shoulder briefly, but did not reply. Appetite whetted, Helen made her way along the row of ground floor maisonettes, many of which, though inhabited, showed little sign of being so. Their curtains were closely drawn; there were no milk-bottles on the doorsteps, nor children's toys left where they had been played with. Nothing, in fact, of *life* here. There *was* more graffiti however, sprayed, shockingly, on the doors of occupied houses. She granted the scrawlings only a casual perusal, in part because she feared one of the doors opening as she examined a choice obscenity sprayed upon it, but more because she was eager to see what revelations the empty flats ahead might offer.

The malign scent of urine, both fresh and stale, welcomed her at the threshold of number 14, and beneath that the smell of burnt paint and plastic. She hesitated for fully ten seconds, wondering if stepping into the maisonette was a wise move. The territory of the estate behind her was indisputably foreign, sealed off in its own misery, but the rooms in front of her were more intimidating still: a dark maze which her eyes could barely penetrate. But when her courage faltered she thought of Trevor, and how badly she wanted to silence his condescension. So thinking, she advanced into the place, deliberately kicking a piece of charred timber aside as she did so, in the hope that she would alert any tenant into showing himself.

There was no sound of occupancy, however. Gaining confidence, she began to explore the front room of the maisonette which had been – to judge by the remains of a disembowelled sofa in one corner and the sodden carpet underfoot – a living-room. The pale-green walls were, as Anne-Marie had promised, extensively defaced, both by minor scribblers – content to work in pen, or even more crudely in sofa charcoal – and by those with aspirations to public works, who had sprayed the walls in half a dozen colours.

Some of the comments were of interest, though many she had already seen on the walls outside. Familiar names and couplings repeated themselves. Though she had never set eyes on these individuals she knew how badly Fabian J. (A. OK.) wanted to deflower Michelle; and that Michelle, in her turn, had the hots for somebody called Mr Sheen. Here, as elsewhere, a man called White Rat boasted of his endowment, and the return of the Syllabub Brothers was promised in red paint. One or two of the pictures accompanying, or at least adjacent to these phrases were of particular interest. An almost emblematic simplicity informed them. Beside the word *Christos* was a stick man with his hair radiating from his head like spines, and other heads impaled on each spine. Close by was an image of intercourse so brutally reduced that at first Helen took it to illustrate a knife plunging into a sightless eye. But fascinating as the images were, the room was too gloomy for her film, and she had neglected to bring a flash. If she wanted a reliable record of these discoveries she would have to come again, and for now be content with a simple exploration of the premises.

The maisonette wasn't that large, but the windows had been boarded up throughout, and as she moved further from the front door the dubious light petered out altogether. The smell of urine, which had been strong at the door, intensified too, until by the time she reached the back living-room and stepped along a short corridor into another room beyond, it was as cloying as incense. This room, being furthest from the front door, was also the darkest, and she had to wait a few moments in the cluttered gloom to allow her eyes to become useful. This, she guessed, had been the bedroom. What little furniture the residents had left behind them had been smashed to smithereens. Only the mattress had been left relatively untouched, dumped in the corner of the room amongst a wretched litter of blankets, newspapers, and pieces of crockery.

Outside, the sun found its way between the clouds, and two or three shafts of sunlight slipped between the boards nailed across the bedroom window and pierced the room like annunciations, scoring the opposite wall with bright lines. Here, the graffitists had been busy once more: The usual clamour of love-letters and threats. She scanned the wall quickly, and as she did so her eye was led by the beams of light across the room to the wall which contained the door she had stepped through.

Here, the artists had also been at work, but had produced an image the like of which she had not seen anywhere else. Using the door, which was centrally placed in the wall, as a mouth, the artists had sprayed a single, vast head on to the stripped plaster. The painting was more adroit than most she had seen, rife with detail that lent the image an unsettling veracity. The cheekbones jutting through skin the colour of buttermilk; the teeth – sharpened to irregular points – all converging on the door. The sitter's eyes were, owing to the room's low ceiling, set mere inches above the upper lip, but this physical adjustment only lent force to the image, giving the impression that he had thrown his head back. Knotted strands of his hair snaked from his scalp across the ceiling.

Was it a portrait? There was something naggingly *specific* in the details of the brows and the lines around the wide mouth; in the careful picturing of those vicious teeth. A nightmare certainly: a facsimile, perhaps, of something from a heroin fugue. Whatever its origins, it was potent. Even the illusion of door-as-mouth worked. The short passageway between living-room and bedroom offered a passable throat, with a tattered lamp in lieu of tonsils. Beyond the gullet, the day burned white in the nightmare's belly. The whole effect brought to mind a ghost train painting. The same heroic deformity, the same unashamed intention to scare. And it worked. She stood in the bedroom almost stupefied by the picture, its red-rimmed eyes fixing her mercilessly. Tomorrow, she determined, she would come here again, this time with high-speed film and a flash to illuminate the masterwork.

As she prepared to leave the sun went in, and the bands of light faded. She glanced over her shoulder at the boarded windows, and saw for the first time that one four-word slogan had been sprayed on the wall beneath them.

Sweets to the sweet, it read. She was familiar with the quote, but not with its source. Was it a profession of love? If so, it was an odd location for such an avowal. Despite the mattress in the corner, and the relative privacy of this room, she could not imagine the intended reader of such words ever stepping in here to receive her bouquet. No adolescent lovers, however heated, would lie down here to play at mothers and fathers; not under the gaze of the terror on the wall. She crossed to examine the writing. The paint looked to be the same shade of pink as had been used to colour the gums of the screaming man; perhaps the same hand?

Behind her, a noise. She turned so quickly she almost tripped over the blanket-strewn mattress.

'Who—?'

At the other end of the gullet, in the living-room, was a scab-kneed boy of six or seven. He stared at Helen, eyes glittering in the half-light, as if waiting for a cue.

'Yes?' she said.

'Anne-Marie says do you want a cup of tea?' he declared without pause or intonation.

Her conversation with the woman seemed hours past. She was grateful for the invitation, however. The damp maisonette had chilled her.

'Yes . . . ' she said to the boy. 'Yes, please.'

The child didn't move, but simply stared on at her.

'Are you going to lead the way?' she asked him.

'If you want,' he replied, unable to raise a trace of enthusiasm.

'I'd like that.'

'You taking photographs?' he asked.

'Yes. Yes, I am. But not in here.'

'Why not?'

'It's too dark,' she told him.

'Don't it work in the dark?' he wanted to know.

'No.'

The boy nodded at this, as if the information somehow fitted well into his scheme of things, and about-turned without another word, clearly expecting Helen to follow.

If she had been taciturn in the street, Anne-Marie was anything but in the privacy of her own kitchen. Gone was the guarded curiosity, to be replaced by a stream of lively chatter and a constant scurrying between half a dozen minor domestic tasks, like a juggler keeping several plates spinning simultaneously. Helen watched this balancing act with some admiration; her own domestic skills were negligible. At last, the meandering conversation turned back to the subject that had brought Helen here.

'Them photographs,' Anne-Marie said, 'why'd you want to take them?'

'I'm writing about graffiti. The photos will illustrate my thesis.'

'It's not very pretty.'

'No, you're right, it isn't. But I find it interesting.'

Anne-Marie shook her head. 'I hate the whole estate,' she said. 'It's not safe here. People getting robbed on their own doorsteps. Kids setting fire to the rubbish day in, day out. Last summer we had the fire brigade here two, three times a day, 'til they sealed them chutes off. Now people just dump the bags in the passageways, and that attracts rats.'

'Do you live here alone?'

'Yes,' she said, 'since Davey walked out.'

'That your husband?'

'He was Kerry's father, but we weren't never married. We lived together two years, you know. We had some good times. Then he just upped and went off one day when I was at me Mam's with Kerry.' She peered into her tea-cup. 'I'm better off without him,' she said. 'But you get scared sometimes. Want some more tea?'

'I don't think I've got time.'

'Just a cup,' Anne-Marie said, already up and unplugging the electric kettle to take it across for a re-fill. As she was about to turn on the tap she saw something on the draining board, and drove her thumb down, grinding it out. 'Got you, you bugger,' she said, then turned to Helen. 'We got these bloody ants.'

'Ants?'

'Whole estate's infected. From Egypt, they are: Pharoah ants, they're called. Little brown sods. They breed in the central heating ducts, you see; that way they get into all the flats. Place is plagued with them.'

This unlikely exoticism (ants from Egypt?) struck Helen as comical, but she said nothing. Anne-Marie was staring out of the kitchen window and into the backyard.

'You should tell them—' she said, though Helen wasn't certain whom she was being instructed to tell, 'tell them that ordinary people can't even walk the streets any longer—'

'Is it really so bad?' Helen said, frankly tiring of this catalogue of misfortunes.

Anne-Marie turned from the sink and looked at her hard.

'We've had murders here,' she said.

'Really?'

'We had one in the summer. An old man he was, from Ruskin. That's just next door. I didn't know him, but he was a friend of the sister of the woman next door. I forget his name.'

'And he was murdered?'

'Cut to ribbons in his own front room. They didn't find him for almost a week.'

'What about his neighbours? Didn't they notice his absence?'

Anne-Marie shrugged, as if the most important pieces of information – the murder and the man's isolation – had been exchanged, and any further enquiries into the problem were irrelevant. But Helen pressed the point.

'Seems strange to me,' she said.

Anne-Marie plugged in the filled kettle. 'Well, it happened,' she replied, unmoved.

'I'm not saying it didn't, I just—'

'His eyes had been taken out,' she said, before Helen could voice any further doubts.

Helen winced. 'No,' she said, under her breath.

'That's the truth,' Anne-Marie said. 'And that wasn't all'd been done to him.' She paused, for effect, then went on: 'You wonder what kind of person's capable of doing things like that, don't you? You wonder.' Helen nodded. She was thinking precisely the same thing.

'Did they ever find the man responsible?'

Anne-Marie snorted her disparagement. 'Police don't give a damn what happens here. They keep off the estate as much as possible. When they do patrol all they do is pick up kids for getting drunk and that. They're afraid, you see. That's why they keep clear.'

'Of this killer?'

'Maybe,' Anne-Marie replied. Then: 'He had a hook.'

'A hook?'

'The man what done it. He had a hook, like Jack the Ripper.'

Helen was no expert on murder, but she felt certain that the Ripper hadn't boasted a hook. It seemed churlish to question the truth of Anne-Marie's story however; though she silently wondered how much of this – the eyes taken out, the body rotting in the flat, the hook – was elaboration. The most scrupulous of reporters was surely tempted to embellish a story once in a while.

Anne-Marie had poured herself another cup of tea, and was about to do the same for her guest.

'No thank you,' Helen said. 'I really should go.'

'You married?' Anne-Marie asked, out of the blue.

'Yes. To a lecturer from the University.'

'What's his name?'

'Trevor.'

Anne-Marie put two heaped spoonfuls of sugar into her cup of tea. 'Will you be coming back?' she asked.

'Yes, I hope to. Later in the week. I want to take some photographs of the pictures in the maisonette across the court.'

'Well, call in.'

'I shall. And thank you for your help.'

'That's all right,' Anne-Marie replied. 'You've got to tell somebody, haven't you?'

*

'The man apparently had a hook instead of a hand.'

Trevor looked up from his plate of tagliatelle con prosciutto.

'Beg your pardon?'

Helen had been at pains to keep her recounting of this story as uncoloured by her own response as she could. She was interested to know what Trevor would make of it, and she knew that if she once signalled her own stance he would instinctively take an opposing view out of plain bloody-mindedness.

'He had a hook,' she repeated, without inflexion.

Trevor put down his fork, and plucked at his nose, sniffing. 'I didn't read anything about this,' he said.

'You don't look at the local press,' Helen returned. 'Neither of us do. Maybe it never made any of the nationals.'

'"Geriatric Murdered By Hook-Handed Maniac"?' Trevor said, savouring the hyperbole. 'I would have thought it very newsworthy. When was all of this supposed to have happened?'

'Some time last summer. Maybe we were in Ireland.'

'Maybe,' said Trevor, taking up his fork again. Bending to his food, the polished lenses of his spectacles reflected only the plate of pasta and chopped ham in front of him, not his eyes.

'Why do you say *maybe*?' Helen prodded.

'It doesn't sound quite right,' he said. 'In fact it sounds bloody preposterous.'

'You don't believe it?' Helen said.

Trevor looked up from his food, tongue rescuing a speck of *tagliatelle* from the corner of his mouth. His face had relaxed into that non-committal expression of his – the same face he wore, no doubt, when listening to his students. 'Do *you* believe it?' he asked Helen. It was a favourite time-gaining device of his, another seminar trick, to question the questioner.

'I'm not certain,' Helen replied, too concerned to find some solid ground in this sea of doubts to waste energy scoring points.

'All right, forget the tale –' Trevor said, deserting his food for another glass of red wine. 'What about the teller? Did you trust her?'

Helen pictured Anne-Marie's earnest expression as she told the story of the old man's murder. 'Yes,' she said. 'Yes; I think I would have known if she'd been lying to me.'

'So why's it so important, anyhow? I mean, whether she's lying or not, what the fuck does it matter?'

It was a reasonable question, if irritatingly put. Why *did* it matter? Was it that she wanted to have her worst feelings about Spector Street proved false? That such an estate be filthy, be hopeless, be a dump where the undesirable and the disadvantaged were tucked out of public view – all that was a liberal commonplace, and she accepted it as an unpalatable social reality. But the story of the old man's murder and mutilation was something other. An image of violent death that, once with her, refused to part from her company.

She realized, to her chagrin, that this confusion was plain on her face, and that Trevor, watching her across the table, was not a little entertained by it.

'If it bothers you so much,' he said, 'why don't you go back there, and ask around, instead of playing believe-in-it-or-not over dinner?'

She couldn't help but rise to his remark. 'I thought you liked guessing games,' she said.

He threw her a sullen look.

'Wrong again.'

The suggestion that she investigate was not a bad one, though doubtless he had ulterior motives for offering it. She viewed Trevor less charitably day by day. What she had once thought in him a fierce commitment to debate she now recognized as mere power-play. He argued, not for the thrill of dialectic, but because he was pathologically competitive. She had seen him, time and again, take up attitudes she knew he did not espouse, simply to spill blood. Nor, more's the pity, was he alone in this sport. Academe was one of the last strongholds of the professional time-waster. On occasion their circle seemed entirely dominated by educated fools, lost in a wasteland of stale rhetoric and hollow commitment.

From one wasteland to another. She returned to Spector Street the following day, armed with a flashgun in addition to her tripod and high-sensitive film. The wind was up today, and it was Arctic, more furious still for being trapped in the maze of passageways and courts. She made her way to number 14, and spent the next hour in its befouled confines, meticulously photographing both the bedroom and living-room walls. She had half expected the impact of the head in the bedroom to be dulled by re-acquaintance; it was not. Though she struggled to capture its scale and detail as best she could, she knew the photographs would be at best a dim echo of its perpetual howl.

Much of its power lay in its context, of course. That such an image might be stumbled upon in surroundings so drab, so conspicuously lacking in mystery, was akin to finding an icon on a rubbish-heap: a gleaming symbol of transcendence from a world of toil and decay into some darker but more tremendous realm. She was painfully aware that the intensity of her response probably defied her articulation. Her vocabulary was analytic, replete with buzz-words and academic terminology, but woefully impoverished when it came to evocation. The photographs, pale as they would be, would, she hoped, at least hint at the potency of this picture, even if they couldn't conjure the way it froze the bowels.

When she emerged from the maisonette the wind was as uncharitable as ever, but the boy was waiting outside – the same child as had attended upon her yesterday – dressed as if for spring weather. He grimaced in his effort to keep the shudders at bay.

'Hello,' Helen said.

'I waited,' the child announced.

'Waited?'

'Anne-Marie said you'd come back.'

'I wasn't planning to come until later in the week,' Helen said. 'You might have waited a long time.'

The boy's grimace relaxed a notch. 'It's all right,' he said, 'I've got nothing to do.'

'What about school?'

'Don't like it,' the boy replied, as if unobliged to be educated if it wasn't to his taste.

'I see,' said Helen, and began to walk down the side of the quadrangle. The boy followed. On the patch of grass at the centre of the quadrangle several chairs and two or three dead saplings had been piled.

'What's this?' she said, half to herself.

'Bonfire Night,' the boy informed her. 'Next week.'

'Of course.'

'You going to see Anne-Marie?' he asked.

'Yes.'

'She's not in.'

'Oh. Are you sure?'

'Yeah.'

'Well, perhaps *you* can help me . . .' She stopped and turned to face the child; smooth sacs of fatigue hung beneath his eyes. 'I heard about an old man who was murdered near here,' she said to him. 'In the summer. Do you know anything about that?'

'No.'

'Nothing at all? You don't remember anybody getting killed?'

'No,' the boy said again, with impressive finality. 'I don't remember.'

'Well; thank you anyway.'

This time, when she retraced her steps back to the car, the boy didn't follow. But as she turned the corner out of the quadrangle she glanced back to see him standing on the spot where she'd left him, staring after her as if she were a madwoman.

By the time she had reached the car and packed the photographic equipment into the boot there were specks of rain in the wind, and she was sorely tempted to forget she'd ever heard Anne-Marie's story and make her way home, where the coffee would be warm even if the welcome wasn't. But she needed an answer to the question Trevor had put the previous night. Do *you* believe it?, he'd asked when she'd told him the story. She hadn't known how to answer then, and she still didn't. Perhaps (why did she sense this?) the terminology of verifiable truth was redundant here; perhaps the final answer to his question was not an answer at all, only another question. If so; so. She had to find out.

Ruskin Court was as forlorn as its fellows, if not more so. It didn't even boast a bonfire. On the third-floor balcony a woman was taking washing in before the rain broke; on the grass in the centre of the quadrangle two dogs were absent-mindedly rutting, the fuckee staring up at the blank sky. As she walked along the empty pavement she set her face determinedly; a purposeful look, Bernadette had once said, deterred attack. When she caught sight of the two women talking at the far end of the court she crossed over to them hurriedly, grateful for their presence.

'Excuse me?'

The women, both in middle age, ceased their animated exchange and looked her over.

'I wonder if you can help me?'

She could feel their appraisal, and their distrust; they went undisguised. One of the pair, her face florid, said plainly: 'What do you want?'

Helen suddenly felt bereft of the least power to charm. What was she to say to these two that wouldn't make her motives appear ghoulish? 'I was told . . .' she began, and then stumbled, aware that she would get no assistance from either woman. '. . . I was told there'd been a murder near here. Is that right?'

The florid woman raised eyebrows so plucked they were barely visible. 'Murder?' she said.

'Are you from the press?' the other woman enquired. The years had soured her features beyond sweetening. Her small mouth was deeply lined; her hair, which had been dyed brunette, showed a half-inch of grey at the roots.

'No, I'm not from the press,' Helen said. 'I'm a friend of Anne-Marie's in Butts' Court.' This claim of *friend* stretched the truth, but it seemed to mellow the women somewhat.

'Visiting, are you?' the florid woman asked.

'In a manner of speaking—'

'You missed the warm spell—'

'Anne-Marie was telling me about somebody who'd been murdered here, during the summer, I was curious about it.'

'Is that right?'

'—do you know anything about it?'

'Lots of things go on around here,' said the second woman. 'You don't know the half of it.'

'So it's true,' Helen said.

'They had to close the toilets,' the first woman put in.

'That's right. They did,' the other said.

'The toilets?' Helen said. What had this to do with the old man's death?

'It was terrible,' the first said. 'Was it your Frank, Josie, who told you about it?'

'No, not Frank,' Josie replied. 'Frank was still at sea. It was Mrs Tyzack.'

The witness established, Josie relinquished the story to her companion, and turned her gaze back upon Helen. The suspicion had not yet died from her eyes.

'This was only the month before last,' Josie said. 'Just about the end of August. It was August, wasn't it?' She looked to the other woman for verification. 'You've got the head for dates, Maureen.'

Maureen looked uncomfortable. 'I forget,' she said, clearly unwilling to offer testimony.

'I'd like to know,' Helen said. Josie, despite her companion's reluctance, was eager to oblige.

'There's some lavatories,' she said, 'outside the shops – you know, public lavatories. I'm not quite sure how it all happened exactly, but there used to be a boy . . . well, he wasn't a boy really, I mean he was a man of twenty or more, but he was . . .' she fished for the words '. . . mentally subnormal, I suppose you'd say. His mother used to have to take him around like he was a four-year-old. Anyhow, she let him go into the lavatories while she went to that little supermarket, what's it called?' She turned to Maureen for a prompt, but the other woman just looked back, her disapproval plain. Josie was ungovernable, however. 'Broad daylight, this was,' she said to Helen. 'Middle of the day. Anyhow, the boy went to the toilet, and the mother was in the shop. And after a while, you know how you do, she's busy shopping, she forgets about him, and then she thinks he's been gone a long time . . .'

At this juncture Maureen couldn't prevent herself from butting in: the accuracy of the story apparently took precedence over her wariness.

'– She got into an argument,' she corrected Josie, 'with the manager. About some bad bacon she'd had from him. That was why she was such a time . . .'

'I see,' said Helen.

'—anyway,' said Josie, picking up the tale, 'she finished her shopping and when she came out he still wasn't there—'

'So she asked someone from the supermarket—' Maureen began, but Josie wasn't about to have her narrative snatched back at this vital juncture.

'She asked one of the men from the supermarket—' she repeated over Maureen's interjection, 'to go down into the lavatory and find him.'

'It was terrible,' said Maureen, clearly picturing the atrocity in her mind's eye.

'He was lying on the floor, in a pool of blood.'

'Murdered?'

Josie shook her head. 'He'd have been better off dead. He'd been attacked with a razor—' she let this piece of information sink in before delivering the *coup de grâce*, '—and they'd cut off his private parts. Just cut them off and flushed them down a toilet. No reason on earth to do it.'

'Oh my God.'

'Better off dead,' Josie repeated. 'I mean, they can't mend something like that, can they?'

The appalling tale was rendered worse still by the *sang-froid* of the teller, and by the casual repetition of 'Better off dead'.

'The boy,' Helen said. 'Was he able to describe his attackers?'

'No,' said Josie, 'he's practically an imbecile. He can't string more than two words together.'

'And nobody saw anyone go into the lavatory? Or leaving it?'

'People come and go all the time—' Maureen said. This, though it sounded like an adequate explanation, had not been Helen's experience. There was not a great bustle in the quadrangle and passageways; far from it. Perhaps the shopping mall was busier, she reasoned, and might offer adequate cover for such a crime.

'So they haven't found the culprit,' she said.

'No,' Josie replied, her eyes losing their fervour. The crime and its immediate consequences were the nub of this story; she had little or no interest in either the culprit or his capture.

'We're not safe in our own beds,' Maureen observed. 'You ask anyone.'

'Anne-Marie said the same,' Helen replied. 'That's how she came to tell me about the old man. Said he was murdered during the summer, here in Ruskin Court.'

'I do remember something,' Josie said. 'There *was* some talk I heard. An old man, and his dog. He was battered to death, and the dog ended up . . . I don't know. It certainly wasn't here. It must have been one of the other estates.'

'Are you sure?'

The woman looked offended by this slur on her memory. 'Oh, yes,' she said. 'I mean if it had been here, we'd have known the story, wouldn't we?'

Helen thanked the pair for their help and decided to take a stroll around the quadrangle anyway, just to see how many more maisonettes were out of operation here. As in Butts' Court, many of the curtains were drawn and all the doors locked. But then if Spector Street *was* under siege from a maniac capable of the murder and mutilation such as she'd heard described, she was not surprised that the residents took to their homes and stayed there. There was nothing much to see around the court. All the unoccupied maisonettes and flats had been recently sealed, to judge by a litter of nails left on a doorstep by the council workmen. One sight *did* catch her attention, however. Scrawled on the paving stones she was walking over – and all but erased by rain and the passage of feet – the same phrase she'd seen in the bedroom of number 14: *Sweets to the sweet.* The words were so benign; why did she seem to sense menace in them? Was it in their excess, perhaps, in the sheer overabundance of sugar upon sugar, honey upon honey?

She walked on, though the rain persisted, and her walkabout gradually led her away from the quadrangles and into a concrete no-man's-land through which she had not previously passed. This was – or had been – the site of the estate's amenities. Here was the children's playground, its metal-framed rides overturned, its sandpit fouled by dogs, its paddling pool empty. And here too were shops. Several had been boarded up now; those that hadn't were dingy and unattractive, their windows protected by heavy wire-mesh.

She walked along the row, and rounded a corner, and there in front of her was a squat brick building. The public lavatory, she guessed, though the signs designating it as such had gone. The iron gates were closed and padlocked. Standing in front of the charmless building, the wind gusting around her legs, she couldn't help but think of what had happened here. Of the man-child, bleeding on the floor, helpless to cry out. It made her queasy even to contemplate it. She turned her thoughts instead to the felon. What would he look like, she wondered, a man capable of such depravities? She tried to make an image of him, but no detail she could conjure carried sufficient force. But then monsters were seldom very terrible once hauled into the plain light of day. As long as this man was known only by his deeds he held untold power over the imagination; but the human truth beneath the terrors would, she knew, be bitterly disappointing. No monster he; just a whey-faced apology for a man more needful of pity than awe.

The next gust of wind brought the rain on more heavily. It was time, she decided, to be done with adventures for the day. Turning her back on the public lavatories she hurried back through the quadrangles to the refuge of the car, the icy rain needling her face to numbness.

The dinner guests looked gratifyingly appalled at the story, and Trevor, to judge by the expression on his face, was furious. It was done now, however; there was no taking it back. Nor could she deny the satisfaction she took in having silenced the interdepartmental babble about the table. It was Bernadette, Trevor's assistant in the History Department, who broke the agonizing hush.

'When was this?'

'During the summer,' Helen told her.

'I don't recall reading about it,' said Archie, much the better for two hours of drinking; it mellowed a tongue which was otherwise fulsome in its self-coruscation.

'Perhaps the police are suppressing it,' Daniel commented.

'Conspiracy?' said Trevor, plainly cynical.

'It's happening all the time,' Daniel shot back.

'Why should they suppress something like this?' Helen said. 'It doesn't make sense.'

'Since when has police procedure made sense?' Daniel replied.

Bernadette cut in before Helen could answer. 'We don't even bother to read about these things any longer,' she said.

'Speak for yourself,' somebody piped up, but she ignored them and went on:

'We're punch-drunk with violence. We don't see it any longer, even when it's in front of our noses.'

'On the screen every night,' Archie put in. 'Death and disaster in full colour.'

'There's nothing very modern about that,' Trevor said. 'An Elizabethan would have seen death all the time. Public executions were a very popular form of entertainment.'

The table broke up into a cacophony of opinions. After two hours of polite gossip the dinner-party had suddenly caught fire. Listening to the debate rage Helen was sorry she hadn't had time to have the photographs processed and printed; the graffiti would have added further fuel to this exhilarating row. It was Purcell, as usual, who was the last to weigh in with his point of view; and – again, as usual – it was devastating.

'Of course, Helen, my sweet—' he began, that affected weariness in his voice edged with the anticipation of controversy '—your witnesses could all be lying, couldn't they?'

The talking around the table dwindled, and all heads turned in Purcell's direction. Perversely, he ignored the attention he'd garnered, and turned to whisper in the ear of the boy he'd brought – a new passion who would, on past form, be discarded in a matter of weeks for another pretty urchin.

'Lying?' Helen said. She could feel herself bristling at the observation already, and Purcell had only spoken a dozen words.

'Why not?' the other replied, lifting his glass of wine to his lips. 'Perhaps they're all weaving some elaborate fiction or other. The story of the spastic's mutilation in the public toilet. The murder of the old man. Even that hook. All quite familiar elements. You must be aware that there's something *traditional* about these atrocity stories. One used to exchange them all the time; there was a certain *frisson* in them. Something competitive maybe, in attempting to find a new detail to add to the collective fiction; a fresh twist that would render the tale that little bit more appalling when you passed it on.'

'It may be familiar to you—' said Helen defensively. Purcell was always so *poised*; it irritated her. Even if there were validity in his argument – which she doubted – she was damned if she'd concede it. '—*I've* never heard this kind of story before.'

'Have you not?' said Purcell, as though she were admitting to illiteracy. 'What about the lovers and the escaped lunatic, have you heard that one?'

'I've heard that . . . ' Daniel said.

'The lover is disembowelled – usually by a hook-handed man – and the body left on the top of the car, while the fiancée cowers inside. It's a cautionary tale, warning of the evils of rampant heterosexuality.' The joke won a round of laughter from everyone but Helen. 'These stories are very common.'

'So you're saying that they're telling me lies—' she protested.

'Not lies, exactly—'

'You said *lies*.'

'I was being provocative,' Purcell returned, his placatory tone more enraging than ever. 'I don't mean to imply there's any serious mischief in it. But you *must* concede that so far you haven't met a single *witness*. All these events have happened at some unspecified date to some unspecified person. They are reported at several removes. They occurred at best to the brothers of friends of distant relations. Please consider the possibility that perhaps these events do not exist in the real world at all, but are merely titillation for bored housewives—'

Helen didn't make an argument in return, for the simple reason that she lacked one. Purcell's point about the conspicuous absence of witnesses was perfectly sound; she herself had wondered about it. It was strange, too, the way the women in Ruskin Court had speedily consigned the old man's murder to another estate, as though these atrocities always occurred just out of sight – round the next corner, down the next passageway – but never *here*.

'So why?' said Bernadette.

'Why what?' Archie, puzzled.

'The stories. Why tell these horrible stories if they're not true?'

'Yes,' said Helen, throwing the controversy back into Purcell's ample lap. '*Why?*'

Purcell preened himself, aware that his entry into the debate had changed the basic assumption at a stroke. 'I don't know,' he said, happy to be done with the game now that he'd shown his arm. 'You really mustn't take me too seriously, Helen. *I* try not to.' The boy at Purcell's side tittered.

'Maybe it's simply taboo material,' Archie said.

'Suppressed—' Daniel prompted.

'Not the way you mean it,' Archie retorted. 'The whole world isn't politics, Daniel.'

'Such naiveté.'

'What's so *taboo* about death?' Trevor said. 'Bernadette already pointed out: it's in front of us all the time. Television; newspapers.'

'Maybe that's not close enough,' Bernadette suggested.

'Does anyone mind if I smoke?' Purcell broke in. 'Only dessert seems to have been indefinitely postponed—'

Helen ignored the remark, and asked Bernadette what she meant by 'not close enough'?

Bernadette shrugged. 'I don't know precisely,' she confessed, 'maybe just that death has to be *near*; we have to *know* it's just round the corner. The television's not intimate enough—'

Helen frowned. The observation made some sense to her, but in the clutter of the moment she couldn't root out its significance.

'Do you think they're stories too?' she asked.

'Andrew has a point—' Bernadette replied.

'Most kind,' said Purcell. 'Has somebody got a match? The boy's pawned my lighter.'

'—about the absence of witnesses.'

'All that proves is that I haven't met anybody who's actually *seen* anything,' Helen countered, 'not that witnesses don't exist.'

'All right,' said Purcell. 'Find me one. If you can prove to me that your atrocity-monger actually lives and breathes, I'll stand everyone dinner at *Appollinaires*. How's that? Am I generous to a fault, or do I just know when I can't lose?' He laughed, knocking on the table with his knuckles by way of applause.

'Sounds good to me,' said Trevor. 'What do you say, Helen?'

*

She didn't go back to Spector Street until the following Monday, but all weekend she was there in thought: standing outside the locked toilet, with the wind bringing rain; or in the bedroom, the portrait looming. Thoughts of the estate claimed all her concern. When, late on Saturday afternoon, Trevor found some petty reason for an argument, she let the insults pass, watching him perform the familiar ritual of self-martyrdom without being touched by it in the least. Her indifference only enraged him further. He stormed out in high dudgeon, to visit whichever of his women was in favour this month. She was glad to see the back of him. When he failed to return that night she didn't even think of weeping about it. He was foolish and vacuous. She despaired of ever seeing a haunted look in his dull eyes; and what worth was a man who could not be haunted?

He did not return Sunday night either, and it crossed her mind the following morning, as she parked the car in the heart of the estate, that nobody even knew she had come, and that she might lose herself for days here and nobody be any the wiser. Like the old man Anne-Marie had told her about: lying forgotten in his favourite armchair with his eyes hooked out, while the flies feasted and the butter went rancid on the table.

It was almost Bonfire Night, and over the weekend the small heap of combustibles in Butts' Court had grown to a substantial size. The construction looked unsound, but that didn't prevent a number of boys and young adolescents clambering over it and into it. Much of its bulk was made up of furniture, filched, no doubt, from boarded-up properties. She doubted if it could burn for any time: if it did, it would go chokingly. Four times, on her way across to Anne-Marie's house, she was waylaid by children begging for money to buy fireworks.

'Penny for the guy,' they'd say, though none had a guy to display. She had emptied her pockets of change by the time she reached the front door.

Anne-Marie was in today, though there was no welcoming smile. She simply stared at her visitor as if mesmerized.

'I hope you don't mind me calling . . .'

Anne-Marie made no reply.

'. . . I just wanted a word.'

'I'm busy,' the woman finally announced. There was no invitation inside, no offer of tea.

'Oh. Well . . . it won't take more than a moment.'

The back door was open and the draught blew through the house. Papers were flying about in the back yard. Helen could see them lifting into the air like vast white moths.

'What do you want?' Anne-Marie asked.

'Just to ask you about the old man.'

The woman frowned minutely. She looked as if she was sickening, Helen thought: her face had the colour and texture of stale dough, her hair was lank and greasy.

'What old man?'

'Last time I was here, you told me about an old man who'd been murdered, do you remember?'

'No.'

'You said he lived in the next court.'

'I don't remember,' Anne-Marie said.

'But you *distinctly* told me—'

Something fell to the floor in the kitchen, and smashed. Anne-Marie flinched, but did not move from the doorstep, her arm barring Helen's way into the house. The hallway was littered with the child's toys, gnawed and battered.

'Are you all right?'

Anne-Marie nodded. 'I've got work to do,' she said.

'And you don't remember telling me about the old man?'

'You must have misunderstood,' Anne-Marie replied, and then, her voice hushed: 'You shouldn't have come. Everybody *knows*.'

'Knows what?'

The girl had begun to tremble. 'You don't understand, do you? You think people aren't watching?'

'What does it matter? All I asked was—'

'I don't know *anything*,' Anne-Marie reiterated. 'Whatever I said to you, I lied about it.'

'Well, thank you anyway,' Helen said, too perplexed by the confusion of signals from Anne-Marie to press the point any further. Almost as soon as she had turned from the door she heard the lock snap closed behind her.

That conversation was only one of several disappointments that morning brought. She went back to the row of shops, and visited the supermarket that Josie had spoken of. There she enquired about the lavatories, and their recent history. The supermarket had only changed hands in the last month, and the new owner, a taciturn Pakistani, insisted that he knew nothing of when or why the lavatories had been closed. She was aware, as she made her enquiries, of being scrutinized by the other customers in the shop; she felt like a pariah. That feeling deepened when, after leaving the supermarket, she saw Josie emerging from the launderette, and called after her only to have the woman pick up her pace and duck away into the maze of corridors. Helen followed, but rapidly lost both her quarry and her way.

Frustrated to the verge of tears, she stood amongst the overturned rubbish bags, and felt a surge of contempt for her foolishness. She didn't belong here, did she? How many times had she criticized others for their presumption in claiming to understand societies they had merely viewed from afar? And here was she, committing the same crime, coming here with her camera and her questions, using the lives (and deaths) of these people as fodder for party conversation. She didn't blame Anne-Marie for turning her back; had she deserved better?

Tired and chilled, she decided it was time to concede Purcell's point. It *was* all fiction she had been told. They had played with her – sensing her desire to be fed some horrors – and she, the perfect fool, had fallen for every ridiculous word. It was time to pack up her credulity and go home.

One call demanded to be made before she returned to the car however: she wanted to look a final time at the painted head. Not as an anthropologist amongst an alien tribe, but as a confessed ghost train rider: for the thrill of it. Arriving at number 14, however, she faced the last and most crushing disappointment. The maisonette had been sealed up by conscientious council workman. The door was locked; the front window boarded over.

She was determined not to be so easily defeated, however. She made her way around the back of Butts' Court and located the yard of number 14 by simple mathematics. The gate was wedged closed from the inside, but she pushed hard upon it, and, with effort on both parts, it opened. A heap of rubbish – rotted carpets, a box of rain-sodden magazines, a denuded Christmas tree – had blocked it.

She crossed the yard to the boarded-up windows, and peered through the slats of wood. It wasn't bright outside, but it was darker still within; it was difficult to catch more than the vaguest hint of the painting on the bedroom wall. She pressed her face close to the wood, eager for a final glimpse.

A shadow moved across the room, momentarily blocking her view. She stepped back from the window, startled, not certain of what she'd seen. Perhaps merely her own shadow, cast through the window? But then *she* hadn't moved; it had.

She approached the window again, more cautiously. The air vibrated; she could hear a muted whine from somewhere, though she couldn't be certain whether it came from inside or out. Again, she put her face to the rough boards, and suddenly, something leapt at the window. This time she let out a cry. There was a scrabbling sound from within, as nails raked the wood.

A dog! – And a big one to have jumped so high.

'Stupid,' she told herself aloud. A sudden sweat bathed her.

The scrabbling had stopped almost as soon as it had started, but she couldn't bring herself to go back to the window. Clearly the workmen who had sealed up the maisonette had failed to check it properly, and incarcerated the animal by mistake. It was ravenous, to judge by the slavering she'd heard; she was grateful she hadn't attempted to break in. The dog – hungry, maybe half-mad in the stinking darkness – could have taken out her throat.

She stared at the boarded-up window. The slits between the boards were barely a half-inch wide, but she sensed that the animal was up on its hind legs on the other side, watching her through the gap. She could hear its panting now that her own breath was regularizing; she could hear its claws raking the sill.

'Bloody thing . . . ' she said. 'Damn well stay in there.'

She backed off towards the gate. Hosts of wood-lice and spiders, disturbed from their nests by moving the carpets behind the gate, were scurrying underfoot, looking for a fresh darkness to call home.

She closed the gate behind her, and was making her way around the front of the block when she heard the sirens: two ugly spirals of sound that made the hair on the back of her neck tingle. They were approaching. She picked up her speed, and came around into Butts' Court in time to see several policemen crossing the grass behind the bonfire and an ambulance mounting the pavement and driving around to the other side of the quadrangle. People had emerged from their flats and were standing on their balconies, staring down. Others were walking around the court, nakedly curious, to join a gathering congregation. Helen's stomach seemed to drop to her bowels when she realized *where* the hub of interest lay: at Anne-Marie's doorstep. The police were clearing a path through the throng for the ambulance men. A second police car had followed the route of the ambulance onto the pavement; two plain-clothes officers were getting out.

She walked to the periphery of the crowd. What little talk there was amongst the onlookers was conducted in low voices; one or two of the older women were crying. Though she peered over the heads of the spectators she could see nothing. Turning to a bearded man, whose child was perched on his shoulders, she asked what was going on. He didn't know. Somebody dead, he'd heard, but he wasn't certain.

'Anne-Marie?' she asked.

A woman in front of her turned and said: 'You know her?' almost awed, as if speaking of a loved one.

'A little,' Helen replied hesitantly. 'Can you tell me what's happened?'

The woman involuntarily put her hand to her mouth, as if to stop the words before they came. But here they were nevertheless: 'The child—' she said.

'Kerry?'

'Somebody got into the house around the back. Slit his throat.'

Helen felt the sweat come again. In her mind's eye the newspapers rose and fell in Anne-Marie's yard.

'No,' she said.

'Just like that.'

She looked at the tragedian who was trying to sell her this obscenity, and said, 'No,' again. It defied belief; yet her denials could not silence the horrid comprehension she felt.

She turned her back on the woman and paddled her way out of the crowd. There would be nothing to see, she knew, and even if there had been, she had no desire to look. These people – still emerging from their homes as the story spread – were exhibiting an appetite she was disgusted by. She was not of them; would never *be* of them. She wanted to slap every eager face into sense; wanted to say: 'It's pain and grief you're going to spy on. Why? Why?' But she had no courage left. Revulsion had drained her of all but the energy to wander away, leaving the crowd to its sport.

Trevor had come home. He did not attempt an explanation of his absence, but waited for her to cross-question him. When she failed to do so he sank into an easy *bonhomie* that was worse than his expectant silence. She was dimly aware that her disinterest was probably more unsettling for him than the histrionics he had been anticipating. She couldn't have cared less.

She tuned the radio to the local station, and listened for news. It came surely enough, confirming what the woman in the crowd had told her. Kerry Latimer was dead. Person or persons unknown had gained access to the house via the back yard and murdered the child while he played on the kitchen floor. A police spokesman mouthed the usual platitudes, describing Kerry's death as an 'unspeakable crime', and the miscreant as 'a dangerous and deeply disturbed individual'. For once, the rhetoric seemed justified, and the man's voice shook discernibly when he spoke of the scene that had confronted the officers in the kitchen of Anne-Marie's house.

'Why the radio?' Trevor casually enquired, when Helen had listened for news through three consecutive bulletins. She saw no point in withholding her experience at Spector Street from him; he would find out sooner or later. Coolly, she gave him a bald outline of what had happened at Butts' Court.

'This Anne-Marie is the woman you first met when you went to the estate; am I right?'

She nodded, hoping he wouldn't ask her too many questions. Tears were close, and she had no intention of breaking down in front of him.

'So you were right,' he said.

'Right?'

'About the place having a maniac.'

'No,' she said. 'No.'

'But the kid—'

She got up and stood at the window, looking down two storeys into the darkened street below. Why did she feel the need to reject the conspiracy theory so urgently? Why was she now praying that Purcell had been right, and that all she'd been told had been lies? She went back and back to the way Anne-Marie had been when she'd visited her that morning: pale, jittery; *expectant*. She had been like a woman anticipating some arrival, hadn't she? – eager to shoo unwanted visitors away so that she could turn back to the business of waiting. But waiting for what, or *whom*? Was it possible that Anne-Marie actually knew the murderer? 'Had perhaps invited him into the house?'

'I hope they find the bastard,' she said, still watching the street.

'They will,' Trevor replied. 'A baby-murderer, for Christ's sake. They'll make it a high priority.'

A man appeared at the corner of the street, turned, and whistled. A large Alsatian came to heel, and the two set off down towards the Cathedral.

'The dog,' Helen murmured.

'What?'

She had forgotten the dog in all that had followed. Now the shock she'd felt as it had leapt at the window shook her again.

'What dog?' Trevor pressed.

'I went back to the flat today – where I took the pictures of the graffiti. There was a dog in there. Locked in.'

'So?'

'It'll starve. Nobody knows it's there.'

'How do you know it wasn't locked in to kennel it?'

'It was making such a noise—' she said.

'Dogs bark,' Trevor replied. 'That's all they're good for.'

'No . . .' she said very quietly, remembering the noises through the boarded window. 'It didn't bark . . .'

'Forget the dog,' Trevor said. 'And the child. There's nothing you can do about it. You were just passing through.'

His words only echoed her own thoughts of earlier in the day, but somehow – for reasons that she could find no words to convey – that conviction had decayed in the last hours. She was not just passing through. Nobody ever just *passed through*; experience always left its mark. Sometimes it merely scratched; on occasion it took off limbs. She did not know the extent of her present wounding, but she knew it more profound than she yet understood, and it made her afraid.

'We're out of booze,' she said, emptying the last dribble of whisky into her tumbler.

Trevor seemed pleased to have a reason to be accommodating. 'I'll go out, shall I?' he said. 'Get a bottle or two?'

'Sure,' she replied. 'If you like.'

He was gone only half an hour; she would have liked him to have been longer. She didn't want to talk, only to sit and think through the unease in her belly. Though Trevor had dismissed her concern for the dog – and perhaps justifiably so – she couldn't help but go back to the locked maisonette in her mind's eye: to picture again the raging face on the bedroom wall, and hear the animal's muffled growl as it pawed the boards over the window. Whatever Trevor had said, she didn't believe the place was being used as a makeshift kennel. No, the dog was *imprisoned* in there, no doubt of it, running round and round, driven, in its desperation, to eat its own faeces, growing more insane with every hour that passed. She became afraid that somebody – kids maybe, looking for more tinder for their bonfire – would break into the place, ignorant of what it contained. It wasn't that she feared for the intruders' safety, but that the dog, once liberated, would come for her. It would know where she was (so her drunken head construed) and come sniffing her out.

Trevor returned with the whisky, and they drank together until the early hours, when her stomach revolted. She took refuge in the toilet – Trevor outside asking her if she needed anything, her telling him weakly to leave her alone. When, an hour later, she emerged, he had gone to bed. She did not join him, but lay down on the sofa and dozed through until dawn.

The murder was news. The next morning it made all the tabloids as a front page splash, and found prominent positions in the heavyweights too. There were photographs of the stricken mother being led from the house, and others, blurred but potent, taken over the back yard wall and through the open kitchen door. Was that blood on the floor, or shadow?

Helen did not bother to read the articles – her aching head rebelled at the thought – but Trevor, who had bought the newspapers in, was eager to talk. She couldn't work out if this was further peace-making on his part, or a genuine interest in the issue.

'The woman's in custody,' he said, poring over the *Daily Telegraph*. It was a paper he was politically averse to, but its coverage of violent crime was notoriously detailed.

The observation demanded Helen's attention, unwilling or not. 'Custody?' she said. 'Anne-Marie?'

'Yes.'

'Let me see.'

He relinquished the paper, and she glanced over the page.

'Third column,' Trevor prompted.

She found the place, and there it was in black and white. Anne-Marie had been taken into custody for questioning to justify the time-lapse between the estimated hour of the child's death and the time that it had been reported. Helen read the relevant sentences over again, to be certain that she'd understood properly. Yes, she had. The police pathologist estimated Kerry to have died between six and six-thirty that morning; the murder had not been reported until twelve.

She read the report over a third and fourth time, but repetition did not change the horrid facts. The child had been murdered before dawn. When she had gone to the house that morning Kerry had already been dead four hours. The body had been in the kitchen, a few yards down the hallway from where she had stood, and Anne-Marie had said *nothing*. That air of expectancy she had had about her – what had it signified? That she awaited some cue to lift the receiver and call the police?

'My Christ . . .' Helen said, and let the paper drop.

'What?'

'I have to go to the police.'

'Why?'

'To tell them I went to the house,' she replied. Trevor looked mystified. 'The baby was dead, Trevor. When I saw Anne-Marie yesterday morning, Kerry was already dead.'

She rang the number in the paper for any persons offering information, and half an hour later a police car came to pick her up. There was much that startled her in the two hours of interrogation that followed, not least the fact that nobody had reported her presence on the estate to the police, though she had surely been noticed.

'They don't want to know—' the detective told her. 'You'd think a place like that would be swarming with witnesses. If it is, they're not coming forward. A crime like this . . .'

'Is it the first?' she said.

He looked at her across a chaotic desk. 'First?'

'I was told some stories about the estate. Murders. This summer.'

The detective shook his head. 'Not to my knowledge. There's been a spate of muggings; one woman was put in hospital for a week or so. But no; no murders.'

She liked the detective. His eyes flattered her with their lingering, and his face with their frankness. Past caring whether she sounded foolish or not, she said: 'Why do they tell lies like that? About people having their eyes cut out. Terrible things.'

The detective scratched his long nose. 'We get it too,' he said. 'People come in here, they confess to all kinds of crap. Talk all night, some of them, about things they've done, or *think* they've done. Give you it all in the minutest detail. And when you make a few calls, it's all invented. Out of their minds.'

'Maybe if they didn't tell you those stories . . . they'd actually go out and do it.'

The detective nodded. 'Yes,' he said. 'God help us. You might be right at that.'

And the stories *she'd* been told, were they confessions of uncommitted crimes? Accounts of the worst-imaginable, imagined to keep fiction from becoming fact? The thought chased its own tail: these terrible stories still needed a *first cause*, a wellspring from which they leapt. As she walked home through the busy streets she wondered how many of her fellow citizens knew such stories. Were these inventions common currency, as Purcell had claimed? Was there a place, however small, reserved in every heart for the monstrous?

'Purcell rang,' Trevor told her when she got home. 'To invite us out to dinner.'

The invitation wasn't welcome, and she made a face.

'Appollinaires, remember?' he reminded her. 'He said he'd take us all to dinner, if you proved him wrong.'

The thought of getting a dinner out of the death of Anne-Marie's infant was grotesque, and she said so.

'He'll be offended if you turn him down.'

'I don't give a damn. I don't want dinner with Purcell.'

'Please,' he said softly. 'He can get difficult; and I want to keep him smiling just at the moment.'

She glanced across at him. The look he'd put on made him resemble a drenched spaniel. Manipulative bastard, she thought; but said: 'All right, I'll go. But don't expect any dancing on the tables.'

'We'll leave that to Archie,' he said. 'I told Purcell we were free tomorrow night. Is that all right with you?'

'Whenever.'

'He's booking a table for eight o'clock.'

The evening papers had relegated The Tragedy of Baby Kerry to a few column inches on an inside page. In lieu of much fresh news they simply described the house-to-house enquiries that were now going on at Spector Street. Some of the later editions mentioned that Anne-Marie had been released from custody 'after an extended period of questioning, and was now residing with friends. They also mentioned, in passing, that the funeral was to be the following day.

Helen had not entertained any thoughts of going back to Spector Street for the funeral when she went to bed that night, but sleep seemed to change her mind, and she woke with the decision made for her.

Death had brought the estate to life. Walking through to Ruskin Court from the street, she had never seen such numbers out and about. Many were already lining the kerb to watch the funeral cortège pass, and looked to have claimed their niche early, despite the wind and the ever-present threat of rain. Some were wearing items of black clothing – a coat, a scarf – but the overall impression, despite the lowered voices and the studied frowns, was one of celebration. Children running around, untouched by reverence; occasional laughter escaping from between gossiping adults – Helen could feel an air of anticipation which made her spirits, despite the occasion, almost buoyant.

Nor was it simply the presence of so many people that reassured her; she was, she conceded to herself, happy to be back here in Spector Street. The quadrangles, with their stunted saplings and their grey grass, were more real to her than the carpeted corridors she was used to walking; the anonymous faces on the balconies and streets meant more than her colleagues at the University. In a word, she felt *home*.

Finally, the cars appeared, moving at a snail's pace through the narrow streets. As the hearse came into view – its tiny white casket decked with flowers – a number of women in the crowd gave quiet voice to their grief. One onlooker fainted; a knot of anxious people gathered around her. Even the children were stilled now.

Helen watched, dry-eyed. Tears did not come very easily to her, especially in company. As the second car, containing Anne-Marie and two other women, drew level with her, Helen saw that the bereaved mother was also eschewing any public display of grief. She seemed, indeed, to be almost elevated by the proceedings, sitting upright in the back of the car, her pallid features the source of much admiration. It was a sour thought, but Helen felt as though she was seeing Anne-Marie's finest hour; the one day in an otherwise anonymous life in which she was the centre of attention. Slowly, the cortège passed by and disappeared from view.

The crowd around Helen was already dispersing. She detached herself from the few mourners who still lingered at the kerb and wandered through from the street into Butts' Court. It was her intention to go back to the locked maisonette, to see if the dog was still there. If it was, she would put her mind at rest by finding one of the estate caretakers and informing him of the fact.

The quadrangle was, unlike the other courts, practically empty. Perhaps the residents, being neighbours of Anne-Marie's, had gone on to the Crematorium for the service. Whatever the reason, the place was eerily deserted. Only children remained, playing around the pyramid bonfire, their voices echoing across the empty expanse of the square.

She reached the maisonnette and was surprised to find the door open again, as it had been the first time she'd come here. The sight of the interior made her light-headed. How often in the past several days had she imagined standing here, gazing into that darkness. There was no sound from inside. The dog had surely run off; either that, or died. There could be no harm, could there, in stepping into the place one final time, just to look at the face on the wall, and its attendant slogan?

Sweets to the sweet. She had never looked up the origins of that phrase. No matter, she thought. Whatever it had stood for once, it was transformed here, as everything was; herself included. She stood in the front room for a few moments, to allow herself time to savour the confrontation ahead. Far away behind her the children were screeching like mad birds.

She stepped over a clutter of furniture and towards the short corridor that joined living-room to bedroom, still delaying the moment. Her heart was quick in her; a smile played on her lips.

And there! At last! The portrait loomed, compelling as ever. She stepped back in the murky room to admire it more fully and her heel caught on the mattress that still lay in the corner. She glanced down. The squalid bedding had been turned over, to present its untorn face. Some blankets and a rag-wrapped pillow had been tossed over it. Something glistened amongst the folds of the uppermost blanket. She bent down to look more closely and found there a handful of sweets – chocolate and caramels – wrapped in bright paper. And littered amongst them, neither so attractive nor so sweet, a dozen razor-blades. There was blood on several. She stood up again and backed away from the mattress, and as she did so a buzzing sound reached her ears from the next room. She turned, and the light in the bedroom diminished as a figure stepped into the gullet between her and the outside world. Silhouetted against the light, she could scarcely see the man in the doorway, but she smelt him. He smelt like candy-floss; and the buzzing was with him or in him.

'I just came to look—' she said, '—at the picture.'

The buzzing went on: the sound of a sleepy afternoon, far from here. The man in the doorway did not move.

'Well . . .' she said, 'I've seen what I wanted to see.' She hoped against hope that her words would prompt him to stand aside and let her pass, but he didn't move, and she couldn't find the courage to challenge him by stepping towards the door.

'I have to go,' she said, knowing that despite her best efforts fear seeped between every syllable. 'I'm expected . . .'

That was not entirely untrue. Tonight they were all invited to Appollinaires for dinner. But that wasn't until eight, which was four hours away. She would not be missed for a long while yet.

'If you'll excuse me,' she said.

The buzzing had quietened a little, and in the hush the man in the doorway spoke. His unaccented voice was almost as sweet as his scent.

'No need to leave yet,' he breathed.

'I'm due . . . due . . .'

Though she couldn't see his eyes, she felt them on her, and they made her feel drowsy, like that summer that sang in her head.

'I came for you,' he said.

She repeated the four words in her head. *I came for you.* If they were meant as a threat, they certainly weren't spoken as one.

'I don't . . . know you,' she said.

'No,' the man murmured. 'But you doubted me.'

'Doubted?'

'You weren't content with the stories, with what they wrote on the walls. So I was obliged to come.'

The drowsiness slowed her mind to a crawl, but she grasped the essentials of what the man was saying. That he was legend, and she, in disbelieving him, had obliged him to show his hand. She looked, now, down at those hands. One of them was missing. In its place, a hook.

'There will be some blame,' he told her. 'They will say your doubts shed innocent blood. But I say – what's blood for, if not for shedding? And in time the scrutiny will pass. The police will leave, the cameras will be pointed at some fresh horror, and they will be left alone, to tell stories of the Candyman again.'

'Candyman?' she said. Her tongue could barely shape that blameless word.

'I came for you,' he murmured so softly that seduction might have been in the air. And so saying, he moved through the passageway and into the light.

She knew him, without doubt. She had known him all along, in that place kept for terrors. It was the man on the wall. His portrait painter had not been a fantasist: the picture that howled over her was matched in each extraordinary particular by the man she now set eyes upon. He was bright to the point of gaudiness: his flesh a waxy yellow, his thin lips pale blue, his wild eyes glittering as if their irises were set with rubies. His jacket was a patchwork, his trousers the same. He looked, she thought, almost ridiculous, with his bloodstained motley, and the hint of rouge on his jaundiced cheeks. But people were facile. They needed these shows and shams to keep their interest. Miracles; murders; demons driven out and stones rolled from tombs. The cheap glamour did not taint the sense beneath. It was only, in the natural history of the mind, the bright feathers that drew the species to mate with its secret self.

And she was almost enchanted. By his voice, by his colours, by the buzz from his body. She fought to resist the rapture, though. There was a *monster* here, beneath this fetching display; its nest of razors was at her feet, still drenched in blood. Would it hesitate to slit her own throat if it once laid hands on her?

As the Candyman reached for her she dropped down and snatched the blanket up, flinging it at him. A rain of razors and sweetmeats fell around his shoulders. The blanket followed, blinding him. But before she could snatch the moment to slip past him, the pillow which had lain on the blanket rolled in front of her.

It was not a pillow at all. Whatever the forlorn white casket she had seen in the hearse had contained, it was not the body of Baby Kerry. That was *here*, at her feet, its blood-drained face turned up to her. He was naked. His body showed everywhere signs of the fiend's attentions.

In the two heartbeats she took to register this last horror, the Candyman threw off the blanket. In his struggle to escape from its folds, his jacket had come unbuttoned, and she saw – though her senses protested – that the contents of his torso had rotted away, and the hollow was now occupied by a nest of bees. They swarmed in the vault of his chest, and encrusted in a seething mass the remnants of flesh that hung there. He smiled at her plain repugnance.

'Sweets to the sweet,' he murmured, and stretched his hooked hand towards her face. She could no longer see light from the outside world, nor hear the children playing in Butts' Court. There was no escape into a saner world than this. The Candyman filled her sight; her drained limbs had no strength to hold him at bay.

'Don't kill me,' she breathed.

'Do you believe in me?' he said.

She nodded minutely. 'How can I not?' she said.

'Then why do you want to live?'

She didn't understand, and was afraid her ignorance would prove fatal, so she said nothing.

'If you would learn,' the fiend said, 'just a *little* from me . . . you would not beg to live.' His voice had dropped to a whisper. 'I am rumour,' he sang in her ear. 'It's a blessed condition, believe me. To live in people's dreams; to be whispered at street-corners; but not have to *be*. Do you understand?'

Her weary body understood. Her nerves, tired of jangling, understood. The sweetness he offered was life without living: was to be dead, but remembered everywhere; immortal in gossip and graffiti.

'Be my victim,' he said.

'No . . .' she murmured.

'I won't force it upon you,' he replied, the perfect gentleman. 'I won't oblige you to die. But think; *think*. If I kill you here – if I unhook you . . .' He traced the path of the promised wound with his hook. It ran from groin to neck. 'Think how they would mark this place with their talk . . . point it out as they passed by and say: "*She* died there; the woman with the green eyes." Your death would be a parable to frighten children with. Lovers would use it as an excuse to cling closer together . . .'

She had been right: this *was* a seduction.

'Was fame ever so easy?' he asked.

She shook her head. 'I'd prefer to be forgotten,' she replied, 'than be remembered like that.'

He made a tiny shrug. 'What do they know?' he said. 'Except what the bad teach them by their excesses?' He raised his hooked hand. 'I said I would not oblige you to die and I'm true to my word. Allow me, though, a kiss at least . . .'

He moved towards her. She murmured some nonsensical threat, which he ignored. The buzzing in his body had risen in volume. The thought of touching his body, of the proximity of the insects, was horrid. She forced her lead-heavy arms up to keep him at bay.

His lurid face eclipsed the portrait on the wall. She couldn't bring herself to touch him, and instead stepped back. The sound of the bees rose; some, in their excitement, had crawled up his throat and were flying from his mouth. They climbed about his lips; in his hair.

She begged him over and over to leave her alone, but he would not be placated. At last she had nowhere left to retreat to; the wall was at her back. Steeling herself against the stings, she put her hands on his crawling chest and pushed. As she did so his hand shot out and around the back of her neck, the hook nicking the flushed skin of her throat. She felt blood come; felt certain he would open her jugular in one terrible slash. But he had given his word. And he was true to it.

Aroused by this sudden activity, the bees were everywhere. She felt them moving on her, searching for morsels of wax in her ears, and sugar at her lips. She made no attempt to swat them away. The hook was at her neck. If she so much as moved it would wound her. She was trapped, as in her childhood nightmares, with every chance of escape stymied. When sleep had brought her to such hopelessness – the demons on every side, waiting to tear her limb from limb – one trick remained. To let go; to give up all ambition to life, and leave her body to the dark. Now, as the Candyman's face pressed to hers, and the sound of bees blotted out even her own breath, she played that hidden hand. And, as surely as in dreams, the room and the fiend were painted out and gone.

She woke from brightness into dark. There were several panicked moments when she couldn't think of where she was, then several more when she remembered. But there was no pain about her body. She put her hand to her neck; it was, barring the nick of the hook, untouched. She was lying on the mattress, she realized. Had she been assaulted as she lay in a faint? Gingerly, she investigated her body. She was not bleeding; her clothes were not disturbed. The Candyman had, it seemed, simply claimed his kiss.

She sat up. There was precious little light through the boarded window – and none from the front door. Perhaps it was closed, she reasoned. But no; even now she heard somebody whispering on the threshold. A woman's voice.

She didn't move. They were crazy, these people. They had known all along what her presence in Butts' Court had summoned, and they had *protected* him – this honeyed psychopath; given him a bed and an offering of bonbons, hidden him away from prying eyes, and kept their silence when he brought blood to their doorsteps. Even Anne-Marie, dry-eyed in the hallway of her house, knowing that her child was dead a few yards away.

The child! That was the evidence she needed. Somehow they had conspired to get the body from the casket (what had they substituted – a dead dog?) and brought it here – to the Candyman's tabernacle – as a toy, or a lover. She would take Baby Kerry with her – to the police – and tell the whole story. Whatever they believed of it – and that would probably be very little – the fact of the child's body was incontestable. That way at least some of the crazies would suffer for their conspiracy. Suffer for *her* suffering.

The whispering at the door had stopped. Now somebody was moving towards the bedroom. They didn't bring a light with them. Helen made herself small, hoping she might escape attention.

A figure appeared in the doorway. The gloom was too impenetrable for her to make out more than a slim figure, who bent down and picked up a bundle on the floor. A fall of blonde hair identified the newcomer as Anne-Marie: the bundle she was picking up was undoubtedly Kerry's corpse. Without looking in Helen's direction, the mother about-turned and made her way out of the bedroom.

Helen listened as the footsteps receded across the living room. Swiftly, she got to her feet, and crossed to the passageway. From there she could vaguely see Anne-Marie's outline in the doorway of the maisonette. No lights burned in the quadrangle beyond. The woman disappeared and Helen followed as speedily as she could, eyes fixed on the door ahead. She stumbled once, and once again, but reached the door in time to see Anne-Marie's vague form in the night ahead.

She stepped out of the maisonette and into the open air. It was chilly; there were no stars. All the lights on the balconies and corridors were out, nor did any burn in the flats; not even the glow of a television. Butts' Court was deserted.

She hesitated before going in pursuit of the girl. Why didn't she slip away now, cowardice coaxed her, and find her way back to the car? But if she did that the conspirators would have time to conceal the child's body. When she got back here with the police there would be sealed lips and shrugs, and she would be told she had imagined the corpse and the Candyman. All the terrors she had tasted would recede into rumour again. Into words on a wall. And every day she lived from now on she would loathe herself for not going in pursuit of sanity.

She followed. Anne-Marie was not making her way around the quadrangle, but moving towards the centre of the lawn in the middle of the court. To the bonfire! Yes; to the bonfire! It loomed in front of Helen now, blacker than the night sky. She could just make out Anne-Marie's figure, moving to the edge of the piled timbers and furniture, and ducking to climb into its heart. *This* was how they planned to remove the evidence. To bury the child was not certain enough; but to cremate it, and pound the bones – who would ever know?

She stood a dozen yards from the pyramid and watched as Anne-Marie climbed out again and moved away, folding her figure into the darkness.

Quickly, Helen moved through the long grass and located the narrow space in amongst the piled timbers into which Anne-Marie had put the body. She thought she could see the pale form; it had been laid in a hollow. She couldn't reach it, however. Thanking God that she was as slim as the mother, she squeezed through the narrow aperture. Her dress snagged on a nail as she did so. She turned round to disengage it, fingers trembling. When she turned back she had lost sight of the corpse.

She fumbled blindly ahead of her, her hands finding wood and rags and what felt like the back of an old armchair, but not the cold skin of the child. She had hardened herself against contact with the body: she had endured worse in the last hours than picking up a dead baby. Determined not to be defeated, she advanced a little further, her shins scraped and her fingers spiked with splinters. Flashes of light were appearing at the corners of her aching eyes; her blood whined in her ears. But there! *there!* the body was no more than a yard and a half ahead of her. She ducked down to reach beneath a beam of wood, but her fingers missed the forlorn bundle by millimetres. She stretched further, the whine in her head increasing, but still she could not reach the child. All she could do was bend double and squeeze into the hidey-hole the children had left in the centre of the bonfire.

It was difficult to get through. The space was so small she could barely crawl on hands and knees; but she made it. The child lay face down. She fought back the remnants of squeamishness and went to pick it up. As she did so, something landed on her arm. The shock startled her. She almost cried out, but swallowed the urge, and brushed the irritation away. It buzzed as it rose from her skin. The whine she had heard in her ears was not her blood, but the hive.

'I knew you'd come,' the voice behind her said, and a wide hand covered her face. She fell backwards and the Candyman embraced her.

'We have to go,' he said in her ear, as flickering light spilled between the stacked timbers. 'Be on our way, you and I.'

She fought to be free of him, to cry out for them not to light the bonfire, but he held her lovingly close. The light grew: warmth came with it; and through the kindling and the first flames she could see figures approaching the pyre out of the darkness of Butts' Court. They had been there all along. Waiting, the lights turned out in their homes, and broken all along the corridors. Their final conspiracy.

The bonfire caught with a will, but by some trick of its construction the flames did not invade her hiding-place quickly; nor did the smoke creep through the furniture to choke her. She was able to watch how the children's faces gleamed; how the parents called them from going too close, and how they disobeyed; how the old women, their blood thin, warmed their hands and smiled into the flames. Presently the roar and the crackle became deafening, and the Candyman let her scream herself hoarse in the certain knowledge that nobody could hear her, and even if they had, would not have moved to claim her from the fire.

The bees vacated the fiend's belly as the air became hotter, and mazed the air with their panicked flight. Some, attempting escape, caught fire, and fell like tiny meteors to the ground. The body of Baby Kerry, which lay close to the creeping flames, began to cook. Its downy hair smoked, its back blistered.

Soon the heat crept down Helen's throat, and scorched her pleas away. She sank back, exhausted, into the Candyman's arms, resigned to his triumph. In moments they would be on their way, as he had promised, and there was no help for it.

Perhaps they would remember her, as he had said they might, finding her cracked skull in tomorrow's ashes. Perhaps she might become, in time, a story with which to frighten children. She had lied, saying she preferred death to such questionable fame; she did not. As to her seducer, he laughed as the conflagration sniffed them out. There was no permanence for him in this night's death. His deeds were on a hundred walls and ten thousand lips, and should he be doubted again his congregation could summon him with sweetness. He had reason to laugh. So, as the flames crept upon them, did she, as through the fire she caught sight of a familiar face moving between the onlookers. It was Trevor. He had forsaken his meal at Appollinaires and come looking for her.

She watched him questioning this fire-watcher and that, but they shook their heads, all the while staring at the pyre with smiles buried in their eyes. Poor dupe, she thought, following his antics. She willed him to look past the flames in the hope he might see her burning. Not so that he could save her from death – she was long past hope of that – but because she pitied him in his bewilderment and wanted to give him, though he would not have thanked her for it, something to be haunted by. That, and a story to tell.

File classification: Sewer Alligators
Location: New York, USA

Title: Croatoan
Writer: *Harlan Ellison*

Briefing: *Sewer Alligators – widespread American legend of giant alligators said to live in sewer systems; a credo or modern fable.* Gabe is a lawyer with a fascination for geology and a passion for seduction. His dual pursuits take him from vast underground caves in Kentucky to the sewers beneath the streets of Manhattan. He knows all about the dangers that are supposed to lurk there – alligators, for a start, flushed down the toilet by their owners when they got too big. But what he *actually* finds is even more horrifying still . . .

Author: The American writer Harlan Ellison has matched his taste for controversy with producing some of the most thought-provoking sf stories ever since he emerged on the scene in the Fifties. A man of enormous energy and vision, he was one of the first writers in the genre to attempt to describe the complexity and dangers of city life in the manner which has now become the focus of the current 'Cyberpunk' movement. This work was inspired by his impressions when he arrived in New York from his native Cleveland and joined a Brooklyn gang, The Barons. Following *Rumble*, published in 1958, he wrote several more books about the violence of urban life, before becoming a magazine editor and scriptwriter on several television series, including *The Alfred Hitchcock Hour* and *The Untouchables*. Subsequent sf novels and stories have seen him acknowledged as a major writer as well as a groundbreaking anthologist with the *Dangerous Visions* series begun in 1967. Ellison has said that a terrible personal experience forms the core of 'Croatoan', but although he has had 'an acquaintance with spelunking and the wonders of the Manhattan sewer system', he insists he is most certainly *not* the narrator of this final word on urban legends.

Beneath the city, there is yet another city: wet and dark and strange; a city of sewers and moist scuttling creatures and running rivers so desperate to be free not even Styx fits them. And in that lost city beneath the city, I found the child.

Oh my God, if I knew where to start. With the child? No, before that. With the alligators? No, earlier. With Carol? Probably. It always started with a Carol. Or an Andrea. A Stephanie. Always someone. There is nothing cowardly about suicide; it takes determination.

'Stop it! Godammit, just *stop* it . . . I said stop . . .' And I had to hit her. It wasn't that hard a crack, but she had been weaving, moving, stumbling: she went over the coffee table, all the fifty-dollar gift books coming down on top of her. Wedged between the sofa and the overturned table. I kicked the table out of the way and bent to help her up, but she grabbed me by the waist and pulled me down; crying, begging me to *do* something. I held her and put my face in her hair and tried to say something right, but what could I say?

Denise and Joanna had left, taking the d&c tools with them. She had been quiet, almost as though stunned by the hammer, after they had scraped her. Quiet, stunned, dry-eyed but hollow-eyed; watching me with the plastic Baggie. The sound of the toilet flushing had brought her running from the kitchen, where she had lain on a mattress pad. I heard her coming, screaming, and caught her just as she started through the hall to the bathroom. And hit her, without wanting to, just trying to stop her as the water sucked the Baggie down and away.

'D-*do* something,' she gasped, fighting for air.

I kept saying Carol, Carol, over and over, holding her, rocking back and forth, staring over her head, across the living room to the kitchen, where the edge of the teak dining table showed through the doorway, the amber-stained mattress pad hanging half over the edge, pulled loose when Carol had come for the Baggie.

After a few minutes, she spiralled down into dry, sand-papered sighs. I lifted her onto the sofa, and she looked up at me.

'Go after him, Gabe. Please. Please, go after him.'

'Come on, Carol, stop it. I feel lousy about it . . .'

'*Go after him, you sonofabitch!*' she screamed. Veins stood out on her temples.

'I *can't* go after him, dammit, he's in the plumbing; he's in the fucking river by now! Stop it, get off my case, let me alone!' I was screaming back at her.

She found a place where untapped tears waited, and I sat there, across from the sofa, for almost half an hour, just the one lamp casting a dull glow across the living room, my hands clasped down between my knees, wishing she was dead, wishing I was dead, wishing everyone was dead . . . except the kid. But. He was the only one who *was* dead. Flushed. Bagged and flushed. Dead.

When she looked up at me again, a shadow cutting off the lower part of her face so the words emerged from darkness, keynoted only by the eyes, she said, 'Go find him.' I had never heard anyone sound that way, ever. Not ever. It frightened me. Riptides beneath the surface of her words created trembling images of shadow women drinking Drano, lying with their heads inside gas ovens, floating face up in thick, red bath water, their hair rippling out like jellyfish.

I knew she would do it. I couldn't support that knowledge. 'I'll try,' I said.

She watched me from the sofa as I left the apartment, and standing against the wall in the elevator, I felt her eyes on me. When I reached the street, still and cold in the predawn, I thought I would walk down to the River Drive and mark time till I could return and console her with the lie that I had tried but failed.

But she was standing in the window, staring down at me.

The manhole cover was almost directly across from me, there in the middle of the silent street.

I looked from the manhole cover to the window, and back again, and again, and again. She waited. Watching. I went to the iron cover and got down on one knee and tried to pry it up. Impossible. I bloodied my fingertips trying, and finally stood, thinking I had satisfied her. I took one step toward the building and realized she was no longer in the window. She stood silently at the curb, holding the long metal rod that wedged against the apartment door when the police lock was engaged.

I went to her and looked into her face. She knew what I was asking: I was asking, *Isn't this enough? Haven't I done enough?*

She held out the rod. No, I hadn't done enough.

I took the heavy metal rod and levered up the manhole cover. It moved with difficulty, and I strained to pry it off the hole. When it fell, it made a clanging in the street that rose up among the apartment buildings with an alarming suddenness. I had to push it aside with both hands; and when I looked up from that perfect circle of darkness that lay waiting, and turned to the spot where she had given me the tool, she was gone.

I looked up; she was back in the window.

The smell of the unwashed city drifted up from the manhole, chill and condemned. The tiny hairs in my nose tried to baffle it; I turned my head away.

I never wanted to be an attorney. I wanted to work on a cattle ranch. But there was family money, and the need to prove myself to shadows who had been dead and buried with their owners long since. People seldom do what they want to do; they usually do what they are *compelled* to do. Stop me before I kill again. There was no rational reason for my descending into that charnel house stink, that moist darkness. No rational reason, but Denise and Joanna from the Abortion Center had been friends of mine for eleven years. We had been in bed together many times; long past the time I had enjoyed being in bed together with them, or they had enjoyed being in bed together with me. They knew it. I knew it. They knew I knew, and they continued to set that as one of the payments for their attendance at my Carols, my Andreas, my Stephanies. It was their way of getting even. They liked me, despite themselves, but they had to get even. Get even for their various attendances over eleven years, the first of which had been one for the other, I don't remember which. Get even for many flushings of the toilet. There was no rational reason for going down into the sewers. None.

But there were eyes on me from an apartment window.

I crouched, dropped my legs over the lip of the open manhole, sat on the street for a moment, then slipped over the edge and began to climb down.

Slipping into an open grave. The smell of the earth is there, where there is no earth. The water is evil; vital fluid that has been endlessly violated. Everything is covered with a green scum that glows faintly in the darkness. An open grave waiting patiently for the corpse of the city to fall.

I stood on the ledge above the rushing tide, sensing the sodden weight of lost and discarded life that rode the waters toward even darker depths. *My God*, I thought, *I must be out of my mind just to be here*. It had finally overtaken me; the years of casual liaisons, careless lies, the guilt I suppose I'd *always* known would mount up till it could no longer be denied. And I was down here, where I belonged.

People do what they are compelled to do.

I started walking toward the arching passageway that led down and away from the steel ladder and the street opening above. Why not walk: aimless, can you perceive what I'm saying?

Once, years ago, I had an affair with my junior partner's wife. Jerry never knew about it. They're divorced now. I don't think he ever found out; she would have had to've been even crazier than I thought to tell him. Denise and Joanna had visited that time, too. I'm nothing if not potent. We flew to Kentucky together one weekend. I was preparing a brief, she met me at the terminal, we flew as husband and wife, family rate. When my work was done in Louisville, we drove out into the countryside. I minored in geology at college, before I went into law. Kentucky is rife with caves. We pulled in at a picnic grounds where some locals had advised us we could do a little spelunking, and with the minimal gear we had picked up at a sporting goods shop, we went into a fine network of chambers, descending beneath the hills and the picnic grounds. I loved the darkness, the even temperature, the smooth-surfaced rivers, the blind fish and water insects that scurried across the wet mirror of the still pools. She had come because she was not permitted to have intercourse at the base of Father Duffy's statue on Times Square, in the main window of Bloomingdale's, or on Channel 2 directly preceding *The Late News*. Caves were the next best thing.

For my part, the thrill of winding down deeper and deeper into the earth – even though graffiti and Dr Pepper cans all along the way reminded me this was hardly unexplored territory – offset even her (sophomoric) appeals to 'take her violently,' there on the shell-strewn beach of a subterranean river.

I *liked* the feel of the entire Earth over me. I was not claustrophic, I was – in some perverse way – wonderfully free. Even soaring! Under the ground, I was soaring!

The walk deeper into the sewer system did not unsettle or distress me. I rather enjoyed being alone. The smell was terrible, but terrible in a way I had not expected.

If I had expected vomit and garbage, this was certainly not what I smelled. Instead, there was a bittersweet scent of rot – reminiscent of Florida mangrove swamps. There was the smell of cinnamon, and wallpaper paste, and charred rubber; the warm odours of rodent blood and bog gas; melted cardboard, wool, coffee grounds still aromatic, rust.

The downward channel levelled out. The ledge became a wide, flat plain as the water went down through drainage conduits, leaving only a bubbling, frothy residue to sweep away into the darkness. It barely covered the heels of my shoes. Florsheims, but they could take it. I kept moving. Then I saw the light ahead of me.

It was dim, flickering, vanished for a moment as something obscured it from my view, moving in front of it, back again, dim and orange. I moved toward the light.

It was a commune of bindlestiffs, derelicts gathered together beneath the streets for safety and the skeleton of camaraderie. Five very old men in heavy overcoats and three even older men in castoff army jackets . . . but the older men were younger, they only *looked* older: a condition of the skids. They sat around a waste barrel oil drum filled with fire. Dim, soft, withered fire that leaped and curled and threw off sparks all in slow motion. Dream-walking fire; somnambulist fire; mesmerized fire. I saw an atrophied arm of flame like a creeper of kangaroo ivy emerge over the lip of the barrel, struggling toward the shadowed arch of the tunnel ceiling; it stretched itself thin, released a single, teardrop-shaped spark, and then fell back into the barrel without a scream.

The hunkering men watched me come toward them. One of them said something, directly into the ear of the man beside him; he moved his lips very little and never took his eyes off me. As I neared, the men stirred expectantly. One of them reached into a deep pocket of his overcoat for something bulky. I stopped and looked at them.

They looked at the heavy iron rod Carol had given me.

They wanted what I had, if they could get it.

I wasn't afraid. I was under the Earth and I was part iron rod. They could not get what I had. They knew it. That's why there are always fewer killings than there might be. People *always* know.

I crossed to the other side of the channel, close to the wall. Watching them carefully. One of them, perhaps strong himself, perhaps merely stupider, stood up and, thrusting his hands deeper into his overcoat pockets, paralleled my passage down the channel away from them.

The channel continued to descend slightly, and we walked away from the oil drum and the light from the fire and the tired community of subterranean castoffs. I wondered idly when he would make his move, but I wasn't worried. He watched me, trying to see me more clearly, it seemed, as we descended deeper into the darkness. And as the light receded he moved up closer, but didn't cross the channel. I turned the bend first.

Waiting, I heard the sounds of rats in their nests.

He didn't come around the bend.

I found myself beside a service niche in the tunnel wall, and stepped back into it. He came around the bend, on my side of the channel. I could have stepped out as he passed my hiding place, could have clubbed him to death with the iron rod before he realized that the stalker had become the stalked.

I did nothing, stayed far back motionless in the niche and let him pass. Standing there, my back to the slimy wall, listening to the darkness around me, utter, final, even palpable. But for the tiny twittering sounds of rats I could have been two miles down in the central chamber of some lost cavern maze.

There's no logic to why it happened. At first, Carol had been just another casual liaison, another bright mind to touch, another witty personality to enjoy, another fine and workable body to work so fine with mine. I grow bored quickly. It's not a sense of humor I seek – lord knows every slithering, hopping, crawling member of the animal kingdom has a sense of humor – for Christ sake even dogs and *cats* have a sense of humor – it's wit! Wit is the answer. Let me touch a woman with wit and I'm gone, sold on the spot. I said to her, the first time I met her, at a support luncheon for the Liberal candidate for D.A., 'Do you fool around?'

'I don't fool,' she said instantly, no time-lapse, no need for rehearsal, fresh out of her mind, 'fools bore me. Are you a fool?'

I was delighted and floored at the same time. I went fumfuh-fumfuh, and she didn't give me a moment. 'A simple yes or no will suffice. Answer this one: how many sides are there to a round building?'

I started to laugh. She watched me with amusement, and for the first time in my life I actually saw someone's eyes twinkle with mischief. 'I don't know,' I said, 'how many sides *are* there to a round building?'

'Two,' she answered, '*in*side and *out*side. I guess you're a fool. No, you may not take me to bed.' And she walked away.

I was undone. She couldn't have run it better if she had come back two minutes in a time machine, knowing what I'd say, and programmed me into it. And so I chased her. Up hill and down dale, all around that damned dreary luncheon, till I finally herded her into a corner – which was precisely what she'd been going for.

'As Bogart said to Mary Astor, "You're good, shweet-heart, very very good." ' I said it fast, for fear she'd start running me around again. She settled against the wall, a martini in her hand; and she looked up at me with that twinkling.

At first it was just casual. But she had depth, she had wiliness, she had such an air of self-possession that it was inevitable I would start phasing-out the other women, would start according her the attention she needed and wanted and without demanding . . . demanded.

I came to care.

Why didn't I take precautions? Again, there's no logic to it. I thought she was; and for a while, she was. Then she stopped. She told me she had stopped, something internal, the gynaecologist had suggested she go off the pill for a while. She suggested vasectomy to me. I chose to ignore the suggestion. But chose not to stop sleeping with her.

When I called Denise and Joanna, and told them Carol was pregnant, they sighed and I could see them shaking their heads sadly. They said they considered me a public menace, but told me to tell her to come down to the Abortion Center and they would put the suction pump to work. I told them, hesitantly, that it had gone too long, suction wouldn't work. Joanna simply snarled, 'You thoughtless cocksucker!' and hung up the extension. Denise read me the riot act for twenty minutes. She didn't suggest a vasectomy; she suggested, in graphic detail, how I might have my organ removed by a taxidermist using a cheese grater. Without benefit of anesthesia.

But they came, with their dilation and curettage implements, and they laid her out on the teak table with a mattress under her, and then they had gone – Joanna pausing a moment at the door to advise me this was the last time, the last time, the very last time she could stomach it, that it was the last time and did I have that fixed firmly, solidly, imbedded in the forefront of my brain? The last time.

And now I was here in the sewers.

I tried to remember what Carol looked like, but it wasn't an image I could fix in my mind half as solidly as I had fixed the thought that this. Was. The. Last. Time.

I stepped out of the service niche.

The young-old bindlestiff who had followed me was standing there, silently waiting. At first I couldn't even see him – there was only the vaguest lighter shade of darkness to my left, coming from around the bend and that oil drum full of fire – but I knew he was there. Even as *he* had known I was there, all the time. He didn't speak, and I didn't speak, and after a while I was able to discern his shape. Hands still deep in his pockets.

'Something?' I said, more than a little belligerently.

He didn't answer.

'Get out of my way.'

He stared at me, sorrowfully, I thought, but that had to be nonsense. I thought.

'Don't make me have to hurt you,' I said.

He stepped aside, still watching me.

I started to move past him, down the channel.

He didn't follow, but I was walking backward to keep him in sight, and he didn't take his eyes off mine.

I stopped. 'What do you want?' I asked. 'Do you need some money?'

He came toward me. Inexplicably, I wasn't afraid he would try something. He wanted to see me more clearly, closer. I thought.

'You couldn't give me nothing I need.' His voice was rusted, pitted, scarred, unused, unwieldy.

'Then why are you following me?'

'Why've you come down here?'

I didn't know what to say.

'You make it bad down here, mister. Why don't you g'wan and go back upside, leave us alone?'

'I have a right to be here.' Why had I said *that?*

'You got no right to come down here; stay back upside where you belong. All of us know you make it bad, mister.'

He didn't want to hurt me, he just didn't want me here. Not even right for these outcasts, the lowest level to which men could sink; even here I was beneath contempt. His hands were deep in his pockets. 'Take your hands out of your pockets, slowly, I want to make sure you aren't going to hit me with something when I turn around. Because I'm going on down there, not back. Come on now, do it. Slowly. Carefully.'

He took his hands out of his pockets slowly, and held them up. He had no hands. Chewed stumps, glowing faintly green like the walls where I had descended from the manhole.

I turned and went away from him.

It grew warmer, and the phosphorescent green slime on the walls gave some light. I had descended as the channel had fallen away deeper under the city. This was a land not even the noble streetworkers knew, a land blasted by silence and emptiness. Stone above and below and around, it carried the river without a name into the depths, and if I could not return, I would stay here like the skids. Yet I continued walking. Sometimes I cried, but I don't know why, or for what, or for whom. Certainly not for myself.

Was there ever a man who had everything more than I had had everything? Bright words, and quick movements, soft cloth next to my skin, and places to place my love, if I had only recognized that it *was* love.

I heard a nest of rats squealing as something attacked them, and I was drawn to a side tunnel where the shining green effluvium made everything bright and dark as the view inside the machines they used to have in shoe stores. I hadn't thought of that in years. Until they found out that the X-rays could damage the feet of children, shoe stores used bulky machines one stepped up onto, and into which one inserted newly shod feet. And when the button was pushed a green X-ray light came on, showing the bones that lay beneath the flesh. Green and black. The light was green, and the bones were dusty black. I hadn't thought of that in years, but the side tunnel was illuminated in just that way.

An alligator was ripping the throats of baby rats.

It had invaded the nest and was feeding mercilessly, tossing the bodies of the ripped and shredded rodents aside as it went for the defenseless smaller ones. I stood watching, sickened but fascinated. Then, when the shrieks of anguish were extinguished at last, the great saurian, direct lineal descendant of Rex, snapped them up one by one and, thrashing its tail, turned to stare at me.

He had no hands. Chewed stumps, glowing faintly green like the walls.

I moved back against the wall of the side tunnel as the alligator belly-crawled past me, dragging its leash. The thick, armoured tail brushed my ankle and I stiffened.

Its eyes glowed red as those of an Inquisition torturer.

I watched its scaled and taloned feet leave deep prints in the muck underfoot, and I followed the beast, its trail clearly marked by the impression of the leash in the mud.

Frances had a five-year-old daughter. She took the little girl for a vacation to Miami Beach one year. I flew down for a few days. We went to a Seminole village, where the old women did their sewing on Singer machines. I thought that was sad. A lost heritage, perhaps; I don't know. The daughter, whose name I can't recall, wanted a baby alligator. Cute. We brought it back on the plane in a cardboard box with air holes. Less than a month later it had grown large enough to snap. Its teeth weren't that long, but it snapped. It was saying: this is what I'll be: direct lineal descendant of Rex. Frances flushed it down the toilet one night after we'd made love. The little girl was asleep in the next room. The next morning, Frances told her the alligator had run off.

The sewers of the city are infested with full-grown alligators. No amount of precaution and no forays by hunting teams with rifles or crossbows or flame throwers have been able to clear the tunnels. The sewers are still infested; workers go carefully. So did I.

The alligator moved steadily, graceful in its slithering passage down one tunnel and into another side passage and down always down, steadily into the depths. I followed the trail of the leash.

We came to a pool and it slid into the water like oil, its dead-log snout above the fetid foulness, its Torquemada eyes looking toward its destination.

I thrust the iron rod down my pant leg, pulled my belt tight enough to hold it, and waded into the water. It came up to my neck and I lay out and began dog-paddling, using the one leg that would bend. The light was very green and sharp now.

The saurian came out on the muck beach at the other side and crawled forward toward an opening in the tunnel wall. I crawled out, pulled the iron rod loose, and followed. The opening gave into darkness, but as I passed through, I trailed my hand across the wall and felt a door. I stopped, surprised, and felt in the darkness. An iron door, with an arched closure at the top and a latch. Studs, heavy and round and smelling faintly of rust, dotted the door.

I walked through . . . and stopped.

There had been something else on the door. I stepped back and ran my fingers over the open door again. I found the indentations at once, and ran my fingertips across them, trying to discern in the utter darkness what they were. Something about them . . . I traced them carefully.

They were letters. 𝕮. My fingers followed the curves. 𝕽. Cut into the iron somehow. 𝕺. What was a door doing down here? 𝕬. The cuts seemed very old, weathered, scummy. 𝕿. They were large and very regular. 𝕺. They made no sense, no word formed that I knew. 𝕬. And I came to the end of the sequence. 𝕹.

CROATOAN. It made no sense. I stayed there a moment, trying to decide if it was a word the sanitation engineers might have used for some designation of a storage area perhaps. Croatoan. No sense. Not Croatian, it was Croatoan. Something nibbled at the back of my memory: I *had* heard the word before, knew it from somewhere, long ago, a vapour of sound travelling back on the wind of the past. It escaped me; I had no idea what it meant.

I went through the doorway again.

Now I could not even see the trail of the leash the alligator had dragged. I kept moving, the iron rod in my hand.

I heard them coming toward me from both sides, and it was clearly alligators, many of them. From side passages. I stopped and reached out to find the wall of the channel. I couldn't find it. I turned around, hoping to get back to the door, but when I hurried back the way I thought I had come, I didn't reach the door. I just kept going. Either I had gone down a fork and not realized the channel had separated, or I had lost my sense of direction. And the slithering sounds kept coming.

Now, for the first time, I felt terror! The safe, warm, enfolding darkness of the underworld had, in an instant, merely by the addition of sounds around me, become a suffocating winding-sheet. It was as if I'd abruptly awakened in a coffin, buried six feet beneath the tightly stomped loam; that clogging terror Poe had always described so well because he had feared it himself . . . the premature burial. Caves no longer seemed comfortable.

I began to run!

I lost the rod somewhere, the iron bar that had been my weapon, my security.

I fell and slid face first in the muck.

I scrabbled to my knees and kept going. No walls, no light, no slightest aperture or outcropping, nothing to give me a sense of being in the world, running through a limbo without beginning, without end.

Finally, exhausted, I slipped and fell and lay for a moment. I heard slithering all around me and managed to pull myself to a sitting position. My back grazed a wall, and I fell up against it with a moan of gratitude. Something, at least; a wall against which to die.

I don't know how long I lay there, waiting for the teeth.

Then I felt something touching my hand. I recoiled with a shriek! It had been cold and dry and soft. Did I recall that snakes and other amphibians were cool and dry? Did I remember that? I was trembling.

Then I saw light. Flickering, bobbing, going up and down just slightly, coming toward me.

And as the light grew closer and brighter, I saw there was something right beside me; the something that had touched me; it had been there for a time, watching me.

It was a child.

Naked, deathly white, with eyes great and luminous, but covered with a transparent film as milky as a membrane, small, very young, hairless, its arms shorter than they should have been, purple and crimson veins crossing its bald skull like traceries of blood on a parchment, fine even features, nostrils dilating as it breathed shallowly, ears slightly tipped as though reminiscent of an elf, barefooted but with pads on the soles, this child stared at me, looked up at me, its little tongue visible as it opened its mouth filled with tiny teeth, trying to form sounds, saying nothing, watching me, a wonder in its world, watching me with the saucer eyes of a lemur, the light behind the membrane flickering and pulsing. This child.

And the light came nearer, and the light was many lights. Torches, held aloft by the children who rode the alligators.

Beneath the city, there is yet another city: wet and dark and strange.

At the entrance to their land someone – not the children, they couldn't have done it – long ago built a road sign. It is a rotted log on which has been placed, carved from fine cherrywood, a book and a hand. The book is open, and the hand rests on the book, one finger touching the single word carved in the open pages. The word is CROATOAN.

On August 13, 1590, Governor John White of the Virginia colony managed to get back to the stranded settlers of the Roanoke, North Carolina, colony. They had been waiting three years for supplies, but politics, foul weather and the Spanish Armada had made it impossible. As they went ashore, they saw a pillar of smoke. When they reached the site of the colony, though they found the stronghold walls still standing against possible Indian attacks, no sign of life greeted them. The Roanoke colony had vanished. Every man, woman, and child, gone. Only the word CROATOAN had been left. *'One of the chiefe trees or postes at the right side of the entrance had the barke taken off, and 5. foote from the ground in fayre Capitall letters was grauen CROATOAN without any crosse or signe of distresse.'*

There was a Croatan island, but they were not there. There was a tribe of Hatteras Indians who were called Croatans, but they knew nothing of the whereabouts of the lost colony. All that remains of legend is the story of the child Virginia Dare, and the mystery of what happened to the lost settlers of Roanoke.

Down here in this land beneath the city live the children. They live easily and in strange ways. I am only now coming to know the incredible manner of their existence. How they eat, what they eat, how they manage to survive, and have managed for hundreds of years, these are all things I learn day by day, with wonder surmounting wonder.

I am the only adult here.

They have been waiting for me.

They call me father.

Acknowledgements

The Editor is grateful to the following authors, agents and publishers for permission to print the stories in this collection:

'The Job' by Richard Laymon. Copyright © 1998 by Richard Laymon and printed for the first time in this book by permission of the author and his agents, International Scripts.

'The Trespassers' by Nigel Kneale. Copyright © 1949 by Nigel Kneale. First published in *Tomato Cain* (Wm.Collins). Reprinted by permission of the author and his agents, The Agency.

'The Gap' by Ramsey Campbell. Copyright © 1980 by Ramsey Campbell. Published in *Alone With The Horrors* (Headline). Reprinted by permission of the author.

'Red Light' by David J. Schow. Copyright © 1986 by David J. Schow. First published in *Twilight Zone*, December 1986. Reprinted by permission of the author.

'The Irish Question' by Graham Masterton. Copyright © 1998 by Graham Masterton and printed for the first time in this book by permission of the author and his agents, International Scripts.

'Girl of my Dreams' by Richard Matheson. Copyright © 1963 by Mercury Press, renewed 1991 by Richard Matheson. Reprinted by permission of the author and his agent, Abner Stein.

'A Modern Magician' by Olaf Stapledon. Copyright © 1979 by Mrs Agnes Stapledon. First published in the *Magazine of Fantasy & Science Fiction*, July 1979. Reprinted by permission of John Stapledon.

'Death of a Sensitive' by Harry Bates. Copyright © 1953 by Gernsback Publications Ltd. No record of copyright renewal.

'Cassandra' by C. J. Cherryh. Copyright © 1978 by Mercury Press. First published in the *Magazine of Fantasy & Science Fiction*, October 1978. Reprinted by permission of the author.

'The Encounter' (aka 'The Venus Hunters') by J. G. Ballard. Copyright © 1967 by J. G. Ballard. From the collection *The Venus Hunters* (Flamingo, an imprint of HarperCollins, London). Reprinted by permission of the author and Margaret Hanbury Literary Agent.

'Men Without Bones' by Gerald Kersh. Copyright © 1958 by Gerald Kersh.

First published in *Esquire*, June 1958. Reprinted by permission of Peters, Fraser & Dunlop Writers' Agents.

'Goldfish Bowl' by Robert A. Heinlein. Copyright © 1942 by Street & Smith Publications Inc. Reprinted by permission of International Scripts.

'Mewhu's Jet' by Theodore Sturgeon. Copyright © 1946 by Street & Smith Publications Inc. First published in *Astounding Science Fiction*, November 1946. Reprinted by permission of the Theodore Sturgeon Literary Trust, c/o Ralph M. Vicinanza Ltd.

'Unicorn Variation' by Roger Zelazny. Copyright © 1981 by Davis Publications Inc. First published in *Isaac Asimov's Science Fiction Magazine*, April 13, 1981. Reprinted by permission of The Amber Corporation c/o Ralph M. Vicinanza Ltd.

'The New Atlantis' by Ursula K. Le Guin. Copyright © 1975 by Ursula K. Le Guin. First published in *The New Atlantis* edited by Robert Silverberg (Hawthorn Books). Reprinted by permission of MBA Literary Agents.

'The Shining Pyramid' by Arthur Machen. Copyright © 1988 by the Estate of Arthur Machen. Reprinted by permission of A. M. Heath & Company, Literary Agents.

'The Bride of Bigfoot' by Kit Reed. Copyright © 1984 by Davis Publications Inc. First published in *Isaac Asimov's Science Fiction Magazine*, July 1984. Reprinted by permission of the author.

'Tulips from Amsterdam' by Ian Watson. Copyright © 1996 by Ian Watson. First published in *Interzone*, August 1996. Reprinted by permission of the author.

'Out of the Fog' by Basil Copper. Copyright © 1970 by Basil Copper. First published in *Argosy*, September 1970. Reprinted by permission of the author.

'The Forbidden' by Clive Barker. Copyright © 1985 by Clive Barker. First published in *Books of Blood, Volume 5* (Sphere Books). Reprinted by permission of Little, Brown Publishers.

'Croatoan' by Harlan Ellison. Copyright © 1975 by Harlan Ellison. Published in *Strange Wine* (Warner Books). Reprinted by arrangement with, and permission of, the author and the author's agent, Richard Curtis Associates Inc.